倍斯特出版事業有限公司
Best Publishing Ltd.

U0077374

Lea
En
So Easy 　倍斯特編輯部◎著

那些年
我們一起熟悉的
英文文法

藏在電影、小說、歌詞裡

本書特別精心挑選

50+ **電影台詞、文學名著、流行歌曲**等的經典名句，

以名人名句為故事背景、**【英文達人小筆記】**的核心文法整理＋基礎**【文法觀念】**

與 **10** 大易混淆的英文文法

引領讀者藉由看名句的趣味學習方式，

瞬間透析英文文法句型公式，強力提升學習效果！

同時幫助讀者自然吸收、加強文法觀念！

編 者 序

英文文法無所不在。

泰勒斯的上張專輯 Red《紅色》裡的多首歌曲仍然猶言在耳，只要一聽到旋律就會忍不住跟著哼 "I Knew You Were a Trouble"《我知道你是大麻煩》，這首關於愛情的歌曲，描述某一方認定兩人相遇有如命運，"You found me" 你就在我最脆弱的時候，" 發現了我 "，然後麻煩就此開始。

歌詞 "You found me" 你發現了我，這裡用的是過去簡單式（simple past tense）。

湯姆漢克斯（Tom Hanks）因主演《阿甘正傳》（Forrest Gump）而獲得奧斯卡男主角獎。這部電影不管看了幾次依然激勵人心，許多台詞還可運用在日常生活中，女主角小珍妮對小阿甘說："Run, Forrest. Run"（快跑，阿甘，快跑啊！），換到馬拉松賽事場景就非常貼切；還有阿甘母親最有名的台詞之一："Miracles happen every day."（奇蹟每天都會發生。），用這句給人打氣加油也非常實用。

"Run! Forrest, Run." 為英文裡的祈使句，而 "Miracles happen every day." 用的則是基本句型 S + Vi（主詞 + 不及物動詞）。

本書便是從 " 英文文法無法不在 " 的概念延伸而來，精選收錄電影台詞、文學名著、熱門歌曲與名人金句，並將之與英文文法概念結合，無非是希望讀者能用那些年熟悉的名句，不知不覺中就學會英文文法。

倍斯特編輯部

CONTENTS

目 次

目 次

1

Part I 句型文法

Unit 1
五大基本句型

✓ 搶先看名句學文法：

1. *Miracles happen every day!* 奇蹟每天都在發生。
   句型一：**S + Vi**（主詞 + 不及物動詞）

2. *Time is money.* 時間就是金錢。
   句型二：**S + Vi + SC**（主詞 + 不及物動詞 + 主詞補語）

3. *You complete me.* 你使我完整。
   句型三：**S + Vt + O**（主詞 + 及物動詞 + 受詞）

4. *People call me Forrest Gump!* 人們叫我阿甘。
   句型四：**S + Vt + O + OC**（主詞 + 及物動詞 + 受詞 + 受詞補語）

5. *(You) show me the money.* 你要讓我賺大錢。
   句型五：**S + Vt + IO + DO**（主詞 + 及物動詞 + 間接受詞 + 直接受詞）

 ## 英文達人小筆記！

　　一個完整的英文句型是由主詞和動詞這二個基本元素所組成的句子，並且能完整表達語意。主詞，是一個句子中想要強調或凸顯的人、事、物；通常由單字詞類中的「名詞」扮演主詞的角色。動詞，則是主詞採取的行為或動作。所以，由主詞＋動詞作為基本原型，依動詞的特性，再加上受詞與補語，可延伸出英文簡單的五大基本句型。

1. 句型一：**S+Vi**（主詞＋不及物動詞）

Miracles happen every day. 奇蹟每天都在發生。

名言背景：這是電影《阿甘正傳》的主角母親對阿甘說的話。阿甘不聰明，經常遭到鄰居同學欺負；而他的母親天性樂觀，總是會安慰鼓勵阿甘，說這句話是期盼阿甘在往後的生活面臨各種困難時，能更有勇氣。

■ 句型一【主詞＋不及物動詞】文法概念解析：句型一中的動詞為不及物動詞，後面不需要有接受動作者（O 受詞），或者補充說明（C 補語）；也就是說，動詞本身的意念就很清楚，可以表達出完整的意思。

1. 觀念說明：

　　a. 不及物動詞（Vi）：

　　　　動作可以獨立發生，不牽涉到別的人或物，這種動詞就叫做「不及物」動詞。

　　　　例：Fishes swim. 魚兒游。

　　b. 沒有受詞或補語：

　　　　不及物動詞的後面不需要有動作接收者（O 受詞），也不需要補充說明（C 補語）。

　　　　例：It rained. 下雨了。

　　c. 可以有修飾語： 主詞或是動詞都可以有修飾語。

　　　　例：Most students laughed loudly. 大部分的學生大聲地笑。（most 修飾 students；loudly 修飾 laughed）。

2. 延伸文法結構：

　　a. S 主詞 + Vi 動詞 + Adv. 副詞：

　　　　後面可以接副詞，副詞片語，或是副詞子句，用來修飾動詞。

　　　　例：I run fast.（fast 修飾 run）。我跑步很快。

　　　　例：Nothing happened last night.（last night 時間副詞）昨晚沒事發生。

　　　　例：Baby laughed when she saw me.（when 副詞子句）寶寶一見我就笑了。

　　b. S 主詞 + Vi 動詞 + Prep. 介系詞 + O 受詞：

不及物動詞後面如有需要加上受詞（O）時，前面需加上介系詞。

例：Don't laugh at me. 不要嘲笑我。

c. S 主詞 + Vi 動詞 + 不定詞 or 不定詞片語：

光是一個不及物動詞，有時可能無法表達完整意思，這時在後面加上不定詞片語，可以更完整傳達語意。

例：Will you come to see me? 你會來看我嗎？

3. 使用特點：

a. 同樣一個動詞，可以作及物動詞（Vt）用，也可作不及物動詞用（Vi），但在句型一中的動詞，永遠只作不及物動詞（Vi）使用。

b. 常用於句型一的動詞有 arrive／bloom／come／cry／go／happen／rain／rise／run／sing／sit／sleep／smile…等。

 絕妙好例句：

1. Nothing happened!（S + Vi）無事發生！
2. Who knows?（S + Vi）誰知道呢？
3. She sings loudly.（S + Vi + Adv.）她大聲唱歌。
4. The handsome man smiled at me.（S + Vi + Prep. + O）那帥哥對我微笑。
5. He ran to catch the bus.（S + Vi + 不定詞片語）他跑去趕公車。

換你選選看：

( ) 1. Jane slept _____ last night. A bad B badly C worse
( ) 2. Time _____. A flies B fly C flying
( ) 3. The show must _____ _____. A went in B go on C going on
( ) 4. Alex _____ the desk. A is sitting B sat on C sits
( ) 5. Tom stopped to listen to her talking. A S+Vi B S+Vi+to
   C S+Vi+Adv.
( ) 6. The sun _____ in the east and _____ in the west. A rise;set
   B rises;sets C rising;setting

答案與中譯解析：

1. 昨晚 Jane 睡得不好。（答：**B** badly，S+Vi+ Adv.，選項 B 為副詞，修飾動詞 slept。）

2. 時間飛逝。（答：**A** flies，S+Vi，time 為第三人稱單數，動詞跟著變化。）

3. 表演還是得繼續。（答：**B** go on，S+Vi+Adv.，助動詞 must 後面的動詞使用 原形動詞，on 做介系詞 用具有繼續之含義。）

4. Alex 坐在桌上。（答：**B**，S + Vi + Prep.+ O。）

5. Tom 停下來聽她說話。（答：B，stopped 後面跟著表示原因的不定詞 to listen，S + Vi + to 不定詞片語。）

6. 太陽東升西落。（答：**B** rises;sets，S + Vi + adv.，the sun 為第三人稱單數， 動詞跟著變化。

2. 句型二： **S + Vi + SC**（主詞 + 不及物動詞 + 主詞補語）

Time is money. 時間就是金錢。

名言背景：由美國著名政治家、科學家班傑明 • 富蘭克林（Benjamin Franklin，1706-1790）所說，之後仍被廣泛引用在不同領域。近年更有 電影《IN TIME 鐘點戰》，便是以 Time is money 時間就是金錢這個概 念而衍生而出的故事，影片中金錢被時間取代，人們所賺與花用的，皆是 以時間為計價單位，富有的人意味著有無窮的時間。

■ 句型二【主詞＋不及物動詞＋主詞補語】文法概念解析：句型二中的動詞為不 及物動詞，後面不需要有接受動作者（O 受詞），但是要加上對主詞的補充說 明（即 SC 主詞補語）；也就是說，動詞本身不能表達完整的意義，需要主詞 補語。

1. 觀念說明：

a. 不及物動詞（Vi）：句型二的動詞為 be 動詞或連綴動詞（Linking Verbs），是一種沒有動作的不及物動詞，主要是用來連接主詞與主詞補 語，動作本身沒有辦法表達語意。

例：He is... 他是…。

例：He looks... 他看起來⋯。

上述兩句，若在動詞之後沒有任何敘述，就無法完整說明想要表達的意思。

b. 主詞補語（SC）：因為動詞本身沒有辦法完整表達語意，因此需要加些詞彙來補充說明或描述主詞，這些用來補充說明的詞彙即稱為主詞補語（SC）。補語可以是名詞、形容詞、動名詞、名詞子句、代名詞、或是不定詞等。

例：He is a teacher. 他是老師。（teacher 為名詞。）

例：He looks happy. 他看起來很高興。（happy 為形容詞。）

2. 使用特點：

a. 常用的連綴動詞：

表示「感覺」的動詞：

smell ／ feel ／ taste ／ sound⋯等。

例：Coffee tastes bitter. 咖啡嚐起來有苦味。

表示「似乎、變得、看起來」的動詞：

become ／ look ／ seem ／ appear ／ remain ／ stay ／ turn ／ fall⋯等。

b. 區分（S＋Vi＋⋯）與（S＋Vi＋SC）句型：

（S＋Vi＋⋯）She appeared suddenly. 她突然出現。

（S＋Vi＋SC）She appeared tired. 她似乎累了。

（S＋Vi＋⋯）He came to see me. 他來看我。

（S＋Vi＋SC）Dream came true. 夢想成真。

絕妙好例句：

1. I am Lisa.（Lisa=SC，名詞 n.）我叫 Lisa。

2. Ryan looks shy.（shy=SC，形容詞 Adj.）Ryan 看起來很害羞。

3. My favorite exercise is jogging.（jogging=SC，動名詞 Ving）我喜歡的運動是慢跑。

4. An iPad was what she wanted for her birthday.（what…=SC 名詞子句）一台 iPad 正是她生日想要的。

5. To see is to believe.（to believe=SC 主詞補語，為不定詞）眼見為憑。

換你選選看：

（　）1. I ＿＿ crazy. A am　B is　C are

（　）2. The pen＿＿＿ ＿＿＿. A is; my　B is mine　C is; me

（　）3. The soup ＿＿＿ ＿＿＿. A tastes; delicious　B tastes; deliciously

（　）4. He seems ＿＿＿. A knows the answer　B to know the answer

（　）5. The lovers ＿＿＿. A kiss　B are kissing　C to kiss

（　）6. The toilet ＿＿＿. A is bad　B is out of order　C is out

答案與中譯解析：

1. 我瘋了。（答：A am，形容詞 crazy 修飾主詞。）

2. 這筆是我的。（答：B is;mine，代名詞 mine 表示 my pen，修飾主詞 The pen。）

3. 這湯嚐起來很美味。（答：A tastes;delicious，形容詞 delicious 說明主詞 The soup。）

4. 他似乎知道答案。（答：B，不定詞 to know the answer 修飾主詞 He。）

5. 情人正在接吻。（答：B，動名詞 kissing 修飾主詞 The lovers。）

6. 馬桶故障。（答：B，片語 out of order 通常用於連綴動詞 be 之後做主詞補語。）

3. 句型三：**S +Vt +O**（主詞＋及物動詞＋受詞）

You complete me. 你使我完整。

名言背景：這是在電影《征服情海》一段影史經典對白，Tom Cruise 對 Renee 告白，"You complete me."，我的世界因你而完整，有情人終成眷屬；而這樣一句情人間深情對話套用在電影《蝙蝠俠：黑暗騎士》的情節裡，當瘋狂的 Joker 對蝙蝠俠說出 "You complete me" 時，就又顯得荒唐又搞笑。

■ 句型三【S 主詞 +Vt 及物動詞 +O 受詞文法】概念解析：句型三中的動詞為及物動詞，要有接受動作者（O 受詞），不需要補語（C）；也就是說，動詞本身需要一個受詞，才能表達完整的意義。

1. 觀念說明：

　　a. 及物動詞（Vt）：句型三的動詞為及物動詞，後面通常必須跟著一個受詞來接受這個動作。

　　　例：I miss you. 我想你。

　　b. 受詞（O）：受詞是指人、事、物用以承受動詞之動作者。跟主詞一樣，受詞都是由名詞類扮演，像是名詞、代名詞、名詞片語、動名詞、不定詞或名詞子句等。

　　　例：I know you.（O 是代名詞）我認識你。

　　　例：Someone opened the door.（O 是名詞）有人開了門。

2. 使用特點：

　　a. 常見的及物動詞： answer ／ ask ／ bring ／ buy ／ carry ／ cook ／ do ／ eat ／ enjoy ／ hate ／ hear ／ know ／ love ／ make ／ sell ／ speak ／ wash…等。

　　　例：She asked a question. 她問了一個問題。

　　b. 大多數的動詞，可作及物動詞用，又可作不及物動詞用，但以下例句中的動詞，永遠只作及物動詞使用。

　　　例：We ate at home.（S + Vi + adv.）我們在家吃飯。

　　　例：I ate lunch.（S + Vt + O）我吃了午飯。

絕妙好例句：

1. I love you.（you 為代名詞 pronoun；當受詞 O）我愛你。
2. Jack stopped drinking.（drinking 動名詞；當受詞 O）傑克戒酒了。
3. We want to buy a house.（to…不定詞；當受詞 O）我們想買一間房子。
4. You don't know what I'm thinking.（what…名詞子句；當受詞 O）你並不知道我在想什麼。
5. I know how to swim.（how…名詞片語；當受詞 O）我知道如何游泳。

 換你選選看：

（　）1. I ＿＿＿ ＿＿＿. A beat him　B beat he　C beat X
（　）2. My friend likes ＿＿＿ the piano. A play　B playing　C plays
（　）3. I hate ＿＿＿ you this bad news. A to tell　B tell　C told
（　）4. I see ＿＿＿ you mean. A thing　B that　C what
（　）5. Everyone wants ＿＿＿. A go　B to go　C going
（　）6. Father is fixing the car. A S+Vt +O　B S+ Vi +SC　C S+Vi

 答案與中譯解析：

1. 我打他。（答：A beat him，O= 代名詞 =him，動詞後面選用受格。）
2. 我朋友喜歡彈鋼琴。（答：B playing，O= 動名詞 = playing。）
3. 我討厭告訴你這壞消息。（答：A to tell，O= 不定詞 =to tell。）
4. 我瞭解你的意思。（答：C what，O= 關係代名詞領導的名詞子句 = what you mean。）
5. 每個人都想去。（答：B，O= 不定詞 =to go。）
6. 父親正在修車。（答：A，O= 名詞 =the car。）

4. 句型四：**S + Vt + O +OC**（主詞 + 及物動詞 + 受詞 + 受詞補語）

My name's Forrest Gump. People call me Forrest Gump.
我的名字是阿甘，人們叫我阿甘。

名言背景：在《Forrest Gump 阿甘正傳》電影裡，每當阿甘認識新的朋友時，都會用這句話自我介紹，這句話幾乎貫穿整部電影。

■ 句型四【S 主詞 +Vt 及物動詞 +O 受詞 +OC 受詞補語】文法概念解析：句型四中的動詞為及物動詞，除了要有接受動作者（O 受詞），還要加上對受詞的補充說明（即 OC 受詞補語）；也就是說，動詞本身除了一個受詞之外，還需要一個受詞補語，說明有關受詞（O）的情況，這樣句子意思才能完整。

1. 觀念說明：

　　a. 及物動詞（Vt）：句型四的動詞為及物動詞，如果只跟著一個受詞來接受動作，整個句子意思感覺不會完整，例如：He makes you...（S + Vt + O）他使我…。這樣的句子雖然有主詞、動詞和受詞，卻無法清楚表達整句的意涵。

　　b. 受詞補語（OC）：　因為動詞本身沒有辦法完整表達語意，這時需要加些東西來補充說明、或描述有關受詞的情況，即稱為受詞補語（OC）。受詞補語可以是形容詞、名詞、不定詞片語（當名詞）、現在分詞（當形容詞）、過去分詞（當形容詞）。

　　　　例：He makes me happy.（S + Vt + O + OC）他使我快樂。

2. 使用特點：

　　a. 常見的及物動詞：believe ／ call ／ consider ／ feel ／ find ／ keep ／ leave ／ name ／ prove ／ think ／ watch…等。

　　　　例：Father gave him a book. 父親給了他一本書。

絕妙好例句：

1. We called him "007". （"007"=OC，名詞 n，補充說明 him） 我們叫他 007。

2. This move made me cry. （cry =OC，名詞 n，補充說明 me）這部電影使我哭了。

3. I found the box empty. （empty=OC，形容詞，補充說明 the box）我發現這盒子是空的。

4. She kept her boyfriend waiting for hours. （waiting=OC，現在分詞，補充說明 her boyfriend）她讓她男友等了幾個小時。

5. I must get this job done. （done=OC，過去分詞，補充說明 this job）我必須把這件事做完。

6. The teacher wants us to read this book. （to read this book=OC，不定詞片語，補充說明 us）老師要我們去讀這本書。

換你選選看：

(　) 1. She asked _____. Ⓐ he his name Ⓑ him his name

(　) 2. She kept _____. Ⓐ the child quiet Ⓑ quiet the child

(　) 3. I found this news _____. Ⓐ interested Ⓑ interesting Ⓒ interest

(　) 4. I prefer _____. Ⓐ the steak well done Ⓑ done well the steak Ⓒ the steak done well

(　) 5. Mother warned us _____. Ⓐ late Ⓑ not to be late Ⓒ be late

(　) 6. He made me _____. Ⓐ changed Ⓑ changing Ⓒ to change

Part I 句型文法

Part II 字詞文法

Part III 文法糾正篇

答案與中譯解析：

1. 她問他的名字。（答：B him his name，OC＝名詞＝his name，動詞後面的人稱要使用受格。）

2. 她讓小孩保持安靜。（答：A the child quiet，OC＝形容詞＝quiet。）

3. 我發現這新聞有趣。（答：B interesting，OC＝形容詞＝interesting（令人覺得有趣），interested 雖然也是形容詞，但具有被動意涵，表示「感到有趣」，interest 為動詞。）

4. 我想要牛排全熟。（答：A the steak well done，OC＝過去分詞＝done。）

5. 母親警告我們別遲到了。（答：B，OC＝不定詞＝not to be late。）

6. 他使我改變了。（答：A，OC＝過去分詞當形容詞用＝changed。）

5. 句型五：**S＋ Vt ＋ IO ＋ DO**（主詞＋及物動詞＋間接受詞＋直接受詞）

（**You**）**show me the money.** 你要讓我賺大錢。

名言背景：《征服情海》情節中，當球員經紀人 Jerry 試圖說服一位脾氣很壞的二線球員 Rod 跟著他時，Rod 要求 Jerry 為他做一件事，就是跟著一起在電話中大喊 "Show me the money"。而後，這句話多被財經相關節目或文章所引用。

■ 句型五【S 主詞 ＋ Vt 及物動詞 ＋ IO 直接受詞 ＋ DO 間接受詞】文法概念解析：句型五中的動詞為及物動詞又稱為授與動詞，後面需要接兩個受詞（O），傳達 "給某人某物" 的句型；也就是說，動詞本身需要二個受詞，才能表達完整的意義。

1. 觀念說明：

　　a. 及物動詞（Vt）：句型五的動詞為及物動詞又稱為授與動詞，後面通常必須跟著二個受詞：間接受詞（IO）與直接受詞（DO）。

　　b. 間接受詞（IO）：通常指人或動物，表示授與的對象；放在直接受詞（DO）前。

　　c. 直接受詞（DO）：通常指事或物，表是授與的東西；放在間接受詞（IO）後。直接受詞可以是名詞、不定詞、名詞片語或名詞子句。

例：I gave you a book.（IO=you，DO=a book）我給你一本書。

2. 使用特點：

a. 常見的授與動詞：bring ／ give ／ lend ／ offer ／ pay ／ send ／ show ／ teach ／ tell ／ write…等。

例：She offered me a job. 她提供我一個工作。

b. 間接受詞（IO）和直接受詞（DO）的排列位置可以互換，但是中間必須要有介系詞，如 to、for 或 of 等介於兩者之間。

例：Chris sent me a letter.（S + Vt + IO + DO）Chris 寄給我一封信。

例：Chris sent a letter to me.（S + Vt + DO + Prep. + IO）Chris 寄了一封信給我。

 絕妙好例句：

1. Mother bought me a gift.（me=IO；a gift=DO，名詞）母親給我買了禮物。

2. He showed her to her seat.（her=IO；to her seat=DO，不定詞）他把她帶到座位上。

3. Will you buy me a drink?（me =IO；a drink=DO，名詞）你要不要請我喝杯酒？

4. I wish you luck.（you=IO；luck=DO 名詞）祝你好運。

5. John bought a coffee to me.（S+Vt+DO+to+IO，a coffee=DO， 名 詞，me=IO）約翰買了一杯咖啡給我。

換你選選看（請選出句中的間接受詞和直接受詞）：

（　　）1. He passed me the ball.

　　　　IO= A He　B passed　C me　D the ball；

　　　　DO= A He　B passed　C me　D the ball

（　　）2. He passed the ball to me.

　　　　IO= A He　B passed　C the ball　D me；

　　　　DO= A He　B passed　C the ball　D me

（　　）3. She showed us how to make a cake.

　　　　IO= A She　B showed　C us　D how to make a cake；

　　　　DO= A She　B showed　C us　D how to make a cake

（　　）4. He bought an iPad for his girlfriend.

　　　　IO= A He　B bought　C an iPad　D his girlfriend；

　　　　DO= A He　B bought　C an iPad　D his girlfriend

（　　）5. I told you not to do that.

　　　　DO= A不定詞　B名詞　C名詞片語

（　　）6. He sent me a card.

　　　　DO= A he　B a card　C me

答案與中譯解析：

1. 他傳給我球。（答：IO= C ，DO= D ，名詞；S + Vt + IO + DO。）

2. 他傳球給我。（答：IO= D ，DO= C ，名詞；S + Vt + DO + prep.（to）+ IO。）

3. 她教我們如何製作蛋糕。（答：IO= C ，DO= D ，名詞片語。）

4. 他給她女友買了台 iPad。（答：IO= D ，DO= C ，名詞；S + Vt + DO + prep.（for）+ IO。）

5. 我告訴過你不要做此事。（答： A ，IO=you，DO=not to do that，不定詞。）

6. 他寄給我一張卡片。（答： B ，IO=me，DO=a card，名詞。）

Unit 2
時態

 搶先看名句學文法：

1. You are beautiful! It's true. 你很美，真的。
   時態一：現在簡單式 **Simple Present Tense**

2. No one is going to hurt you. 沒有人能傷害你。
   時態二：現在進行式 **Present Progressive Tense**

3. You have been the one for me. 你是我今生的唯一。
   時態三：現在完成式 **Present Perfect Tense**

4. I have been waiting for you. 我一直都在等你。
   時態四：現在完成進行式 **Present Perfect Progressive Tense.**

5. You found me. 你發現了我。
   時態五：過去簡單式 **Simple Past Tense**

6. I was dreaming of the past. And my heart was beating fast. 我昨晚夢到過去，心跳不已。
   時態六：過去進行式 **Past Progressive Tense**

7. You hid your skeletons when I had shown you mine. You woke the devil that I thought you'd left behind. 當我向你展現自我時，你卻隱藏了自己的軀體。你喚醒了那頭我以為你已擺脫的惡魔。
   時態七：過去完成式 **Past Perfect Tense**

8. I had been trying to emulate Barbara Walters since the start of my TV career. 自我電視生涯開始，我就以 **Barbara Walters** 為我試圖模仿的對象。
   時態八：過去完成進行式 **Past Perfect Progressive Tense**

9. *Take a breath, I'll pull myself together... You'll never know.* 深呼吸，我會振作起來…，你永遠也不會知道。

　　時態九：未來簡單式 **Simple Future Tense**

10. *I'll be missing you.* 我會一直想你。

　　時態十：未來進行式 **Future Progressive Tense**

11. *When you learn to tap this resource, you will truly have defeated age.* 當你學會使用這個資源時，你將真的戰勝年老。

　　時態十一：未來完成式 **Future Perfect Tense**

12. *"Next July I will have been doing this for 50 years, "Springsteen says.* "到明年 **7** 月，我的演唱生涯就要滿 **50** 年了。

　　時態十二：未來進行完成式 **Future Perfect Progressive Tense**

 英文達人小筆記！

　　英文對時間的表示有三種，分別為過去（Past），現在（Present），未來（Future）。對狀態的表示有四種，分別為簡單式（Simple）、進行式（Progressive）、完成式（Perfect）以及完成進行式（Perfect Progressive）。透過狀態與時間的交叉組合，可形成英文的 12 種時態。

	過去（Past）	現在（Present）	未來（Future）
簡單式（Simple）	過去簡單式 Past Simple	現在簡單式 Present Simple	未來簡單式 Future Simple
進行式（Progressive）	過去進行式 Past Progressive	現在進行式 Present Progressive	未來進行式 Future Progressive
完成式（Perfect）	過去完成式 Past Perfect	現在完成式 Present Perfect	未來完成式 Future Perfect
完成進行式（Perfect Progressive）	過去完成進行式 Past Perfect Progressive	現在完成進行式 Present Perfect Progressive	未來完成進行式 Future Perfect Progressive

Part I 句型文法

Part II 字詞文法

Part III 文法訂正篇

1. 時態一：現在簡單式 Simple Present Tense

You are beautiful. It's true! 你很美麗，是真的！

名言背景：摘自於英國創作型歌手 James Blunt 的代表作品 You're Beautiful，收錄於專輯 Back to Bedlem。這首歌於 2005 年一推出便攀升至英國流行歌曲排行榜的冠軍，並且停留 6 週；2006 年在美國 "Billboard Hot 100" 單曲排行榜上，排行榜首；隨後更橫掃全世界的流行樂排行榜。

1. 使用時機：

    a. 反覆性的動作或習慣：說明動作重覆或是習慣。

       例：I drink a cup of coffee every morning. 我每天早上喝咖啡。

    b. 一般性真理：說明普遍相信的真理事實。

       例：The sun rises in the East. 旭日東昇。

    c. 事實或狀態：陳述事實或表達現在的狀況。

       例：She is a teacher. 她是老師。

2. 文法結構：

    a. 肯定句：

       I. 主詞 S + 動詞 V + …

       例：You drink coffee. 你喝咖啡。

       II. 主詞 S + Be 動詞 + …

       例：She is a teacher. 她是老師。

    b. 否定句：

       I. 主詞 S + 助動詞 + not + 動詞 V + …

       例：You do not（don't）drink coffee. 你不喝咖啡。

       II. 主詞 S + Be 動詞 + not + …

       例：She is not（isn't）a teacher. 她不是老師。

    c. 疑問句：

       I. 助動詞 + 主詞 S + 動詞 V + …

       例：Do you drink coffee? 你喝咖啡嗎？

       II. Be 動詞 + 主詞 S + …

       例：Is she a teacher? 她是老師嗎？

3. 使用特點：

　　a. 肯定句的動詞前不加助動詞。

　　b. 主詞 S 為第三人稱（he ／ she ／ it），動詞 V 字尾要加上 s ／ es；助動詞要用 does。

　　c. 否定句與疑問句的動詞不做變化，只有助動詞隨主詞變化。

　　d. 常使用於現在簡單式的時間副詞：every day ／ often ／ always ／ sometimes ／ never。

　　e. is not = isn't；are not = aren't；do not = don't

 絕妙好例句：

1. John walks to school every day.（V=walks，現在式表重覆動作）John 每天走路去上學。

2. The Moon goes around the Earth.（V=goes，現在式表真理）月亮繞著地球。

3. She is not here now.（is + not，現在式表事實或狀態） 她現在不在這裡。

4. The party starts at 7 o'clock.（V=starts，現在式表事實或狀態）舞會 7 點開始。

5. Do you collect stamp?（V=collect，現在式表習慣）你集郵嗎？

換你選選看（選出正確的動詞時態）：

（　　）1. I ＿＿ in Taiwan now. Ａ lived　Ｂ living　Ｃ live

（　　）2. She ＿＿ she is right. Ａ think　Ｂ thinks　Ｃ thought

（　　）3. He ＿＿ his daughter. Ａ loving　Ｂ loves　Ｃ love

（　　）4. The train ＿＿＿every morning at 8 o'clock. Ａ leaves　Ｂ leave　Ｃ leaving

（　　）5. Do you＿＿ your passport with you? Ａ have　Ｂ has　Ｃ had

（　　）6. Pet always＿＿ his wallet. Ａ forget　Ｂ forgets　Ｃ forgot

答案與中譯解析：

1. 我現在住在台灣。（答案選 C，V=live，現在簡單式表事實或狀態。）

2. 她認為她是對的。（答案選 B，V=thinks，現在簡單式表事實或狀態，此外，think 表示看法時，只能用現在簡單式。）

3. 他愛他女兒。（答案選 B，V=loves，現在簡單式表事實或狀態。）

4. 火車每天早上八點離開。（答案選 A，V=leaves，現在簡單式表反覆性動作或習慣。）

5. 你有帶護照嗎？（答案選 A，V=have，現在簡單式表事實或狀態。）

6. Pet 總是忘記他的皮夾。（答案選 B，V=forgets，現在簡單式表反覆性動作或習慣。）

2. 時態二：現在進行式 **Present Progressive Tense**

No one is going to hurt you. 沒有人能傷害你。

引言背景：摘自美劇影集《The Vampire Diaries，吸血鬼日記》，改編自作者 L. J. Smith 同名小說，2009 年於 CW 電台首播。這句話在劇中很常出現，不論是 Damon 對著獵物進行催眠蠱惑的話語，還是 Stefan 安撫受驚嚇的 Elena 時說的話。

　　1. 使用時機：

　　　　a. 動作正在進行或發生：強調 " 現在／當下 " 正在進行的動作，且這個動作有可能會繼續發展下去。

　　　　　例：We are watching TV now. 我們正在看電視。

　　　　b. 計畫性的未來動作：現在進行式也可以用來表示已經計畫，並且即將發生的未來動作。後面通常會加上表示未來的時間副詞，如：tonight ／ tomorrow ／ next Friday ／ at noon... 等。

　　　　　例：I am going to the theatre tonight. 我晚上要去電影院。

　　2. 文法結構：

　　　　a. 肯定句：主詞 S ＋（am ／ are ／ is）＋現在分詞（V-ing）＋…

　　　　　例：They are eating dinner. 他們正在吃晚餐。

b. 否定句：主詞 S+（am ／ are ／ is）＋ not ＋現在分詞（V-ing）＋…

例：They are not（aren't）eating dinner. 他們沒再吃晚餐。

c. 疑問句：（Am ／ Are ／ Is）＋主詞 S ＋現在分詞（V-ing）＋…

例：Are they eating dinner? 他們正在吃晚餐嗎？

3. 使用特點：

a. 用 Be 動詞（am ／ are ／ is）為助動詞。

b. 動詞使用使用現在分詞，也就是在原形動詞字尾加上 "-ing"

c. 常使用於現在進行式的時間副詞：now, right now, just now, at this moment...

 絕妙好例句：

1. He is playing football now.（V=play，進行式表動作正在進行／發生）他現在正在踢足球。

2. I am preparing for my exam.（V=prepare，進行式表動作正在進行／發生）我正在準備考試。

3. She is going to Hong Kong next Friday.（V=go，進行式表計畫性的未來動作）她下週五即將去香港。

4. Are you coming with us to that store?（V=come，進行式表計畫性的未來動作）你要跟我們去那家店嗎？

5. Jane is not talking on the phone now.（V=talk，進行式表動作正在進行／發生）Jane 現在沒有在講電話。

換你選選看（選出正確的動詞時態）：

（　　）1. I ＿＿＿＿for London tomorrow morning. Ⓐ am leaving　Ⓑ leave　Ⓒ left

（　　）2. They ＿＿＿＿the printer. Ⓐ checks　Ⓑ are checking　Ⓒ are check

（　　）3. She ＿＿＿＿＿ to the park. Ⓐ is not going　Ⓑ is go　Ⓒ isn't goes

(   ) 4. ＿＿＿ they ＿＿＿ to help? Ⓐ Are; trying   Ⓑ Are; to try   Ⓒ Do; trying

(   ) 5. Look! They ＿＿＿＿＿. Ⓐ coming   Ⓑ are come   Ⓒ are coming

(   ) 6. My sister is ＿＿＿＿ with us. Ⓐ not live   Ⓑ not living   Ⓒ does not live

📁 答案與中譯解析：

1. 我明早動身去英國。（答：Ⓐ am leaving，現在進行式表示計畫性的未來動作。）

2. 他們正在檢查印表機。（答：Ⓑ are checking，現在進行式表示動作正在進行／發生。）

3. 她沒有要去公園。（答：Ⓐ is not going，現在進行式表示動作正在進行／發生。）

4. 他們是想幫忙嗎？（答：Ⓐ Are; trying，現在進行式表示動作正在進行／發生。）

5. 看！他們來了！（答：Ⓒ are coming，現在進行式表示動作正在進行／發生。）

6. 我姊姊不和我們住在一起。（答：Ⓑ not living，現在進行式表示動作正在進行／發生。）

3. 時態三：現在完成式 Present Perfect Tense

You have been the one for me. 你是我今生的唯一。

名言背景：摘自於英國歌手 James Blunt，於 2004 年發行的首張專輯 Back to Bedlem 的其中一首 "Goodbye My Lover" 歌詞內容；這首歌一推出，隨即攀升至英國單曲排行榜第三名的位置。透過 James Blunt 獨特的嗓音，道出離別的悲傷，因為已經分手，所以歌詞內容運用了很多的現在完成式時態。

■【現在完成式 Present Perfect 文法解析】：現在完成式（Present Perfect），強調的是過去與現在的關係，主要在表達動作在過去不確定的時間發生，持續一段時間直到現在的狀態，動作已完成／未完成、經驗與持續性的動作。

1. 使用時機：

　　a. 動作已完成：強調某個動作／事件，已經完成、剛剛完成或者未完成的狀態

　　　　例：Pete has done this project. Pete 已經完成這個案子。

　　b. 過去經驗：說明過去曾經歷的經驗。

　　　　例：Pete has done this project before. Pete 曾做過這個案子。

　　c. 持續性的動作／事件：說明動作／事件從過去發生一直到現在，並且有可能還會繼續下去。

　　　　例：Pete has done this project for one month. Pete 做這個案子已經有一個月了。

2. 文法結構：

　　a. 肯定句：主詞 S ＋ 助動詞（have ／ has）＋ 過去分詞（P.P.）＋ ⋯

　　　　例：She has fixed the problem. 她已經解決問題。

　　b. 否定句：主詞 S ＋ 助動詞（have ／ has）＋ not ＋ 過去分詞（P.P.）＋ ⋯

　　　　例：She has not（hasn't）fixed the problem. 她還沒解決問題。

　　c. 疑問句：助動詞（Have ／ Has）＋ 主詞 S ＋ 過去分詞（P.P.）＋ ⋯

　　　　例：Has she fixed the problem? 她已經解決問題了嗎？

3. 使用特點：

　　a. 不管肯定句、否定句或是疑問句，加上助動詞（have ／ has），依主詞選擇適合的助動詞，第三人稱助動詞選用 has，其餘用 have。

　　b. 動詞使用過去分詞；規則動詞字尾加上 "-ed"，不規則性動詞變化，則另參照列表。

　　c. 常使用於現在完成式的時間副詞： just ／ yet ／ never ／ already ／ since ＋（過去某一時間到現在 or 過去式子句）／ for ＋（一段時間）。

　　d. have not = haven't；has not = hasn't

4. 區分（have ／ has）＋ been to 與（have ／ has）＋ gone to 用法：

a. been to 表示某人曾經去過某地方且已經回來，人現在就在這裡。

例：He has been to London before. 他曾去過倫敦。

b. gone to 表示某人已經去某地方但是還沒回來，人現在不在這裡。

例：He has gone to London. 他已經去倫敦了。

絕妙好例句：

1. He has played football for 2 hours.（V=play，完成式表示持續性的動作／事件）他已經踢了 2 個小時的足球了。

2. I have prepared for my exam since last week.（V=prepare，完成式表示持續性的動作／事件）從上週開始，我已經在準備考試了。

3. She has never been to Hong Kong.（been to，完成式表示過去經驗）她從未去過香港。

4. They have not come to the party.（V=come，完成式表示動作已完成／未完成）他們還沒來到這個舞會。

5. My mother has lived here for 20 years.（V=live，完成式表示持續性的動作／事件）我的母親在這裡已經住了 20 年。

換你選選看（選出正確的動詞時態）：

（　）1. I ＿＿＿ my brother for a long time. A have not seen　B am seeing　C saw

（　）2. She ＿＿＿＿ her answers for 5 times. A checks　B has checked　C is checking

（　）3. ＿＿＿she ＿＿＿＿ to the park? A Has; walking　B Has; walked　C Is; walked

（　）4. ＿＿＿ you ever ＿＿＿ that girl? A Have; seeing　B Have; saw　C Have; seen

（　）5. My sister ＿＿＿＿ with us for 2 years. A has live　B has lived　C has living

答案與中譯解析：

1. 我已經很久沒有見到我哥了。（答：Ⓐ have not seen，現在完成式表示持續性的動作／事件。）

2. 她已經檢查她的答案 5 次了。（答：Ⓑ has checked，現在完成式表示動作已完成／未完成。）

3. 她已經走到公園了嗎？（答：Ⓑ Has; walked，現在完成式表示動作已完成／未完成。）

4. 你曾經見過那個女孩嗎？（答：Ⓒ Have; seen，現在完成式表示過去經驗。）

5. 我姊姊和我們住在一起已經兩年了。（答：Ⓑ has lived，現在完成式表示持續性的動作／事件。）

4. 時態四：現在完成進行式 Present Perfect Progressive Tense

I have been waiting for you. 我一直都在等你。

名言背景：摘自美國音樂創作歌手 Ben Harper 於 2006 年發行的專輯 Both Side of The Gun，歌曲名稱為 Waiting for you，整首歌詞大多是運用現在完成進行式的時態；這是一首甜蜜浪漫的情歌，特別適合在戀愛剛開始的階段。

■【現在完成進行式 **Present Perfect Progressive** 文法解析】：現在完成進行式 Present Perfect Progressive，主要在表達動作在過去不確定的時間發生，一直到現在，動作還在持續進行，或者是剛剛結束；強調的是動作的持續性。

1. 使用時機：

動作的持續性：說明動作在過去已經發生，說話的當下，動作還在持續進行中，或剛剛結束。

例：We have been standing here for 1 hour. 我們站在這裡已經一個小時了。

2. 文法結構：

a. 肯定句：主詞 S + 助動詞（have／has）+ 助動詞 been + 現在分詞（V-ing）+ …

Part I 句型文法

Part II 字詞文法

Part III 文法糾正篇

> 例：I have been sitting on a sofa for a while. 我已經坐在沙發上有段時間了。

b. 否定句：主詞 S ＋ 助動詞（have／has）＋ not ＋ 助動詞 been ＋ 現在分詞（V-ing）＋⋯

> 例：She has not been fixing the problem since last night. 自從昨晚，她就沒有在試著解決問題。

c. 疑問句：助動詞（Have／Has）＋ 主詞 S ＋ 助動詞 been ＋ 現在分詞（V-ing）＋⋯

> 例：Has she been fixing the problem？ 她有一直在試著解決問題嗎？

3. 使用特點：

a. 有兩個助動詞（have／has）以及 been，只有助動詞（have／has）跟著主詞變化。

b. 用 "how long" 表示動作持續多長時間。

c. 常使用於現在完成式的時間副詞：since ＋（過去某一時間到現在 or 過去式子句）／ for ＋（一段時間）／ lately／ recently。

4. 現在完成式 VS. 現在完成進行式：

5. 現在完成式與現在完成進行式兩者主要都在表示動作發生在過去，一直持續到現在，但是強調的重點不同：

a. 現在完成式，大多時候主要在表示動作已經完成，強調結果。

> 例：Pete has done this project. Pete 已經完成這個計畫。

b. 現在完成進行式，大多時候主要在表示動作還在進行，強調動作的持續性。

> 例：Pete has been doing this project. Pete 還在做這個計畫。

絕妙好例句：

1. He has been playing football for 2 hours.（V=play，完成進行式表動作的持續性）。他已經連續踢了 2 個小時的足球。

2. I have been preparing for my exam since last week.（V=prepare，完成進行式表動作的持續性）。 從上週開始，我都在準備考試。

3. She has not been feeling well lately.（V=feel，完成進行式表動作的持續性）。她最近一直覺得不舒服。

4. I have been watching you.（V=watch，完成進行式表動作的持續性）。我一直在注意著你。

5. Mother has been living here for 20 years.（V=live，完成進行式表動作的持續性）。母親一直在這裡住了 20 年。

換你選選看（選出正確的動詞時態）：

( ) 1. I _____ my brother for a long time. A have not been seeing B have seeing C have been seen

( ) 2. She _____ so hard. A has been worked B has been working C has working

( ) 3. We _____ since last month. A have been dated B have dating C have been dating

( ) 4. You_____ to the teacher for last 5 minutes? A have not been listening B not have been listening C have been not listening

( ) 5. How long _____ you _____ here? A have; be staying B are; staying C have; been staying

( ) 6. Sandy _____ this book lately. A is reading B reads C has been reading

答案與中譯解析：

1. 我已經很久沒有見到我哥了。（答：A have not been seeing，現在完成進行式表示動作的持續性。）

2. 她一直努力工作。（答：B has been working，現在完成進行式表示動作的持續性。）

3. 從上個月開始我們一直在約會（答：C have been dating，現在完成進行式表示動作的持續性。）

4. 從過去五分鐘到現在，你一直都沒有在聽課。（答：A have not been listening，現在完成進行式表示動作的持續性。）

5. 你在這裡待多久了。（答：C have; been staying，現在完成進行式表示動作的持續性。）

6. Sandy 最近一直在看這本書。（答：C has been reading，現在完成進行式表示動作的持續性。）

5. 時態五：過去簡單式 Simple Past Tense

You found me. 你發現了我。

名言背景：摘自美國鄉村音樂創作歌手 Taylor Swift 於 2012 年底發行的單曲 "I Knew You Were a Trouble"，收錄於專輯《Red》，推出首週即排上美國 Billboard Hot 100 第三名，隨後更攀上冠軍行列。"I knew you were trouble when you walked in."（當你走進來時，我就知道你會是個麻煩），內容主要有關失戀，大多用過去簡單式的時態敘事；You found me 是一句很實用的句子，可以應用到很多場合。

■【過去簡單式 Simple Past 文法解析】：過去簡單式 Simple Past，主要表達過去發生的動作、事實、習慣，並且動作在過去的時間已經結束。

　1. 使用時機：

　　a. 過去的動作／狀態：表示動作發生在過去並且已經結束。

　　　例：He watched a football game yesterday. 他昨天看了場足球賽。

　　b. 過去的習慣：表示過去的習慣，現在沒有這個習慣。

　　例：I studied French when I was a child. 我小時候曾學過法文。

　c. 過去的事實：表示過去發生的事實，現在已經停止。

　　例：He liked onion before. 他以前喜歡洋蔥。

2. 文法結構：

　a. 肯定句：

　　主詞 S ＋ 動詞 V-ed（規則或不規則動詞）＋…

　　例：She worked hard. 她過去努力工作。

　　主詞 S ＋ Be 動詞（was ／ were）＋…

　　例：She was a teacher. 她曾是老師。

　b. 否定句：

　　主詞 S ＋ 助動詞（did）＋ not ＋ 動詞 V ＋…

　　例：You didn't drink coffee. 你過去不喝咖啡。

　　主詞 S ＋ be 動詞（was ／ were）＋ not ＋…

　　例：She was not a teacher. 她以前不是老師。

　c. 疑問句：

　　助動詞（Did）＋ 主詞 S ＋ 動詞 V ＋…

　　例：Did you drink coffee? 你以前喝咖啡嗎？

　　Be 動詞（were ／ was）＋ 主詞 S ＋…

　　例：Was she a teacher? 她以前是老師嗎？

3. 使用特點：

　a. 肯定句的動詞前不加助動詞，規則動詞字尾加 "-ed"，不規則動詞則依動詞變化來使用。

　b. 不管主詞 S 人稱，助動詞用都 "did"。Be 動詞（was ／ were），則依據主詞作變化；主詞為第一、三人稱時，使用 "was"，主詞第二人稱或複數，使用 "were"。

　c. 否定句與疑問句的動詞，都用原形動詞。

　d. 常使用於過去簡單式的時間副詞：yesterday，last ＋（week，night，...），ago

絕妙好例句：

1. He played football before.（V=play，過去式表過去的事實）他以前踢過足球。
2. I prepared for my exam last week.（V=prepare，過去式表過去的動作狀態）我在上週為考試而做準備。
3. She did not feel well yesterday.（V=feel，過去式表過去的動作狀態）她昨天覺得不舒服。
4. I loved you.（V=love，過去式表過去的事實）我曾愛過你。
5. My mother lived here.（V=live，過去式表過去的事實）我的母親以前住這。

換你選選看（選出正確的動詞時態）：

（　　）1. I _____ to my brother. A didn't talk　B have talking　C am talk
（　　）2. She _____ so hard long time ago. A worked　B has been woking　C works
（　　）3. We _____ last month. A are dating　B dated　C will date
（　　）4. You _____ your car yesterday. A don't wash　B didn't washed　C didn't wash
（　　）5. _____ you _____ milk when you were a child? A Do; drink　B Did; drink　C Did; drank
（　　）6. Alice _____ shy before. A was　B is　C were

答案與中譯解析：

1. 我沒和我哥說話。（答：A did not talk，過去簡單式表示過去的動作／狀態。）
2. 她很久以前努力工作過。（答：A worked，過去簡單式表示過去的事實。）
3. 從上個月我們曾約會過（答：B dated，過去簡單式過去的動作／狀態。）
4. 你昨天沒有洗車。（答：C didn't wash，過去簡單式表示過去的動作／狀態。）

5. 你小時候喝牛奶嗎？（答：B Did;drink，過去簡單式表示過去的習慣。）

6. Alice 以前很害羞 .（答：A was，過去簡單式表示過去的事實。

6. 時態六： 過去進行式 **Past Progressive Tense**

I was dreaming of the past. And my heart was beating fast.

我昨晚做夢夢到過去，而我的心跳地非常快。

名言背景：選自於約翰藍儂的歌曲 Jealous Guy（忌妒的男人）。約翰藍儂是一名英國音樂人、歌手及作曲，以身為披頭四團員揚名全球。與他的妻子小野洋子同為激進和平主義者與視覺藝術家，影響當今流行音樂深遠。

■【過去進行式 **Past Progressive** 文法解析】：過去進行式 Past Progressive，主要在表達過去某個「特定」時間點上，「正在進行」的動作／狀態。

  1. 使用時機：

    a. 過去正在發生的動作／狀態：表示在過去某特定時間點上，動作／狀態正在進行。

      例：He was watching a football game at 10 p.m. last night. 他昨晚 10 點正在看足球賽。

    b. 兩個動作同時發生：表示過去某個特定時間點上，剛好兩個動作正在平行進行。

      例：While he was watching a football game, she was talking on the phone. 當他看足球賽時，她正在講電話。

    c. 經常搭配過去簡單式：主要表達兩個動作都發生在過去，一個進行中的動作，被另一個動作／事件介入。

      例：He was watching a football game when she called. 當她來電時，他正在看足球賽。

  2. 文法結構：

    a. 肯定句：

      主詞 S + 助動詞（was ／ were）+ 動詞 V-ing + …

      例：She was watching TV at 7 p.m. 昨晚 7 點她正在看電視。

b. 否定句：

主詞 S + 助動詞（was ／ were）+ not + 動詞 V-ing + …

例：She wasn't watching TV at 7 p.m. 昨晚 7 點她沒有在看電視。

c. 疑問句：

助動詞（Was ／ Were）+ 主詞 S + 動詞 V-ing + …

例：Was she watching TV at 7 pm？ 昨晚 7 點的時候，她在看電視嗎？

3. 使用特點：

a. Be 動詞（was ／ were）為助動詞，主要動詞字尾加 "-ing"。

b. 助動詞（was ／ were），則依據主詞 S 作變化；主詞為第一、三人稱時，使用 "was"，主詞第二人稱或複數，使用 "were"。

c. 常使用於過去簡單式的時間副詞：when，while。

d. was not = wasn't；were not = weren't

 絕妙好例句：

1. Andy was playing football when I arrived.（V=play、arrive，搭配過去簡單式）當我到的時候，Andy 正在踢足球。

2. I was preparing for my exam at 7 p.m..（V=prepare，過去正在進行的動作狀態）我在晚上 7 點時，準備著我的考試。

3. She was not cooking when I visited her.（V=cook、visit，搭配過去簡單式）我昨天拜訪她時，她沒有在煮飯。

4. My mother was travelling to London last week when I called her.（V=travel、call，搭配過去簡單式）上週當我打給我媽時，她正好在倫敦旅遊。

5. Pete was sitting there while I was shopping at the store.（V=sit、shop，兩個動作同時發生）當我在店裡購物時，Pete 就坐在那裡。

換你選選看（選出正確的動詞時態）：

（　　）1. I _____ to my brother. **A** was talking　**B** were talking　**C** talking

（　　）2. When you _____, I _____ to my brother. **A** came; was talking　**B** come; am talking　**C** coming; talked

（　　）3. We _____ at 7pm last night. **A** are dating　**B** were dating　**C** dated

（　　）4. We _____ , while you _____ to party. **A** were dating; go　**B** were dating; were going　**C** dated; go

（　　）5. Thomas _____ and I _____ , either. **A** was not work; was not work　**B** was not working; was not working　**C** was work; was work

（　　）6. _____ you _____ , when I called last night? **A** Are; sleeping　**B** Were; sleeping　**C** Did; sleep

答案與中譯解析：

1. 我當時正在跟我哥說話。（答：**A** was talking，過去進行式表示過去正在進行的動作狀態。）

2. 當你來的時候，我正在和我哥說話。（答：**A** came;was talking，過去進行式搭配過去簡單式一起使用，表示動作的先後關係。）

3. 我們昨晚 7 點正在約會。（答：**B** were dating，過去進行式表示過去某時間點正在進行的動作狀態。）

4. 你們去舞會的時候，我們在約會。（答：**B** were dating;were going，兩個動作在過去同時發生。）

5. 湯瑪斯當時沒有在工作，我也是。（答：**B** was not working、was not working，兩個動作在過去同時發生。）

6. 昨晚我打給你時，你正好在睡覺嗎？（答：**B** Were;sleep，過去進行式搭配過去簡單式一起使用，表示動作的先後關係）

Part I 句型文法

Part II 字詞文法

Part III 文法糾正篇

7. 時態七：過去完成式 **Past Perfect Tense**

You hid your skeletons when I had shown you mine. You woke the devil that I thought you'd left behind. 當我向你展現自我時，你卻隱藏了自己的軀體。你喚醒了那頭我以為你已經擺脫了的惡魔。

名言背景：電影《吸血鬼獵人：林肯總統》 *Abraham Lincoln: Vampire Hunter* 的主題曲，Linkin Park（聯合公園）為其量身訂做的歌名為 Powerless（無能為力），吸血鬼獵人是一部 2012 年美國電影，改編自 2010 年的同名小説，作者為 Seth Grahame Smith 為美國一位暢銷小説作家及電影監製。

■【過式完成式 **Past Perfect** 文法解析】：過式完成式 Past Perfect，主要在表達動作／狀態在過去的時間開始，並且過去時間已經完成；簡單來説所有的動作與狀態，都在 "過去" 的時空背景下，開始、進行到結束。

1. 使用時機：

    a. 表達二個過去動作的先後順序，與過去簡單式 Past Simple 使用，第一個先發生的動作使用 "過式完成式 **Past Perfect**"，第二個則使用 "過去簡單式 Past Simple"；提供一個容易的記住的口訣 "先完成後簡單"。

    例：Pete had never cooked before he went to college. Pete 上大學前，從未下過廚。

    第一個動作：Pete had never cooked.（過去完成式）

    第二個動作：He went to college.（過去簡單式）

2. 文法結構：

    a. 肯定句：

    主詞 S ＋ 助動詞（had）＋ 過去分詞（P.P.）…

    例：I had lived in Taiwan before I moved to USA. 我搬去美國前，一直住在台灣。

    b. 否定句：

    主詞 S ＋ 助動詞（had）＋ not ＋ 過去分詞（P.P.）＋ …

    例：I had not lived in Taiwan before I moved to USA. 我搬去美國

前，不住在台灣。

c. 疑問句：

助動詞（had）＋主詞 S ＋過去分詞（P.P.）＋…

例：Had you lived in Taiwan before you moved to USA. 你搬去美國前，是住在台灣嗎？

3. 使用特點：

a. 用助動詞（has／have）的過去式 "had"，不隨著主詞 S 作變化。

b. 動詞使用過去分詞；規則動詞字尾加上 "-ed"，不規則性動詞變化，則另參照列表。

 絕妙好例句：

1. Vicky was hungry; she had not eaten for 8 hours.（1st action 過去完成式，V=eat）Vicky 餓了，她已經 8 個小時沒吃飯了。

2. John had had that mobile phone for 4 years before it broke down.（1st action 過去完成式，V= have）John 在他的手機壞掉前，已經使用它 4 年了。

3. Had Anne talked to Mother before she cooked dinner?（1st action 過去完成式，V= talk）Anne 煮晚餐前有跟母親說話嗎？

4. I had never visited London before I went there in 2010.（1st action 過去完成式，V= visit）我在 2010 年去倫敦的，之前從來沒去過。

5. I had worked all day before my friends came to pick me up.（1st action 過去完成式，V= work）我朋友來接我時，我之前已經工作一整天了。

換你選選看（選出正確的動詞時態）：

（　　）1. Jane knew the movie because she _____ it before. A has seen
B had seen　C has been seeing

（　　）2. Before I ran to my sister's house, I _____ her. A has called
B has been calling　C had called

（　　）3. By the time the rain began, she _____. A had arrived　B has arrived　C has been arrived

（　　）4. I _____ Olivia for 2 years before I met her in France. A had not seen　B has not seen　C has not been seeing

（　　）5. We _____ enough, so we lost the basketball game. A has not practiced　B had not practiced　C has not been practicing

（　　）6. ____ Frank _____ the instructions before they use this notebook? A Had; read　B Has; read　C Has; been reading

答案與中譯解析：

1. Jane 知道這部電影因為他之前已經看過了。（答：B had seen，第一個先發生的動作使用過式完成式。）

2. 在我跑去我姐姐家之前，我已經打過電話給她了。（答：C had called，第一個先發生的動作使用過式完成式。）

3. 雨開始下之前她已經抵達了。（答：A had arrived，第一個先發生的動作使用過式完成式。）

4. 我在法國碰到 Olivia，在之前我已經有 2 年沒見過她了。（答：A had not seen，第一個先發生的動作使用過式完成式。）

5. 我們之前練習的不夠，所以我們才會輸了這場球賽。（答：B had not practiced，第一個先發生的動作使用過式完成式。）

6. Frank 在使用手提電腦前，有先讀過使用說明嗎？（答：A Had; read，第一個先發生的動作使用過式完成式。）

8. 時態八：過去完成進行式 **Past Perfect Progressive Tense**

I had been trying to emulate Barbara Walters, since the start of my TV career. Barbara Walters，她是我自電視生涯開始，即試圖模仿的對象。

名言背景：脫口秀主持人、20 世紀最富有的美國黑人 Oprah（歐普拉）在史丹佛大學 2008 年畢業典禮的演講，Oprah 在演講裡分享 3 個人生經驗，是有關感覺、失敗、及尋找快樂。

■【過去完成進行式 **Past Perfect Progressive** 文法解析】：過去完成進行式 Past Perfect Progressive，主要在表達動作／狀態在過去的時間開始，且持續一段時間；簡單來說所有的動作與狀態，都在「過去」的時空背景下，開始並且持續進行；強調「過去動作的持續性」。

1. 使用時機：

　　表達二個過去動作的先後順序，與過去簡單式 Past Simple 使用，第一個先發生的動作已經持續一段時間，用「過去完成進行式 Past Perfect Progressive」；第二個動作則使用「過去簡單式 Past Simple」；提供一個容易的記住的口訣「先完成進行後簡單」。

　　　例：We had been standing here for over 1 hour when she finally arrived. 當她終於抵達的時候，我們站在這裡已經一個多小時了。

　　　第一個動作：We had been standing here for over 1 hour.（過去完成進行式）

　　　第二個動作：when she finally arrived.（過去簡單式）

2. 文法結構：

　　a. 肯定句：

　　　主詞 S + 助動詞（had）+ 助動詞 been + 現在分詞（V-ing）⋯

　　　例：I had been waiting for him for a while when he showed up. 當他出現時，我已經等了一會了。

　　b. 否定句：

　　　主詞 S + 助動詞（had）+ not + 助動詞 been + 現在分詞（V-ing）⋯

　　　例：I had not been waiting for him for a while when he showed

up. 當他出現時，我沒有等了一會了。

  c. 疑問句：

   助動詞（had）＋主詞 S ＋助動詞 been ＋現在分詞（V-ing）…

   例：Had you been waiting for him for a while when he showed up? 當他出現時，你已經等了一會了嗎？

 3. 使用特點：

  a. 有兩個助動詞 had 以及 been，兩者都不隨著主詞 S 作變化。

  b. 動詞使用現在分詞（V-ing）。

  c. 常使用於現在完成式的時間副詞：for ／ since ／ the whole day ／ all day。

👑 絕妙好例句：

1. They had been talking for over hours before father came home.（1st action 過去完成進行式，V＝ talk）當父親回家時，他們已經聊了好幾個小時。

2. John had been using that mobile phone for 4 years before it broke down（1st action 過去完成進行式，V＝ use）John 在他的手機壞掉前，已經使用它 4 年了。

3. Had Anne been eating for last few days? She lost a lot of weight.（1st action 過去完成進行式，V＝ ear）Anne 過去幾天有吃東西嗎？她瘦了很多。

4. I had not been visiting London before I went there in 2010 again?（1st action 過去完成進行式，V＝ visit） 我在 2010 年再去倫敦的，之前已經很久沒有去過了。

5. I had been working all day before my friends came to pick me up.（1st action 過去完成進行式，V＝ work） 我朋友來接我時，我之前已經工作一整天了。

換你選選看（選出正確的動詞時態）：

（　　）1. Jane knew the movie because she _____ it several times.
　　　　 Ⓐ were seeing　Ⓑ has been seeing　Ⓒ had been seeing

（　　）2. Before I ran to my sister's house, I _____ her for million times.
　　　　 Ⓐ has called　Ⓑ had been calling　Ⓒ has been calling

（　　）3. It _____ all day, when she arrived. Ⓐ had been raining
　　　　 Ⓑ has rained　Ⓒ was raining

（　　）4. I _____ Olivia for 2 years before I met her in France. Ⓐ had
　　　　 not been seeing　Ⓑ has not seen　Ⓒ was not seeing

（　　）5. We _____ enough, so we lost the basketball game. Ⓐ were
　　　　 not practicing　Ⓑ has not practiced　Ⓒ had not been practicing

（　　）6. ____ Frank _____ for 12 hours when I came home? Ⓐ Had; been
　　　　 sleeping　Ⓑ Has; slept　Ⓒ Was; sleeping

 答案與中譯解析：

1. Jane 知道這部電影因為她之前已經看過很多遍了。（答：Ⓒ had been seeing，第一個先發生的動作已經持續一段時間，使用過去完成進行式。）

2. 在我跑去我姊家之前，我已經打過電話無數次給她了。（答：Ⓑ had been calling，第一個先發生的動作已經持續一段時間，使用過去完成進行式。）

3. 當她已經抵達時，已經下了整天的雨了。（答：Ⓐ had been raining，第一個先發生的動作已經持續一段時間，使用過去完成進行式。）

4. 我在法國碰到 Olivia，在之前我已經有 2 年沒見過她了。（答：Ⓐ had not been seeing，第一個先發生的動作已經持續一段時間，使用過去完成進行式。）

5. 我們之前練習的不夠，所以我們才會輸了這場球賽。（答：Ⓒ had not been practicing，第一個先發生的動作已經持續一段時間，使用過去完成進行式。）

6. Frank 在我回家之前已經睡了 12 小時了嗎？（答：Ⓐ Had; been sleeping，第一個先發生的動作已經持續一段時間，使用過去完成進行式。）

9. 時態九：未來簡單式 Simple Future Tense

Take a breath, I'll pull myself together... You'll never know... 深呼吸，我會振作起來 ... 你永遠也不會知道 ...

名言背景：摘自歌曲 Save You，收錄於 2008 年發行的同名專輯 Simple Plan 中。Simple Plan（簡單計劃樂團），是一支於 1999 年在加拿大魁北克地區成立的流行龐克樂團。

■【未來簡單式 Simple Future 文法解析】：未來簡單式 Simple Future，說的是「未來」，主要在表達未來將會發生的動作或即將存在的狀態。

1. 使用時機：

a. 未來的行動的意願：對未來行動的決定，說之前並沒有任何計畫與決定。

例：I will make dinner tonight. 我今晚會做晚餐。

b. 表達承諾：對未來的作出承諾。

例：I will be careful. Don't worry! 我會小心的，別擔心！

c. 對未來的預測／假設：預測未來可能會發生的事情。

例：She will win this game. 她會贏得這次比賽。

d. 未來成真／確認的事實：未來即將發生，成為不可改變的事實、確認的未來。

例：She will be 18 next month. 她下個月即將滿 18 歲。

2. 文法結構：

a. 肯定句：

主詞 S + 助動詞（will）+ 動詞 V +⋯

例：I will call you this weekend. 我週末將會打電話給你。

b. 否定句：

主詞 S + 助動詞（will）+ not + 動詞 V +⋯

例：I will not call you this weekend. 我週末不會打電話給你。

c. 疑問句：

助動詞（will）+ 主詞 S + 動詞 V +⋯

例：Will you call me this weekend? 你週末會打電話給我嗎？

3. 使用特點：

    a. 助動詞用 "will"，不隨著主詞 S 作變化。

    b. 動詞使用原形動詞。

    c. 常使用於現在完成式的時間副詞：tomorrow ／ next+（hour, year,）
...etc.

4. 另一個表示未來的句型 "Be going to"：

    主詞 S + 助動詞（am ／ are ／ is）+ going to + 動詞 V + ⋯

    a. 表示對未來的計畫、想法與打算，不管未來有沒有可能實現。

       例：I am going to call you this weekend.（打算）我打算這週末打電話給你。

       例：I will call you this weekend.（意願）我這週末會打給你。

    b. 也可以用作 "預測" 未來，跟 "will-furture" 的 "預測未來" 的作用相同。

       例：She is going to win this game. 她將要贏得這次比賽。

       例：She will win this game. 她將會贏得這次比賽。

    c. 確定行動會在未來發生。

       例：I am going to read this book tonight. 我今晚準備讀這本書。

 絕妙好例句：

1. I will help you later.（V= help，表示意願）我待會幫你。

2. It will rain tomorrow.（V=rain，表示預測）明天預計會下雨。

3. I will take care of myself.（V=take，表式承諾）我會照顧好我自己。

4. Kevin will return next week.（V= return，表示未來的事實）Kevin 下週將回來。

5. My boss is going to take few days off.（V=take，表示打算）我老闆打算放幾天假。

換你選選看（選出正確的動詞時態）：

（　　）1. _____you marry me? Ａ Will　　Ｂ Are　　Ｃ Do

（　　）2. I _____ in London tomorrow. Ａ am　　Ｂ will be　　Ｃ was

（　　）3. Pat _____ this competition. Ａ will not win　　Ｂ is wining
　　　　　Ｃ wins

（　　）4. _____ you meet May at coffee shop tomorrow. Ａ Will　　Ｂ Are
　　　　　Ｃ Do

（　　）5. I _____her. Ａ will not going to help　　Ｂ am helping　　Ｃ am not
　　　　　going to help

 答案與中譯解析：

1. 你願意嫁給我嗎？（答：Ａ Will，未來簡單式表示意願、承諾。）

2. 明天我將會在倫敦（答：Ｂ will be，未來簡單式表示未來的事實。）

3. Pat 不會贏得這個比賽的。（答：Ａ will not win，未來簡單式表示預測。）

4. 你明天將會和 May 在咖啡店碰面嗎？（答：Ａ Will，未來簡單式表示意願。）

5. 我不打算幫她。（答：Ｃ am not going to help，未來簡單式表示打算，will 以
　可以用 be going to 代替。）

6. 各位先生女士，今晚我們請總統先生出場。（答：Ｂ will invite，未來簡單式表
　示未來的事實。）

10. 時態十：未來進行式 Future Progressive Tense

I'll Be Missing You . 我會一直想你。

名言背景：這首歌是 1997 年 Puff Daddy 寫給意外過世的好友
Notorious B.I.G 的曲子，參與和聲的有團體 112，以及 B.I.G. 的遺孀—
Faith Evans。這首歌改編自 70 年代名曲 *Every Breath You Take* 原作
者是警察合唱團（Police），吹牛老爹將這首歌改成輕快的嘻哈風，收錄
在專輯 No Way Out 中。Puff Daddy 也曾經在黛安娜王妃的紀念音樂會

上（2007 年 7 月 1 日），向全世界演唱這首歌。

■【未來進行式 **Future Progressive** 文法解析】：未來進行式 Future Progressive，主要在表達在 "未來某一個特定時間點" 上，動作／事件即將進行或者還在持續進行中；強調未來動作的持續。

1. 使用時機：

　　未來特定的時間點上，動作將會進行，或持續進行；通常動作／事件，已經事先被規劃，確認會在未來的某個特定時間發生。

　　　　例：I will be making dinner at 8 o'clock tonight.　今晚 8 點的時候，我將會在那時候做晚餐。

2. 文法結構：

　　a. 肯定句：

　　　　主詞 S ＋ 助動詞（will）＋ 助動詞（be）＋ 現在分詞（動詞 V-ing）＋ …

　　　　例：I will be calling you this Sunday. 我週日將會打電話給你。

　　b. 否定句：

　　　　主詞 S ＋ 助動詞（will）＋ not ＋ 助動詞（be）＋ 現在分詞（動詞 V-ing）＋ …

　　　　例：I will not be calling you this Sunday. 我週日將不會打電話給你。

　　c. 疑問句：

　　　　助動詞（will）＋ 主詞 S ＋ 助動詞（be）＋ 現在分詞（動詞 V-ing）＋ …

　　　　例：Will you be calling me this Sunday? 你週末將會打電話給我嗎？

3. 使用特點：

　　a. 有二個助動詞 "will" 與 "be"，都不用隨著主詞 S 作變化。

　　b. 動詞使用現在分詞（V-ing）。

👑 絕妙好例句：

1. We will be going to party this Friday night.（V= go，表示動作將進行中）
   這週五晚上，我們將會去舞會。

2. At this time tomorrow, we will be leaving for Taipei.（V=leave，表示動作將進行中）明天這個時候，我們將動身前往台北。

3. Next week, she will be working for her new boss .（V=work，表示動作將進行中）她下週即將替她新老闆工作。

4. Kevin will not be returning next Monday.（V= return，表示動作將進行中）Kevin 下週一將不會回來。

5. Will Mary be taking few days off from tomorrow?（V=take，表示動作將進行中） 從明天開始，May 將會休幾天假嗎？

✏️ 換你選選看（選出正確的動詞時態）：

(   ) 1. _____ she _____ him in one year? A Will; be marrying   B Is marrying   C Does; marry

(   ) 2. _____ Bill _____ lunch with us at 6pm tonight? A Will; being eating   B Will; be eating   C Will; eating

(   ) 3. The storm _____ soon. A coming   B will be coming   C is coming

(   ) 4. Petty _____ to Italy this fall. A will not going   B is not going   C will not be going

(   ) 5. _____ you _____ the car tomorrow morning? A Are; using   B Will; be using   C Will; using

(   ) 6. They _____ on the beach this time next week. A will sitting   B will be sitting   C are sitting

答案與中譯解析：

1. 她一年內會嫁給他嗎？（答：△ Will; be marrying，未來進行式表示事情預先被規劃，即將進行中。）

2. Bill 今晚 6 點會和我們一起晚餐嗎？（答：Ⓑ will; be eating、未來進行式表示事情預先被規劃。）

3. 暴風雨即將來臨。（答：Ⓑ will be coming、未來進行式表示動作將進行中。）

4. Petty 今年秋天將不會去義大利。（答：Ⓒ will not be going，未來進行式表示動作將進行中。）

5. 你明早會用車嗎？（答：Ⓑ Will;be using，未來進行式表示動作將進行中。）

6. 下週的這個時間，他們會坐在海灘上。（答：Ⓑ will be sitting，未來進行式表示動作將進行中。）

11. 時態十一：未來完成式 Future Perfect Tense

When you learn to tap this source, you will truly have defeated age. 當你學會使用這個資源時，你將真的已經戰勝年老。

名言背景：Sophia Loren（索非婭 · 羅蘭）為義大利著名女演員，以《兩婦人》電影於 1961 年獲得奧斯卡最佳女主角。那一年，她與瑪麗蓮夢露、碧姬芭鐸一起被封 「世界上最性感的女人」。除了奧斯卡最佳女主角獎和奧斯卡終身成就獎，她在全世界已獲得 50 個國際獎項。她在 1999 年被美國電影學會選為百年來最偉大女演員第 21 名。

■ 【未來完成式 **Future Perfect Tense** 文法解析】：
    未來完成式 Future Perfect Tense，主要在表達在 " 未來某一個特定時間點 " 之前，動作／事件已經發生、結束或完成；簡單來說，預設在未來的時空下，動作已經發生、結束或完成的狀態。

    1. 使用時機：
        預設在未來特定的時間點之前，動作／事件已經發生、結束或完成的狀態。
        例：I will have written this letter by tomorrow.　我會在明天前，寫完這封信。

Part I 句型文法　*Part II* 字詞文法　*Part III* 文法糾正篇

2. 文法結構：

    a. 肯定句：

        主詞 S ＋ 助動詞（will）＋ 助動詞（have）＋ 過去分詞（p.p.）＋ …

        例：I will have called you by this Sunday. 我週日前將會打電話給你。

    b. 否定句：

        主詞 S ＋ 助動詞（will）＋ not ＋ 助動詞（have）＋ 過去分詞（p.p.）＋ …

        例：I will not have called you by this Sunday. 我週日前將不會打電話給你。

    c. 疑問句：

        助動詞（will）＋ 主詞 S ＋ 助動詞（have）＋ 過去分詞（p.p.）＋ …

        例：Will you have called me by this Sunday? 你這週末前就會打電話給我嗎？

3. 使用特點：

    a. 有二個助動詞 "will" 與 "have"，都不用隨著主詞 S 作變化。

    b. 動詞使用過去分詞（p.p.）。

    c. 使用的時間副詞片語或子句的動詞，要用 "現在簡單式"。

 絕妙好例句：

1. By 7pm, his wife will have cooked dinner.（V= cook，表示動作預計已經完成）在 7 點之前，他太太將煮好飯了。

2. When you arrive, the bus will have left.（V=leave，表示動作預計已經完成）當你抵達的時候，巴士估計已經離開了。

3. She will have met for her new boss by next week.（V=meet，表示動作預計已經完成）下週之前，她就會見過她的新老闆了。

4. Kevin will not have returned from his holiday next Monday.（V= return，表示動作預計完成）Kevin 下週一還不會從休假中回來。

5. Will Mary have taken few days off by next month?（V=take，表示動作預計已經完成）下個月之前，May 將會休幾天假嗎？

換你選選看（選出正確的動詞時態）：

(　) 1. _____ she _____ him by next year? **A** Will; have married
B Will; have been married　**C** Will; being married

(　) 2. Bill _____ lunch when we come home at 1pm. **A** will have eaten
B is eating　**C** will eat

(　) 3. May _____ at office by 9 am. **A** will arrive　**B** will have
arrived　**C** arrived

(　) 4. Petty _____ to Italy by next fall. **A** is not going　**B** will
not go　**C** will not have gone

(　) 5. _____ you _____ the new car by next year? **A** Will; have
bought　**B** Are; buying　**C** Did; buy

(　) 6. They _____ this project before the deadline. **A** are complete
B will have completed　**C** completed

答案與中譯解析：

1. 明年之前，她已經嫁給他了嗎？（答：**A** Will; have married，未來完成式表示動作預計已經完成。）

2. 當我們下午 1 點回家時，Bill 將已經吃完午餐了。（答：**A** will have eaten，未來完成式表示動作預計已經完成，時間副詞用現在簡單式。）

3. 9 點之前，May 將已經到辦公室了。（答：**B** will have arrived，未來完成式表示動作預計已經完成。）

4. Petty 明年秋天之前，將不會去義大利。（答：**C** will not have gone，未來完成式表示動作預計已經完成。）

5. 明年之前你已經買了車嗎？（答：**A** Will; have bought，未來完成式表示動作

Part I 句型文法

Part II 字詞文法

Part III 文法糾正篇

預計已經完成。）

6. 在截止日前，他們將已經完成這個案子。（答：B will have completed，未來完成式表示動作預計已經完成。）

12. 時態十二：未來完成進行式 Future Perfect Progressive

"Next July I will have been doing this for 50 years,"
Springsteen says. 到明年 7 月，我的演唱生涯就要滿 50 年了。

名言背景：Bruce Springsteen（布魯斯·史普林斯汀）暱稱 The Boss 是美國搖滾歌手、創作者與吉他手。他創作出詩人般的歌詞，並常以家鄉紐澤西為創作主軸。

■【未來完成進行式 Future Perfect Continuous 文法解析】：未來完成進行式 Future Perfect Continuous，主要在表達動作／事件，在過去發生，一直持續到現在，並且延續到未來某一個特定時間點，動作／事件還可能會持續下去；也就是過去發生的動作／事件，橫跨現在與未來的時空，強調動作的持續。

1. 使用時機：

動作的持續：在未來特定的時間點之前，動作／事件已經開始並且持續一段時間，有可能會繼續下去。

例：Within 10 minutes, I will have been waiting the bus for an hour. 十分鐘之內，我將會已經等了 1 小時公車了。

2. 文法結構：

a. 肯定句：

主詞 S + 助動詞（will）+ 助動詞（have）+ 助動詞（been）+ 現在分詞（V-ing）+ …

例：In 10 minutes, I will have been waiting the bus for an hour. 再過十分鐘，我即將等了 1 小時公車了。

b. 否定句：

主詞 S + 助動詞（will）+ not + 助動詞（have）+ 助動詞（been）+ 現在分詞（V-ing）+ …

例：I will have not been studying for ten years; it's time to go back to school. 我將要已經近十年沒有學習了，該是回學校進修的時候。

  c. 疑問句：

   助動詞（will）＋ 主詞 S ＋ 助動詞（have）＋ 助動詞（been）＋ 現在分詞（V-ing）＋⋯

   例：Will you have been waiting 1 hour for bus in ten minutes? 再過十分鐘，你們就將等了 1 小時公車了嗎？

 3. 使用特點：

  a. 有三個助動詞 "will"、"have" 以及 "been"，都不用隨著主詞 S 作變化。

  b. 動詞使用現在分詞（V-ing）。

  c. 使用的時間副詞片語或子句的動詞，要用 " 現在簡單式 "。

絕妙好例句：

1. By 7pm he comes home, his wife will have been cooking dinner.（V= cook，表示動作的持續）在 7 點他回來之前，他太太將還在煮飯。

2. I will have been working here for 8 years next week.（V=work，表示動作的持續）下星期我在這裡工作即將滿 8 年。

3. Pat will have been playing football all day long.（V=play，表示動作的持續）Pat 將幾乎踢了一整天的足球了。

4. Kevin will not have been using the car.（V= use，表示動作的持續）Kevin 將不會用車。

5. Will Mary have been taking her vacation for a month?（V=take，表示動作的持續） May 下個月將會繼續休假嗎？

換你選選看（選出正確的動詞時態）：

( ) 1. _____ she _____ him for 5 year by end of next month? A Will; have been marrying B Is; marrying C Does; marry

( ) 2. Bill _____ lunch when we come home. A was eating B will have been eating C will be eating

( ) 3. We _____ Wii for 12 hours by midnight. A have played B play C will have been playing

( ) 4. Petty_____ to Italy by next fall. A will not have been staying B will not staying C is not staying

( ) 5. _____ we _____in USA long enough to get the citizenship next year? A Will; have been living B Are; staying C Are; be staying

( ) 6. They _____for over an hour by the time Thomas arrives. A is talking B are talking C will talk D will have been talking

答案與中譯解析：

1. 到下個月底，她嫁給他即將滿 5 年了嗎？（答：A Will; have been marrying，未來完成進行式表示從過去到未來動作的持續。）

2. 當我們回家時，Bill 將繼續在吃午餐。（答：B will have been eating，未來完成進行式表示動作的持續，副詞子句動詞用現在簡單式。）

3. 到凌晨我們玩 Wii 即將持續了 12 小時。（答：C will have been playing，未來完成進行式表示動作的持續。）

4. 到明年秋季，Petty 將不會繼續待在義大利。（答：A will not have been staying，未來完成進行式表示動作的持續。）

5. 我們在美國居住的時間是否有足夠到明年就可以拿到公民身份？（答：A Will; have been living，未來完成進行式表示動作的持續。）

6. 他們在 Thomas 來之前，他們聊了即將超過一個小時。（答：D will have been talking，未來完成進行式表示動作的持續，副詞子句動詞用現在簡單式）

Unit 3
祈使句

 搶先看名句學文法：

Run, Forest! Run.　跑，阿甘，快跑！
為祈使句。

 英文達人小筆記！

　　祈使句可用於命令要求、表示禮貌委婉、請求、允許或建議的情況；肯定句為（Do...；Let's...）、否定句則為（Don't...；Let us not...）的句型。另外，當祈使句用於寫作時，則要特別注意「逗號」的位置。

關於祈使句的詳細說明：

Run, Forrest! Run! 跑，阿甘，快跑！

名言背景：在電影 Forest Gump《阿甘正傳》的開端，因為阿甘的個性，小時候遭受不少欺負，每回這時候，青梅竹馬 Jenny 總是對著阿甘大喊 "Run, Forrest! Run! "，幫助阿甘躲過危險，不知是不是因為這樣長期的鍛鍊，造就阿甘之後美式足球輝煌的成績。其實，祈使句在電影的場景中，經常出現，尤其是動作片或者是警匪片呢！像是 Don't move! 下回留意看看吧！…

■ 【祈使句 **Imperative Mood** 文法解析】：祈使句 Imperative Mood，主要是用來表達命令、請求、禁止、建議或勸告等等的句子。主詞 S 有時候會被省略。

1. 使用時機：

    a. 表示命令或要求：

        例：Stand Up! 起立→一般動詞

        例：Be quiet! 安靜 → Be 動詞

    b. 表示禮貌委婉：通常加 "please"，或用附加問句表示，如 will ／ won't you，would ／ could you…等。

        例：Please stand up! 請起立→一般動詞

        例：Be quiet, please! 請安靜→ Be 動詞

    c. 表示請求、允許或建議：通常用 "Let" 表示允許，用 "Let's"（=Let us）表示建議。

        例：Let him go! 讓他走！

        例：Let's go to see the movie. 讓我們一起去看電影。

    d. 表示條件：通常在祈使句後，加上 "and" 或 "or" 的子句，表示條件。

        例：Study hard, and you will succeed.（and 表示正面）努力學習然後你會成功。

        例：Study hard, or you will fail.（or 表示負面）努力學習要不然你會失敗。

2. 文法結構：

    a. 肯定句

       Ⅰ. 原形動詞 V +…

       Ⅱ. Be 動詞 + ...

       Ⅲ. Let + 受詞 O + 原形動詞 V

       Ⅳ. Let's + 原形動詞 V + ...

          例：Let's go to play basketball! 我們一起去打籃球吧！

    b. 否定句可用以下幾種表示：

       Ⅰ. Don't（Do not）+ 原形動詞 V + ...

Don't + be + ...

例：Don't be so silly. 別傻了。

Ⅱ. No + 名詞（N）or 動名詞

Ⅲ. Never + 動詞原形

Ⅳ. Don't + Let + 受詞 O + 原形動詞 V

Ⅴ. Let's + not + 原形動詞 V + ...

例：Don't do that again. 不要再這樣做。

c. 疑問句附加問句字眼 will ／ won't you，can ／ could ／ would ／ you.... 等字眼。

例：Come here a moment, could you? 你到這裡一會兒，可能嗎？

例：Could you come here for a moment? 你能夠到這裡來一下嗎？

3. 使用特點：

a. 祈使句的主詞 S 大部分時候會被省略，如要強調時「主詞 S」放句尾，前面要加「逗號」。

例：Be quiet, Tom! 安靜 Tom ！

b. 表示禮貌委婉的字眼如 "please"，以及附加問句，都可以放在句首或句尾，只是放句尾時前面要加上「逗號」。

例：Give me a book, would you? 你可以給我一本書嗎？

c. 肯定句前如加上 "Do"，可以強調語氣。

例：Do have another cup of coffee! 再喝杯咖啡吧！

 絕妙好例句：

1. Let's go!（表示建議）我們走吧！

2. Take him home, Pet!（表示要求）帶他回家，Pet ！

3. Never do that again!!（表示命令）別再做那種事了！！

4. Be patient, kid!（表示勸告）有耐心，孩子！！

5. Have a cup of tea, will you?（表示禮貌委婉）來杯茶嗎？

換你選選看：

(　　) 1. Marry me! _____ my wife, May!　Ａ To be　Ｂ Be　Ｃ Being

(　　) 2. _____ in, please!　Ａ Come　Ｂ To come　Ｃ Coming

(　　) 3. Let's _____open the window. It's raining now!　Ａ don't
　　　　　 Ｂ not　Ｃ isn't

(　　) 4. _____it!　Ａ Don't touch　Ｂ Touching　Ｃ Aren't
　　　　　 touch

(　　) 5. _____ yourself comfortable!　Ａ Do to make　Ｂ To do
　　　　　 make　Ｃ Do make

(　　) 6. _____ a lie, or the police will keep you here!　Ａ Don't tell
　　　　　 Ｂ Don't to tell　Ｃ To don't tell

答案與中譯解析：

1. 嫁給我，成為我的妻，May！（答：Ｂ Be，表示請求。）

2. 請進！！（答：Ａ Come，禮貌委婉。）

3. 讓我們不要開窗，現在下雨了！（答：Ｂ，表示建議，Let's not+V。）

4. 別碰它！（答：Ａ，表示命令。）

5. 請自便！！（答：Ｃ，表示禮貌委婉。）

6. 別說謊，否則警察將留你在這裡！（答：Ａ，表示警告。）

Part I 句型文法

Part II 字詞文法

Part III 文法糾正篇

Unit 4
主動式與被動式

 搶先看名句學文法：

Now life has killed the dream I dreamed.
如今現實的生活已經扼殺了我昔日的夢想。 為主動完成式。

 英文達人小筆記！

主動式語態（Active Voice）與被動式語態（Passive Voice）依執行動作者來決定。若主詞為人，且由人執行動作，則為主動語態，例如：I opened the door. 我開了門；被動語態則以接受動作者為主，例如：The door was opened by me. 門被我開了。此時接受動作者為門，門是被打開的狀態，因此為被動語態。

關於現在現在完全式主動式詳細說明：

Now life has killed the dream I dreamed. 如今現實的生活已經扼殺了我昔日的夢想。

名言背景：聽起來很耳熟嗎？*I Dreamed a Dream* 是一首來自音樂劇《悲慘世界》的歌曲，為劇中角色 Fantine 於第一幕演唱的獨唱歌曲。這首歌曲是一首哀歌，演唱角色 Fantine 當時十分痛苦、垂死和很貧窮，並回想起以往的美好時光。　2009 年英國選秀節目讓蘇珊大嬸（Susan Boyle）一夕成名的歌就是這首 *I Dreamed a Dream*，她的初賽片段在 Youtube 上觀看次數高達 1 億人次以上。

■【被動式文法解析】：英文句子依主詞與動詞的互動關係，可以分為兩種語態：主動語態（Active Voice）與被動語態（Passive Voice）；主動或被動，主要是以動詞的角度來看主詞，是動詞的執行者或接受者。

　A. 主動式語態（Active Voice）：主詞 S 是動詞 V 的執行者。

　　I opened the door. 我開了門

　　S（執行者）＋ V ＋ O（接受者）

　B. 被動式語態（Passive Voice）：主詞 S 是動詞 V 的接受者。

　　Door was opened by me. 門被我開了。

　　S（接受者）＋ Be 動詞＋ p.p. ＋ by ＋ O（執行者）

如果，主詞（S）的角色是動作的執行者，那麼就是主動式語態，英文句子大部分的句型，都是以主動式語態呈現；然而有時候，為了強調動作接受者的重要性，主詞（S）的角色成為動作的接受者，就是被動式語態了。

1. 使用時機：

　　a. 強調動詞的接收者：　當執行者與接受者相比，更想要強調「接受者」。

　　　例：The last book was bought by him. 最後一本書被他買走了。

　　b. 不知道誰是執行者，或是不願意說出執行者時：

　　　例：This book was bought. 最後一本書被買走了。

　　c. 禮貌性修辭：有時用被動語氣更能表示禮貌委婉的語氣。

　　　例：Your application was rejected. 你的申請被拒。

2. 文法結構：

　　a. 肯定句：

　　　主詞 S（接受者）＋助動詞（Be 動詞）＋過去分詞（p.p.）＋ by ＋受詞 O ＋…

　　　例：The last book was not bought. 最後一本書未被買走。

　　b. 否定句：

　　　主詞 S ＋助動詞（Be 動詞）＋ not ＋過去分詞（p.p.）＋ by ＋受詞 O

例：The last book was bought. 最後一本書被買走了。

c. 疑問句：

助動詞（Be 動詞）＋主詞 S ＋過去分詞（p.p.）＋ by ＋受詞 O ？

例：Was the book bought by him? 最後一本書被他買走了嗎？

3. 使用特點：

a. 在被動語態中，執行者被「降級」到受詞的地位，前面須加 "by" ，有時可以省略，尤其是在執行者不重要、不知道或者是不方便提的情況下。

b. Be 動詞的單複數，隨主詞 S 變化。

c. 主要動詞用過去分詞形式，且只有及物動詞（Vt）才能形成被動語態。

4. 各時態的被動式語態變化：

a. 現在簡單式（Simple Present）：主詞 S ＋ Be 動詞＋過去分詞（p.p.）＋ by ＋受詞＋…

主動＝ Tom takes out the garbage every night. Tom 每天晚上都會丟垃圾。

被動＝ The garbage is taken out by Tom every night. 每天晚上 Tom 都要拿出垃圾來倒。

b. 現在進行式（Present Progressive）：主詞 S ＋ Be 動詞＋ being ＋過去分詞（p.p.）by ＋受詞＋…

主動＝ Sara is opening the window now. Sara 現在打開窗戶。

被動＝ The window is being opened by Sara now. 現在窗戶被 Sara 打開。

c. 現在完成式（Present Perfect）：主詞 S ＋ have ／ has ＋ been ＋過去分詞（p.p.）＋ by ＋受詞＋…

主動＝ He has taken these photos. 他拍了這些照片了。

被動＝ These photos has been taken by him. 這些照片是由他拍攝的。

d. 現在完成進行式（Present Perfect Progressive）：主詞 S ＋ has ／ have ＋ been ＋ being ＋過去分詞（p.p.）＋ by ＋受詞＋…

主動＝ Recently, John has been doing the work. 最近，John 一直在

工作。

被動＝ Recently, the work has been being done by John. 最近，工作都是由 John 負責。

e. 過去進行式（Past Progressive）：主詞 S ＋ was ／ were ＋ being ＋ 過去分詞（p.p.）＋ by ＋受詞＋…

主動＝ I was teaching Jane when you came. 你來的時候我正在教 Jane。

被動＝ Jane was being taught by me when you came. 你來的時候，Jane 正在被我教導中。

f. 過去完成式（Past Perfect）：主詞 S ＋ had ＋ been ＋過去分詞 （p.p.）＋ by ＋受詞＋…

主動 ＝ George had repaired many cars before he received his mechanic's license. George 已經修過許多車了，在他拿到技師執照之前。

被動＝ Many cars had been repaired by George before he received his mechanic's license. 許多車已經被 George 整修過，在他拿到技師執照之前。

g. 未來簡單式（Simple Future）：主詞 S ＋ will ＋ be ＋過去分詞 （p.p.）＋ by ＋受詞＋…

主動＝ I will love you. 我會愛你。

被動＝ You will be loved（by me）. 你會被人愛。（被我）

h. 未來完成式（Future Perfect）：主詞 S ＋ will ＋ have ＋ been ＋過去分詞（p.p.）＋ by ＋受詞＋…

主動＝ Sue will have completed her new book before the deadline. Sue 將在截止日期前完成了她的新書。

被動＝ Sue's new book will have been completed（by her）before the deadline. Sue 的新書已在截止日期前完成了。

👑 **絕妙好例句：**

1. My car was stolen（by someone）.（V = steal，執行者未知）我的車被偷了。

2. The same joke has been heard twice by me.（V = hear，強調接受者 = the same joke）同樣的笑話我已經聽過 2 次了。

3. Will the house be built here?（V = build，執行者未知）這房子將要蓋在這裡嗎？

4. This famous song will not be sung by Tony.（V = sing，強調接受者 = This famous song）Tony 將不會演唱這首名曲。

5. Will this project be finished by John in time?（V = finish，強調接受者 = this project）這個案子可以準時被 John 完成嗎？

✏️ **換你選選看：**

（ ）1. The old lady _____ by the dog. Ⓐ was bitten Ⓑ bitten Ⓒ is biting

（ ）2. Will my apology_____（by you）? Ⓐ be accept Ⓑ is accepted Ⓒ be accepted

（ ）3. The contract _____ by both parties. Ⓐ will sign Ⓑ has signed Ⓒ has been signed

（ ）4. This car will not _____. It's too old. Ⓐ been stolen Ⓑ be stolen Ⓒ stolen

（ ）5. Your application _____. Ⓐ received Ⓑ has received Ⓒ was received

（ ）6. Pat _____ to give up this job. Ⓐ was compelled Ⓑ compelled Ⓒ had compelled

答案與中譯解析：

1. 老婦人被狗咬了。（答：Ⓐ was bitten，V = bit、強調接受者 = the old lady。）

2. 我的道歉會被接受嗎？（答：Ⓒ be accepted，V = accept 、強調接受者 = my apology。）

3. 合同已被雙方簽署。（答：Ⓒ has been signed，V = sign、強調接受者 = the contract。）

4. 這輛車不會被偷，太舊了。（答：Ⓑ be stolen，V = steal 、執行者未知。）

5. 您的申請已收到。（答：Ⓒ was received，被動式表示禮貌委婉的語氣。）

6. Pat 被迫離職。（答：Ⓐ was compelled，執行者未知）

Part I 句型文法

Part II 字詞文法

Part III 文法糾正篇

Unit 5
比較句

 搶先看名句學文法：

Walking with a friend in the dark is better than walking alone in the light. 在黑暗中有朋友相伴行走比在光亮中獨自而行還要好。

為比較句型。

 英文達人小筆記！

學會懂得使用相似（the same、alike、similar…; as...as、the same...）與相異（different、unlike…; not as ...as、different from）等單字與片語，進而活用於寫作中，增加句子的活潑度。

關於比較句的詳細說明：

Walking with a friend in the dark is better than walking alone in the light. 在黑暗中有朋友相伴行走比在光亮中獨自而行還要好。

名言背景：海倫凱勒（Helen Keller），知名的美國作家，也是一名教育家、慈善家與社會運動人士。最為人所知的就是她克服自我本身的殘疾，激勵許多人心的人生歷程。本單元的標題出自看不見這個世界的海倫凱勒更是能貼切的讓讀者感受到這光明與黑暗的比較。單元標題的例句，是在比較 "walking with a friend in the dark" 在黑暗中有朋友相伴行走與 "walking alone in the light" 在光亮裡獨自而行這兩件事情，句型為 A is better than B。雖然一般人都會比較偏好走在光亮的地方，但是即使如此，一個人走在光亮處但是沒有人陪伴還是不為大多數人的選擇。另外一方面，那些走在黑暗裡卻有朋友陪伴的人其實是多了安全感甚至是安慰。個人的延伸解讀是人在成功耀眼的時候，如果身旁沒有人可以分享光榮，還比不起在低潮的時候，在黑暗中有人拉你一把。

■ 比較句的文法解析：

A. 表達相似與不同的單字：

1. 表達相似的單字

These oranges are the same. 這些柳橙都一樣。

These oranges are alike. 這些柳橙很像。

These oranges are similar. 這些柳橙很類似。

These oranges smell similarly. 這些柳橙聞起來差不多。

This orange is like that orange. 這顆柳橙很像那顆柳橙。

2. 表達不同的單字

The pen and the pencil are different. 這筆與鉛筆不同。

The pen and the pencil are unalike ／ not alike. 這筆與鉛筆不一樣。

The pen and the pencil are dissimilar. 這筆與鉛筆不相似。

The pen and the pencil look differently. 這筆與鉛筆看起來不一樣。

The pen is unlike the pencil. 這筆是不像鉛筆。

B. 表達相似與不同的片語：

1. 使用 as…as, the same…as, like 等表達相似

This pear is as big as that pear. 這顆梨子跟那顆梨子一樣大。

This pear has the same flavor as that pear. 這顆梨子跟那顆梨子有一樣的味道。

This pear looks like that pear. 這顆梨子看起來像那顆梨子。

This pear is similar to that pear. 這顆梨子跟那顆梨子很相似。

This pear is like that pear. 這顆梨子像那顆梨子。

2. 使用 not as…as, different…from, unlike 表達不同

The peach is different from／than the pear. 這桃子跟梨子不同。

This peach is not as sweet as this pear. 這桃子不像這梨子一樣甜。

The peach is more flavorful than the pear. 這桃子比梨子更有味道。

The peach is more like an apple than the pear. 這桃子比較像蘋果不像梨子。

The peach in contrast to the pear is sweet. 這桃子比較起梨子是甜的。

C. 表達相似與不同的連接副詞

1. 連接副詞表達相似

This van is big. Similarly, that car is also spacious.
這個廂型車很大。相似地，那台車也是空間大。

This van is big. In the same way, that car is also spacious.
這個廂型車很大。同樣地，那台車也是空間大。

This steak is delicious. Likewise, that lamb is very flavorful.
這塊牛排很美味。一樣地，那塊羊肉很有味道。

This steak is delicious. Equally, that lamb is very flavorful.
這塊牛排很美味。相同地，那塊羊肉很有味道。

This steak is flavorful. In a similar manner, that lamb is very tasty.
這塊牛排很有味道。相似地，那塊羊肉非常好吃。

2. 連接副詞表達不同

The house is big. In contrast, the apartment is small.
這房子很大。相反地，這公寓很小。

Some people think a tomato is vegetable. On the contrary, others think a tomato is fruit.
有些人認為番茄是蔬菜。相對地，其他人認為番茄是水果。

While／Whereas potatoes are nutritious, French fries are not.

雖然馬鈴薯營養很高，薯條卻不是。

Potatoes are very nutritious. However, French fries are not.

馬鈴薯營養很高。然而薯條卻不是。

On the one hand potatoes are highly nutritious; on the other hand, it takes much time to cook.

馬鈴薯一方面營養很高。另一方面卻要花很多時間調理。

D. 形容詞比較級

　　1. 比較形容詞（－er）

　　　This peach is better than that one.　這顆桃子比那一顆好。

　　　This peach is redder than the other one.　　這顆桃子比那一顆紅。

　　2. 比較形容詞（more）

　　　This pear is more beautiful than that one. 這顆梨子比那一顆漂亮。

　　　This pear is more flavorful than the other one. 這顆梨子比另外一顆有味道。

 絕妙好例句：

1. **The more... the more...**

用一組相關連接詞（correlative conjunction）連結兩個對等的子句

例：

The more we find out the truth, **the more** we feel terrified.

我們知道越多真相時，我們感到越害怕。

The more the wave rose, **the faster** we ran. 這浪升得越高，我們跑得越快。

The more he talked to the witness, **the less** he believed her.

他跟這證人談得越多，他就越不相信她。

The more time we have spent on the project, **the fewer** obstacles we find in the process.

我們在這計畫中花得時間越多，我們就會在過程中找到越少阻礙。

2. **Prefer & Would rather**

先注意 prefer 的用法

例：

a. I prefer coffee to tea. 我喜歡咖啡勝於茶。→ coffee 跟 tea 是單純兩個名詞。

b. I prefer drinking coffee to drinking tea. 我喜歡喝咖啡勝於喝茶。→ drinking coffee 跟 drinking tea 是動名詞所形成的兩件事，跟比較上一句兩個名詞是相同觀念。

c. I prefer to drink coffee rather than（drink）tea. 我喜歡喝咖啡勝於喝茶。→這一句子則是比較兩個動作 drink coffee 與 drink tea。

Prefer to…than…與 would rather…than…是同樣的句型，所接的都是原形動詞

例：

I'd rather stay at home tonight than go to the cinema. 我寧願待在家裡勝於去電影院。

＝ I prefer to stay at home than go to the cinema.

3. **....as many／much as...**

Linda has **as many shoes as** her older sister does. Linda 跟她姐姐有一樣多的鞋。

→ as many…as 接可數名詞

I drink **as much tea as** I drink coffee every day. 我每天喝一樣多的茶跟咖啡。

→ as much…as 接不可數名詞

The living cost here is not **as high as** in the city. 這裡的物價沒有像城市那麼高。

→ as…as 中間可加形容詞作比較

The senior employee doesn't work as hard as the newcomer. 這資深員工沒像新進人員工作一樣努力。→ as…as 中間也可加副詞作比較

As many as（Up to） 5 people were missing in this incident. 多達五人在這意外中失蹤。

→ as many ／ much as ＋數量＝ up to ＋數量，表示有多達…之多

4. 倍數＋ **adj** ／ **adv** ＋ **than**

The man weighs **three times heavier than** his wife. 這男人體重是他太太三倍。

＝ The man has **three times the weight of his wife's.**

I work **twice harder than** you do. 我工作比你雙倍地努力。

5. **A is to B as C is to D**

Water is to plants as reading is to me. 閱讀對我來說就跟水對植物一樣重要。

→這是在比喻 water is to plants 水對植物來說就像 reading is to me 閱讀對我一樣重要。

＝ Water is to plants what reading is to me.

＝ As water is to plants, so is reading to me.

＝ Reading to me is like water to plants.

Part I 句型文法

Part II 字詞文法

Part III 文法糾正篇

換你選選看：

(   ) 1. The dress she buys from that store is _____ than the one from this store. A beautifuler   B more beautiful   C much beautiful

(   ) 2. The car has the same color _____ the truck. A as   B than   C to

(   ) 3. I prefer _____ to _____ . A drive a car; ride a bike   B driving a car; riding a bike   C drove a car; rode a bike

(   ) 4. The more time I spend on practicing my English, _____ I become in speaking and listening. A the well   B better   C the better

(   ) 5. Sylvia doesn't do _____ exercise as her doctor tells her to do. A as much   B as many   C as

(   ) 6. She makes three times _____（more／much）than she used to. A much   B more   C as

答案與中譯解析：

1. 她在那一家店買的洋裝比這一家店買的好看。（答：B more beautiful 。）
2. 這車子跟卡車的顏色一樣。（答：A as 。）
3. 我喜歡開車勝於騎腳踏車。（答：B driving a car; riding a bike，prefer+V-ing。）
4. 我花越多時間在練習我的英文上，我在口說與聽力上就變得越好。（答：C the better。）
5. Sylvia 並沒有做跟她醫生叫她做的運動一樣多。（答：A as much。）
6. 現在她賺的薪水是她以前所賺的三倍。（答：B more。）

Part I 句型文法

Part II 字詞文法

Part III 文法糾正篇

Unit 6
附屬子句

 搶先看名句學文法：

The World is a book, and those who do not travel read only a page. 這個世界就像一本書，而那些不旅行的人只讀了一頁。

本句使用附屬子句，其中 **"who do not travel"** 為一形容詞子句在修飾 **those**（**people**）。

 英文達人小筆記！

　　在深入了解附屬子句的各種結構之前，了解附屬子句本身與其餘子句的定義差別將對於文法裡的許多句型結構與句子的連接將有更清楚的觀念。

關於附屬子句的詳細說明：

The World is a book, and those who do not travel read only a page. 這個世界就像一本書，而那些不旅行的人只讀了一頁。

名言背景：聖奧古斯丁（St. Augustine）（354－430）是早期西方的神學家與哲學家。在許多年前，旅遊還是極度不方便的年代，將足跡踏遍各地的渴望已存在人們的心中。在中文，也有非常相似的句子，「行萬里路勝讀萬卷書」，所以不論在東西方的思想裡，都認同旅行是想要了解這個世界，認識各地的風俗民情的最好方法。

■ 附屬子句文法解析：

A. 獨立子句與非獨立子句（Independent and Dependent Clauses）：

首先，讓我們先來了解子句的定義。一個子句是由一組字所組合而成，其中有名詞或代名詞所代表的主詞，也有動詞或其他詞性的單字。那甚麼時候一個子句可以形成一個完整的句子呢？讓我們看看下面兩個例句：

When I studied in the library yesterday

I studied in the library yesterday

這兩個句子都有主詞（I）、動詞（studied）、介系詞（in）、當作介系詞受詞的名詞（the library）與時間副詞（yesterday）。但很明顯的第一個例句的意思尚未完整的表達完畢（當我昨天在圖書館念書的時候），而第二個句子相對地已經有完整的意思（我昨天在圖書館念書）。一個完整可獨立存在的句子（sentence）又稱做獨立子句（dependent clause），就像上面所舉出的第二個例句。而像第一個例句，意思尚未表達完整，無法單獨獨立構成一個句子，所以又稱做非獨立子句（independent clause）。加上標點符號會更清楚看出兩者的差別：

When I studied in the library yesterday,

I studied in the library yesterday.

而非獨立子句要如何形成一個句子呢？它必須要連結一個獨立子句來讓它的意思完整。如以下例句：

When I studied in the library yesterday, I found that I left the notes at home.

當我昨天在圖書館念書的時候，我發現我把筆記放在家裡。

而因為非獨立子句無法單獨存在，必須與一個獨立子句連接，所以又稱做為附屬子句（subordinate clause），而所連接的獨立子句則又為主要子句（main clause）。連接附屬子句與主要子句的連接詞則稱為從屬連接詞（subordinating conjunction）。

B.附屬子句（Subordinate Clause）：

根據附屬子句在句子中的使用，可分成三大類，形容詞子句、副詞子句與名詞子句。形容詞、副詞、與名詞子句的功能與性質就與形容詞、副詞、與名詞本身相同。

1. 副詞子句（**Adverb Clause**）

就跟副詞的功能一般，副詞子句（Adverb Clause）可修飾動詞、形容詞或副詞，或者是一個片語或子句。副詞子句跟副詞一樣可能出現在句子中的任何位置。

例：After the meeting was over, John decided to meet with his teammates to discuss the report. 在會議結束之後，John 決定跟他的組員碰面討論這份報告

→副詞子句 After the meeting was over 在這裡也為時間子句，在介紹 John decided…這件事情發生的時間點。

a. 副詞子句的種類與所使用的從屬連接詞

時間	after, before, when, while, as, once, by the time（that）, as soon as, since, until, whenever, the first time（that）, the next time（that）, the last time（that）, every time（that）
因果	because, since, as, as long as, so long as, due to the fact that, now that
對比	Although = though = even though, whereas, while
條件	if, even if, only if, unless, in case（that）, providing（that）, provided（that）, in the event（that）, as long as
目的	so that, in order that, lest
讓步	whether, no matter, no matter wh- = wh-ever（whenever, whoever, wherever, whatever, whichever, however）
限制	as far as, in that
狀態	as, as if

b. When vs. While

例1：

The phone rang **when** Cindy opened the door. Cindy 開門時電話響了。→ When 連接的句子裡如果都是簡單式，when 之後的動作先發生。在這個例句中，Cindy opened the door 先發生，the phone rang 在之後發生。

例2：

When my friend called, we were having dinner. 當我朋友打電話來時，我們正在吃晚餐。

While we were having dinner, my friend called. 當我們正在吃晚餐時，我朋友打電話來。

→這裡以兩個不同的時態來表示兩個事件的時間關係。進行式代表持續進行的動作（we were having dinner），而在進行的當中，發生了另一件事件（my friend called）。

這時候在連接詞的選擇上，when 習慣接在簡單句之前，而 while 則是大多數放在進行式之前。

例3：

While she was studying hard for the test, her friends were having a party in the house. 當她正在努力念書準備考試的時候，她的朋友正在房子裡開派對。→ While 在這裡則是連接兩個進行式。

While some people are suffering from hunger, others are wasting much food. 當有些人受到飢餓的折磨，其他人卻在浪費許多食物。

→這裡的 while 也當作直接對比的連接詞。

c. 標點符號的使用

例：

1. We all went to bed early **because** we were all exhausted. 我們都很早睡因為我們都累壞了。

2. **Because** we were all exhausted, we went to bed early. 因為我們都累壞了，我們都很早睡。

→在字義解釋上就可以看出附屬子句 because we were all exhausted 與主要子句 we all went to bed early 之間主與從的關係。而這個主從關係，也可以在之前獨立與非獨立子句的解釋了解到，因為非獨立子句無法單獨存在，必須依附另一獨立子句。所以在標點符號的使用上，如果附屬子句在主要子句之前，兩個子句需用逗號隔開。如是主要子句開始的句子，中間則不需要逗號隔開。

3. David buys it anyway **although** the suit is pricey. David 還是買了雖然這西裝很貴。

= **Although** the suit is pricey, David buys it anyway. 雖然這西裝很貴，David 還是買了。

比較：The suit is pricey, **but** David buys it anyway. 這西裝很貴，但是 David 還是買了。

→之前說明了附屬子句裡標點符號的使用必須參照附屬子句與主要子句的位置。但 but 屬於對等連接詞（請參照連接詞單元），中間一定需用逗號分開，而對等連接詞與從屬連接詞不同的是對等連接詞所連接的為兩個獨立子句，其中並沒有主與從的關係。

d. 副詞子句中的時態使用

例：

1. After I finish this project, I will take a short trip to Tainan. 在我完成這個專案後，我將到台南做短暫的旅遊。

2. We are going to give them a tour of our house first when the guests arrive tonight. 我們將先帶他們參觀我們的房子當客人今天晚上抵達的時候。

→當句子中表達不同未來時間發生的動作時，時間子句需使用現在時態。

3. I will walk to work if it doesn't rain tomorrow. 我將會走路上班如果明天不下雨的話。＝ I will walk to work unless it rains tomorrow. 我將會走路上班除非明天下雨的話。

4. He will get the job done as long as he stops chatting and texting to his friends. 他將會把事情做好只要他停止傳簡訊跟朋友聊

天。

5. In case you（should）need to have a discussion with me, I'll give you my office number.　萬一你需要跟我討論一下，我將會給你我的辦公室號碼。

→ If, as long as, in case（that）所引導的副詞子句又稱為條件子句。使用可能的條件的副詞子句中使用的是現在時態，主要子句則是表達將會發生的結果，使用的是未來時態。關於條件子句的用法，請參考假設語氣的單元。

2. 形容詞子句（**Adjective Clause**）

　　a. 形容詞子句（Adjective Clause）（關係子句 Relative Clause）修飾名詞或代名詞。為了讓形容詞子句與所修飾的名詞或代名詞關係明確，形容詞子句總是跟在所修飾的名詞或代名詞之後。

　　例：Our meeting, which starts at two in the afternoon, discusses the importance of the budget cut. 我們在下午兩點的會議，討論預算縮減的重要性。

　　→形容詞子句 which starts at two in the afternoon 用來修飾 our meeting。

　　b. 形容詞子句功能即為像形容詞，作用在修飾名詞。形容詞子句的位置一定是放在所修飾的名詞之後。而連接形容詞子句的連接詞又稱做關係代名詞（Relative pronoun）。使用何種關係代名詞決定在之前所修飾的名詞為人、地方、時間或事物。首先先來認識關係代名詞的種類：

關係代名詞	例句
which →事物	The food which we ate yesterday was delicious. 我們昨天吃的食物美味極了。
that →人或事物	I've never talked to the man that is standing there. 我從來沒跟正站在那裡的男人說過話。
who（m）→人	She is the teacher who（m）I told you about. 她就是我之前跟你提過的老師。
where →地方	This is the school where I studied before. 這是我之前念書的學校。
when →時間	It's so hard to find a day when everyone has time available. 很難去找到一天每個人都有空的時間。
whose →所有	I know the student whose painting won the competition. 我認識這個贏繪畫比賽的學生。

c. 使用形容詞子句來結合句子：

方法：首先在不同句子裡，找出同為討論的名詞，然後再決定哪一句為主。

The teacher is nice.

He is in the classroom.

→ the teacher 跟 he 兩者是同一事物，所以在合併這兩個句子的時候，the teacher 即為句子中的主角，即是句子的主詞。再來就是決定要以哪一句子為主。如果是以第一句為主要子句，第二句則是要變成形容詞子句跟在修飾的名詞之後：

例：The teacher who is in the classroom is nice. 那個在教室的老師很和善。如果第二句為主要子句，則是將第一句變成形容詞子句跟在修飾的名詞之後：The teacher who is nice is in the classroom. 那個很和善的老師在教室裡。

3. 名詞子句（**Noun Clause**）

a. 名詞子句（Noun Clause）擔任句子中主詞、受詞或補語的角色。
許多時候名詞子句用於非直接或稱間接引用句（indirect speech or
reported speech）。

例：Who is your favorite author? 你最喜歡的作者是誰？

例：Could you tell me who your favorite author is? 你可以告訴我
你最喜歡的作者是誰嗎？→第二句將第一句的問句引用在句子中，
並將其改為一名詞子句，作為 tell 的間接受詞。

b. 名詞在句中可能為主詞或受詞（請參照名詞子句）。相同的觀念可想
見形容詞子句所修飾的名詞可能在句子中是擔任主詞、動詞的受詞、或
介系詞的受詞。這中間的差別將會決定其中的關係代名詞是否可以省略：

1. 所修飾的名詞作為主詞時，關係代名詞不可省略：

The dress is red.

It is in the closet.（it = the dress 在此為句子的主詞）

→ The dress which is in the closet is red.

→ The dress that is in the closet is red.

2. 所修飾的名詞作為動詞的受詞時，關係代名詞可省略：

The woman was my classmate.

I saw her.（her = the woman 在此為動詞 saw 的受詞）

→ The woman who（m）I saw was my classmate.（因修飾的名詞
作為受詞時，關係代名詞 who 可用受格型式 whom 或是一般的 who）

→ The woman that I saw was my classmate.

→ The woman（X）I saw was my classmate.（省略關係代名詞）

所修飾的名詞作為介系詞的受詞時，關係代名詞可省略：

The bicycle is on sale.

I am looking at it.（it = the bicycle 在此為介系詞 at 的受詞）

→ The bicycle at which I am looking is on sale.（介系詞放置於形
容詞子句之前為較為正式的英語用法）

→ The bicycle which I am looking at is on sale.

→ The bicycle that I am looking at is on sale.

→ The bicycle（X）I am looking at is on sale.（省略關係代名詞）

c. 名詞子句成為疑問句的用法

英文基本句型：S＋V＋O（主詞＋動詞＋受詞），其中除了動詞 V 之外，其餘主詞 S 與受詞 O 為名詞或代名詞。

在了解英文基本句型與其中構成要素之後，各位還記得之前介紹子句的觀念中，一個子句包含了主詞、動詞以及其他可能詞性的單字。主詞在動詞（包含 be 動詞與助動詞）之前形成了一般句，包括肯定與疑問句。而將動詞（包含 be 動詞與助動詞）放置與主詞之前，則是形成了疑問句或是倒裝句。

例：

What should we do? 疑問句：我們該怎麼做？

I wonder what we should do? →因為這疑問句要放在句中擔任動詞 wonder 的受詞，所以將疑問句 What should we do? 改成一般句 what we should do 為一名詞子句，就像名詞一般作 wonder 的受詞。

d. 名詞子句在句中的位置

將 Where is he? →問句放在句子中變成名詞子句的用法：

名詞子句為動詞的受詞

I don't know where he is. 我不知道他在哪裡。

名詞子句為介系詞片語後的受詞

We never ask about where he is. 我們從來不去問他在哪裡。

名詞子句為主詞

Where he is remains a mystery. 他在哪裡仍然是個謎。

其他例子：

1. Where the bus station is? 你可以跟我講車站在哪裡嗎？

→ Can you tell me where the bus station is?

2. When does the next train come? 你知道下一班火車什麼時候到嗎？

→ Do you know when the next train comes?

注意：改成名詞子句之後即變成一般句。現在簡單式單數的第三人稱主詞（非單數的我或你）動詞人需加 s 或 es。

3. Where did you go last night?

→ You should tell me where you went last night. 你應該告訴我你昨晚去哪裡了？

注意：改成名詞子句時時態需保持一致。do ／ does ／ did 這三個助動詞先去掉，再將主詞放置與動詞之前。其餘助動詞與 be 動詞則放置在主詞之後。

4. Can she finish the project on time?

→ We really need to know if? ／ whether she can finish the project on time. 我們真的需要知道她是否可以如期完成這個專案。

注意：疑問句如果是 Yes ／ No 問句，也就是 be 動詞或助動詞為首的疑問句，名詞子句則是以 if 或 whether 作連接。

換你選選看：

(　) 1. I got a birthday present from my family. _____ I opened it, I _____ a surprise. Ⓐ When; found　Ⓑ When; was finding Ⓒ While; found

(　) 2. _____ the weather condition was so bad, I didn't go to school. Ⓐ Although　Ⓑ Because　Ⓒ Though

(　) 3. You'll feel tried at work tomorrow _____ you stay up all night. Ⓐ unless　Ⓑ if　Ⓒ or

(　) 4. Catherine is the lawyer _____ handled my case. Ⓐ which Ⓑ whose　Ⓒ who

(　) 5. The teacher _____ class is 2A has much patience to her students. Ⓐ whose　Ⓑ whom　Ⓒ who

(　) 6. The drink _____ you gave me is not a soda. Ⓐ what Ⓑ which　Ⓒ whose

答案與中譯解析：

1. 我收到一個我家人給我的生日禮物。當我打開時，我發現一個驚喜。（答：Ａ When; found，when 之後接簡單式，所接的動作 I opened it 先開始，再來是 I found a surprise。）

2. 因為天氣狀況如此地糟，我沒有去學校（答：Ｂ Because。because 在句子中表達正確意思。）

3. 你明天上班將會覺得很累，如果你整晚熬夜的話。（答：Ｂ if。）

4. Catherine 是之前處理我案子的律師。（答：Ｃ who。）

5. 那老師是 2A 的老師，她對學生很有耐心。（答：Ａ whose。）

6. 你之前給我的飲料不是汽水。（答：Ｂ which。）

■ 文法加油站：

　　A. 句子中逗號使用方法：在英語中，只要是用逗號隔開的子句，放在句子中間，功能就是在做補充説明，這個觀念就像同位語的觀念。

　　例：

1. Tokyo, which is the capital of Japan, is a very modern city.（which is the capital of Japan 是一非限定形容詞子句。Tokyo 已經是一特定的城市，其後的形容詞子句只是在補充説明，不需再作限定縮小範圍。）

2. Tokyo, the capital of Japan, is a very modern city.（the capital of Japan 是一同位語。也是在補充説明 Tokyo。）東京，日本的首都。是一個很現代化的城市

　　重點：在使用逗號時，不可使用關係代名詞 that，也不可省略關係代名詞。

　　例：

1. The man who（m）／ that ／（X）I met yesterday works at this company. 我昨天遇到的那個男人在這個公司上班。→限定用法

2. Mr. Thompson, who（m）I met yesterday, works at this company. Mr. Thompson，我昨天遇到的人，在這家公司上班。

→非限定，有逗號時，不可使用 that，也不可省略關係代名詞

B. 限定與非限定用法（**Restrictive and Nonrestrictive Adjective Clause**）關於限定與非限定的差別，首先先來看一下這兩個句子其中句義的差別：

1. There are 30 students in this class. 20 students passed the test. For those 20 students, they can get a certificate. 班上有 30 個學生，其中 20 個有通過考試。那 20 個通過的學生可以得到證書。

2. The students who passed the test can get a certificate. →這是限定的用法。首先 the students 是指這班上 30 個學生，利用形容詞子句 who passed the test 來限定縮小範圍到通過考試的那 20 個學生。

3. The students, who passed the test, can get a certificate. →這是非限定的用法。the students 在此已經是指通過考試的那 20 個學生，形容詞子句 who passed the test 只是在做補充說明，並不會改變前面 the students 的範圍。

3. 以 that 連接的名詞子句

句型	例句	其它
動詞＋that（that 可省略）	I believe that I can make it. = I believe I can make it. 我相信我可以辦到。	think, feel, hope, know, understand, agree, decide, discover, hear, notice, remember
S＋be＋adj.＋that（可省略）	I'm glad that you've found your wallet. = I'm glad you've found your wallet. 我很慶幸你有找到你的錢包。	sorry, happy, sure, surprised, worried, aware, afraid, angry, certain, disappointed, proud

It + be + adj. + that（可省略）	It's obvious that Oscar doesn't like his new teacher. = It's obvious Oscar doesn't like his new teacher. 很明顯地 Oscar 不喜歡他的新老師。	clear, possible, strange, true, wonderful, important, strange
That －名詞子句作為主詞	（接上句）= That Oscar doesn't like his new teacher is oblivious.	

Part I 句型文法

Part II 字詞文法

Part III 文法糾正篇

Unit 7
假設語氣

 搶先看名句學文法：

Hold fast to dreams, for if dreams die, life is a broken-winged bird that cannot fly. 意指緊抓住你的夢想，不要讓它們流走或消失，因為如果夢想熄滅或死去的話，生命就像一隻折翼的鳥，無法在天空中飛翔。

if 出現，為假設語氣句型。

 英文達人小筆記！

假設語氣並不僅有 **if**（假設）的意思，在英文文法中，還有「萬一」的意味。另外假設還有各種用法，像是 " 有可能成為事實的假設 "、" 與現在、過去事實相反 " 的假設，用法容易混淆，要小心。

關於假設語氣的詳細說明：

Hold fast to dreams, for if dreams die, life is a broken-winged bird that cannot fly.

意指緊抓住你的夢想，不要讓它們流走或消失，因為如果夢想熄滅或死去的話，生命就像一隻折翼的鳥，無法在天空中飛翔。

名言背景：這是一篇美國詩人 Langston Hughes 寫的短詩。"Hold fast to your dreams" 意指緊抓住你的夢想，不要讓它們流走或消失。"for if dreams die" 因為如果夢想熄滅或死去的話 "life is a broken-winged bird" 生命就像一隻折翼的鳥，"that cannot fly" 無法在天空中飛翔。這首短詩非常有詩意的但卻有力地比喻出夢想對人們的重要。不論年齡或背景，對於這個世界的好奇與新鮮都是啟發我們對於更多事物的想像力，也是我們不侷限自我勇於夢想以及追求實現的原動力。

■ 假設語氣文法解析：假設語氣裡主要句型為 If 條件子句所形成的不同條件狀況，以下是四種不同的條件子句所構成的假設句型：

1. 觀念說明：

   a. 句型一（Conditional 0）：

     If I am late, I take the taxi to work. 如果我遲到的話，我搭計程車上班。

     → 這是指經常發生的事件。

     if－子句與主要子句皆為現在時態。在這種情況下，if 可以用 when 取代：

     → When I am late, I take taxi to work. 當我遲到的時候，我搭計程車上班。

   b. 句型二（Conditional 1）：

     If it rains, we will stay at home. 如果下雨的話，我們將會待在家裡。

     → 這是在指可能會發生的事件，只要達到 if－子句裡的條件，主要子句裡的事情就會成真。這裡的 if－子句使用現在簡單式，而主要子句則是使用未來簡單式，或是使用助動詞 shall／can／may。

   c. 句型三（Conditional 2）：

     If he worked harder, he would get the raise. 如果他工作更認真的話，他會得到加薪。

     但事實上→ He doesn't get the raise.

     → 這是與現在或未來事實相反的假設，if－子句中使用過去簡單式，而主要子句裡則根據句子的意思使用 would／should／could／might＋V。

Part I 句型文法

Part II 字詞文法

Part III 文法糾正篇

d. 句型四（Conditional 3）：

If I had known the truth, I would have chosen to believe him. 如果我知道事實的話，我會選擇相信他。

但事實上（在過去）→ I didn't know the truth so I didn't believe him.

→ 這是與過去事實相反的假設，if- 子句中使用過去完成式（had + p.p.），而主要子句裡則根據句子的意思使用 would ／ should ／ could ／ might + have + p.p.。

2. 使用時機：

a.「萬一」的假設

b. 有可能成為事實的假設

c. 與現在事實相反

d. 與過去式事實相反

e. 過去事實想法與現在事實混用

f. If 省略

g. Hope vs. Wish

3. 使用特點：

a.「萬一」的假設：

A. **Should** 在 **if-** 子句的用法：以 **should** 作一假設的語氣，作萬一解釋。

例：

If anyone should visit the company, please make an appointment in advance.

＝ If anyone visits the company, please make an appointment in advance.

萬一任何人要參觀公司，請事先預約。

If she should be here tomorrow, I will explain the whole thing to her.

萬一她明天在這裡，我會跟她解釋全部的事情。

比較→ If she is here tomorrow, I will explain the whole thing to here.

如果她明天在這裡，我會跟她解釋全部的事情。

使用 should 在 if－子句（If she should be here tomorrow）比較起使用現在時態（If she is here tomorrow）發生的機率較低。

B.「萬一」的其他用法：

例1：In case（that）the little baby（should）see a doctor, the parents will take a day off tomorrow. 萬一小嬰兒要看醫生，這父母明天將會請假。

例2：What should I do if I forget to bring my passport? 萬一我忘記帶護照，我該怎麼辦？

= What if I forget to bring my passport? 萬一我忘記帶護照，怎麼辦？

b. 有可能成為事實的假設：

比較假設句型一（Conditional 0）與句型二（Condition 1）：

句型一（**Conditional 0**）：

If－子句現在式＋主要子句現在式

例：If I have time, I usually walk the dog in the park. 如果我有時間，我通常會帶狗去公園散步。→ 平常經常性會發生的事件。

句型二（**Conditional 1**）：

If－子句現在式＋主要子句未來式或使用 shall／can／may

例：If I have time, I will walk the dog in the park tomorrow. 如果我有時間，我明天會帶狗去公園散步。→ 必須符合 if－子句裡的條件才會發生。

c. 與現在事實相反：

與現在或未來事實相反 Unreal Conditional＝句型三（Conditional 2）：

If－子句過去式＋主要子句 would／should／could／might＋V

注意：**if**－子句過去式中的 **be** 動詞一律使用 **were**。

例1：

If I had wings, I would fly to anywhere that I wanted to be.

如果我有翅膀的話，我會飛到任何我想到的地方。

這一類的句子時常在做不可能的假設。人類不可能有翅膀，所以用這個假設語氣來代表與現實相反的情形。

= I don't have wings so I won't fly to anywhere that I want to be.

我沒有翅膀，所以我不會飛到任何我想到的地方。

例2：

I would give everyone more vacation days if I were the boss.

我會給每個人更多有薪假如果我是老闆的話。

→ 這是與現在事實完全相反的的假設，代表我不是老闆，也不會給每個人有薪假。

= I won't give everyone more vacation days since I'm not the boss. 我不會給每個人更多有薪假既然不我是老闆。

例3：

If I won the lottery, I would buy a house. 如果我中樂透的話，我將會去買房子。

→ If I won the lottery, I could buy a house. 如果我中樂透的話，我就可以去買房子。

這兩個句子的差別為 would 代表期望與想做的事，而 could 為 could be able to，表示達到某種能力。

d. 與過去事實相反：

與過去事實相反 Past Conditional＝ 句型四（Conditional 3）：

If－子句過去完成式（had + p.p.）＋主要子句 would ／ should ／ could ／ might + have + p.p.

例1：

I wouldn't have gone to the meeting if you had told me that it was cancelled. 我就不會去那會議如果你跟我說它取消的話。

真實發生→ I went to the meeting because you didn't tell me that it was cancelled. 我去了那會議因為你沒跟我說它取消了。

例2：

We would have shopped at that store if the salesperson had been nice to us. 我們會在那一間店消費如果店員對我們好的話。

真實發生→ We didn't shop at that store because the salesperson wasn't nice to us. 我們沒在那一間店消費因為店員對我們不好。

過去式助動詞 should，could，would 加 have p.p. 可表示對過去曾經或不曾發生的事情一個相反的假設，表達後悔之意。主要結構為：should have ／ could have ／ would have ＋ p.p.

例1：

I should have applied for the job. 我應該要申請那工作。

真實發生→ I didn't apply for the job. 我沒有申請那工作。 *should have 代表這件事是一個好主意，但是卻沒有做。

例2：

I shouldn't have missed the deadline. 我不應該錯過期限。

真實發生→ I missed the deadline. 我錯過了期限。 *shouldn't have 表示這件事不應該去做，但是卻去做了。

例3：

I could have taken the opportunity. 我其實可以把握這機會。

真實發生→ I didn't take the opportunity. 我沒有把握這機會。 *could have 代表本來可能可以做的選擇，但是沒有去做。

例4：

I would have helped you. 我本來會幫你的。

真實發生→ You didn't ask me for help 你沒有請求我的幫忙。

注意：would have 表示本來願意或將會發生的事情。

注意：should have，could have，would have 在句子中經常以縮寫型式 should've，could've，would've 出現，在口語中則是念成 shoulda，coulda，woulda。

e. **過去事實相反與現在事實混用：**

A. 先與過去事實相反，後與現在事實相反：

例1：

I didn't eat breakfast this morning. →過去（我今天早上沒有吃早餐。）

I feel hungry now! →現在（我現在感到餓了！）

→ If I had eaten breakfast this morning, I would not feel hungry now.

如果我今天早上有吃早餐的話，我現在就不會感到餓了。這個句子是現在事實相反結合與過去事實相反。if－子句要使用過去完成式（had+p.p.）。

例2：

I didn't eat breakfast this morning → If I had eaten breakfast this morning.

以及與現在事實相反主要子句 would ／ should ／ could ／ might + V。

I feel hungry now → I would not feel hungry now.

B. 先與現在事實相反，後與過去事實相反：

例：

He is not a responsible employee. →現在（他不是一個負責的員工。）

He did not finish the work on time. →過去（他沒有準時完成工作。）

→ If he were a responsible employee, he would have finished the work on time. 他如果是個好員工的話，他之前就會把工作準時完成。

這個句子是過去事實相反結合與現在事實相反。if－子句要使用過去式。

f. **If 省略**：

If- 子句中如有出現 should, were, had，可省略 if，再將 should，were，had 倒裝至主詞之前

例：

Should it rain tomorrow, we will cancel the company picnic.

= If it should rain tomorrow, we will cancel the company picnic.

萬一下雨的話,我們將會取消公司野餐。

Were your father here, he would be so proud of you.

= If your father were here, he would be so proud of you.

如果你父親在這裡,他會為你感到非常地驕傲。

Had you been in the same situation, you would have also told the truth

= If you had been in the same situation, you would have also told the truth

如果你之前在同樣的情況下,你也會說實話的。

g. **Hope vs. Wish**:

A. **Hope**(針對過去的事情,使用過去簡單式)

例:

I hope she found the company. 我希望她有找到那公司。

I hope he passed the driving test. 我希望他有通過駕駛考試。

B. **Hope**(針對現在的事情,使用現在簡單或現在進行式)

例:

I hope everyone is alright. 我希望每個人都沒事。

I hope my friends are having fun at the party. 我希望我的朋友都正在派對上玩的開心。

C. **Hope**(針對未來的事情,較常用現在簡單式,但也可以使用未來簡單式)

例:

I hope she comes to visit us next year. 我希望她明年可以來拜訪我們。

= I hope she will come to visit us next year.

重點:Wish 的用法跟假設語氣是一樣的觀念

D. **Wish**(針對過去的事情,使用過去完成式)

例:

He wishes he had passed the driving test. 他但願他有通過考試。

→ He didn't pass the driving test.（與過去事實相反）

E. Wish（針對現在的事情，使用過去簡單式）

例：

I wish I had a million dollars. 我但願我有一百萬。

→ I don't have a million dollars.（與現在事實相反）

F. Wish（針對未來的事情，使用 would）

例：

I wish he would quit smoking soon. 我但願他會盡早戒菸。

→ Maybe he will quit smoking soon.（對未來事件的假設）

換你選選看：

（　　）1. If it's cold, what _____ you usually wear? Ⓐ are　Ⓑ did
　　　　　Ⓒ do

（　　）2. If you like the book, you _____ keep it. Ⓐ will　Ⓑ may
　　　　　Ⓒ usually

（　　）3. If the train _____, I will miss the seminar. Ⓐ delays
　　　　　Ⓑ should be delaying　Ⓒ delayed

（　　）4. We _____ so much money on shopping last week.
　　　　　Ⓐ shouldn't spent　Ⓑ shouldn't have spent　Ⓒ won't have spent

（　　）5. If I _____ all night last night, I would not be tired now.
　　　　　Ⓐ didn't not stay　Ⓑ haven't stay　Ⓒ had not stayed up

（　　）6. I hope she _____ a good job soon. Ⓐ gets　Ⓑ has got　Ⓒ is
　　　　　getting

答案與中譯解析：

1. 如果下雨時，你通常會穿什麼？（答：C。）

2. 如果你喜歡這書的話，你可以留著。（答：B。）

3. 萬一火車誤點的話，我將會錯過研討會。（答：A。）

4. 我們上星期不應該花這麼多錢在血拼上。（答：B，和過去事實相反，主要子句 would／should／could／might＋have＋p.p.。）

5. 如果我昨晚沒有整晚熬夜的話，我現在就不會累了。（答：C，和過去事實相反，If子句使用過去完成式。）

6. 我希望她能盡快找到工作。（答：A，動詞 hope 針對未來的事情，可使用現在簡單式或未來簡單式。）

Part I 句型文法

Part II 字詞文法

Part III 文法糾正篇

Unit 8
疑問句

 搶先看名句學文法：

Student: "Dr. Einstein, aren't these the same questions as last years'."

Dr. Einstein: "Yes. But this year the answers are different."

學生：「愛因斯坦教授，這不是去年的考卷嗎？」

愛因斯坦：「對，但是答案跟去年的不一樣。」

學生的問題（動詞＋名詞的結構）為疑問句型。

 英文達人小筆記！

　　疑問句主要分為三種，一為 Be 動詞為首，二為助動詞（如 do、does）為首，三為情態助動詞為主（如 may、should、could）為首，第四種以五大疑問句，也就是 where、when、what、who 和 how 為首。

關於疑問句的詳細說明：

Student: "Dr. Einstein, aren't these the same questions as last years'."

Dr. Einstein: "Yes. But this year the answers are different."

學生：「愛因斯坦教授，這不是去年的考卷嗎？」

愛因斯坦：「對，但是答案跟去年的不一樣。」

名言背景：愛因斯坦是二十世紀偉大的科學家。他一直思考與世界有關的物理問題。有一天他在他所任教的大學給學生出期末考考卷，學生質疑反應題目與去年期末考考題相同，愛因斯坦回答說：是的，但答案與去年不同。愛因斯坦意在告訴學生不要拘泥於固有的框架與答案，要跳脫出來，才有新視野。

■ **疑問句的文法解析**：英文疑問句分為三種：（一）以 be 動詞為句首（二）以助動詞為句首（三）以疑問詞為句首。

　　1. 以 **be** 動詞為句首：

　　a.　中文翻譯為「是」的動詞為英文的 be 動詞。例如：is，am，are，was，were。有這些動詞的句子，移動 be 動詞到句首成為疑問句。

be 動詞與主詞一致表如下：

I 我	am ╱ was	we 我們	are ╱ were
You 你	are ╱ were	you 你們	are ╱ were
he ╱ she ╱ it 他╱她╱它	is	they 他們	are ╱ were

例：

He is a good student. → Is he a good student?

他是一位好學生→他是一位好學生嗎？

　　2. 以助動詞為句首：句子若有一般動詞，變成疑問句時，助動詞放在句首，主詞後面的動詞變成原型動詞，成為疑問句。

　　a. 當主詞為第三人稱單數時，助動詞為 does。第三人稱單數：he〈他〉、she〈她〉、it〈它〉。

例：

He has a new book. → Does he have a new book?

他有一本新書。→ 他有一本新書嗎？

b. 第一人稱單數、複數和第二人稱單數、複數，第三人稱複數，助動詞為 do。第一人稱：I〈我〉、we〈我們〉。第二人稱：you〈你〉、you〈你們〉、they〈他們〉。

例：

You finished your homework. → Did you finish your homework?

你完成你的家庭作業。→ 你完成你的家庭作業嗎？

c. 過去式的助動詞一律用 did。

例：

He went to school yesterday. → Did he go to school yesterday?

他昨天去學校。→ 他昨天去學校嗎？

3. 以情態助動詞為句首：情態助動詞為 **may**〈可以／祝願〉，**can**〈能夠／可以〉，**must**〈必須〉，**should**〈應該〉，**could**〈能夠〉，**would**〈會／願意〉，**will**〈將〉，**might**〈可以〉，這些情態助動詞有其特定的意義以表達特定的態度和意見。而這些情態助動詞不能單獨存在，必須和原形動詞一起使用，不會因主詞人稱或數量不同而有所不同。在疑問句中，情態助動詞當句首。

例1：

He can speak English. → Can he speak English?

他可以說英語。→他可以說英語嗎？

例2：

He should tell the truth. → Should he tell the truth?

他應該說實話→他應該說實話嗎？

4. 以疑問詞為句首：英文有五大疑問詞當疑問句句首為 **where**，**when**，**what**，**who** 和 **how**。助動詞以主詞一致，其句型為：

a. 疑問詞 + be 動詞 + 主詞？

例：Where is my book? 我的書在哪裡？

b. 疑問詞 ＋ 助動詞 ＋ 主詞 ＋ 原型動詞？

例：What do you think? 你想什麼？

c. 特例！ 以 Which one 為疑問詞句首，用於人或事的二選一選擇。

例：Which one do you like, Jenny or Jean?

你喜歡哪一個，Jenny 還是 Jean ？

 絕妙好例句：

1. Are they new students?（be 動詞當句首）他們是新學生嗎？

2. Does John walk to school every day?（現在式助動詞 does 當句首，第三人稱 單數當主詞）約翰每天走路學校嗎？

3. Do they have a good time?（現在式助動詞 do 當句首，第三人稱複數當主詞） 他們玩的愉快嗎？

4. Did he eat his lunch?（過去式助動詞 did 當句首）他吃過午餐嗎？

5. How are you?（疑問詞當句首）你好嗎？

6. Which one do you like? Coffee or tea?（疑問詞當句首，有兩個選項）你喜歡 哪一個？咖啡還是茶？

換你選選看：

( ) 1. _____ he a good teacher? A Are   B Is   C Does

( ) 2. _____ he take a bus to school every day? A Do   B Does   C Is

( ) 3. _____ do they come from? A Where   B When   C What

( ) 4. _____ you have a good sleep last night? A Do   B Does
C Did

( ) 5. _____ do you like your steak? A What   B How   C When

( ) 6. _____ time is it? A When   B Where   C What

答案與中譯解析：

1. 他是一位好老師嗎？（答：B Is，第三人稱單數 he 當主詞，be 動詞為 is。）

2. 他每天搭公車上學嗎？（答：B Does，第三人稱單數 he 當主詞，助動詞為 does。）

3. 他們來自哪裡？（答：A Where，come from 與地點相關，疑問詞選用表示詢問地點的 where。）

4. 你昨晚睡的好嗎？（答：C Did，過去式疑問句以 did 當句首。）

5. 你想要你的牛排幾分熟？（答：B，由題意判斷選擇疑問詞 how。）

6. 現在是幾點？（答：C What，由題意判斷選擇疑問詞 what。）

Part I 句型文法

Part II 字詞文法

Part III 文法勘正篇

Unit 9
附加問句

 搶先看名句學文法：

A toothbrush is a non-lethal object, isn't it? 牙刷是一支非致命的東西，不是嗎？

看到 **isn't it**，就要聯想到 " 附加問句 "。

 英文達人小筆記！

　　附加問句（如 Isn't it? Aren't they?）表示「（不）是嗎？」，的反問法來徵求對方的意見，也有強調的語氣在裡面。由於是反問，因此附加的簡短問句要和主要句子的屬性相反，也就是若主要句子為「肯定直述句」，則附加的簡短問句就是「否定」；反之，若主要句子為「否定直述句」，則附加的簡短問句就是要「肯定」的。

關於附加問句的詳細說明：

A toothbrush is a non-lethal object, isn't it? 牙刷是一支非致命的東西，不是嗎？

名言背景：此句話出自美國電影《刺激 1995》（The Shawshank Redemption）是一部 1994 年上映的美國電影，電影中的男主角安迪由提姆·羅賓斯飾演，男配角由摩根·費里曼飾演，劇情主要圍繞著安迪在獄中的生活，闡述希望、自由、體制化等概念。此句話為摩根·費里曼給劇中男主角一把牙刷的一句話：牙刷是一支非致命的東西，不是嗎？

附加問句文法解析：附加問句是放在直述句後的問句，表示「（不）是嗎？」、「是嗎？」、「對嗎？」。直述句是肯定句時，附加問句為否定。直述句是否定句時，附加問句為肯定。附加問句的主詞需與直述句主詞的人稱代名詞一致。

1. 使用時機：

　　a. **Be** 動詞的附加問句：

　　直述句的動詞為 be 動詞時，句型如下：

　　　　主詞＋肯定句，be 動詞否定式縮寫＋主詞之代名詞？

　　　　例：Angela is smart, isn't she? Angela 是聰明的，不是嗎？

　　　　主詞＋否定句，be 動詞肯定式＋主詞之代名詞？

　　　　例：The school isn't big, is it? 這所學校不大，對吧？

　　b. 一般動詞的附加問句：

　　直述句的動詞為一般動詞時，句型如下：

　　　　主詞＋一般動詞肯定句，助動詞否定式縮寫＋主詞之代名詞？

　　　　例：He likes jogging in the park, doesn't he? 他喜歡在公園裡慢跑，不是嗎？

　　　　主詞＋一般動詞否定句，助動詞肯定式＋主詞之代名詞？

　　　　例：You didn't believe me, did you? 你不相信我，對吧？

2. 文法重點：

　　a. 主詞是 **I** 時，附加問句為 **am I not, am not** 不能縮寫，口語常用代替 **aren't I**。

　　　　例：I am beautiful, am I not? 我是漂亮的，不是嗎？

　　b. 情態助動詞 **will ／ can ／ should** 的附加問句與完成式助動詞 **have** 的附加問句。主詞＋有助動詞肯定句，助動詞否定式縮寫＋主詞之代名詞？

　　　　例：You can't ride a bicycle, can you? 你不會騎腳踏車，不是嗎？

c. 主詞＋有助動詞否定句，助動詞肯定式＋主詞之代名詞？

　　例：She has gone to Japan, hasn't she? 她已經去日本，不是嗎？

d. 直述句有 **have ／ has to** 時，附加問句助動詞為 **do ／ does**。

　　例：They have to go to school quickly, don't they? 他們必須快速回學校，不是嗎？

e. 若直述句的主詞為 **there**，附加問句主詞為 **there**。若直述句的主詞為 **this** 和 **that**，附加問句主詞為 **it**。若直述句的主詞為 **these** 和 **those**，附加問句主詞為 **they**。

　　例：There is a bank near here, isn't there? 附近有一間銀行，不是嗎？

　　　　This is a good book, isn't it? 這是一本好書，不是嗎？

　　　　Those are your pencils, aren't they? 那些是你的鉛筆，不是嗎？

f. 若直述句有否定意味的字，如：**no**、**no one**、**nobody**、**nothing**、**few**（很少，用於可數名詞）、**little**（很少，用於不可數名詞）、**seldom**（不常）、**never**（從不）等，附加問句為肯定句。

　　例：He never plays basketball with you, does he? 他從沒與你打籃球，對吧？

　　　　Few students were present yesterday, were they? 昨天很少學生出席，不是嗎？

g. 特例！！

1. 若直述句的主詞為 **something**、**everything**、**nothing**、**anything**、虛主詞 **it**、不定詞、動名詞，附加問句主詞為 **it**。

　　例：Everything is perfect, isn't? 每件事都完美，不是嗎？

　　　　It is wonderful to meet you here, isn't it? 在這裡遇見你真棒，不是嗎？

　　　　Eating less doesn't make you healthier, does it? 吃少一點並不會使你更健康，對吧？

2. 若直述句的主詞為 everyone、everybody、no one、nobody，主

要子句動詞用單數動詞，附加問句的主詞用複數代名詞 they，動詞用複數動詞。

　　例：Everybody looks happy, don't they? 每個人看起來快樂，不是嗎？

3. 祈使句的附加問句一律為 **will you**。

　　例：Please open the window, will you? 請打開窗戶，好嗎？

4. 有邀請意味的祈使句，附加問句為 **won't you**。

　　例：Have some tea, won't you? 喝些茶，好嗎？

5. **Let's not** 的附加問句為 **OK** 或 **all right**。**Let's...** 的附加問句為 **shall we**。

　　例：Let's go back home, shall we? 讓我們回家去，好嗎？

6. **too... to...** 的附加問句為否定式。

　　例：He is too short to play basketball, isn't he? 他太矮以致於不能打籃球，不是嗎？

 絕妙好例句：

1. Your parents are always here for you, aren't they?（be 動詞的否定式附加問句）你的父母親永遠在你身邊，不是嗎？

2. You have never been to Canada, have you?（有否定意味字詞 never 的附加問句）你從未去過加拿大，不是嗎？

3. Everyone has to finish one project, don't they?（直述句有 have／has to 時，附加問句助動詞為 do／does）每個人必須完成一個計畫，對吧？

4. I am your best friend, am I not?（主詞是 I 時，附加問句為 am I not）我是你最好的朋友，不是嗎？

5. Don't lie to us, will you?（祈使句的附加問句一律為 will you）不要對我們說謊，好嗎？

6. Andy wants to be a scientist in the future, doesn't he?（一般動詞的否定式附加問句）Andy 想要在將來成為一位科學家，是嗎？

7. Going to bed early is good for your health, isn't it?（動名詞當直述句的主詞）早睡有益你的健康，不是嗎？

換你選選看：

( ) 1. He is tired because he worked very late last night, _____? A didn't he B isn't he C did he

( ) 2. Rachel likes to drink a cup of coffee after lunch, _____? A does she B doesn't she C doesn't Rachel

( ) 3. Playing computer games is interesting, _____? A is it B doesn't it C isn't it

( ) 4. You have to arrive at the train station before 6 pm, _____? A haven't you B don't you C aren't you

( ) 5. There is going to be a show on TV tomorrow, _____? A won't it B will there C isn't there

( ) 6. Have some coffee, _____? A won't you B isn't it C will you

答案與中譯解析：

1. 他很累，因為他昨晚工作到很晚，不是嗎？（答：B isn't he，be 動詞 is 不變，主要子句為肯定，附加問句為否定。）

2. Rachel 喜歡在午餐後喝杯咖啡，不是嗎？（答：B doesn't she，有一般動詞的肯定句，附加問句為助動詞否定式縮寫，主詞為 Rachel，附加問句使用人稱代名詞。）

3. 玩電腦遊戲很有趣，不是嗎？（答：C isn't it，動名詞當直述句的主詞，附加問句主詞為 it。）

4. 你們必須在六點前抵達車站，不是嗎？（答：B don't you，直述句中的 have ／ has to 表示「必須」，為一般動詞，附加問助動詞為 do ／ does。）

5. 明天電視將會有個秀，不是嗎？（答：C isn't there，直述句的主詞為 there，附加問句主詞為 there。附加問句為助動詞否定式縮寫。）

6. 來杯咖啡，好嗎？（答：A won't you，有邀請意味的祈使句，附加問句為 won't you。）

Part I 句型文法

Part II 字詞文法

Part III 文法糾正篇

Unit 10
間接問句

 搶先看名句學文法：

I can see how it might be possible for a man to look down upon the earth and be an atheist, but I cannot conceive how a man could look up into the heavens and say there is no God. 我可以了解當一個人從天上看地球時那一個人可能是無神論者。但我不認為當一個人抬頭看上天時，會說沒有上帝的存在。

當 **how** 出現在句中時，問句的作用變得不明顯，而成為間接問句。

 英文達人小筆記！

　　間接問句放在句中時，須注意主詞動詞的位置，其性質為名詞子句，架構為疑問句（如 if、whether，與五大疑問句：where、when、what、who 和 how）＋主詞與動詞。

關於間接問句的詳細說明：

I can see how it might be possible for a man to look down upon the earth and be an atheist, but I cannot conceive how a man could look up into the heavens and say there is no God.

我可以了解當一個人從天上看地球時那一個人可能是無神論者。但我不認為當一個人抬頭看上天時，會說沒有上帝的存在。

名言背景：Abraham Lincoln 亞伯拉罕‧林肯是美國最偉大的總統其中之一。他在 1861 年當選美國總統，當時美國因應是否解放黑奴問題，南北發生衝突，引發了南北戰爭。林肯主張廢奴隸制度，後來他所領導的北方獲得勝。林肯宣佈廢除奴隸制度，使美國從南北長期分裂中恢復了統一。此段話為林肯談論有關無神論，他說當一個人從天上看地球時那一個人可能是無神論者。但他不認為當一個人抬頭看上天時，會說沒有上帝的存在。

■ **間接問句文法解析**：當一個問句放入句子中間而非句首時，即構成間接問句，為一「名詞子句」，作為前面動詞或介詞的受詞。間接問句後面的標點符號視主要子句決定。當疑問句成為間接問句時，疑問句中的主詞、助動詞與動詞的位置將會有變化。其變化如下：

1. 使用時機：

　　a. 有 be 動詞的間接問句

　　　間接問句的動詞為 be 動詞時，句型如下：

　　　　　主要子句＋疑問詞＋主詞＋ be 動詞

　　　　　要訣：只要將疑問句中的 be 動詞與主詞對調，成為直述句句型。

　　　例：I don't know that.

　　　　　Who is he?

　　　　　→ I don't know who he is.（間接問句中，be 動詞與主詞對調）

　　　　　我不知道他是誰。

　　b. 有一般動詞的間接問句

　　　間接問句的動詞為一般動詞時，句型如下：

主要子句＋疑問詞＋主詞＋一般動詞

要訣：一定要將疑問句中的助動詞去掉，動詞恢復成原來的時態，成為直述句句型。也就是如果去掉的助動詞為過去式，則動詞就必須恢復成為過去式。若去掉的助動詞為 does，間接問句的動詞就必須加 s 或 es。

例：I don't know that.

Where did he go?

→ I don't know where he went.（去掉的助動詞為過去式，動詞 go 恢復成為過去式 went）我不知道他去哪裡。

c. 沒有疑問詞的疑問句：沒有疑問詞的 yes-no 疑問句，分為三種：

1. 以 be 動詞為句首的 yes-no 疑問句，句型如下：

主要子句＋ if ／ whether ＋主詞＋ be 動詞

要訣：將 yes-no 疑問句中的 be 動詞與主詞對調，成為直述句句型，在間接問句前面加 if ／ whether（是否）。

例：I don't know that.

Is she a good teacher?

→ I don't know if ／ whether she is a good teacher.

（be 動詞與主詞對調，在間接問句前面加 if ／ whether）我不知道她是否是一位好老師。

2. 以 do、did、does 為句首的 yes-no 疑問句，句型如下：

主要子句＋ if ／ whether ＋主詞＋原來時態的動詞

要訣：將 yes-no 疑問句中的 do、did、does 助動詞去掉，成為直述句句型在間接問句前面加 if ／ whether（是否）。

例：Please tell me.

Did he finish his homework?

→ Please tell me if ／ whether he finished his homework.（did 助動詞去掉，在間接問句前面加 if ／ whether，動詞變成原時態）請告訴我他是否完成他的家庭作業。

3. 以情態助動詞 can、will 等為句首的 yes-no 疑問句，句型如下：

主要子句＋ if ／ whether ＋主詞＋情態助動詞＋原型動詞

要訣：將 yes-no 疑問句中的 can、will 等情態助動詞移到主詞後面，成為直述句句型，在間接問句前面加 if ／ whether（是否）。

例：He didn't tell me.

Could I eat my breakfast there?

→ He didn't tell me if ／ whether I could eat my breakfast there.（將情態助動詞移到主詞後面，在間接問句前面加 if ／ whether）他沒告訴我是否可以在那裡吃早餐。

2. 若間接問句句首字詞為 when ／ if，則須注意是否為副詞子句，則時態將須注意。間接問句的時間。若為未來式，則須用現在式代替未來式。

當 when 和 if 意思是（何時）和（是否），則該間接問句為名詞子句，其後動詞的時態與一般用法相同，亦即若時間為未來，則仍用未來式。

若 when 和 if 意思是（當…的時後）和（假如），則該間接問句為副詞子句，且時態為未來式時，其動詞的時態則須用現在式代替未來式。

例1：

When will he come back tomorrow?

→ Please tell me when he will come back tomorrow.（when 的意思為「何時」，間接問句，為名詞子句用未來式。）仍請告訴我明天他何時回來。

例2：

Please tell me the truth.

When will he come back tomorrow?

→ Please tell me the truth when he comes back tomorrow.（when 的意思為「當…的時候」，間接問句為副詞子句，用現在式代替未來式。）

當他明天回來時，請告訴我實情。

3. 特例！！

有些間接問句本身是主詞或修飾主詞，此類問句原本就沒有「倒裝」，故不用恢復成直述句。

例：Do you know?

What made him so happy?

→ Do you know what made him so happy?

你知道什麼使得他如此快樂？

 絕妙好例句：

1. Do you know how he goes to school?（間接問句中助動詞 does 去掉，變成直述句，主詞為第三人稱單數，動詞 go ＋ es）你知道他如何上學的嗎？

2. He forgot how many students there were in the classroom.（間接問句中 were there 改成 there were，變成直述句。）他忘記有多少學生在教室裡。

3. Do you know what he did at his birthday party?（間接問句中助動詞 did 去掉，變成直述句，動詞 do 變成過去式 did。）你知道在他的生日派對中他做什麼？

4. Tell me if ／ whether he can speak English.（yes-no 疑問句變成間接問句，將情態助動詞 can 到間接問句主詞後面，變成直述句，間接問句句首加 if ／ whether。）告訴我他是否會説英文。

5. Do you remember how old he is?（間接問句中 be 動詞與主詞對調）你記得他年紀多大了？

6. Do you know what is wrong with him?（間接問句 what 本身是主詞，此類問句原本就沒有「倒裝」）你知道他怎麼了嗎？

 換你選選看：

（　　）1. Do you know ＿＿＿＿ yesterday? Ⓐ what he did　Ⓑ what did he Ⓒ what did he do

（　　）2. Do you know＿＿＿＿? Ⓐ when is the TV show　Ⓑ when the TV show is　Ⓒ when does the TV show be

（　　）3. I don't know＿＿＿＿. Ⓐ I should go where　Ⓑ where should I go

ⒸⒸ where I should go

( ) 4. Do you know _____? Ⓐ what is the matter with him Ⓑ what the matter is with him Ⓒ who is he

( ) 5. I want to know _____. Ⓐ if he can finish this project Ⓑ can he finish this project Ⓒ when can he finish this project

( ) 6. I will send him a present _____? Ⓐ when he will pass the exam next week Ⓑ when will he pass the exam next week Ⓒ when he passes the exam next week

 答案與中譯解析：

1. 你知道他昨天做什麼嗎？（答：Ⓐ，間接問句中助動詞 did 去掉，變成直述句，動詞 do 變成過去式 did。）

2. 你知道電視表演是什麼時候？（答：Ⓑ，間接問句中 be 動詞與主詞位置對調。）

3. 我不知道我應該去哪裡。（答：Ⓒ，間接問句中動詞與主詞位置對調。）

4. 你知道他怎麼了？（答：Ⓐ，間接問句 what 本身是主詞，此類問句原本就沒有「倒裝」。）

5. 我想知道他是否可以完成那個計劃。（答：Ⓐ，Yes-no 疑問句變成間接問句，將情態助動詞 can 到間接問句主詞後面，變成直述句，間接問句句首加 if ／ whether。）

6. 等他下週通過考試時，我將送他一個禮物。（答：Ⓒ，when 的意思是「當…的時候」，則該間接問句為副詞子句，且時態為未來式時，其動詞的時態則須用現在式代替未來式。）

Unit 11
分詞構句

 搶先看名句學文法：

A kind heart is a fountain of gladness, making everything in its vicinity freshen into smile. 一顆善良的心就像欣喜的噴泉，使周遭的每一件事都顯出清新的笑容。

making 這裡為分詞構句的用法。

 英文達人小筆記！

　　分詞構句的原貌為形容詞或副詞子句，架構為關係代名詞（如 which、that or who）＋動詞，來修式前方的人事物，若要變成分詞構句時，關代這時就要省略，動詞會成為現在分詞或過去分詞。分詞構句能讓句子富有變化性，同時也有精簡、優美的效果。

關於分詞構句的詳細說明：

A kind heart is a fountain of gladness, making everything in its vicinity freshen into smile.

一顆善良的心就像欣喜的噴泉，使周遭的每一件事都顯出清新的笑容。

名言背景：華盛頓•歐文 Washington Irving（1783-1859），是美國著名作家、短篇小說家、也是一名律師，曾當過政府官員，是對西班牙與英國的外交官。這一句子是指一顆善良的心就像欣喜的噴泉，使周遭的每一件事都顯出清新的笑容。句子中原本有一形容詞子句 "which makes everything in its vicinity freshen into smiles" 來修飾 A kind heart。這一句形容詞子句省略 which 以及將 makes 改成 making 形成了一分詞構句。

■ **分詞構句文法解析**：分詞構句可以由形容詞子句或副詞子句簡化，或將兩個句子合併，將其中一主詞省略。（形容詞子句的用法請參照第六單元附屬子句。）

A. 簡化形容詞子句

1. 省略關係代名詞與 be 動詞

例1：I've never talked to the man ~~that is~~ standing there.　我從來沒跟正站在那裡的男人說過話。→ I've never talked to the man standing there.

例2：The topics ~~which are~~ discussed in class are related to the current events.　上課討論的話題與時事相關。→ The topics discussed in class are related to the current events.

2. 省略關係代名詞並將一般動詞改成 Ving

例1：The singer ~~who made~~ his debut album a big hit has created more popular songs. 這位初張專輯就造成轟動的歌手一直推出受人歡迎的歌曲。→ The singer making his debut album a big hit has created more popular songs.

例2：Anyone ~~who wants~~ to attend the conference has to sign up early.　所有想參加這個研討會的人必須及早登記。→ Anyone wanting to attend the conference has to sign up early.

Part I 句型文法

Part II 字詞文法

Part III 文法糾正篇

3. 形容詞子句若是有其他主詞則無法簡化

例1：The woman who I saw was my classmate. 我看到那女人是我以前的同學。→ The woman I saw was my classmate.（只可省略關係代名詞）

例2：Everyone liked the pie that I made. 每個人都喜歡我做的派。→ Everyone liked the pie I made.

4. 非限定形容詞子句簡化時變成同位語

例1：We visited Penghu, ~~which are~~ islands located in the Taiwan Strait. 我們之前拜訪澎湖，是位於台灣海峽的島。→ We visited Penghu, islands located in the Taiwan Strait.（Penghu = islands located in the Taiwan Strait）

B. 簡化副詞子句（副詞子句的用法請參照第六單元附屬子句）

1. 如何簡化副詞子句

確定副詞子句與主要子句兩個主詞是同一主詞才可簡化

a. 省略副詞子句中的主詞與 be 動詞

例：While ~~I was~~ having dinner, I heard the phone ring. 當我在吃晚餐時，我聽到電話響。→ While having dinner, I heard the phone ring.

b. 省略副詞子句中的主詞並將一般動詞改成 Ving

例：After ~~I finished~~ the assignment, I went to the party. 在做完這工作後，我去了派對。→ After finishing the assignment, I went to the party.

2. 不同的種類的副詞子句的簡化

a. 表達時間關係的副詞子句 after, before, since, when, while

例：Before I came to Taiwan, I lived in the United States. 我來台灣之前，我住在美國。→ Before coming to Taiwan, I lived in the United States.

b. while 連接的句子，while 也可省略

例：While ~~I was~~ having dinner, I heard the phone ring. 當我在吃

晚餐時，我聽到電話響。

→ While having dinner, I heard the phone ring.

→ Having dinner, I heard the phone ring.

c. 表達因果關係的副詞子句 because 也可省略

例1：~~Because he wants~~ to make more money, he's looking for a second job. 因為他想要多賺些錢，他正在找第二份工作。

→ Wanting to make more money, he's looking for a second job.

例2：~~Because I didn't want~~ to hurt her feeling, I didn't tell her the truth. 因為我不想傷害她的感受，我沒有告訴她實話。

→ Not wanting to hurt her feeling, I didn't tell her the truth.

例3：~~Because I have lived~~ in that city before, I have many friends there. 因為我之前住過那城市，我有很多朋友在那。

→ Having lived in that city before, I have many friends there.

例4：~~Because I had read~~ the book, I didn't want to read it again. 因為我之前已經讀過那本書了，我不想再讀一遍。

→ Having read the book, I didn't want to read it again.

例5：~~Because she was~~ nervous about flying, she couldn't sleep that night. 因為她對搭飛機很緊張，她那一晚都睡不著。

→ Being nervous about flying, she couldn't sleep that night.

→ Nervous about flying, she couldn't sleep that night.（be 動詞可省略）

d. when 所形成的副詞子句，簡化的子句前可加 upon 或 on

例：~~When she heard~~ the news, she was so surprised! 當她聽到這消息時，她十分的驚訝！

→ When hearing the news, she was so surprised.

→ Upon hearing the news, she was so surprised.

→ On hearing the news, she was so surprised.

3. 合併句子再簡化

要合併句子再簡化時，首先要確定兩個句子的主詞一樣。再來決定那一個主要子句。

a. 省略主詞與 be 動詞

例1：

~~I was~~ watching a horror movie last night.

I didn't feel scared at all. → 主要子句

合併成為→ Watching a horror movie last night, I didn't feel scared at all. 昨晚看恐怖電影，我一點都不覺得害怕。

例2：

~~The teacher was~~ interrupted by the students all the time.

He finally got upset. → 主要子句

合併成為→ Interrupted by the students all the time, the teacher finally got upset. 一直被學生打斷，這老師終於生氣了。

（合併之後主詞只出現過一次，所以不用代名詞。）

例3：

~~The car is~~ the fastest car in the world.

Needless to say, it's very expensive. → 主要子句

合併成為 → Being the fastest car in the world, needless to say, the car is very expensive. 做為世界上最快的車，不用說，這一定很貴。

（如果 be 動詞之後是說明主詞的補語，be 動詞不可省略，改成 being）

b. 省略主詞並將一般動詞改成 Ving

例1：

~~Richard has~~ eaten too much.

He feels sick. → 主要子句

合併成為→ Having eaten too much, Richard feels sick. Richard 吃太多東西感覺想吐。

例2：

~~Judy~~ comes from a small town.

She is fascinated by the interesting nightlife in Taipei. → 主要子句

合併成為→ Coming from a small town, Judy is fascinated with the interesting nightlife in Taipei. 來自從一個小鎮來的 Judy 對台北有趣的夜生活很嚮往。

c. 簡化後的句子可以放在不同的位置

例：

Judy comes from a small town.

She is fascinated by the interesting nightlife in Taipei. → 主要子句

合併後可成為：

→ Coming from a small town, Judy is fascinated with the interesting nightlife in Taipei.

→ Judy, coming from a small town, is fascinated with the interesting nightlife in Taipei.

→ Judy is fascinated with the interesting nightlife in Taipei, coming from a small town.

Part I 句型文法

Part II 字詞文法

Part III 文法糾正篇

✏️ **換你選選看（選出正確的分詞構句）：**

( ) 1. The girl who is talking on the phone is my best friend.

    Ⓐ The girl talking on the phone is my best friend.

    Ⓑ The girl talked on the phone is my best friend.

    Ⓒ The girl is talking on the phone is my best friend.

( ) 2. His company, which was based in New York, filed bankruptcy last week.

    Ⓐ His company, basing in New York, filed bankruptcy last week.

    Ⓑ His company, has based in New York, filed bankruptcy last week.

    Ⓒ His company, based in New York, filed bankruptcy last week.

( ) 3. Something that smells bad may be rotten.

    Ⓐ Something smelling bad may be rotten.

    Ⓑ Something smells bad may be rotten.

    Ⓒ Something smelled bad may be rotten

( ) 4. Have you read the crime novel which is written by J.K. Rowling?

    Ⓐ Have you read the crime novel written by J.K. Rowling?

    Ⓑ Have you read the crime novel writing by J.K. Rowling?

    Ⓒ Have you read the crime novel was written by J.K. Rowling?

( ) 5. _____ in the car crash, Chris stayed in hospital for three months. Ⓐ Severely being injured   Ⓑ Severely injured   Ⓒ Severely injuring

( ) 6. ____ _____ the topic, the student didn't know what to say in the discussion. Ⓐ Not caught   Ⓑ Not being caught   Ⓒ Not catching

答案與中譯：

1. 這個正在講電話的女生是我最好的朋友。（答：A 。）
2. 他的公司，設立於紐約，上星期宣佈破產。（答：C 。）
3. 聞起來很糟的東西有可能就是壞掉了！（答：A 。）
4. 你有讀過 J.K. Rowling 寫的犯罪小說嗎？（答：A 。）
5. 在車禍中嚴重受傷，Chris 在醫院待了三個月。（答：B 。）
6. 沒有聽到主題，學生不知道要在討論中説甚麼。（答：C 。）

Unit 12
倒裝句

 搶先看名句學文法：

Seldom, very seldom, does complete truth belong to any human disclosure; seldom can it happen that something is not a little disguised or a little mistaken. 完整的真相很少被揭露出來，偽裝與誤認是常發生的。

非以主詞＋動詞基本架構起頭，而是以 **Seldom** 副詞為首的句子，是為倒裝句。

 英文達人小筆記！

常見的倒裝句有 Not only ＋ V（不僅僅）、hardly ＋ V ...（幾乎沒有） 或 Only by Ving…（唯有…）等句型，和一般主詞（名詞屬性）＋ 動詞的架構不同，這類倒裝句的句型都以副詞（如地方副詞）為首，有強調的意涵，用在寫作上也有讓人眼睛一亮的效果（但還是要小心，千萬別濫用為妙）。

關於倒裝句的詳細說明：

> **Seldom, very seldom, does complete truth belong to any human disclosure; seldom can it happen that something is not a little disguised or a little mistaken.** 完整的真相很少被揭露出來，偽裝與誤認是常發生的。

名言背景：珍·奧斯汀（Jane Austen），1775 － 1817，19 世紀英國小説家，世界文學史上最具影響力的女性文學家之一，其最著名的作品是《傲慢與偏見》和《理性與感性》，以細緻入微的觀察和活潑文字描述十九世紀的女性生活著稱。本段為珍·奧斯汀在《艾瑪》中説完整的真相很少被揭露出來，偽裝與誤認是常發生的。

■ **否定副詞倒裝／地方副詞倒裝文法解析**：在英文中為了強調句子的某一部分，將一般敘述句的主詞與動詞位置改變，成為倒裝句。本單元將討論副詞倒裝句與地方副詞倒裝句。

A. 否定副詞倒裝

1. 當句首是否定詞，其後面句子則用倒裝句，句型如下：

否定副詞 ＋	have ／ has ／ had be 動詞 助動詞	＋主詞＋ p.p. ＋主詞＋形容詞／名詞 ＋主詞＋原形動詞

2. 常用否定副詞與片語如下：

1	never=not at all=by no means=in no way=on no account 絕不
2	hardly=scarcely=rarely　幾乎不
3	few ／ little 幾乎沒有，seldom 很少
4	not until　直到…才… no sooner…than…　一…就… not only…but（also）　不但…而且…

例：

1. Hardly did anyone know the secret. 幾乎沒有任何一個人知道那個秘密。

2. Never have they seen such a situation. 他們從未看過如此這種情況。

3. By no means would you help him pay back the money. 你絕不會幫他還那筆錢。

4. Not until the age of forty did he make his dream come true. 直到四十歲他才完成他的夢想。

5. Not only did he come, but he saw her. 他不只是來，而且看到她。

B. Only 的倒裝句型

3. 當 only 當句子的句首時，主要子句用倒裝句。句型如下：

Only by（副詞子句／副詞片語…）＋ did ＋ 主詞

例：Only by working hard did he finish his project. 只有藉由努力工作他完成他的計畫。

C. 表也／也不的倒裝句，句型如下：

1.	肯定句 , and 主詞 ＋ be 動詞／助動詞 , too.
	＝肯定句 , and so ＋倒裝句 .
	＝肯定句 . So ＋倒裝句 .

2.	否定句 , and ＋主詞＋ be 動詞／助動詞 ＋ not, either.
	＝否定句 , nor ＋倒裝句
	and neither
	＝否定句 . Nor ＋倒裝句
	Neither

例1：

I am a student, and he is, too.

＝ I am a student, and so is he.

＝ I am a student. So is he.

我是一個學生，他也是。

例2：

I am not a teacher, and he is not, either.

＝ I am not a teacher, nor is he.

＝ I am not a teacher, and neither is he.

= I am not a teacher. Neither is he.

我不是一位老師，他也不是。

例3：

He likes music, and I do, too.

= He likes music, and so do I.

= He likes music. So do I.

他喜歡音樂，我也是。

例4：

He didn't finish his homework, and I didn't, either.

= He didn't finish his homework, nor did I.

= He didn't finish his homework, and neither did I.

= He didn't finish his homework. Nor did I.

= He didn't finish his homework. Neither did I.

他沒完成他的家庭作業，我也沒有。

特例！！

So 之後的句子如果不倒裝，則表示同意。

例：Helen is a good student. So she is.　Helen 是一位好學生。她的確
　　是。

D. 強調地方副詞的倒裝句

1. 當句首是（1）地方副詞 There ／ Here，（2）表地方的介副詞，（3）
表位置的副詞片語時，其後面的主要子句須為倒裝句。句型如下：

> There ／ Here ＋ be 動詞／一般動詞＋主詞（名詞）
> There ／ Here ＋主詞（代名詞）＋ be 動詞／一般動詞

請注意當主詞是名詞與代名詞時，句子排列方式的差異性。而 be 動詞／
一般動詞單複數形式依主詞決定。

2. 表地方介副詞，如：up, down, off, away….

3. 表位置的副詞片語，如：at the door, on the table….

例：

Here comes the bus. 公車來了。

Here you are. 你在這裡。

Up flies the balloon. 氣球往上飛。

At the door waited the parents. 父母親在門口等。

E. 表讓步的倒裝句型

1. 當一般句子句首為 Although，為了語氣強調，亦可用倒裝句。其句型如下：

> Although ＋主詞＋ be 動詞＋形容詞，名詞＋ 一般動詞（主要子句）
> ＝形容詞／名詞／副詞＋ as ／ though ＋主詞＋ be 動詞 ＋（主要子句）

例：Although he is poor, he is happy.

= Poor as ／ though he is, he is happy.

雖然他是貧窮的，他是快樂的。

2. 當名詞放句首，冠詞要省略。

例： Although he is a child, he acts like an adult.

= Child as ／ though he is, he acts like an adult.

雖然他是一個小孩，他舉止像大人。

絕妙好例句：

1. Here you are.（There ／ Here ＋主詞（代名詞）＋ be 動詞／一般動詞）你在
   這裡。

2. Out rushed the students.（表位置的副詞片語時＋ be 動詞／一般動詞＋主詞
   （名詞）學生們衝出去。

3. You do not feel comfortable, and I don't, either.（否定句，and ＋主詞＋ be
   動詞／助動詞＋ not、 either）你覺得不舒服，我也是。

   Not until Jenny visited him did she realize how ill he was.（Not until ＋…
   助動詞＋主詞＋原形動詞）直到 Jenny 探望他，她才了解他病得多重。

4. Seldom did I go shopping in the supermarket on Saturdays.（否定副詞＋助
   動詞＋主詞＋原形動詞）我很少星期六到超級市場購物。

5. Little did he know that the police were after him all the time.（否定副詞＋
   助動詞＋主詞＋原形動詞）他一點都不知道警察一直都在追他。

換你選選看：

( ) 1. Only when one is away from home_____.

    Ⓐ one realize how home is nice

    Ⓑ one can realize how nice home is

    Ⓒ does one realize how nice home is

( ) 2. Jane can hardly eat it, _____.

    Ⓐ May can, too.

    Ⓑ neither can't May

    Ⓒ nor can May

( ) 3. Sick _____ he was, he went to the meeting as usual.

    Ⓐ in spite

    Ⓑ though

    Ⓒ although

( ) 4. _____she left the house than it began to snow.

    Ⓐ Sooner no had

    Ⓑ Sooner had no

    Ⓒ No sooner had

( ) 5. Along the side of the road _____ the palm trees.

    Ⓐ is

    Ⓑ has

    Ⓒ are

( ) 6. At the bottom of the stairs _____ a door that leads to the garden.

    Ⓐ has

    Ⓑ is

    Ⓒ are

答案與中譯解析：

1. 只有當一個人離開家，才了解家是多麼好。（答：C，Only 當句首，主要主子句須倒裝。倒裝句句型為助動詞＋主詞＋原型動詞。）

2. Jane 幾乎不吃它，May 也不。（答：C，hardly 為有否定意味的字詞，「也不」的倒裝句型為 nor／neither＋助動詞＋主詞。）

3. 他雖然生病，他一如往常去參加會議。（答：B，表讓步子句的倒裝句型，形容詞／名詞／副詞＋ as／though＋主詞＋ be 動詞＋主要子句。）

4. 她一離開房子天氣就下雪。（答：C，no sooner＋had＋主詞＋p.p. …than＋子句。）

5. 沿著道路的一邊是棕櫚樹。（答：C，表位置的副詞片語＋主詞（代名詞）＋be 動詞／一般動詞。）

6. 在樓梯底部有一個門指向花園。（答：B，表位置的副詞片語＋主詞（代名詞）＋ be 動詞／一般動詞。）

Unit 13
虛主詞句型

 搶先看名句學文法：

It is not enough to win a war; it is more important to organize the peace. 贏得戰爭是不夠的，組織和平才是更重要的。

這兩句皆以 **It is** 為開頭，重點放在 **to win a war** 以及 **to organize the peace**，這時的 **It is** 就為虛主詞。

 英文達人小筆記！

虛主詞句型除了以 It is… 為開頭，也有 It takes… 為首的句型，這類的句型都要看到最後才會了解句子的重點。

關於虛主詞句型的詳細說明：

It is not enough to win a war; it is more important to organize the peace. 贏得戰爭是不夠的，組織和平才是更重要的。

名言背景：亞里斯多德是古希臘哲學家，柏拉圖的學生。他的著作包含許多學科，包括了物理學、形上學、詩歌（包括戲劇）、邏輯學、政治、政府、以及倫理學等。和柏拉圖、蘇格拉底一起被譽為西方哲學的奠基者。

使用虛主詞的句型有：

1. It takes + 人 + 時間 + to V..

   = 人 + spend + 時間 + V-ing

   = 人 + take（s）+ 時間 + to V

   ake 在此句型中文意思為「花…多少時間」，其後接不定詞片語。虛主詞 it 代表句子中的不定詞片語。

   例：

   It took me five hours to read this book.

   = I spent five hours reading this book.

   = I took five hours to read this book.

   我花了五小時讀這本書。

2. It is + adj.（修飾事物的形容詞）+ for + 人 + to V

   It is + adj.（修飾人的形容詞）+ of + 人 + to V

   It is + adj.（必要、緊要、重要等形容詞 + that + S +（should）+ 原 V

   a. 虛主詞 it 代表句子中的不定詞片語。It is adj. + of + 人 + to V 的句型用於讚美或責備某人，此類形容詞如下：

   > nice、kind 、honest 、polite 、impolite 、wrong
   > bad 、foolish 、stupid 、generous 、wise …等

   例：

   It is really kind of you to help the poor girl.

    = You are so kind to help the poor girl.

   你真是仁慈來幫忙這位貧窮的女孩。

   b. 虛主詞 it 代表句子中的不定詞片語。It is adj. + for + 人 + to V 的句型，其中文涵意為「…事對某人是…」。此類形容詞如下：

   > difficult 、easy 、possible 、necessary 、enough
   > unnecessary 、convenient 、inconvenient 、polite…等

   例：

   It is impossible for him to finish the project.

完成這個計劃對他而言是不可能的。

c.It is + adj.（必要、緊要、重要等形容詞）+ that + S +（should）+ 原 V

虛主詞 it 代表句子中的 that 子句，此類形容詞如下：

> necessary、important、essential、urgent …等

例：

It is important that you（should）follow the directions.

遵守指示對你們而言是重要的。

d.It is no wonder + that 子句，中文意思為「…一點也不為奇；難怪」，此句型中的 it is 和 that 常被省略。

例：

 It is no wonder that he didn't want to come back.

= No wonder he didn't want to come back. 難怪他不想回來。

👑 絕妙好例句：

1. It is difficult for me to speak in public.（It is + adj.「修飾事物的形容詞」+ for + 人 + to V）對我而言，在公開場合演講是困難的。

2. It is wise of you to answer this hard question. （It is + adj.「修飾人的形容詞」+ of + 人 + to V）你是有智慧能回答這個困難的問題。

3. It is no wonder that he wanted to stay at home.（It is no wonder + that 子句，中文意思為「…一點也不為奇；難怪」）難怪他想待在家。

4. It took him fifty minutes to arrive at the train station.（It takes + 人 + 時間 + to V..，虛主詞 it 代表句子中的不定詞片語。）他花五十分鐘到達火車站。

5. It is important that Jane passed the final exam.（It is + adj.「必要、緊要、重要等形容詞」+ that + S +（should）+ 原 V，虛主詞 it 代表句子中的 that 子句）Jane 通過期末考試重要的。

6. It is good for you to take a walk for thirty minutes every day.（It is adj. + for + 人 + to V 的句型，其中文涵意為「…事對某人是…」。）每天散步三十分鐘對你是好的。

換你選選看：

( ) 1. _____ is impossible to run as fast as the light. Ⓐ This　Ⓑ It
　　　Ⓒ That

( ) 2. It _____ him one day to clean his room. Ⓐ cost　Ⓑ spent
　　　Ⓒ took

( ) 3. ____ is no _____ that you want to go to Canada with me. Ⓐ It;
　　　wonder　Ⓑ That; wonder　Ⓒ It; why

( ) 4. It is necessary ____ you ____ finish your homework on time.
　　　Ⓐ for; for　Ⓑ for; to　Ⓒ to; for

( ) 5. It is generous ____ you ____ send me such a valuable present.
　　　Ⓐ of; to　Ⓑ for; to　Ⓒ of; for

( ) 6. It _____ me three days _____ for the test. Ⓐ spent;
　　　preparing　Ⓑ takes; to prepare　Ⓒ took; to prepare

 答案與中譯解析：

1. 要跑得像光一樣快是不可能的。（答：Ⓑ，It is + adj.「修飾事物的形容詞」 +
to V。）

2. 他花一天時間打掃他的房間。（答：Ⓒ，It takes + 人 + 時間 + to V..，虛主詞
it 代表句子中的不定詞片語。）

3. 難怪你想跟我一起去加拿大。答：Ⓐ，It is no wonder + that 子句，中文意思
為「…一點也不為奇；難怪」。）

4. 準時完成功課對你來說是必要的。（答：Ⓑ，It is adj. + for + 人 + to V 的句
型，其中文涵意為「…事對某人是…」。）

5. 你真慷慨送我如此貴重的禮物。（答：Ⓐ，It is + adj.「修飾人的形容詞」 + of
+ 人 + to V。）

6. 我花三天準備考試。（答：Ⓒ，It takes + 人 + 時間 + to V..，中文意思是「我
花三天準備這場考試」。）

Unit 14
強調語氣句型

 搶先看名句學文法：

The glory of friendship is not the outstretched hand, not the kindly smile, nor the joy of companionship; it is the spiritual inspiration that comes to one when you discover that someone else believes in you and is willing to trust you with a friendship. 友誼不是伸展開的手，不是仁慈的微笑，不是陪伴的喜悅；而是心靈的激勵，此激勵是來自於你發現有人願意以友誼之情來相信你、信賴你。

It is ... that ... 為強調語氣句型。

 英文達人小筆記！

It is ... that ... 為強調語氣句型，that 子句用於說明前面強調部分，為真主詞，it 為形式主詞。

關於強調語氣句型的詳細說明：

The glory of friendship is not the outstretched hand, not the kindly smile, nor the joy of companionship; it is the spiritual inspiration that comes to one when you discover that someone else believes in you and is willing to trust you with a friendship. 友誼不是伸展開的手，不是仁慈的微笑，不是陪伴的喜悅；而是心靈的激勵，此激勵是來自於你發現有人願意以友誼之情來相信你、信賴你。

名言背景：拉爾夫·沃爾多·愛默生（Ralph Waldo Emerson，1803－1882），生於波士頓，為美國思想家、文學家。愛默生雖是個深奧的作家，但他的演講仍然有很多人來聽。愛默生的作品，是以其日記中對針對事物觀察後的意見為主，在他還在哈佛大學就讀時已有寫日記的習慣，那些日記都被愛默生精心地編號索引。後來他修訂並潤飾演講內容，放在他的散文及一些其他作品中。

■　強調語氣的句型有：

1. It is ＋ 強調部份 ＋ that ＋ 其餘部分

　　說明：that 子句用於說明前面強調部份，為真主詞，it 為形式主詞。

　　例：

　　It was yesterday that my car was stolen.

　　就是昨天我的車子被偷了。

2. 主詞 ＋ 動詞 ＋ it ＋ 受詞補語 ＋ to 原型動詞

　 that ＋ 主詞 ＋ 動詞

　　說明：it 為形式受詞，代表後面的不定詞片語或 that 子句，受詞補語補充說明 it，受詞補語為形容詞或名詞。It 前面的動詞有 "make、take、think、find、believe、consider…"

　　例：

　　We consider it difficult to finish this big project on time.

　　我們認為如期完成這個計劃是困難的。

3. 含 it 的慣用語：

    a. take it for granted that ＋ 子句視⋯為理所當然

      例：

      We take it for granted that parents take care of their children.
      我們視父母親照顧小孩為理所當然。

    b. make it a　rule ／ custom　to ＋ 動詞習慣於⋯

      例：

      They make it a rule to go to the library every Sunday.
      他們習慣於每週日去圖書館。

    c. 否定字 not 放在不定詞之前，not to ＋ 原型動詞

      例：

      He thinks it hard not to get on the Internet.
      他認為不上網是困難的。

👑 絕妙好例句：

1. It was John that sent some cake to the school.（It is ＋ 強調部份 ＋ that ＋ 其餘部分）就是約翰送蛋糕到學校。

2. We consider it our duty to obey the school rules.（主詞 ＋ 動詞 ＋ it ＋ 受詞補語 ＋ to 原型動詞）我們認為遵守校規是我們的義務。

3. He seemed to take it for granted that he acted as a class leader.（take it for granted that ＋ 子句視⋯為理所當然）他似乎認為自己行為舉止像班長是理所當然。

✏️ 換你選選看：

（　　）1. It is Susan that ＿＿＿＿ about to head for Taipei. Ⓐ is　Ⓑ am
          Ⓒ are

（　　）2. They found ＿＿＿＿ easy to make cupcakes by themselves. Ⓐ that

　　　　　　　　Ⓑ it　Ⓒ this

(　　) 3. They considered it _____ not to join the club. Ⓐ loss　Ⓑ lost
　　　　　　Ⓒ their loss

(　　) 4. She took it for granted all _____ for her.
　　　　　　Ⓐ that her husband did
　　　　　　Ⓑ her husband
　　　　　　Ⓒ that her husband was

(　　) 5. She_____ to eat an apple for breakfast every day. Ⓐ makes
　　　　　　rules　Ⓑ makes it be a rule　Ⓒ makes it a rule

(　　) 6. It was yesterday ____the accident happened. Ⓐ this　Ⓑ that
　　　　　　Ⓒ it

📁 **答案與中譯解析：**

1. 就是 Susan 打算要前往台北。（答：Ⓐ，that 子句主詞為子句前面的 I，所以 be 動詞為 am。）

2. 他們發現自己做杯子蛋糕是容易的。（答：Ⓑ，it 為形式受詞，代表後面的不定詞片語或 that 子句。）

3. 他們認為沒加入那個社團是他們的損失。（答：Ⓒ，在「主詞＋動詞＋it＋受詞補語 +to 原型動詞／ that ＋主詞＋動詞」的句型中，受詞補語可為形容詞或名詞。）

4. 她認為她先生為她所作的一切是理所當然。（答：Ⓐ，take it for granted that+ 子句視⋯為理所當然。）

5. 她習慣每天早餐吃一顆蘋果。（答：Ⓒ，「make it a rule to ＋動詞」＝習慣於⋯。）

6. 意外發生的時間就在昨天。（答：Ⓑ，It is ＋強調部份＋ that ＋其餘部分。）

Unit 15
特殊句型

 搶先看名句學文法：

I was too absorbed to be responsive. 我太投入以致於無法回應。

too...to 為常見的英文句型，意為太…而無法…。是慣用句型，英文文法裡有許多這樣套用公式的句型，我們在這裡歸類為特殊句型。

 英文達人小筆記！

　　特殊句型除了 too..to 外，還有 so...that...、why not ... 等，接下來會有詳細的說明與例句。

關於特殊句型的詳細說明：

I was too absorbed to be responsive. 我太投入以致於無法回應。

名言背景：大亨小傳（The Great Gatsby）是美國作家法蘭西斯·史考特·基·費茲傑羅於 1925 所寫的一部以 1920 年代的紐約市及長島為背景的短篇小說。本書以第一人稱—尼克—敘述男主角蓋茲一生的故事。蓋茲雖生活於紙醉金迷的奢侈豪門世界中，卻一心追求自己的浪漫愛情夢想，故事一直圍繞蓋茲心中的執著，卻也為自己帶來悲劇的命運。此句是男主角蓋茲說的，其意思是：我太投入以致於無法回應。

■ 特殊句型與其架構、例句：

1. ...too...to

    a. 句型如下：

        S + be 動詞 + too + 形容詞 + to + 原型動詞

        S + 一般動詞 + too + 副詞 + to + 原型動詞

    b. 中文意思為「⋯太⋯以致於不能⋯」，當句子的動詞為 be 動詞時，too
       後面接形容詞，to 後面接原型動詞。當句子的動詞為一般動詞時，too
       後面接副詞，to 後面接原型動詞。此句型有否定的意思。

    c. ...too...to+ 原型 V..=so...that...can't

       例：

       He is too short to play basketball 他太矮以致於不能打籃球。

       He is too young to go to school. 他太小以致於不能上學。

2. so...that...

    a. 句型如下：

        S + be 動詞 + so + 形容詞 +（a ／ an+ N）+ that 子句

        S + 一般動詞 + so + 副詞 + that 子句

    b. 中文意思為「如此⋯以致於⋯」（引號內粗體），當句子的動詞為 be 動
       詞時，so 後面接形容詞，that 後面接子句。當句子的動詞為一般動詞
       時，so 後面接副詞，that 後面接子句。

       例：

       She is so beautiful（a girl）that everyone likes her.
       她是如此美麗的（一個女孩）以致於每個人喜歡她

       He runs so fast that nobody can catch up with him.
       他跑得如此快以致沒有人可以趕上他。

3. Why not+ 原型動詞：中文意思為有兩種：（a）「為何不可」、（b）「為
   什麼不行」。

    a. 「為何不可」，表示同意。從下面的例子可知：

       A: Do you mind my borrowing your book?

       B: Why not?

A：你介意我借你的書嗎？

B：為何不可？

b. 「為什麼不行」，表示疑問。從下面的例子可知：

A: He can't go to the meeting with you.

B: Why not?

A: 他不能和你去參加會議？

B: 為什麼不行？

此處的 why not 和 why 可互換，表疑問。

4. How come+ 子句

a. 中文意思是「為什麼；怎麼回事」但 How come 是表驚訝，不需要對方的回答。但 Why 是需要對方的回答。

b. How come 和 why 的中文意思一樣，但 How come 比較口語化。How come 後接名詞子句。

例：

A: I am sorry for being late. 我很抱歉遲到了。

B: How come you are late? 咦，你怎麼遲到了。

5. What do you think + S+ V?

當主要子句為 Do you think（guess, believe）表達自我主觀判斷的動詞，則疑問詞置於句首，do you think（guess, believe）置於其後。助動詞 do, did, does 去掉，動詞恢復為原來時態。

例：

What did he do last night?

Do you think?

→ What do you think he did last night? 你認為他昨晚作了什麼？

絕妙好例句：

1. The book is too difficult to understand.（too + adj.to + 原型動詞，太…以致於不能…）這本書太難以致於不能了解。

2. The plan is too good to be true.（too + adj.to + 原型動詞，太…以致於不能…）這個計劃太好以致於不是真的。

3. Johnny is so kind that every girl likes him.（so…that + 子句, 如此…以致於…）Jonny 是如此仁慈以致於每個女孩都喜歡他。

4. It happened so fast that nobody could solve the problem.（so…that + 子句, 如此…以致於…）它發生得太快以致於沒有人可以解決那個問題。

5. Why not go to the party with us?（Why not+ 原型動詞）為什麼不跟我們去參加派對？

6. How come you are afraid of him? He is not bad at all.（How come+ 子句）為什麼你怕他？他一點都不壞。

7. Where do you think he went?（當主要子句為 do you think 表達自我主觀判斷的動詞，則疑問詞置於句首，do you think 置於其後。）你認為他去哪裡？

Part I 句型文法

Part II 字詞文法

Part III 文法糾正篇

換你選選看：

( ) 1. The activity is ___ exciting _____ he wants to join it again. A so; because   B too; to   C so; that

( ) 2. A: Please keep quiet. B:_____ we need to keep quiet? A How come   B How will   C How go

( ) 3. _____ come with us? The activity is very interesting. A Why   B Why not   C How come

( ) 4. He walked ___ fast _____ nobody wanted to be with him. A so... that   B too... to   C so... as to

( ) 5. The game is _____ dangerous for us _____ it again. A so... that...   B too... to playing   C too... to play

( ) 6. He focused _____ much on his study _____ he forget what he should do next. A very... on   B so... that   C too... to

答案與中譯解析：

1. 那個活動是如此刺激以致於他想再次加入。（答：C，so…that＋子句，如此… 以致於…。）

2. A：請保持安靜。　B：為什麼要保持安靜？（答：A，How come＋子句。）

3. 為什麼不跟我們一起去？那活動很有趣。（答：B，Why not＋原型動詞。）

4. 他走得如此快以至於沒人想要和他再一起。（答：A，so…that＋子句，如此… 以致於…。）

5. 這比賽對我們而言太危險了以致於不能再比一次。（答：C，too＋adj.to＋原 型動詞，太…以致於不能…。）

6. 這比賽對我們而言太危險了以致於不能再比一次。（答：B，so…that＋子句， 如此…以致於…。）

Part II 字詞文法

Unit 16
可數／不可數名詞

 搶先看名句學文法：

I honestly have no idea how to live without you. 沒有你，我真的不知如何活下去。

no idea，一點辦法都沒有，**idea** 為名詞。名詞隨處可見，本單元將介紹可數及不可數名詞。

 英文達人小筆記！

可數名詞若為複數時，一般來說都會聯想到名詞＋s／es／ies，後面的動詞也會隨單複數而改變。但有時可數與不可數名詞並不容易分辨，尤其是集合名詞，如 the police, the Chinese 等，這類集合名詞單複數同形，所以是特別需要注意，後面的動詞變化通常會依句意決定單、複數。接下來會有詳細的說明與例句。

關於可數／不可數的詳細說明：

I honestly have no idea how to live without you. 沒有你，我真的不知如何活下去。

名言背景：新月是美國作家 Stephenie Meyer 所著《暮光之城》系列小

説的第二集，描寫女主角貝拉、吸血鬼愛德華與狼人雅各之間的愛情故事。此劇的意思是「沒有你，我真的不知如何活下去。」

■ **可數／不可數名詞／集合名詞／名詞片語文法解析：**

名詞為人、事、時、地、物等。分為「可數」與「不可數名詞」。集合名詞是由單數或複數人或項目所組成，有時為單複數同行的名詞 依語意來決定其單複數。名詞片語則由兩個字詞以上組成的名詞片語，有名詞之功能。

A. 可數名詞：有固體形體，可用 1、2、3…數字計算，可數名詞可為：規則名詞與不規則名詞。

1. 規則名詞：

單數名詞成為複數名詞，其規則分為三種：

a. 字尾加 s。

b. 單數名詞字尾為 " 子音 +y"，去 y 加 ies。

c. 單數名詞字尾為 " 母音 +y"，則直接加 s。

d. 單數名詞字尾為 "s，x，z，sh，ch"，字尾加 es。

e. 單數名詞字尾為 "f，fe" 則去 f ／ fe 字尾加 ves。

f. 單數名詞字尾為 " 子音 +o" 字尾加 es。（七）單數名詞尾為 " 母音 +o" 字尾加 s。

2. a~f 例子如下：

a. 字尾加 s

book	books	書
girl	girls	女孩
road	roads	道路
hour	hours	小時

b. 單數名詞字尾為 " 子音 +y"，去 y 加 ies：

party	parties	派對
city	cities	城市
body	bodies	身體
library	libraries	圖書館

c. 單數名詞字尾為 "母音 +y" ，則直接加 s：

key	keys	鑰匙
day	days	天
holiday	holidays	假日

d. 單數名詞字尾為 "s，x，z，sh，ch" ，字尾加 es：

watch	watches	手錶
box	boxes	箱子
glass	glasses	玻璃

e. 單數名詞字尾為 "f，fe" 則去 f ／ fe 字尾加 ves：

half	halves	一半
wife	wives	妻子
knife	knives	刀子

f. 單數名詞字尾為 "子音 +o" 字尾加 es：

tomato	tomatoes	番茄
hero	heroes	英雄

g. 單數名詞尾為 "母音 +o" 字尾加 s：

radio	radios	收音機
zoo	zoos	動物園

h. 特例！！有些名詞單複數變化不規則例子如下：

foot	feet	腳
tooth	teeth	牙齒
goose	geese	鵝
child	children	小孩
mouse	mice	老鼠
woman	women	女人
man	men	男人
ox	oxen	公牛

B. 不可數名詞：不可數名詞分三種：

　　a. 抽象名詞（如：happiness 快樂，love 愛，friendship 友誼）

　　b. 專有名詞（如：Taiwan 台灣，September 九月，The Great Wall 萬里長城）

　　c. 物質名詞（如：coffee 咖啡，air 空氣，water 水）

　　d. 不可數名詞之前通常不加冠詞，也沒有複數形。動詞需用單數形動詞或 be 動詞。

C. 集合名詞：由單數或複數人或項目所組成，有時為單複數同形的名詞 依語意來決定其單複數。例子如下：

the police	警方（複數集合名詞）
Chinese	中國人（單複數同形）
cattle	牛群（複數集合名詞）
family	家庭、家人
class	班級、班上同學、課程

例：

　　The cattle are gazing in the field. 牛群正在牧場吃草。

　　My family is a big family. 我的家庭是一個大家庭。

　　My class is made up of fifty students. 我的班是由五十位學生組成。

D. 名詞片語：由兩個字詞以上組成有名詞之功能，但不含主詞與動詞的的片語，既為名詞片語。如所有格加名詞、複合名詞既為其中之的例子，例子如下：

a girl's bicycle	名詞的所有格 + 名詞	一位女孩的腳踏車
Tom and Jane's father	共同所有格 + 名詞	湯姆和珍的父親
the legs of the table	無生物所有格 + 名詞	桌子的腳
a friend of mine	雙重所有格 + 名詞	我的一位朋友

a good student	形容詞 + 名詞	一位好學生
flashlight	名詞 + 名詞	手電筒
toothpaste	名詞 + 名詞	牙膏
seat belt	名詞名詞	座位安全帶
full moon	名詞名詞	滿月
mother-in-law	名詞 + 介系詞 + 名詞	岳母、婆婆

 絕妙好例句：

1. Mr. Wang is a friend of my father's.

（名詞片語 a friend of mine）王先生是我父親的一位朋友。

2. My family are all teachers.

（family 在本句是家人為複數，動詞用複數動詞 are）我的家人都是老師。

3. There are five geese on the pond.

（goose 鵝，複數為不規則變化 geese）有五隻鵝在池塘上。

4. Sam is drinking some water.

（水為不可數名詞，為單數名詞）Sam 正在喝一些水。

5. I am a Chinese.

（中國人 Chinese 單複數同型）我是一位中國人。

6. For most people, love is very important in the world.

（愛 love 是不可數名詞，用單數動詞 is）對多數人來説，愛是世界上一件非常重要的東西。

7. My dad bought two deer last month.

（deer 為單複數同型的名詞，不用加 s）我父親上個月買了兩隻鹿。

8. There are six knives in the kitchen.

（knife 複數為不規則變化 knives）有六把刀在廚房裡。

換你選選看：

( ) 1. He ate too much _____. A fruits B fruit C a fruit

( ) 2. There are three _____ in the university. A library B libraries
C librarys

( ) 3. My class _____ smaller than John's. There are only ten students
in my class. A is B are C does

( ) 4. The air in the mountain _____ very fresh. A are B is C does

( ) 5. He likes to eat _____. A fries potatos B fishes ad beefs
C frozen meat

( ) 6. _____ are asked to brush their _____ before going to bed.
A Child, tooth B Child, teeth C Children, teeth

答案與中譯解析：

1. 他吃太多水果了。（答：B，水果為不可數名詞，複數不可加 s。）

2. 有三間圖書館在這所大學裡。（答：B，library 字尾為子音 +y"，複數要子去
y 加 ies。）

3. 我的班級比 John 的班級還小。只有十個人在我的班上。（答：A，class 意思為
班級，單數名詞。）

4. 山裡的空氣非常新鮮。（答：B，air 為不可數名詞，需單數 be 動詞 is。）

5. 他喜歡吃冷凍肉類。（答：C，potato 複數為 potatoes； fish 和 beef 都為不可
數名詞，不可加 es 或 s。）

6. 孩子們被要求在睡前刷牙。（答：C，child 為不規則變化的名詞，複數為
children；tooth 為不規則變化的名詞，複數為 teeth。）

Part I 句型文法

Part II 字詞文法

Part III 文法糾正篇

Unit 17
動詞

☑️ 搶先看名句學文法：

1. You are beautiful. 你是美麗的。

are：**Be** 動詞。

2. You had a bad day. 我今天倒楣透頂。

had ：一般動詞 **Ordinary Verb**

3. I can`t help feeling. We could have had it all. 我不禁心生感觸，我們本該擁有一切。

can't help：動詞片語 **Phrasal Verb**

4. I can`t breathe! I feel dizzy. 我無法呼吸！我感到頭暈…

feel：感官動詞 **Sense verb**

5. I`m tired of trying. 我懶得再去嘗試了。

be tired of ：情緒動詞 **Emotional Verb**

6. Let it be! 算了吧！

Let：使役動詞 **Causative Verb**

7. Life is a tragedy when seen in close-up, but a comedy in long-shot. 人生從特寫鏡頭看是悲劇，從遠鏡頭看是喜劇。

is：連綴動詞 **Linking Verb**

英文達人小筆記！

Be 動詞在英文裡面的身分特殊，它可以當主要動詞，也可以當助動詞用。

1.Be 動詞：

You are beautiful. 你是美麗的。

名言背景：You are beautiful. 你是美麗的。 上尉詩人 James Blunt，一曲成名的一首歌 "You are beautiful"。這首歌成為 2005 年最熱門單曲，風靡全球；除了在英國流行歌曲停留了 6 週的冠軍外，更奪得美國 Billboard TOP100 的冠軍寶座；在各國音樂排行榜上也交出漂亮成績單，創下驚人銷量。歌詞開頭的兩句 "My life is brilliant. My love is pure...." 是基本的 Be 動詞句型，簡單好學。

■ **Be 動詞文法解析：**

A. Be 動詞為主要動詞（Main Verb）時：

1. 觀念說明：

a. be 動詞跟一般的動詞不同，它不表現任何動作，而是表達一種存在、狀態、情境、或是地位。

例：I am a teacher. 我是一位教師。

b. Be 動詞總共有 8 個，分別為 am ／ are ／ is, was ／ were, be ／ being ／ been。

a. 原形 =be，不隨主詞變化

Be 動詞為主要動詞使用時，如句型有助動詞時，要用原形。例：I will be with you. 我會在你身邊。

b. 現在式 = am ／ are ／ is，隨主詞變化

單數 = I am, you are, she ／ he ／ it is

複數 = we are, you are, they are

Part I 句型文法

Part II 字詞文法

Part III 文法糾正篇

c. 過去式 = was ／ were，隨主詞變化

單數 = I was, you were, she ／ he ／ it was

複數 = we were, you were, they were

d. 進行式 = 現在分詞（動名詞 Be+ing）=being，不隨主詞變化

單數 = I am ／ was+ being, you are ／ were+ being, she ／ he ／ it +is ／ was+ being

複數 = we are ／ were+ being, you are ／ were+ being, they are ／ were+ being

e. 完成式 = 過去分詞 =been，不隨主詞變化

單數 = I have ／ had+ been, you have ／ had+ been, she ／ he ／ it has ／ have+ been

複數 =（we, you, they）+have+ been

f. Be 動詞主要表達的是中文的「是」或「很」的意思，若 be 動詞表達的「很」的意思，那麼主詞補語（SC）後面要接形容詞。例：You are beautiful.（S+be+SC）你很美。

2. 文法結構：

a. 肯定句：主詞（S）＋ Be 動詞＋受詞補語（SC）

例：You are a teacher. 你是一位教師。

b. 否定句：主詞（S）＋ Be 動詞＋ not ＋主詞補語（SC）

例：You are not a teacher. 你不是一位教師。

c. 疑問句：Be 動詞＋主詞（S）＋主詞補語（SC）

例：Are you a teacher? 你是一位教師嗎？

B. Be 動詞為助動詞（Auxiliary Verb）時：

1. 觀念說明：

a. 協助主要動詞形成進行式，包括現在、過去與未來進行式

1. 現在進行式：主詞（S）＋助動詞 be（am ／ are ／ is）＋現在分詞（V-ing）

例：I am reading a book. 我正在看書。

2. 過去進行式：主詞（S）＋助動詞 be（am ／ are ／ is）＋＋現在分

詞（V-ing）

例：I was reading a book. 我正在看書（指過去）。

3.未來進行式：主詞（S）＋ 助動詞（will）＋助動詞 be ＋現在分詞（V-ing）

例：The world will be watching the World Cup. 全球將會觀賞世界杯。

b.協助主要動詞成為被動語態

1.主詞 ＋ 助動詞 be ＋ 過去分詞（p.p.）

例：The famous book was written by John. 這本名書是由 John 所寫。

 絕妙好例句：

1. Am I bothering you?（Be 動詞＝助動詞） 我打擾你了嗎？
2. Philip is known as a great actor.（Be 動詞＝助動詞，被動式）Philip 是位知名的演員。
3. It was a nice day yesterday.（Be 動詞＝主要動詞）昨天是美好的一天。
4. I will be a college student soon.（Be 動詞＝主要動詞）我很快就會成為大學生。
5. She is in the library.（Be 動詞＝主要動詞）她在圖書館。

換你選選看：

（　）1. The baby _____ sleeping. A is　B are　C am
（　）2. Tom _____a singer. A is not　B are not　C am not
（　）3. The door_____. A is open　B has been opened　C has opened
（　）4. Kitty _____bad again. A was being　B be　C are being
（　）5. She _____very cute. A am　B is　C are

（　　）6. She ＿＿ known as a great musician. <u>A</u> am　<u>B</u> is　<u>C</u> are

 答案與中譯解析：

1. 寶寶正在睡覺。（答：<u>A</u>，Be 動詞＝助動詞，現在進行式，第三人稱單數，be 動詞為 is。）

2. Tom 不是歌手。（答：<u>A</u>，Be 動詞＝主要動詞，第三人稱單數，be 動詞為 is。）

3. 門已經被打開了。（答：<u>B</u>，Be 動詞＝助動詞，現在完成式結合被動語態的使用。）

4. Kitty 又不乖了。（答：<u>A</u>，was＝助動詞，being ＝主要動詞。）

5. 她非常可愛。（答：<u>B</u>，Be 動詞＝主要動詞，第三人稱單數，be 動詞用 is。）

6. 她是一位有名的音樂家。（答：<u>B</u>，Be 動詞＝助動詞，第三人稱單數，be 動詞用 is。）

2. 一般動詞 Ordinary Verb

You had a bad day. 你有一個糟糕的一天。

名言背景：這是城市琴人 Daniel Powter，第一首鋼琴流行單曲 *Bad Day* 的歌詞，這首歌的曲風因符合現代大眾的口味，而且歌詞又有鼓勵的效果，廣受大眾喜愛。這首歌最早為 2005 年華納唱片公司為可口可樂歐洲市場廣告的選曲，是很輕鬆又容易學的英文歌曲。

■ **一般動詞文法解析：** 一般動詞指的是除了 Be 動詞或是助動詞以外的動詞型態。

　a. 不及物動詞 VS. 及物動詞

　　1. 不及物動詞（Intransitive Verbs=Vi）：動詞本身可以獨立表達完整意思，後面不需要受詞。

　　　a. 完全不及物動詞：動詞後面完全不需要受詞（O）與任何補語。

　　　例：A funny thing happened. 一件好笑的事發生了。

　　　b. 不完全及物動詞：不需要受詞（O），但是需要補語（C），才能完整表達意思。

例：She looks pretty. 她看起來很漂亮。

2. 及物動詞（Transitive Verbs=Vt）動詞後面須要有受詞，接受動作。

完全及物動詞：動詞後面需要受詞 O，承受動作，但是不須要補語 C。

例：I love you. 我愛你。

不完全及物動詞：動詞後面不但要有受詞 O，還要有受詞補語（OC）。

例：I asked him a question. 我向他問了一個問題。

授與動詞：動詞須要有 2 個受詞 O，間接受詞（IO 通常指人）與直接受詞（DO 通常只事物）才能完整表達意思，常見的授與動詞為 give、buy。

例：I gave you a book. 我給你一本書。

b. 一般動詞變化

1. 規則動詞 VS. 不規則動詞

規則動詞（Regular Verbs）：動詞在原式、過去式與過去分詞的時態變化上有規則可循。

最常見的是在動詞後面加 "**ed**"。

例：原形 =work, 過去式 =worked, 過去分詞 = worked。

動詞字尾已有 **e** 時，直接加 "**d**" 即可。

例：原形 =move, 過去式 =moved, 過去分詞 = moved

字尾是「子音＋ **y**」時，須先去掉 **y**，再加 "**ied**"。

例：原形 =study, 過去式 =studied, 過去分詞 = studied

字尾是「短母音＋子音」時, 須重覆字尾，再加 "**ed**"。

例：原形 =stop, 過去式 =stopped, 過去分詞 = stopped

不規則動詞（Irregular Verbs）：動詞的原形、過去式與過去分詞的時態變化無規則可循，但仍有幾種形態：

三種時態全部相同

例：原形 =hit, 過去式 =hit, 過去分詞 = hit

過去式與過去分詞相同

例：原形 =bring, 過去式 =bought, 過去分詞 = bought

Part I 句型文法

Part II 字詞文法

Part III 文法糾正篇

原形與過去分詞相同

例：原形 =come, 過去式 =came, 過去分詞 = come

三種時態全部不相同

例：原形 =begin, 過去式 =began, 過去分詞 = begun

2. 動詞在句子中的變化： 一般動詞的單複變化，須隨主詞變化。單數主詞，搭配單數動詞；複數主詞搭配複數動詞。

　　a. 現在式：第三人稱以及單數主詞，後面動詞字尾須加 s ／ es ／去 y+ies

　　例：

　　原形 =work, 單數 =works　She works at home.

　　原形 =go, 單數 =goes　She goes to school.

　　原形 =try, 單數 = tries　She tries her best.

　　b. 過去式的單複：無論何種人稱，單、複數都用同型。

　　c. 不管否定句或疑問句，一般動詞的人稱，單、複數都是用原形，只有助動詞隨主詞變化。

　　d. 一般動詞在現在分詞與進行式的變化上，一般在動詞字尾加上 "ing"。

　　例：原形 =work, 現在分詞 =working

 ## 絕妙好例句：

1. Tommy read a good article last week.

（Vt=read，read，read，不規則變化，過去式 read。）Tommy 上週讀了一篇好文章。

註：read 屬不規則動詞變化，雖是拼法一樣，但是讀音不同。

2. Sue has worked in the restaurant for 2 years.

（Vi=work，worked，worked，規則變化，過去分詞，單複數由助動詞變化。）Sue 在餐廳工作已經有 2 年了。

3. The doctor is saving the child's life.

（Vt=save，saved，saved，saving，規則變化，現在分詞，單複數由助動詞變化。） 醫生正在拯救小孩的生命。

4. She picks me a good book.

（Vt=pick，picked，picked，兩個受詞，規則變化，單數動詞加 "-s"。） 她為我挑了一本好書。

5. Birds flew across the blue sky.（Vi=fly，flew， flown，不規則變化，過去式 flew。） 鳥群飛過湛藍的天空。

 換你選選看：

（　　）1. The baby was＿＿＿＿when I ＿＿＿＿in. Ａ sleeping; went
　　　　Ｂ sleep; go　Ｃ slept; goes

（　　）2. The bus＿＿＿＿. Ａ stop　Ｂ stopped　Ｃ stopping

（　　）3. He ＿＿＿＿the ball. Ａ catch　Ｂ doesn't caught　Ｃ didn't catch

（　　）4. She ＿＿＿＿for a help at midnight.（Ａ cried　Ｂ crying　Ｃ was
　　　　cried

（　　）5. Mother ＿＿＿＿ right now. Ａ cooked　Ｂ is cooking　Ｃ is
　　　　cooked

（　　）6. He ＿＿＿ mountain climbing. Ａ go　Ｂ went　Ｃ going

 答案與中譯解析：

1. 我走進去時寶寶正在睡覺。（答：Ａ，過去進行式，第三人稱單數助動詞變化；Vi=go，went，gone，不規則變化，過去式。）

2. 公車停了。（答：Ｂ，Vi=stop，stopped，stopped，規則變化，過去式，單複數不變。）

3. 他沒有接到球。（答：Ｃ，Vt=catch，caught，caught，不規則變化，過去式，第三人稱單數助動詞變化。）

4. 她在深夜哭喊求幫助。（答：Ａ，Vi=cry，cried，cried，規則動詞，過去式，單複數不變 。）

5. 母 親 正 在 煮 飯。（答： B ，Vi=cook，cooked，cooked， 現 在 進 行 式 cooking，第三人稱單數助動詞變化。）

6. 他去爬山。（答： B ，Vi=go，went，gone，現在進行式 going，第三人稱單數助動詞變化。）

3. 動詞片語 Verb Phrase

I can't help feeling. We could have had it all.

我不禁心生感觸，我們本該擁有一切。

名言背景：摘自於歌曲 *Rolling In The Deep*，為英國創作行女歌手 Adele 於 2011 年發行的專輯《21》的歌曲。這首歌一推出即在美國 Billboard100（告示牌 100）上連續 7 週穩居冠軍寶座。這首歌集結多種曲風，搭配上 Adele 渾厚的嗓子，在全球創下驚人銷量，並拿下多項獎項。

■ 動詞片語 Verb Phrase（V.P.）文法解析：動詞片語（Verb Phrase）主要是一個主要動詞與一個或一個以上的助動詞所形成，主要用來表時態、語態、疑問、或否定。

a. 一個或一個以上的助動詞結構

1. 一個助動詞

動詞片語＝助動詞＋主要動詞

例：

They are talking loudly.（V.P.=are talking，現在進行式）

My car is broken by my brother.（V.P.=is broken，被動式語態）

2. 二個助動詞

動詞片語＝助動詞＋助動詞＋主要動詞

例：He has been working hard.（V.P.=has been working，現在完成進行式）

3. 三個助動詞

動詞片語＝助動詞＋助動詞＋助動詞＋主要動詞

例：I will have been waiting for him.（V.P.=will have been

waiting，未來完成進行式）

b. 動詞片語有時會被隔離

1. 肯定句

動詞片語＝主詞＋副詞＋主要動詞

例：I will always love you. 我會永遠愛你（V.P.=will love，被副詞 always 隔離）

2. 疑問句

動詞片語＝助動詞＋主詞＋主要動詞

例：Have you done your homework? 你做完功課了嗎？（V.P.=have done，被主詞 you 隔離）

3. 否定句

動詞片語＝主詞＋助動詞＋not＋主要動詞

例：I don't care. 我不在乎。（V.P.=do care，被 not 隔離）

 絕妙好例句：

a. Mike must eat my cake.（V.P.=must eat）Mike 一定吃了我的蛋糕。

b. Am I bothering you?（V.P.=am bothering）我打擾你了嗎？

c. She has not finished this project.（V.P.= has finished）她還沒完成這個案子。

d. Will Mary have taken few days off by next month?（V.P.=will have taken）下個月之前，May 將會休幾天假嗎？

e. The same joke has been heard twice by me.（V.P.=has been heard）同樣的笑話我已經聽過 2 次了。

 換你選選看：

（　　）1. Don't buy that house. V.P.=_____ Ⓐ don't buy Ⓑ do buy Ⓒ buy

(　) 2. He is reading the book. V.P.=＿＿＿＿＿ A is reading B read
C is

(　) 3. We will be going to party this Friday night. V.P.
=＿＿＿＿＿＿＿ A will be B be going C will be going

(　) 4. Your application was rejected. V.P.=＿＿＿＿＿＿＿ A was
rejected. B was C rejected

(　) 5. I had not lived in Taiwan before I moved to USA. V.P.=＿＿＿＿
A had not lived. B had lived C lived

(　) 6. She ＿＿＿ Japan. V.P.=＿＿＿＿＿ A has been to B been
to C was to

答案與中譯解析：

1. 別買那棟房子。（答：B，V.P.= do buy。）

2. 他正在看書。（答：A，V.P.=is reading。）

3. 這週五晚上，我們將會去舞會。（答：C，V.P.=will be going。）

4. 您的申請被拒。（答：A，V.P.=was rejected，被動式。）

5. 我搬去美國前，不住在台灣。（答：B，V.P.=had lived。）

6. 她曾經去過日本。（答：A，V.P.=has been to）

4. 感官動詞 Sense Verb

I can't breathe! I feel dizzy.... 我無法呼吸！我感到頭暈 ....

名言背景：這天，Sally 突然抽走 Linus 的毯子，Linus 無法忍受形影不離的毯子離開身邊，像毒癮發作似的不斷顫抖 ....。My blanket! I gotta have that blanket! I can't breathe!.... Peanuts《花生漫畫》是一部美國報紙連環漫畫，作者是查爾斯·舒爾茨（Charles M. Schulz）。《花生漫畫》是漫畫發展史上首部多角色系列漫畫，從 1950 年 10 月 2 日開始發行，到 2000 年 2 月 13 日作者病逝之時為止。漫畫以小孩生活為題材，觀察這個簡單又複雜的世界。漫畫的主要角色為小狗史努比（Snoopy）

和查理·布朗（Charlie Brown）、莎莉（Sally Brown）、奈勒斯（Linus Van Pelt）、露西（Lucy Van Pelt）、謝勒德（Schroeder）等。

■ 感官動詞 **Sense Verb** 文法解析：感官動詞 Sense Verb 主要描述視覺（see）、聽覺（hear）、知覺（feel）等等的感受與動作。

a.　感官動詞有：see／hear／feel／notice／watch／look at／listen to／observe／perceive

1. 強調事實完整過程，用原形動詞（V）

句型：感官動詞 + 受詞 O + 原形動詞 V

使用主動語態

強調動作的完整性、真實性，如看見了或聽見了某事。

例：He saw a bird fly. 他看到鳥在飛。

2. 強調動作正在進行，用現在分詞（V-ing）

句型：感官動詞 + 受詞 + 現在分詞（V-ing）

使用主動語態

強調動作的連續性、進行性，看到或聽見某事時，動作正在進行。

例：He saw a bird flying. 他看到鳥正在飛。

3. 表示被動語態的用法

用過去分詞表示：感官動詞 + 受詞 + 過去分詞（P.P.）

例：The boy's parents see him pushed away.　那男孩的父母看到他被推開。

感官動詞用被動式表示：感官動詞（被動式）+ 現在分詞（V-ing）

例：The boy was seen pushing away.（有人）看到男孩被推開。

用不定詞 to 表示：感官動詞（被動式）+to+ 原形動詞 V

例：The boy was seen to push away.（有人）看到男孩被推開。

 絕妙好例句：

1. I hear someone knocking on the door.（強調動作正進行，主動）我聽到有人正在敲門。

2. He saw the girl fall down.（強調事實，主動）他看到這女孩跌倒。

3. I felt the wind blowing.（強調動作正進行，主動）我感覺風再吹。

4. She looked at him leave.（強調事實，主動）她注視著他離開。

5. I did not perceive anyone come in.（強調事實，主動）我沒有察覺到任何人進來。

 換你選選看：

（　　）1. Did you see a strange man ＿＿＿＿ there five minutes ago? A sitting　B sit　C sat

（　　）2. They were seen ＿＿＿＿＿. A arrive　B to arrive　C arriving

（　　）3. David didn't notice baby ＿＿＿＿. A cry　B cried　C crying

（　　）4. When I mentioned Amy, I noticed ＿＿＿＿. A him smiling　B he to smile　C he smiling

（　　）5. He was seen ＿＿＿＿ Tom's house. A enter　B to enter　C entered

（　　）6. I ＿＿＿ her waiting in front of the bookstore. A seen　B see　C saw

答案與中譯解析：

1. 五分鐘前，你有看到一位陌生男人坐在那裡嗎？（答：B，強調事實，主動。）

2. 他們被看見到來了。（答：B，被動式語態，用 to 表示。）

3. David 沒有注意到寶寶正在哭。（答：C，強調動作正進行，主動。）

4. 當我提到 Amy 時，我注意到他正露出微笑。（答：A，強調動作正進行，主動。）

5. 他被看到進到 Tom 的房間。（答：B，被動式語態，用 to 表示。）

6. 我看到她在書店前面等。（答：C，強調事實，主動。）

5. 情緒動詞 Emotional Verb

I'm tired of trying. 我懶得再去嘗試了。

名言背景：歌曲 *Tired* 收錄於《19》首張專輯，發行於 2008 年，是以 Adele 當時的年齡命名，在這專輯裡，她寫了很多歌曲，入選《英國排行榜》第一位。《泰晤士報》將這首歌喻為「重要的藍眼睛靈魂」的記錄。這首歌詞的意境其實是很讓人心碎的，但是卻搭配俏皮輕快的節奏。

■ 情緒動詞 **Emotional Verb** 文法解析：

情緒動詞 Emotional Verb，主要用來表達人或物的喜怒哀樂。

　　a. 情緒動詞

　　　1. 常用情緒動詞及動詞變化

情緒動詞（原形）	現在分詞（-ing）當形容詞用（令人感到 ...）	過去分詞（-ed）當形容詞用（某人感到 ...）
interest（使有趣）	interesting	interested（in）
bore（使無聊）	boring	bored（with, by）
excite（使興奮）	exciting	excited（about）
tire（使疲）	tiring	tired（of, with）
surprise（使驚訝）	surprising	surprised（at）
confuse（使困惑）	confusing	confused（about）
satisfy（使滿意）	satisfying	satisfied（with）
amuse（使有趣）	amusing	amused（at）
worry（使擔憂）	worrying	worried（about）
disappoint（使失望）	disappointing	disappointed（at, with, about）

Part I 句型文法

Part II 字詞文法

Part III 文法訂正篇

2. 句型用法

　　a. 一般動詞用法

　　　　主詞 S（事／物）＋情緒（V）＋受詞 O（人）

　　　　意思：使某人感到…

　　　　例：This movie interests me. 這電影使我感到興趣。

　　b. 現在分詞用法

　　　　主詞 S（事／物）＋be＋情緒（V-ing）＋to＋受詞 O（人）

　　　　意思：令人感到 ... 或者"事物"對我而…

　　　　例：This is movie is interesting to me. 這電影使我感到有興趣。

　　c. 過去分詞用法

　　　　主詞 S（人）＋be＋情緒（-ed）＋介系詞＋受詞 O（人／事／物）

　　　　意思：人對某人／事感到…

　　　　受詞可以是名詞、動名詞（Ving）

　　　　例1：I am interested in this movie. 我對這部電影有興趣。

　　　　例2：I am interested in jogging. 我對慢跑有興趣。

　　d. 情緒動詞當形容詞用

　　　　1. 過去分詞（V-ed）當形容詞使用，用來修飾人。

　　　　例：This movie made me interested. 這部電影令我感到有興趣。

　　　　2. 現在分詞（V-ing）當形容詞使用，用來修飾物。

　　　　例：This is an interesting movie. 這是部有趣的電影。

 絕妙好例句：

1. The world cup excited all people.（一般動詞用法）世界杯賽事令所有人興奮。

2. People are satisfied with the new President.（過去分詞用法）人們對新總統感到滿意。

3. The news was surprising to me.（現在分詞用法）這新聞令人感到驚訝。

4. Pat is bored with reading this book.（過去分詞用法）Pat 對讀這本書感到無

聊。

5. How did Sue feel about the music concert? She was disappointed.

（當形容詞用，修飾人 V-ed） Sue 覺得這音樂會如何？她很失望。

 換你選選看：

（　　）1. We are confused ＿＿＿ his reaction. A with　B of　C in
（　　）2. Math is a ＿＿＿＿＿class. A bored　B bore　C boring
（　　）3. May is worried ＿＿＿＿her child. A of　B in　C about
（　　）4. Tom was ＿＿＿＿football. A interested in playing
　　　　　B interesting　C interested
（　　）5. They are ＿＿＿ the ＿＿＿NBA game last night. A excited,
　　　　　excited.　B excited about, excited.　C excited about,
　　　　　exciting
（　　）6. This new is ＿＿＿ to her. A surprised　B surprising　C surprise

答案與中譯解析：

1. 我們對他的反應感到困惑。（答：A，過去分詞用法。）

2. 數學是門很無聊的課程。（答：C，現在分詞當形容詞用。）

3. May 擔心他小孩。（答：C，過去分詞用法。）

4. Tom 對踢足球感興趣。（答：A，過去分詞用法）

5. 他們對昨晚興奮的 NBA 球賽感到興奮。（答：C，過去分詞用法，exciting 當形容詞用，修飾 NBA。）

6. 她對這則消息感到很震驚。（答：B，現在分詞做形容詞使用。）

6. 使役動詞 Causative Verbs

Let it be! 算了吧！

名言背景：*Let it be* 的歌詞簡單但是很有寓意，這首歌曲收錄於 1970 年在英國發行的 *Let It Be* 專輯，是英國搖滾樂團 The Beatles（披頭四）發行第十二張錄音室專輯。披頭四樂團被公認為英國音樂在 1960 年代「英國入侵」美國的代表樂團。其音樂風格源自 1950 年代的搖滾，之後開拓了各種曲風，其音樂性之創新深深影響了之後的歐美樂壇發展，尤其是藍儂與麥卡尼這一雙子星搭檔更是音樂樂史上最佳唱作搭檔之一。

■ **使役動詞 Causative Verbs 文法解析**：使役動詞 Causative Verbs 是表示主詞要求或強迫某人（受詞 O）去做事情，有使、令、讓、幫、叫、允許等意義。

a. 使役動詞包括：常用使役動詞有：make, let, have, get, want, permit, allow, order, help…等。

b. 用法：

1. 表示主動，第二動詞用原形（V）

主詞 S + 使役動詞 + 受詞 O +（not）+ 動詞 V

make, has／have, let

有主動意味，讓受詞（O）去…

例：He made me laugh. 他使我笑了。

2. 表示主動，後加不定詞 to

主詞 S + 使役動詞 + 受詞 O +（not）+ to + 動詞（V）

get, want, permit, allow, order, help

有主動意味，讓受詞（O）去…

例：I got Tom to go home early. 我讓 Tom 早點回家。

3. 表示被動，第二動詞用過去分詞（P.P.）

主詞 S + 使役動詞 + 受詞 O +（not）+ 過去分詞（P.P.）

make, has／have, get

有被動意味，讓受詞（O）被…

例：I have my care washed. 我叫人洗車。

絕妙好例句：

1. The manager makes me wait here.（動詞原形）經理讓我等在這裡。
2. Mother let me not enter.（動詞原形，否定句）母親讓我不要進來。
3. I get him to stay.（加不定詞）我要他留下。
4. I'll have your luggage sent to your room.（過去分詞，被動）我會將您的行李送到你房間。
5. Sue let me use her kitchen.（動詞原形）Sue 讓我使用她的廚房。

 換你寫寫看：

1. The teacher ordered him_____. A not go　B don't go　C not to go
2. The news make me_____. A excited　B exciting　C excite
3. She got her hand_____. A burned　B burning　C to burn
4. My mom _____ me finish my homework. A making　B need　C makes
5. Father helped me _____ the car. A to fix　B fixing　C fixed
6. She _____ her father proud. A have　B had　C is

 答案與中譯解析：

1. 老師命令他不要走。（答：C，動詞原形，否定。）
2. 這則新聞讓我很興奮。（答：A，過去分詞做形容詞用，表示「感到興奮」。）
3. 她讓他的手被燒到。（答：A，過去分詞，被動。）
4. 我媽要我做完家庭作業。（答：C，動詞原形。）
5. 父親幫我修車。（答：A，加不定詞）
6. 她使他爸爸感到驕傲。（答：B，動詞過去式）

7. 連綴動詞 Linking Verbs

Life is a tragedy when seen in close-up, but a comedy in long-shot. 從特寫鏡頭看人生是悲劇，從遠鏡頭看人生是喜劇。

名言背景：卓別林（1889-1977）是一位英國喜劇演員及反戰人士，後來也成為一名非常出色的導演，尤其在好萊塢電影的早期和中期時，他非常成功和活躍。他奠定了現代喜劇電影的基礎。

■ 連綴動詞 **Linking Verbs** 文法解析：連綴動詞（Linking Verbs）本身的意思不完全，主要用來連接、補充説明主詞（補語），後面不需要受詞，及是五大句型中主詞（S+ 動詞 V+ 主詞補語 SC）。主詞補語可以是形容詞、名詞或介系詞片語來説明主詞的的情況，讓整個句子的意思變得完整。

a. 常見連綴動詞：

Be 動詞類（狀態）：am ／ are ／ is, was ／ were, be ／ being ／ been

感官動詞類：look ／ sound ／ smell ／ taste ／ feel

轉變動詞類：become ／ get ／ grow ／ turn

b. 用法：

1. 主詞 S + 連綴動詞（L.V.）+ 形容詞（Adj.）

   I. Be 動詞類：am ／ are ／ is, was ／ were, be ／ being ／ been

     狀態：沒有進行式、被動式

   例：You are beautiful. 你很漂亮。

   II. 感官動詞類：表示（…起來／變成…）look ／ sound ／ smell ／ taste ／ feel

   沒有進行式、被動式

   例：You look beautiful. 你看起來很漂亮。

   III. 轉變動詞類：Become ／ get ／ grow ／ turn

     可用進行式，常用 Be+Ving 的用法，表示「漸漸…；愈來愈…」。

   例：Her face turns red. 她的臉變紅。

2. 主詞 S+ 連綴動詞（L.V.）+ like（像）+ 名詞（N）

   Like 為介系詞，表示「像…」之意。

   用於感官動詞類 look ／ sound ／ smell ／ taste ／ feel

意思為看起來像…、聽起來像…、聞起來像…、吃起來像…、感覺起來
像…

　　例：It looks like pizza. 它看起來像披薩。

3. 問答句： How & What

　　問1：How ＋助動詞＋主詞（S）＋連綴動詞（L.V.）？

　　答1：主詞（S）＋連綴動詞（L.V.）＋形容詞（Adj）

　　例：How do you feel? I feel very good.（你感覺如何？我覺得很好）

　　問2：What ＋助動詞＋主詞（S）＋連綴動詞（L.V.）＋ like?

　　答2：主詞（S）＋連綴動詞（L.V.）＋ like ＋名詞（N）

　　例：What does it look like? It looks like pizza. 它看起來像甚麼？ 它
看起來像披薩。

 絕妙好例句：

1. The steak tastes delicious.（S ＋ L.V. ＋ Adj.）這牛排吃起來美味。
2. Sue doesn't look like her mother.（S ＋ L.V. ＋ like ＋ N）Sue 看起來不像她
媽媽。
3. Playing tennis sounds fun.（S ＋ L.V. ＋ Adj.）打網球聽起來好玩。
4. Father is getting old.（S ＋ L.V.-ing ＋ Adj.， 進 行 式 ）
父親漸漸變老。
5. What does the drink taste like? It tastes like tea.（S ＋ L.V. ＋ like ＋ N.）這
飲料喝起來像什麼？ 它喝起來像茶。

換你選選看：

(   ) 1. The weather _____ warm this morning. Ⓐ become
      Ⓑ became   Ⓒ becoming

(   ) 2. Her voice _____ a duck. Ⓐ sounds like   Ⓑ sounds   Ⓒ like

(   ) 3. How do I look? You _____. Ⓐ awful look   Ⓑ look awful
      Ⓒ awful

(   ) 4. Her voice _____ happy. Ⓐ smalls   Ⓑ becomes   Ⓒ sounds

(   ) 5. Do you feel better? No, I don't. My headache _____. Ⓐ get
      better   Ⓑ is getting worse   Ⓒ got worse

(   ) 6. The coffee ____ bitter. Ⓐ taste   Ⓑ tastes   Ⓒ tasting.

答案與中譯解析：

1. 今天早上天氣變溫暖了。（答：B，表示轉變，S + L.V. + Adj.。）

2. 她的聲音聽起來像隻鴨子。（答：A，感官連綴動詞，S + L.V. + like + N。）

3. 我看起來如何？你看起來很糟糕。（答：B，感官連綴動詞，S + L.V. + Adj.。）

4. 她的聲音聽起來高興。（答：C，感官連綴動詞，S + L.V. + Adj.。）

5. 你覺得好些了嗎？沒有，我的頭痛愈來愈嚴重了（答：B，轉變連綴動詞，進行式。）

6. 咖啡嚐起來很苦。（答：B，感官連綴動詞，S + L.V. + Adj.。）

Unit 18
形容詞

 搶先看名句學文法：

Imagination is more important than knowledge. 想像力比知識還要重要。

important 為形容詞。

 英文達人小筆記！

本單元重點為形容詞的位置、形容詞的作用、連綴動詞的用法與最高級與比較級的變化。

關於形容詞的詳細說明：

Imagination is more important than knowledge. 想像力比知識還要重要。

名言背景：愛因斯坦（Albert Einstein）對於宇宙萬物擁有許多知識，他的科學研究可以說影響了我們對時間與空間的了解。他告訴世人 " 想像力比知識還要重要 "。因為知識將我們限制在我們現在所了解的事情上，而想像力卻讓人們想要知道的更多。

A. 形容詞的位置

1. 形容詞一般來說用來形容名詞，放置於名詞之前：

　　例1：She is a woman.　She is a beautiful woman.

　　　　她是一個女人。　她是個美麗的女人。

　　例2：They are students.　They are diligent students.

　　　　他們是學生。　他們是勤奮的學生。

　　例3：We need some food.　We need some flavorful food.

　　　　我們需要些食物。我們需要些美味的食物。

　放在形容詞之前的 a 或 an 由形容詞的字首字母決定。子音開頭的字前加 a，母音開頭的字前加 an。至於 the 在子音開頭的字前發音為／ð／，在母音開頭的字前為／ði／。

　　例1：She is a woman.

　　→ She is a nice woman.

　　→ She is an interesting woman.

　　例2：We like the room.

　　→ We like the ／ð／ red room.

　　→ We like the ／ði／ empty room.

2. 形容詞也可以放在主詞與 be 動詞之後來補充說明主詞當補語：

　　例1：The movie was boring.

　　例2：The actress is tall and elegant.

　　例3：He has been very helpful.

3. 形容詞除了可以放在 be 動詞之後，也可以放在一般動詞之後，而這一類的動詞稱為連綴動詞（Linking Verbs）。

　　a. 關於感覺或感官：feel，taste，look，smell，appear，seem，sound

　　　　例1：They seem happy. 他們似乎很開心。

　　　　例2：The idea sounds good. 這個想法聽起來很好。

　　b. 表示改變狀態，變成：become，turn，go，get，grow；證實：prove

例1：

I get worried easily. 我很容易緊張。

例2：

The food has gone bad. 食物已經壞了。

c.　　表示保持，維持：remain，keep，stay

例1：

Please stay calm. 請保持冷靜。

例2：

We'll not keep silent in this case. 我們不會在這件事上保持沉默。

4. 有一些形容詞會接在動詞與受詞的後面來補充說明受詞當受詞補語。

例1：

I've never found this class interesting. 我永遠不會覺得這門課很有趣。

例2：

You can't leave the children hungry. 你不可以任由孩子們飢餓。

5. 有一些形容詞只接在動詞之後。

例1：

He never likes to be alone. 他從來就不喜歡單獨一個人。

例2：

They really look alike. 他們真的長很像。

B.比較級 & 最高級形容詞

1. 變化方法

　　a. 單音節形容詞

　　　比較級：加 er（cheaper）

　　　最高級：加 est（the cheapest）

　　b. 單音節形容詞 "e" 結尾

　　　比較級：加 r（nicer）

　　　最高級：加 st（the nicest）

　　c. 單音節形容詞 " 子音 – 母音 – 子音 " 結尾

比較級：重複子音結尾加 er（hotter）

最高級：重複子音結尾加 est（the hottest）

d. 雙音節形容詞 "y" 結尾

比較級：把 "y" 去掉加 ier（happier）

最高級：把 "y" 去掉加 iest（the happiest）

e. 多音節形容詞

比較級：加 more ／ less（more ／ less beautiful）

最高級：加 the most ／ the least（the most ／ least beautiful）

f. 不規則形容詞

good - better - the best

bad - worse - the worst

far - further - the furthest

2. 使用時機

a. 使用比較級形容詞比較兩件事物（比較級形容詞＋ than）

例1：

Jane is thinner than Billie. Jane 比 Billie 還要瘦。

例2：

It's more expensive to travel by train than by bus. 搭火車旅遊比搭公車旅遊還要貴。

例3：

My house is smaller than my friend's house.

我家的房子比我朋友家的房子還要小。

b. 使用最高級容詞來比較一件與其他同種類的事物

例1：

Jane is the tallest in the class. Jane 是班上最高的。

例2：

He's the best baseball player in the team.

他是球隊裡最厲害的球員。

例3：

This is the most expensive hotel I've ever stayed in. 這是我待過最貴的旅館。

c. 使用 as ＋ adj ＋ as 來敘述兩件事物相同之處。

例1：

He's as tall as me. 他跟我一樣高。

例2：

Joe's car is as fast as mine. Joe 的車子像我的車子一樣快。

d. 使用 not as ＋ adjective ＋ as 來敘述兩件事物不盡相同之處。

例1：

Joe's car is not as fast as mine. Joe 的車子不像我的車子一樣快。

e. 重複比較級形容詞來敘述在改變的狀態。

例1：

These exams are getting harder and harder every year. 考試每年變得越來越難。

例2：

She gets more and more beautiful every time I see her. 我每次看到她，她都變得越來越美。

f. 修飾 more or less

不可數名詞	可數名詞
There is more traffic.	There are more cars.
There is much more traffic.	There are many more cars.
There is a lot ／ a little more traffic.	There are a lot ／ a little more cars.
There is more and more traffic.	There are more and more cars.
There is less traffic.	There are fewer cars.
There is far less traffic.	There are far fewer cars.

There is less and less traffic.　　There are fewer and fewer cars.

g. 使用 much，a lot，far，a little，a bit，slightly 修飾比較級形容詞。

例1：

He is much richer than I am. 他比我有錢許多。

例2：

My sister's hair is slightly longer than mine. 我姐姐的頭髮比我的長一點。

h. 使用 by far，easily，nearly 修飾最高級形容詞。

例1：

It is by far the best restaurant in town. 這是目前鎮上最好的餐廳。

例2：

Michael is nearly the oldest in the class. Michael 幾乎是班上最老的。

i. 最高級形容詞前若是所有格則不加 the。

例1：

His strongest point is his diligence. 他最大的優點是他的勤勉。

 換你選選看：

（　）1. This chair is ＿＿＿＿ than the old one. A comfortable　B most comfortable　C more comfortable

（　）2. This is the ＿＿＿＿movie they have ever seen. A exciting　B most exciting　C more exciting

（　）3. Linda is ＿＿＿＿ than Kate. A pretty　B prettier　C more pretty

（　）4. You are ＿＿＿＿here than there. A safe　B more safe　C safer

（　）5. Annie is the ＿＿＿＿ child in the family. A youngest　B younger

C young

（　　）6. That TV set is the _____ of all. A cheapest   B cheaper
C cheap

 答案與中譯解析：

1. 這張椅子比舊的那一張更舒服。（答：C，兩個音節以上的形容詞，比較及用 more。）

2. 這是他們看過最刺激的電影。（答：B，most exciting 表示「最刺激」。）

3. Linda 比 Kate 更漂亮。（答：B，字尾 y，去 y + ier。）

4. 你在這裡會比在那裡更安全。（答：C，字尾 e 直接加 r。）

5. Annie 是家中最小的小孩。（答：A，youngest 表示「最年輕」。）

6. 那電視組是裡面最便宜的。（答：A，cheapest 表示「最便宜」。）

C. 特殊形容詞

所有格形容詞 **Possessive Adjectives**：

單／複數	人稱	所有格形容詞	例句
單數	第一	my	This is my book.
	第二	your	I like your hair.
	第三	his ／ her ／ its	His name is Joseph.
複數	第一	we	We have sold our car.
	第二	your	Your children are lovely.
	第三	their	The students thanked their teacher.
單／複數		whose	Whose phone did you use?

在聽力中，以下是容易混淆的字：

your ＝ 你或你們的 you're ＝ you are

its ＝ 它的 it's ＝ it is 或 it has

their = 他們的 they're = they are there = 地方副詞
whose = 誰的 who's = who is 或 who has

 換你選選看：

(　　) 1. I have a car. _____ color is red. Ⓐ Its　Ⓑ It's　Ⓒ It has
(　　) 2. The students didn't do _____ homework. Ⓐ they's　Ⓑ their　Ⓒ their's
(　　) 3. Sophia loves _____ grandmother. Ⓐ she has　Ⓑ she's　Ⓒ her
(　　) 4. Marco is from Italy. _____ wife is from France. Ⓐ Her　Ⓑ His　Ⓒ Its
(　　) 5. I like shopping. _____ friends usually go shopping with me. Ⓐ My　Ⓑ Mine　Ⓒ I's
(　　) 6. We like to invite people to stay overnight in _____ house. Ⓐ our　Ⓑ we's　Ⓒ ours

答案與中譯解析：

1. 我有一台車。它的顏色是紅色。（答：Ⓐ，its 表示「它的」。）
2. 學生們沒有做他們的回家作業。（答：Ⓑ，their 表示「他們的」。）
3. Sophia 很愛她的祖母。（答：Ⓒ，her 表示「她的」。）
4. Marco 是從義大利來的。他的太太是從法國來的。（答：Ⓑ，his 表示「他的」。）
5. 我喜歡購物。我的朋友經常跟我去買東西。（答：Ⓐ，my 表示「我的」。）
6. 我們喜歡邀請人來我們家過夜。（答：Ⓐ，our 表示「我們的」。）

D. 數量形容詞

常見的數量形容詞：

	可數	不可數
任何	any	any
一些	some; a few	some; a little
所有	all	all
沒有	no	no
足夠	enough	enough
很多	a lot of; many	a lot of; much
很少	few; not many	little; not much

some 與 any 的用法：

some 一般使用在肯定句，可用於可數與不可數名詞之前。

例1：I have some friends. 我有一些朋友。

例2：They are looking for some furniture. 他們再找一些家俱。

any 一般使用在否定句與疑問句，可用於可數與不可數名詞之前。

例1：Karen hasn't bought any shoes lately.

Karen 最近還沒買任何鞋子。

例2：Do we have any water left in the house?

家裡還有殘留任何水嗎？

注意：some 也可以用在疑問句中，當作請求（request）或提供（offer）

例1：Could I have some water?（request）我可以喝一些水嗎？

例2：Would you like some bread?（offer）你需要一些麵包嗎？

✏️ **換你選選看：**

（　　）1. Is there _____ juice in the fridge? Ⓐ some　Ⓑ any

（　　）2. I'm afraid I don't have _____ answers to life's problems.
Ⓐ some　Ⓑ any

（　　）3. Could I have ＿＿＿＿ coke? Ⓐ some　Ⓑ any

 答案與中譯解析：

1. 冰箱裡還有任何果汁嗎？（答：Ⓑ，any 用於問句與否定句。）

2. 我恐怕我對人生的問題沒有任何的答案。（答：Ⓑ，any 用於問句與否定句。）

3. 我可以喝一些可樂嗎？（答：Ⓐ，some 用於疑問句，具有請求的意味。）

E. 分詞形容詞

動詞加上 **-ing** 與 **-ed** 形成分詞形容詞：

	過去分詞（Vpp） 用於描述感覺與接受動作的經驗者	現在分詞（Ving） 用於描述造成動作的人與事
The lesson interests Anne.	Anne is very interested in the lesson.	The lesson is interesting（to Anne）.
The movie bored Bob.	Bob was bored by the movie.	Bob didn't enjoy the movie because it was boring.

常見的分詞形容詞：

amazed	amazing	exhausted	exhausting
amused	amusing	fascinated	fascinating
annoyed	annoying	frightened	frightening
bored	boring	frustrated	frustrating
charmed	charming	interested	interesting
confused	confusing	puzzled	puzzling
convincing	convincing	relaxed	relaxing
damaged	damaging	satisfied	satisfying
depressed	depressing	shocked	shocking

disappointed	disappointing	terrified	terrifying
embarrassed	embarrassing	tired	tiring
excited	exciting	thrilled	thrilling

 換你選選看：

1. The manger has never been _____with her work. A satisfying B satisfied

2. The news was so _____ that they all burst into tears. A shocking B shocked

3. Cleaning the house is so _____. I think I need to take a break. A tiring B tired

 答案與中譯解析：

1. 經理從來對她的工作沒有滿意過。（答：B，過去分詞用於描述感覺與接受動作的經驗者。）

2. 這消息如此的震驚他們全都哭了。（答：A，現在分詞用於描述造成動作的人與事。）

3. 打掃房子如此地累人。我想我需要休息一下。（答：A，現在分詞用於描述造成動作的人與事。）

F. 複合形容詞

　　1. 主動語態的句子將動詞改成現在分詞（Ving）

　　　　例1：The woman looks good. 她是個長相好看的女人。

　　　　　　She is a good-looking woman.（adj + Ving）

例2：The car runs fast. 這是一台跑很快的車。

It is a fast-running car.（adv + Ving）

例3：The project consumes time. 這是一個耗時的計畫。

It is a time-consuming project.（N + Ving）

2. 被動語態的句子將動詞改成過去分詞（Vpp）

例1：The house is painted red. 這是一個漆成紅色的房子。

It is a red-painted house.（adj + Vpp）

例2：They passengers were seriously injured in the incident.

這些在事故中受傷嚴重的乘客。

There were seriously-injured passengers in the incident.

（adv. + Vpp）

例3：This machine is operated by coins.

這是一台投幣式的機器。

It is a coin-operated machine.（N + Vpp）

3. 特殊複合形容詞：形容詞後加上名詞加 -ed（adj. + Ned）

例1：He was a cold-blooded person and showed no emotion.

他是一個冷血的人且不帶任何情緒。

例2：I wish you could be more open-minded. It's so hard to

communicate with you.

我希望你可以更心胸開闊點。跟你溝通真的很困難。

例3：All my colleagues are kind-hearted. They show much

support when I have some family crisis.

我所有的同事都很心地善良。當我家庭出現危機時他們都很支持

我。

G. 形容詞字尾 Adjective Suffixes

名詞變為形容詞：

字尾	意義	範例
-AL	相關	accident – accidental; person – personal; region – regional universe –universal
-ARY	相關	caution – cautionary; moment – momentary; compliment – complimentary
-FUL	充滿	beauty – beautiful; delight – delightful; skill – skillful; success – successful
-IC	具有…本質	base – basic; photograph – photographic; science – scientific
-ICAL	具有…本質	history – historical; magic – magical; logic – logical; practice – practical
-ISH	狀態	fool – foolish; child – childish; girl – girlish; self – selfish
-LESS	沒有；相反	friend – friendless; power – powerless; use – useless hope – hopeless; worth – worthless
-LIKE	相似	life – lifelike; child – childlike; bird – birdlike; lady – ladylike
-LY	相似	friend – friendly; cost – costly; month – monthly; day – daily
-OUS	狀態	danger – dangerous; mystery – mysterious; poison – poisonous
-Y	相似	dirt – dirty; mess – messy; rain – rainy; fun – funny spot – spotty

動詞變為形容詞：

字尾	意義	範例
-ABLE	可以；可能	agree – agreeable; expand – expandable; pass – passable; remark – remarkable
-IBLE	可以；可能	access – accessible; flex – flexible force – forcible; sense – sensible
-ANT	表現…動作	please – pleasant; resist – resistant; ignore – ignorant; rely – reliant
-ENT	表現…動作	differ – different; depend – dependent; confide – confident; urge – urgent
-IVE	造成…動作	attract – attractive; create – creative; destruct – destructive; posses – possessive
-ING	造成…動作	amuse – amusing; excite – exciting; confuse – confusing; surprise –surprising
-ED	接受…動作	amuse – amused; excite – excited; confuse – confused; surprise – surprised

H. 相似單字比較

例1：We have two dependent children.（需要依靠的）

We have two dependable children. （可以依靠的）

例2：He is a loving teacher. （會付出愛的）

He is a lovable teacher. （讓人喜愛的）

例3：She is a sensible person. （講理的）

She is a sensitive person. （敏感的）

例4：Henry is a worthy team member.（有價值的）

Henry is a worthless team member. （沒有價值的）

例5：We had a fun time at the movies. （有趣的）

We saw a funny movie. （好笑的）

Part I 句型文法

Part II 字詞文法

Part III 文法糾正篇

Unit 19
副詞

 搶先看名句學文法：

Money can add very much to one's ability to lead a constructive life, not only pleasant for oneself, but, hopefully, beneficial to others. 金錢可以增加一個人的能力去過著有意義的生活，不只是個人的享受，但是，希望對他人有助益。

　　hopefully 為副詞。

 英文達人小筆記！

　　副詞（Adverb）在英文句子中，用來修飾動詞、形容詞、副詞和句子。另外副詞則分有情狀副詞、地方副詞與時間副詞，接下來會有詳細的說明與例句。

關於副詞的詳細說明：

Money can add very much to one's ability to lead a constructive life, not only pleasant for oneself, but, hopefully, beneficial to others. 金錢可以增加一個人的能力去過著有意義的生活，不只是個人的享受，但是，希望對他人有助益。

名言背景：身為洛克斐勒家族的成員，這個來自於一個富可敵國的家族企業身負著強烈的社會責任感。一生投入慈善事業和藝術事業，大衛洛克斐勒相信，金錢可以增加一個人的能力去過著有意義的生活，不單只是個人的享受，更重要的是幫助他人。這個句子裡使用了副詞 hopefully 來修飾形容詞 beneficial。而兩個形容詞所形成的片語 pleasant for oneself 與 beneficial to others 則是用 not only…but…來做連接。

■ 副詞的文法解析：

A. 副詞的功能

1. 修飾動詞

The cars moved slowly in traffic. 車子在車陣中移動緩慢。

I can't even remember his name. 我甚至不記得他的名字。

She has handled the case carefully. 她謹慎處理這件案子。

2. 修飾形容詞

The food is very good here. 這裡的食物很讚。

The man said, "I feel absolutely fine."
「我感覺好極了。」那男人說。

It's never too late to be who you want to be.
成為你想要成為的人，永遠不會太遲。

3. 修飾副詞

They speak German pretty well. 他們的德文講得非常好。

Taiwanese people have worked too hard. 台灣人工作太拼了。

I took the test fairly confidently. 我相當有自信地考完了試。

4. 修飾句子

Unfortunately, we couldn't find the answer.
不幸地，我們沒有找到答案。

Surprisingly, he didn't show up on time.
讓人驚訝的是，他並沒有準時現身。

Indeed, we all make mistakes sometimes.
的確，我們有時會犯錯。

B. 副詞的種類

1. 情狀副詞

　　a. 情狀副詞用來修飾動詞，說明這動作是如何發生的或發生的情形。

　　例1：

　　He reads slowly.　他看得很慢。

　　How does he read?　他看書看得如何？　slowly（慢）

　　例2：

　　She sings beautifully. 她歌唱地很優美。

　　How does she sing? 她唱歌唱得如何？　beautifully（優美）

　　b. 情狀副詞一般放在動詞後面，如果是放在動詞前面則是在作副詞的強調。

　　例1：

　　My aunt calmly told everyone about her illness.
　　我的阿姨很冷靜地告訴大家她生病了。

　　例2：

　　She quickly finished her project.
　　她很快地完成她的計畫。

　　c. 有些特定的狀態副詞則一定放在動詞的後面（well, badly, hard, fast）。

　　例1：

　　Wilson did badly on the test.
　　Wilson 考試考得不好。

　　例2：

　　The only path to success is working hard.
　　成功的唯一途徑是努力地工作。

　　d. 動詞後面如果有受詞，狀態副詞一般放在動詞與受詞的後面。

　　例：

　　We celebrated cheerfully his birthday.
　　要改成　We celebrated his birthday cheerfully.

我們很愉快地慶祝他的生日。

e. 如果句子中不只一個動詞，那麼副詞的位置會影響到句子的意思。

例1：

Lisa immediately decided to leave the party.

immediately 修飾 decided

Lisa 很快地決定要離開派對。

例2：

Lisa decided to leave the party immediately.

immediately 修飾 to leave the party

Lisa 決定要趕緊地離開派對。

例3：

The teacher quietly asked the students to finish the assignments.

quietly 修飾 asked

老師小聲地請學生完成作業。

例4：

The teacher asked the students to finish the assignments quietly.

uietly 修飾 to finish the assignments

老師請學生安靜地完成作業。

換你選選看：

(　　) 1. Sylvia can type very _____. A fast　B fastly　C quickly

(　　) 2. He looked _____ inside the room. A careful　B careless
C carefully

(　　) 3. She ran away _____ . A nervous　B nervously
C nervousness

(　　) 4. The teacher explained the lesson _____. A slower　B slow

Ⓒ slowly

（　）5. They meet ＿＿＿＿＿. Ⓐ regularly　Ⓑ regular　Ⓒ regularity

（　）6. She plays the piano ＿＿＿. Ⓐ goodly　Ⓑ good　Ⓒ well

📁 答案與中譯解析：

1. Sylvia 打字可以很快。（答：Ⓐ，fast 為副詞，修飾動詞 type。）

2. 他小心地看著房間裡面。（答：Ⓑ，carefully 為副詞，修飾動詞 look。）

3. 她緊張地跑掉了。（答：Ⓑ，nervously 為副詞，修飾動詞 run away。）

4. 老師慢慢地解釋課程。（答：Ⓒ，slowly 為副詞，修飾動詞 explain。）

5. 他們定期地開會。（答：Ⓐ，regularly 為副詞，修飾動詞 meet。）

6. 她鋼琴彈得很好。（答：Ⓒ，well 為 good 的副詞，修飾動詞 play。）

2. 地方副詞

　　a. 描述動作發生的地方，一般放在動詞或受詞之後。

　　　例：

　　　I looked everywhere ／ around ／ up ／ down ／ away.

　　　John is going in ／ out ／ back ／ home.

　　b. 單純描述一地方的地方副詞前面不需加介系詞。

　　　例：

　　　We need to get some fresh air inside ／ outside.

　　　Please put it here ／ there ／ upstairs ／ downstairs.

　　c. here 跟 there 的用法：

　　　here 跟 there 常與一些介系詞連用來確切表達一個地方的位置。

　　　如：

　　　down here、down there；

　　　over here、over there；

　　　under here、under there；

　　　up here、up there

Here 跟 There 可作倒裝來強調地方，注意如果主詞是代名詞時則不能倒裝。

例：

Here comes the bus. 公車來了。

There she goes. 她走了。

d. 字尾為 -bound 或 -wards 表示行進的方向。

如：

Backwards、forwards（向後，向前）；

Upwards、downwards（向上地，向下地）；

Inwards、outwards（向內地，向外地）；

例：

Why are you walking backwards?

你為什麼要向後走？

The birds flew upwards.

鳥往上飛。

但注意 towards 是介系詞不是地方副詞。

例：

The man is running towards the bridge.

那男人往橋那邊游去。

She walks slowly towards me.

她慢慢地走向我。

e. 同時表達方向與地方的副詞：Ahead、abroad、overseas、sideways、indoors 與 outdoors

例：

I will run ahead and stop them.

我會跑向前並且阻止他們。

I used to study and work abroad.

我曾經在海外讀書與工作過。

換你選選看：

(　　) 1. The department store is _____there. A X　B over　C on

(　　) 2. She has not been ____ here. A X　B over　C in

(　　) 3. We were looking for you ____ . A anywhere　B everywhere
　　　　　C there and here

(　　) 4. Is there a post office_____? A near　B nearly　C nearby

(　　) 5. We must _____. A walk back home　B walk back to home
　　　　　C to walk back home

(　　) 6. He _____ me. A fast run towards　B run towards fast　C run
　　　　　fast towards

答案與中譯解析：

1. 百貨公司就在那裡。（答：B，over there 表示「就在那裡」。）

2. 她沒有來過這裡。（答：A，has been here 表示「來過這裡」。）

3. 我們之前在四處找你。（答：B，everywhere 表示「到處」；　C應改為 here
and there，表示「各處」。）

4. 這附近有郵局嗎？（答：C，nearby 表示「在附近」。）

5. 我們必須走路回家。（答：A，home 前面不加 to；must 和動詞之間不加
to。）

6. 他飛快地跑向我。（答：C，towards 是介系詞不是地方副詞。）

　　3. 時間副詞

　　　　a. 時間副詞分成三大類

　　　　何時發生：today、later、now、last year、next month、many
　　　　　　　　　years ago

　　　　發生多久： all day、not long、for a while、since、last year

　　　　多久發生一次：sometimes、frequently、never、often、yearly

b. 何時發生的時間副詞一般放在句子最後。問句使用 When。

例1：

When did they go to Japan?

他們什麼時候去日本？

They went to Japan two years ago.

他們兩年前去過日本。

例2：

When are you going to see the movie?

你什麼時候要去看電影。

I'm going to see the movie tomorrow.

我明天會去看電影。

c. 但不同的位置的時間副詞則是在作不同的強調。

例：

Later, Gloria will have some coffee.

強調時間副詞 later

Gloria will later have some coffee.

這是用在較正式的寫作中

Gloria will have some coffee later.

一般用法，沒有特殊強調

d. 發生多久的時間副詞一般放在句子最後。問句使用 How long。

例1：

How long did you watch TV? 你們看電視看多久？

We watched TV all day. 我們看電視看了一整天。

例2：

How long will she be staying in Paris? 她將在巴黎待多久？

Sue will be staying in Paris for a while. 她將在巴黎待一陣子。

e. for 跟 since 與完成式連用。for 後是加一段時間，since 則是動作開始的時間點。

例：

She has been a chef for ten years.

她已經擔任主廚有十年了。

She has been a chef since 2003.

她自從 2003 年擔任主廚。

f. 多久發生一次的時間副詞，一般為頻率副詞，位置為 be 動詞或助動詞之後，一般動詞之前。問句使用 how often。

例1：

How often do you eat fast food? 你多久吃一次速食？

I rarely eat fast food. 我很少吃速食。

He never drinks coffee.（一般動詞之前）他從不喝咖啡。

例2：

She is never late for work.（be 動詞之後）

她上班從不遲到。

例3：

You must always fasten your seat belt.（助動詞之後）

你必須每次都繫好安全帶。

例4：

I have never forgotten my first trip to the United States.（助動詞之後，一般動詞之前）

我永遠都不會忘記我第一次去美國旅行。

g. 常見的頻率副詞：

always　100%

almost always　95%

usually　80%

often、frequently　70%

sometimes　50%

seldom、occasionally、rarely　20%

hardly ever　5%

never 0%

h. 有些頻率副詞可放在句首或句尾。例如 usually 可以放在句首,而 sometimes 可以放在句首或句尾。

例1:

Usually she goes to dinner alone.

她經常自己去吃晚餐。

例2:

I email my friends in Japan sometimes.

= Sometimes I email my friends in Japan.

有時候我會發電子郵件給我在日本的朋友。

i. 帶有否定意義的頻率副詞如 seldom、occasionally、rarely、hardly ever、never 可放在句首,但句子需倒裝。

例1:

I have never read such an inspiring book.

=Never have I read such an inspiring book.

我從來沒看過這麼啟發人的書。

例2:

He is rarely noticed.

=Rarely is he noticed.

他幾乎很少被注意。

j. 一些頻率副詞如 often、frequently 可放在句尾,前面再加上表達程度的副詞如 very、pretty、quite。

例1:

I talk to her at work very often.

我在工作時常常與她交談。

例2:

They have disagreement with each other quite frequently.

他們常常意見相左。

k. a lot 可放在句尾與 often 或 frequently 是相同意思。not much 否

Part I 句型文法

Part II 字詞文法

Part III 文法糾正篇

定句則是 not often 或 not frequently。

例1：

I go to Tainan a lot. = I often go to Tainan.

我常常去台南。

例2：

We don't go out much. = We don't often go out.

我們不常出去。

1. 確切說明多久發生一次的時間副詞一般放在句子最後。

例1：

He visits his family once a week.

他拜訪他的家人一週一次。

例2：

The magazine is published weekly.

這本雜誌一週發行一次。

m. Daily、weekly、monthly、quarterly、yearly（=annual）也可以當成形容詞使用。

例1：

Where is the weekly sales report?

每週特價報在哪裡？

例2：

I've got the daily news updates by email.

我信箱有每日新聞更新。

n. yet & still：yet 表示仍未，尚未完成的動作，經常使用在完成式，放置於句尾。still 表示仍然，一般用在肯定與疑問句中，位置為 be 動詞或助動詞之後，一般動詞之前。

例1：

A: Have you finished your work yet?

A: 你完成你的工作了嗎？

B: Not yet. B：還沒。

例2：

She hasn't met the manager yet.

她還沒見到經理。

例3：

The professor still thinks it's your fault.

教授仍然覺得這是你的錯。

例4：

She is still waiting at the school.

她還在學校等。

例5：

Do you still work for the same company?

你還在同一個公司工作嗎？

o. 如果有不同種類的時間副詞，則使用以下順序排列：

1. 發生多久

2. 多久發生一次

3. 何時發生

例：

They work for five hours every day. 1+2

He had to see the doctor once a week last month. 2+3

The meeting will last 90 minutes tomorrow. 1+3

She went to a program for six hours every weekend last year. 1+2+3

 換你選選看：

( ) 1. He said he has known you _____ a long time. Ⓐ for Ⓑ since Ⓒ still

( ) 2. They moved away from here many years _____. Ⓐ yst Ⓑ ago Ⓒ yet

(   ) 3. I have _____ tried to cover the truth. Ⓐ still   Ⓑ yet   Ⓒ never

(   ) 4. Is Natasha _____ here? I need to speak to her. Ⓐ never
　　　　 Ⓑ yet   Ⓒ still

(   ) 5. I haven't seen my family _____ last month. Ⓐ ago   Ⓑ since
　　　　 Ⓒ for

(   ) 6. We haven't had any problems _____. Ⓐ yet   Ⓑ still
　　　　 Ⓒ never

📁 答案與中譯解析：

1. 他說他已經認識你很久一段時間了。（答：Ⓐ，for+ 時間總數。）

2. 他們很多年前從這裏搬走。（答：Ⓑ，many years ago 表示「很多年以前」。）

3. 我從來沒有試著掩蓋真相。（答：Ⓒ，never 表示「從不」。）

4. Natasha 還在這裡嗎？我需要跟她談一下。（答：Ⓒ，still 表示「仍舊」。）

5. 我自從上個月就沒有見到我的家人。（答：Ⓑ，since+ 時間起點。）

6. 我們還沒有任何的問題。（答：Ⓐ，yet 表示「尚未」。）

　　4. 程度副詞

　　　　a. 程度副詞可用來修飾動詞、形容詞與另一副詞，常見的程度副詞
　　　　　有：Almost、nearly、quite、just、too、enough、hardly、
　　　　　scarcely、completely、very、extremely、especially、
　　　　　particularly、pretty、quite、fairly

　　　　b. 程度副詞的位置一般是放在所修飾的單字前。

　　　　　例1：

　　　　　The weather was extremely cold. 修飾形容詞 cold
　　　　　天氣非常地冷。

　　　　　例2：

　　　　　He said, "Thank you very much." 修飾副詞 much
　　　　　他說：「非常謝謝你。」

例3：

Mr. White was just leaving.　修飾動詞 leaving

Mr. White 才剛走。

c. enough 表示足夠，放在形容詞或副詞之後。

例1：

Is your coffee hot enough?　修飾形容詞 hot

你的咖啡夠熱嗎？

例2：

Monty didn't work hard enough.　修飾副詞 hard

Monty 工作沒有很努力。

d. enough 如果放在名詞前，為限定詞（determiner），可修飾可數
與不可數名詞。

例1：

We have enough books.　修飾可數名詞 books

我們有足夠的書。

例2：

He doesn't have enough food.　修飾不可數名詞 food

他沒有足夠的食物。

e. too 代表太過，放在形容詞或副詞之前。

例1：

This coffee is too hot.　修飾形容詞 hot

這咖啡太燙了。

例2：

He works too hard.　修飾副詞 hard

他工作太認真了。

f. enough 與 too 修飾形容詞之後可加 for 某人或某事。

例1：

The new secretary is not experienced enough for the job.

新任的秘書不夠有經驗去勝任這工作。

例2：

The sweater was too big for her.

這件毛衣對她而言太大。

g. not adj ／ adv + enough to V 表示不夠程度去做某件事。too adj + to V 意思為太…以致無法…

例1：

He didn't study hard enough to pass the test.

他沒有足夠努力讀書以致不能通過考試。

例2：

The girl was not old enough to get married.

=The girl was too young to get married.

那女孩年紀還不夠大，以致於不能結婚。

h. very 表示非常，放在形容詞或副詞之前。

例1：

The lady is very elegant. 修飾形容詞 elegant

這女士非常地優雅。

例2：

He worked very quickly. 修飾副詞 quickly

他工作非常地快。

i. not very 可與另一相反意義形容詞或副詞同義。

例：

He worked slowly.

他工作慢。

= He didn't work very quickly.

他工作沒有很快。

j. very 表達事實，too 則是陳述問題。

例1：

They walk very fast.

他們走很快。

例2：

They walk too fast!

他們走太快！

5. 表示可能性的副詞

    a. 常見可能性的副詞有：

    Certainly、definitely、maybe、possibly、clearly、obviously、perhaps、probably

    b. maybe 與 perhaps 一般放在句首。

        例1：

        Perhaps the weather will be fine.

        或許天氣會變好。

        例2：

        Maybe it won't rain.

        或許不會下雨。

    c. 其它常見表示可能性的副詞放在動詞之前，be 動詞之後。

        例1：

        He is certainly coming to the meeting.

        他一定會來參加這個會議。

        例2：

        We will possibly go to England next year.

        我們有可能明年會去英國。

        例3：

        They are definitely at school.

        他們絕對在學校。

        例4：

        She was obviously very surprised.

        她明顯地非常驚訝。

Part I 句型文法

Part II 字詞文法

Part III 文法糾正篇

6. 地方與位置的副詞

    a. 用介系詞表示位置

    He was standing at the door. 他站在門口。

    I can't find it in the drawer. 我在抽屜找不到那東西。

    b. 表示方向

    Walk past the park and keep going. 穿過公園然後繼續走。

    Go straight ahead and turn left. 往前直走然後左轉。

    c. 表示距離

    Hsinchu is 65 kilometers from Taipei. 新竹距離台北 65 公里。

    Hsinchu is not far away from Taipei. 新竹距離台北不遠。

7. 連接副詞

    a. 連接副詞一般是用在句子間的轉折詞，常見的連接副詞有：

時間	對比	增加	結果
then meanwhile henceforth afterward later soon	however nevertheless still on the other hand instead rather otherwise	likewise moreover furthermore besides in addition	consequently hence then therefore thus accordingly as a result

    b. 連接副詞連接句子時可以出現在句子中不同的位置。句子間可以使用句號或分號，使用句號時句首字母需大寫，分號時則不用。連接副詞在句子中必須用逗號隔開。

    例1：

    My sister likes chocolate cookies; however, she doesn't eat many of them.

    例2：

    My sister likes chocolate cookies; she doesn't, however, eat many of them.

例3：

My sister likes chocolate cookies; she doesn't eat many of them, however.

換你選選看：

(　　) 1. You have to stop smoking; _____, you'll die early.
　　　　A however　B therefore　C otherwise

(　　) 2. Golf is a very fun sport; _____, it's very expensive.
　　　　A otherwise　B on the other hand　C however

(　　) 3. Tony never watches what he eats; _____, he gets really heavy. A therefore　B otherwise　C on the other hand

(　　) 4. This is a very useful tool; _____, it's easy to carry around.
　　　　A in addition　B therefore　C on the other hand

(　　) 5. I would like to see the new movie this weekend; _____, I might not have enough time to do that. A therefore　B however C otherwise

(　　) 6. She swept the floor; _____ I did the dishes. A meanwhile B however　C therefore

答案與中譯解析：

1. 你必須要戒菸；不然你會很早死掉。（答：C，otherwise 表示「不然」。）

2. 高爾夫是很有趣的運動；另一方面它相當的貴。（答：B，on the other hand 表示「另一方面」。）

3. Tony 從來沒有注意他吃的食物；所以他變得很胖。（答：A，therefore 表示「所以」。）

4. 這是一個很實用的工具；除此之外它攜帶方便。（答：A，in addition 表示「除此之外」。）

5. 我想要這周末看那新的電影；然而我可能會沒有時間去做那件事。（答：B，however 表示「然而」。）

6. 她掃地，同時，我在洗碗。（答：A，meanwhile 表示「同時」。）

8. 副詞的比較級

a. –ly 副詞

形容詞	副詞	比較級	最高級
quiet	quietly	more quietly	the most quietly
careful	carefully	more carefully	the most carefully
happy	happily	more happily	the most happily

例1：

Mary drives more carefully than John does.

Mary 開車比 John 還要小心。

例2：

Of all the drivers, Mary drives the most carefully.

在這麼多駕駛人中，Mary 開車最小心。

b. 形容詞與副詞同形

形容詞	副詞	比較級	最高級
hard	hard	harder	the hardest
fast	fast	faster	the fastest
early	early	earlier	the earliest

例1：

My brother gets up earlier than I do.

我哥哥起床比我早。

例2：

My brother gets up the earliest of all the family.

我的哥哥是家裡起床最早的。

c. 不規則副詞

形容詞	副詞	比較級	最高級
good	well	better	the best
bad	badly	worse	the worst
far	far	farther／further	the farthest／furthest

例1：

I did worse on the test than Leo did.

我考試考得比 Leo 差。

例2：

On that test, I did the worst in the class.

那次考試，我考得全班最差。

Unit 20
動名詞

 搶先看名句學文法：

I just can't stop loving you. 我就是無法停止愛你。
stop 後面要加 **V-ing**。**V-ing** 稱為動名詞。

 英文達人小筆記！

現在分詞的作用為「形容詞」；而動名詞為「名詞」。動名詞是由「動詞（V）＋ ing」所組成的，在句子中要當作名詞來看。以下有動名詞的詳細解析與例句。

關於動名詞的詳細說明：

I just can't stop loving you. 我就是無法停止愛你。

名言背景：這張單曲發行於 1987 年，收錄於專輯《Bad》，由 Michael Jackson 和歌手 Siedah Garret 合唱的情歌。在《Bad》這張專輯中，Michael 發行了 7 張單曲，其中有 5 首登上美國 Billboard Top 100 的冠軍寶座，可以說是成果輝煌的一張專輯。"I just can't stop loving you" 是其中的一首冠軍歌曲，這首歌曾於 2012 年於美國著名影集 Glee 的「麥克傑克森特輯」中，由 Finn 與 Rachel 再度演唱。

■ **動名詞（Gerunds）文法解析**：動名詞（Gerunds）是由「原形動詞＋ing」組成，是具有動詞性質的「名詞」；已經轉為名詞的動名詞可以當句子的主詞（S）、受詞（O）、或補語（C）。而和現在分詞（V-ing）不同的地方，現在分詞是帶有形容詞的性質，而動名詞則為具有名詞的功用。

A. 動名詞的特性

　　1. 組成：動詞原形 +ing，將原本的動詞轉化為名詞。

　　　　例：Read=Reading，look=looking，am ／ are ／ is=being

　　2. 保有動詞的特性：動名詞後面可加受詞、補語、副詞修飾語、時態與被動式。

　　　　a. 動名詞 + 受詞

　　　　　　例：Playing basketball is good for you. 打籃球對你很好。

　　　　b. 動名詞 + 補語

　　　　　　例：Being idle is the cause of his failure. 懶惰是造成他失敗的原因。

　　　　c. 動名詞 + 副詞

　　　　　　例：Dancing every day makes me healthy. 每天跳舞使我健康。

　　　　d. 動名詞的時態

　　　　　　簡單式動名詞（doing，being）：與主要動詞時間一致，或是表示未來。

　　　　　　例：I am sure of his coming. = I am sure that he will come. （表示未來）我確定他會來。

　　　　e. 完成式動名詞（having + p.p.）：

　　　　　　表示動名詞的時間比主要句子的動詞更早發生的事件。

　　　　　　例：Excuse me for not having answered your letter at once. 很抱歉未能即刻回覆您信件。

　　　　f. 動名詞被動式

　　　　　　簡單被動式動名詞（being+ P.P.）

　　　　　　例：I don't like being treated like that. 我不喜歡被這樣對待。

　　　　　　完成被動式動名詞（having been+ P.P.）

例：I remember having been told that story. 我記得聽過這個故事。

g. 具有名詞的性質

名詞前可放的詞類也適用於動名詞前。

例：I hate all this arguing. 我討厭這爭論。

動名詞的單複數（純名詞）。

1. 動名詞若只表示單一事件時，則後面接單數動詞。

例：Reading book is my hobby. 閱讀是我的嗜好。

2. 動名詞有兩個以上時，主詞視為複數，和複數動詞連用。

例：Reading and cooking are my hobbies. 閱讀與下廚是我的嗜好。

動名詞前可加「所有格」，仍帶有動詞特性。

例：Please excuse my coming late. 抱歉我來晚了。

B. 動名詞的用法

a. 當主詞（S）：主詞（動名詞 V-ing）＋動詞（V）＋形容詞 Adj ／名詞 N

1. 動名詞當主詞時，後面接單數動詞。

2. 兩個動名詞當主詞，使用複數動詞。

例1：Getting up early is good for health. 早起有益健康。

例2：Reading and cooking make me happy. 閱讀與下廚讓我快樂。

b. 當主詞補語（SC）：主詞（S）＋Be 動詞（V）＋動名詞（V-ing）

動名詞放在 beV 的後面，代表與主詞是同一件事。

例：My job is solving problem. 我的工作是解決問題。

c. 當受詞（O）：當動詞的受詞

主詞（S）＋動詞（V）＋受詞（O 動名詞）（多為及物動詞）

例：I like reading and cooking. 我喜歡閱讀與下廚。

d. 接動名詞的動詞

mind 介意	practice 練習	begin 開始	suggest 建議
finish 完成	enjoy 喜愛	risk 風險	admit 承認
suggest 建議	avoid 避免	deny 否認	resist 抵抗
delay 延遲	stop 停止	postpone 延遲	keep 保持
imagine 想像	consider 考慮	escape 逃避	catch 抓住
quit 離開	regret 遺憾	complete 完成	miss 錯過
appreciate 感激	resume 繼續	spend 花費	find 發現

例1：I must avoid doing that again.（Vt+Ving）我一定要避免再這麼做了。

例2：I don't mind staying here alone.（Vt+Ving）我不介意單獨待在這裡。

例3：She admits having a crush on him.（Vt+Ving）她承認對他有好感了。

e. 當介系詞的受詞：

主詞（S）＋動詞（V）＋介系詞＋受詞（O 動名詞 V-ing）

介系詞後接動名詞

f. 接動名詞的片語

be afraid of 恐怕	be good at 擅長	be interested in 興趣	be worried about 擔心
worry about 擔心	dream of／about 夢想	talk about 談論	be careful about 小心
be fond of 喜歡	be responsible for 負責	be capable of 能力	be tired of 疲倦
believe in 相信	object to 反對	thanks for 感謝	be used to 習慣

例1：

He is fond of mountain climbing.（V + of + V-ing）他喜歡爬山。

例2：

I am good at playing the piano.（V+ at+ V-ing）我擅長彈琴。

例3：

He worried abou tmaking mistakes.（V+ about+ V-ing） 他擔心犯錯。

3. 常見慣用語

a. There is no Ving = It's impossible to + V（…是不可能的…）

　　例：There is no telling what will happen in the future. 要知道未來會發生什麼事是不可能的。

　　　　= It's impossible to tell what will happen in the future.

b. It is no use + Ving = It's of no use to + V.（…是沒有用的…）

　　例：There is no use crying over spilt milk. 覆水難收。

　　　　=It's of no use to cry over spilt milk.

c. can't help + Ving = can't but + 原形 V.（…不得不…）

　　例：I can't help falling in love with you. 我情不自禁愛上你。

　　　　=I can't but fall in love with you.

d. On + Ving... , S + V-ed...=

As soon as S + V-ed, S + V-ed...（一…就…）

　　例：On hearing the bad news, she burst into tears. 一聽到這壞消息，她的眼淚就流出來了。

　　　　=As soon as she heard the bad news, she burst into tears.

e. feel like + Ving= would like + 不定詞（想要…）

　　例：I feel like buying a new car. 我有想要買部新車。

　　　　=I would like to buy a new car.

f. 省略介系詞：be busy（in）+ V-ing...（忙於…），be worth（of）+

Ving...（值得 ...）

例：This movie is worth（of）seeing. 這部電影值得看。

g. go+Ving...（去做…），一般用於戶外運動或休閒活動

例：They go（shopping, swimming, dancing...）every Sunday. 他
們每週日去（逛街、游泳、跳舞…）。

h. do + Ving...（做）

例：She does the（cooking, cleaning, traveling...）她（下廚、打
掃、旅行…）。

i. how ／ what about + Ving....（你認為……如何？）

例：What ／ How about playing tennis together this afternoon? 今
天下午一起打網球你認為如何呢？

j. What do you say to+ V（……意下如何？）

例：What do you say to join me for dinner? 跟我一起吃晚餐意下如
何？

絕妙好例句：

1. Seeing is believing.（believing= 主詞補語 SC）眼見為憑。

2. Swimming is a good exercise.（Gerunds=Swimming= 主詞 S）游泳是個好運動。

3. Meggie enjoys riding her bike.（Gerunds=riding= 動詞的受詞）Meggie 喜歡騎腳踏車。

4. You just keep on going straight.（Gerunds=going= 介詞 on 的受詞）你只要繼續一直往前走。

5. I don't like being disturbed while reading.（Gerunds=being disturbed= 動詞的受詞，被動式）我不喜歡在讀書時被打擾。

換你選選看：

(　　) 1. can't help _____ asleep during that boring speech. Ⓐ fall　Ⓑ to fall　Ⓒ falling

(　　) 2. _____ something to eat _____better than nothing. Ⓐ To have; are　Ⓑ Having; is　Ⓒ Having; are

(　　) 3. I look forward to_____ you soon. Ⓐ see　Ⓑ be seen　Ⓒ seeing

(　　) 4. Do you mind _____ on the air conditioner? It's hot in here. Ⓐ to turn　Ⓑ turn　Ⓒ turning

(　　) 5. It's no use _____. Ⓐ complaining　Ⓑ their complaining　Ⓒ complaining

(　　) 6. _____ is a good exercise. Ⓐ Jog　Ⓑ To jogging　Ⓒ Jogging

 答案與中譯解析：

1. 在聽無聊的演講時，我忍不住睡著了。（答：Ⓒ，Gerunds= 動詞 help 的受詞，常見慣用語 can't help + Ving.）

2. 有吃總比沒吃好。（答：Ⓑ，Gerunds= 主詞，使用單數動詞。）

3. 期待再相見。（答：Ⓒ，Gerunds= 介詞 to 的受詞。）

4. 你介意開冷氣嗎？這裡好熱。（答：Ⓒ，Gerunds= 動詞 mind 的受詞。）

5. 抱怨是沒有用的。（答：Ⓐ，It is of on use Ving 常用慣用語。）

6. 慢跑是一個很好的運動。（答：Ⓒ，Gerunds=Jogging= 主詞 S。）

Part I 句型文法

Part II 字詞文法

Part III 文法糾正篇

Unit 21
不定詞

 搶先看名句學文法：

I love to travel, but hate to arrive.

我喜歡旅行，但不喜歡到達目的地。

to + V 為不定詞的用法。

 英文達人小筆記！

不定詞（Infinitives）由「to+ 原形動詞」組成，因是動詞演變而來，所以具有動詞特性，也扮演著名詞（N）、形容詞（Adj.）、（Adv.）的角色。因此 定詞可以拿來當主詞（S）、受詞（O）、或補語（C）。

關於不定詞的詳細說明：

I love to travel, but hate to arrive. 我喜歡旅行，但不喜歡到達目的地。

名言背景：摘自亞伯 · 愛因斯坦（Albert Einstein）是 20 世紀猶太裔理論物理學家，創立了相對論；被譽為是「現代物理學之父」及二十世紀世界最重要科學家之一。他卓越的科學成就和原創性使得「愛因斯坦」一詞成為「天才」的同義詞。這句話可以表達顯示出愛因斯坦非常喜愛於研究的過程。

■ **不定詞文法解析**：不定詞（Infinitives）由「to+ 原形動詞」組成，因是動詞演變而來，所以具有動詞特性，也扮演著名詞（N）、形容詞（Adj.）、（Adv.）的角色。因此定詞可以拿來當主詞（S）、受詞（O）、或補語（C）。

A. 不定詞的特性

　　1. 組成：to＋動詞原形（V）

　　　　a. 否定在 to 前加 not= not to＋V

　　　　例：I decide not to speak to Tom. 我決定不跟 Tom 講話了。

　　　　b. 有時會將 "to" 省略，所以會分為兩類 "有 to 不定詞"，與 "無 to 不定詞"。

　　　　c. 感官動詞（如：see，hear，feel...）

　　　　例：I saw him（to）swim yesterday.

　　　　d. 使役動詞（如：make，let，have...）

　　　　例：I let him（to）go.

　　2. 保有動詞的特性：不定詞後面可加受詞、補語、副詞修飾語。也有時態與被動式。

　　　　a. 不定詞＋受詞

　　　　例：To learn English is difficult for me. 學英語對我來說是困難的。

　　　　b. 不定詞＋補語

　　　　例：To be honest, I like you. 老實說，我喜歡你。

　　　　c. 不定詞＋副詞

　　　　例：I want you to come early. 我希望你能早點來。

　　3. 不定詞的時態

　　　　a. 簡單式（to V）：不定詞與主要動詞時間一致。

　　　　例：I decide to learn English. 我決定學英文。

　　　　b. 進行式（to be＋V-ing）：在主要動詞時間中，動作正在進行。

　　　　例：It's nice to be sitting here with you. 跟你一起坐在這 真好。

　　　　c. 完成式（to have＋p.p.）：不定詞的時間比主要動詞更早發生的事件。

Part I 句型文法

Part II 字詞文法

Part III 文法糾正篇

例：He seems to have missed the train. 他好像沒有趕上火車。

4. 不定詞的被動式：

a. 簡單式：（not）+ to be + p.p.

例：No one likes to be found faults with. 沒有人喜歡被人找缺點。

b. 完成式：（not）+ to have + p.p.

例：Something seems to have been forgotten. 好像有東西被忘掉 。

B. 不定詞的用法

1. 當名詞（N）

2. 當主詞（S）：

a. 不定詞當主詞時，後面接單數動詞

b. 兩個以上不定詞當主詞，使用複數動詞

c. 可用"虛主詞 it"作替代，把真正的主詞放在句尾：

句型 =It is + adj +（for, of）+ N + to-V

例：It is difficult for me to learn English.（S=to learn....）

　　= To learn English is difficult（for me）.

　　學英語對我來說是困難的。

3. 當受詞（N）：

a. 當一般動詞的受詞

句型 =S + V +（受詞 O）+（not）+ to-V

例：He asked me to mail the letter.（S + V + O + to-V）

　　他叫我去寄那封信。

例：I plan to visit Paris.（S + V + to-V）

　　我計畫去巴黎。

b. 可用"虛受詞 it"作替代，把真正的受詞放在句尾

句型 =S + V + it +（adj, N）+ to-V

例1：

　　I think it is better to leave.（O=it=to leave）

　　我認為離開比較好。

4. 當補語（C）

    a. 主詞補語（S.C）

    例：His dream is to become a scientist. 他夢想做一個科學家。

    b. 受詞補語（O.C）

    例：He taught me to speak English. 他教我說英語。

5. 當形容詞（Adj.）：

    a. 用來修飾名詞的不定詞，一定要放在被修飾名詞的後面。

    及物動詞（Vt）用法＝（代）名詞＋to-Vt

    例：I want some water to drink.（adj=to drink）

        我要一些喝的水。

    不及物動詞（Vi）用法＝（代）名詞＋to -Vi＋介詞

    例：He needs a chair to sit on .

        他需要一張椅子坐。

6. 當副詞（Adv.）可以修飾動詞、形容詞、其它副詞、或一整個子句。

    a. 表目的，修飾動詞：

    （not）to＋V＝so as（not）to＋V＝in order（not）to＋V

    例：I came to buy a book. 他來買一本書。

        ＝I came in order to buy a book.（to-V 修飾動詞 come）

    b. 表結果，修飾形容詞與副詞

        表正面結果：（如此／太…以致於…）

        so＋（adj, adv）＋as to＋V＝（adj, adv）＋enough＋to＋V

    例：He studied hard enough to pass the exam.

        他很用功以致於能通過考試。

        ＝He studied so hard as to pass the exam.（to-V 修飾副詞 hard）

        表負面結果：（太怎樣…以致於不能…）

        too＋（adj, adv）＋to V＝（太…以致於不能…）

        ＝ not＋（adj, adv）＋enough＋to＋V

例：He is too weak to stand up.

他太虛弱了以致於沒法站立。

= He is not strong enough to stand up.

（to-V 修飾形容詞 weak，strong）

c. 表原因／理由

主詞（S，人）＋ be 動詞＋ adj＋ to-V

表示情緒（喜怒哀樂等）或態度的形容詞之後加上不定詞（to-V），可以表達情感的原因，主要以人為主詞。

例：I am sorry to give you trouble.

抱歉給您添麻煩。

7. 常見後面接不定詞的形容詞：

be pleased to 高興	be ready to 樂意	be sorry to 抱歉
be delighted to 高興	be prepared to 準備	be afraid to 恐怕
be lucky to 幸運	be anxious to 焦慮	be likely to 可能
be upset to 心煩	be eager to 渴望	be certain to 確信
be disappointed to 失望	be willing to 願意	be surprised to 驚訝
be proud to 驕傲	be careful to 小心	be excited to 興奮

8. 修飾整個子句（又叫做獨立不定詞）

例：To tell you the truth, I don't like you at all.

說實話，我並不喜歡你。

9. 不定詞的疑問句：

a. 疑問句（Wh-）＋ to-V ＝名詞片語

b. 疑問句 ＝how, when, what, where, whom

c. 名詞片語有「名詞」的性質，可以做主詞、受詞或補語

例1：I don't know what to say.（當受詞）

我不知道該說什麼。

例2：My question is how to make coffee.（主詞補語）

我的問題是如何煮咖啡。

10. 常接不定詞的動詞：

a. 動詞 V+ to-V

afford 負擔	consent 同意	manage 管理	refuse 拒絕
agree 同意	decide 決定	mean 意欲	seem 似乎
appear 顯露	demand 要求	need 需要	struggle 掙扎
arrange 安排	deserve 值得	offer 提供	swear 發誓
ask 詢問	expect 期待	plan 計畫	threaten 威脅
beg 乞求	fail 失敗	prepare 準備	volunteer 自願
care 想要	hesitate 猶豫	promise 承諾	wait 等待
claim 主張	hope 希望	pretend 假裝	want 希望

例1：I decide to go.（to-V 當 N 受詞）

我決定去。

b. 動詞 V+ 名詞或代名詞 + to-V：

allow 允許	dare 膽敢	instruct 指式	remind 提醒
ask 詢問	encourage 鼓勵	invite 邀請	require 要求

beg 乞求	expect 期待	need 需要	teach 指導
cause 導致	forbid 禁止	order 命令	tell 告訴
challenge 挑戰	force 強迫	permit 允許	urge 催促
convince 說服	hire 雇用	persuade 說服	want 想要

例2：I allow him to come in.（to-V 當 N 受詞補語）
我允許他進來。

 絕妙好例句：

1. I am very happy to meet you.（to-V 當副詞）很高興見到你。
2. I expect to be invited to the party.（to-V 被動式）我期待被邀請參加舞會。
3. Where to go is up to you?（Wh 疑問句名詞片語，當主詞）隨你想去哪？
4. It is important to be on time.（主詞 =it=to be on time）準時是很重要的。
5. The story is easy enough for a kid to read.（to-V 當副詞，表結果）這故事 夠簡單，小孩也能讀。

換你選選看：

（　　）1. To know is one thing; _____ is another.
　　　　A do　B doing　C to do

（　　）2. She seemed _____ out of her mind. A to be　B being　C is

（　　）3. I don't have a key _____ this door.
　　　　A unlocking　B unlock　C to unlock

（　　）4. My pocket is too small _____ my wallet.
　　　　A to insert　B insert　C inserting.

（　　）5. He promised _____ late again.
　　　　A does not be　B not be　C not to be

（　　）6. The little boy is happy _____ to the birthday party.
　　　　A to be invited　B to invite　C being invited

答案與中譯解析：

1. 知道是一回事，做是另一回事。（答：C，to-V＝名詞＝主詞。）
2. 她似乎神經錯亂了。（答：A，to-V＝主詞補語。）
3. 我沒有開這扇門的鑰匙。（答：C，to-V＝形容詞，修飾 a key。）
4. 我的口袋太小，以致於無法放入我的皮夾。（答：A，to-V＝副詞，修飾形容詞 adj。）
5. 他答應不會再遲到。（答：C，否定句 not 放在 to-V 前。）
6. 小男孩很高興被邀請參加生日派對。（答：A，to-V 被動式。）

Unit 22
動名詞與不定詞的比較

 搶先看名句學文法：

To be or not to be, that is a question.
是或不是，這是一個問題。
to + V 為不定詞的用法，本單元將 **to + V** 與 **V-ing** 作比較。

 英文達人小筆記！

動名詞（**Gerund**）與不定詞（**Infinitives**）的比較文法解析：動名詞（**Gerund**）與不定詞（**Infinitives**）都是由動詞轉換而來，在句子中雖具有動詞的特性，卻扮演著名詞、形容詞、或副詞的角色。

關於動名詞（**Gerund**）與不定詞（**Infinitives**）的詳細比較與說明：

To be or not to be, that is a question. 是或不是，這是一個問題。

名言背景：莎士比亞（William Shakespeare）著作中名句很多，相信最多被人引用的算是這句了，在 Hamlet《哈姆雷特》中第三幕主角的獨白。哈姆雷特一直在煩惱要不要殺了他的母親和繼父，心中充滿矛盾，不知如何處理這錯綜複雜關係的情況下，用這句獨白道出了哈姆雷特的悲傷、矛盾和無奈，猶豫掙扎。

■　動名詞（**Gerund**）與不定詞（**Infinitives**）的比較文法解析：

A.　動名詞與不定詞的比較

1. 用法特性比較表：

用法	動名詞（V-ing）	不動詞（to-V）
名詞（N）	作主詞（S） 作受詞（O）：動詞 , 介系詞 作補語（SC）：主詞	作主詞（S） 作受詞（O）：動詞 作補語（C）：主詞補語（SC） 受詞補語（OC）
形容詞（adj）	N / A	可用來修飾名詞
副詞（adv）	N / A	修飾動詞（V） 修飾形容詞（adj） 修飾其它副詞（adv） 修飾整個子句

例：Seeing is believing.

　　眼見為憑。

　　= To see is to believe.

2. 虛主詞（it）與動名詞、不定詞的互換

　a. 動名詞當主詞可以用不定詞或虛主詞代替

例：Learning English is difficult.

　　學英語是困難的。

　　= To learn English is difficult.

　　= It is difficult to learn English.

3. 動名詞與不定詞的時態：

時態	動名詞（V-ing）	不定詞（to-V）
簡單式	V-ing	to V
進行式	N / A	to be + V-ing
完成式	having + p.p.	to have + p.p.

4. 動名詞與不定詞的被動語態：

時態	動名詞（V-ing）	不定詞（to-V）
簡單被動式	being + p.p.	to be + p.p.
完成被動式	having been + p.p.	to have been + p.p.

B. 動詞後加動名詞還是不定詞

1. 動詞可用動名詞或不定詞，句子意義相同。

like 喜歡	begin 開始	intent 意圖
love 愛	start 開始	neglect 忽略
hate 討厭	cease 停止	learn 學習
dislike 不喜歡	continue 繼續	plan 計畫
prefer 較喜歡	can't stand 不能忍受	can't bear 無法忍受

例：I like to listen to jazz. ＝ I like listening to jazz.

我喜歡聽爵士樂。

2. 動詞可用動名詞或不定詞，句子意義不同。

	說明	Ex.
stop 停止	V-ing 停下做某件事 To- V 停下來去做某事	He stops smoking. 他停止抽菸〈戒菸〉。 He stops to smoke. 他停下來抽菸。
remember 記得	V-ing 記得已做的事情 To- V 記得未做的事情	I remember mailing the letter. 我記得寄過那封信。 I remember to mail the letter. 我要記得去寄那封信。
forget 忘記	V-ing 忘記已做過的事情 To- V 忘記要去做的事情	He forgot doing his homework. 他忘記做過了功課。 He forgot to do his homework. 他忘記要做功課了。

regret 遺憾	V-ing 後悔做過的事情 To- V 抱歉要去做的事情	I regret telling you these. 我後悔告訴你這些。 I regret to tell you these. 我很遺憾要告訴你這些。
Go on 繼續	V-ing 繼續做相同的事 To- V 接著做不同的事	He went on talking for one hour. 他連續講了一個小時。 After reading, he went on to write. 讀完書之後，他接著寫字。

Part I 句型文法

Part II 字詞文法

Part III 文法糾正篇

👑 絕妙好例句：

1. The most important thing is to give back the money.（to-V= 主詞補語）
   Giving back the money is the most important thing.（Ving= 主詞）
   It is important thing to give back the money.（虛主詞 =it；主詞 =to give....）
   將錢還回去是最重要的事。

2. She stops to write to me.（to write= 受詞）她停下來寫信給我。She stop writing to me.（writing= 受詞）她不再寫信給我了。

3. I have a lot of homework to do.（to-V= 形容詞用，修飾 O=homework）我有很多家庭作業要做。

4. She is in charge of teaching English in our school.（Ving= 介系詞 of 的受詞）她在我們學校負責教英文。

5. Please decide which to choose.（to-V= 受詞）請決定要選哪個。

換你選選看：

(　) 1. I save some money in order _____ a new car. Ⓐ buying　Ⓑ buy
　　　Ⓒ to buy

(　) 2. My sister is good at _____. Ⓐ cooking　Ⓑ to cook　Ⓒ cooks

(　) 3. He is too stubborn_____ with you. Ⓐ agree　Ⓑ agreeing
　　　Ⓒ to agree

(　) 4. Are you interested_____ tennis? Ⓐ in playing　Ⓑ to play
　　　Ⓒ play

(　) 5. She likes _____ romantic novels. Ⓐ too reading　Ⓑ reading
　　　Ⓒ read

(　) 6. It is difficult for him _____ Japanese. Ⓐ to learn　Ⓑ learning
　　　Ⓒ learn

答案與中譯解析：

1. 我存錢為了買新車。（答：Ⓒ，to-V = 副詞用法修飾動詞，表目的。）

2. 我姐姐很會煮飯。（答：Ⓐ，V-ing = 介系詞的受詞。）

3. 他太頑固了以致於無法同意你。（答：Ⓒ，too... to-V = 副詞修飾形容詞 stubborn。）

4. 你對打網球有興趣嗎？（答：Ⓐ，V-ing = 介系詞 in 的受詞。）

5. 她喜歡讀言情小說。（答：Ⓑ，like 後面可接不定詞或動名詞。）

6. 對他而言，學習日文很困難。（答：Ⓐ，to-V 做主詞時，可以用虛主詞 it 代替。）

Unit 23
語態助動詞

 搶先看名句學文法：

I Can't Catch You.
我抓不住你。

can't 在這裡為助動詞，但什麼是語態？讓本單元告訴您。

 英文達人小筆記！

本單元有 can、could；will、would；may、might；shall、should；must、need 與 had better 的詳細說明與例子，助動詞在這裡不再只是時態的分別，而有語氣的分別，懂得細分其中的不同，就能正確傳達要求、命令或是請求協助。

關於語態助動詞的詳細說明：

I Can't Catch You. 我抓不住你。

名言背景：出處於嘟噹六便士合唱團（Sixpence None the Richer）的歌曲 *I Can't Catch You*。講出這個團名的時候，也許知道的人並不會太多，但如果提到結婚典禮熱門曲 *Kiss Me* 就是他們唱的，相信不少人就會露出恍然大悟的表情。此樂團以輕快甜美的歌曲熱播全球。

■ 語態助動詞的文法解析：

A. can

1. 表達可能或能力

   John can speak Spanish. （能力）

   John 可以説西班牙文。

   I cannot hear you. （能力）

   =I can't hear you.

   我聽不到你。

   Can you talk to me? （可能）

   你可以跟我説嗎？

2. can 一般用在現在式或未來式

   A: Can you help me with my homework? （現在）

   A: 你可以幫我做功課嗎？

   B: Sorry. I'm busy now. I can help you tomorrow. （未來）

   B: 對不起。我現在在忙。我明天可以幫你。

3. 表達要求與命令

   通常 can 在表達要求或命令時為問句的型式，但這並非一個真正的問句，而是一種較為強烈的要求的語氣。

   Can you make some coffee, please?

   可以給我咖啡嗎？

   Can you be here in a minute?

   你可以現在就到嗎？

4. can 可用於徵詢或給予允許

   A: Can I smoke in this room?

   A: 我可以在這房間抽菸嗎？

   B: You can't smoke here, but you can smoke in the garden.

   B: 你不可以在這裡抽菸，但是你可以在花園抽菸。

5. 注意：在詢問是否可以做一件事時，may, could, can 表達不同的正式與禮貌的程度。

May I help you? 最正式與最有禮貌的用法

請問我可以幫你嗎？

Could I talk to you for a second? （禮貌的請求。could 在此沒有代表過去的時態）

請問可以跟你談一下嗎？

Can I see what you're making? 一般與朋友或認識的人所使用的語氣

可以讓我看你在做什麼嗎？

6. could 表達過去的能力

My grandmother could speak five languages.

我祖母過去可以說五種語言。

When we arrived home, we could not open the door.

= When we arrived home, we couldn't open the door.

當我們到家時，我們打不開門。

Could you understand what he was saying?

你可以理解他當時在說什麼嗎？

7. could 表達請求。相較 can 之下較為正式與禮貌

Could you tell me where the bank is, please?

請問你可否告訴我銀行在哪裡嗎？

Could you send me an email, please?

請問你可否寄 email 給我？

8. can、could，與 be able to 的比較

a. be able to 一樣表達有能力去做某件事情，但可以運用在不同的時態中。而 can 一般則只使用現在與未來時態的表達，could 則是用在過去時態。

I was able to fly an airplane. （過去式）

我之前就能夠開飛機了。

I will be able to fly an airplane very soon. （未來式）
我很快將可以開飛機。

I have been able to fly an airplane since I was at college. （完成式）

我從大學的時候我就已經會開飛機。

b. be able to 後面可加不定詞

I would like to be able to fly an airplane.

我想要能夠開飛機。

換你選選看：

( ) 1. We _____ go to the party. We're going to a wedding.

    A won't be able to

    B couldn't

    C can't be able to

( ) 2. A: Can you lend me some money?

    B: Sorry. I _____. I haven't got any either.

    A can't

    B won't

    C am not able to

( ) 3. I didn't hear what you said. _____ repeat it again?

    A Can I

    B Can you

    C May I

( ) 4. I've left my wallet at my place. _____ borrow some money from you?

    A Do you

    B Can you

    C Could I

( ) 5. _____ you make some coffee, please?

    A Could

    B Might

    C Did

答案與中譯解析：

1. 我們沒辦法去參加派對。我們要去一場婚禮。（答：A，由時間判斷選擇 will 為助動詞。）

2. A：你可以借我一些錢嗎？ B：抱歉，我不行。我也沒有任何錢。（答：A，回答時根據問句使用一樣的助動詞。）

3. 我之前沒聽到你說甚麼。你可以再說一遍嗎？（答：B，表示請求。）

4. 我把錢包放在家裡了。我可以跟你借一些錢嗎？（答：C，表示請求。）

5. 可以請你煮些咖啡嗎？（答：A，表示請求。）

    B. will & would

       1. will 表未來式，would 則是過去以為會發生的事

         We'll be there soon.

         我們很快就會到那裡。

         I thought we would be there soon.

         我原本以為我們會很快到那裡。

       2. will 可以表示提供承諾

         I will think of you all the time when I leave here.

         我離開後我將會常常想你。

         We will come and see you next week.

         我下星期將會去看你。

       3. will 表達意願，would 則是用在過去時態

         I will do it if you want me to.

         我會幫你做這些只要你希望我做。

         The baby wouldn't stop crying last night.

         嬰兒昨晚哭得不停。

       4. will 與 would 都可以作為請求的問句，would 比 will 更有禮貌

         Will you do me a favor?

         你可以幫我個忙嗎？

Would you pass me the pepper?

可以請你幫我傳一下胡椒嗎？

5. would 的相關片語

a. would you mind（not）+ Ving…是有禮貌的請求別人做某件事。如果是願意的，回答時則是用否定語氣來表示不介意。

　A: Would you mind opening the window?

　A: 請問你介意我打開窗嗎？

　B: No, I wouldn't. ／ Of course not. ／ Not at all. ／ No problem. ／ Sure

　B： 不，不會介意。／當然不會介意。／沒關係。／沒問題。／當然可以。

b. would you mind if I + 過去式…是在請求允許。准許時也是用否定語氣來表示不介意。

　Would you mind if I opened the window?

　請問你介意我開窗嗎？

　Would you mind if we used the restroom?

　請問你介意我用化妝室嗎？

c. would you like…或 would you like to…表達提供某件事情或邀請。

　Would you like to come visit us?

　請問你可以拜訪我嗎？

　Would you like another drink?

　請問你還要其他飲料嗎？

d. I would like…或 I would like to... 表示想要的事物或想做的事 = I want 或 I want to

　I'd like that one please.

　我想要這個。

　I'd like to go home now.

　我現在想要回家。

e. I would rather 表示偏好

I'd rather have some tea.

我比較想要茶。

I'd rather ask him to leave now.

我寧願現在就請他離開。。

f. I would think 或 I would imagine 是在提供想法或意見

It's very difficult I would imagine.

我可以想見這很困難。

I would think that's the right answer.

我想這是正確的答案。

換你選選看：

( ) 1. It's so hot! Would you _____ to drink some water?

  Ⓐ care

  Ⓑ mind

  Ⓒ like

( ) 2. A: Do you want to go out for a drink?

  B: Actually, I'd _____, if you don't mind.

  Ⓐ prefer not

  Ⓑ rather not

  Ⓒ don't want

( ) 3. I really need to go now. Would you mind _____ early?

  Ⓐ leaving

  Ⓑ if I leaving

  Ⓒ if I left

( ) 4. A: Do you want to see a movie tonight?

  B: That'd be great! I'd _____.

  Ⓐ rather not

Ⓑ love to

Ⓒ prefer to

（　　）5. A: Would you mind saying that again?

　　　　B: _____.

　　　　Ⓐ Yes, I wouldn't.

　　　　Ⓑ No, I would.

　　　　Ⓒ No, of course.

（　　）6. Would you mind if I ____ beside you?

　　　　Ⓐ sit

　　　　Ⓑ sitting

　　　　Ⓒ sat

 答案與中譯解析：

1. 好熱喔！你想要喝一些水嗎？（答：Ⓒ，would like 表示「想要」。）

2. A：你想出去喝一杯嗎？ B：我寧願不要，如果你不介意的話。（答：Ⓑ，would rather not 表示「寧願不要」。）

3. 我真的需要走了。你介意我先離開嗎？（答：Ⓒ，Would you mind if+ 過去式動詞表示「請求允許」。）

4. A: 你今天晚上想看電影嗎？ B: 那太好了！我願意。（答：Ⓑ，would love to 表示「願意」。）

5. A: 你介意再說一遍嗎？ B: 不，當然不會。（答：Ⓑ，問句用 would 問，答句也用 would 回答）

6. 如果我坐你旁邊，你會介意嗎？（答：Ⓒ，Would you mind if+ 過去式動詞表示「請求允許」）

C. may & might

1. may 使用在我們不是很確定一件事情的時候

There may not be many people for today's class.

今天的課可能不會有很多人。

We may be late for the meeting.

我們今天會議可能會遲到。

2. may 可用來表達很有禮貌的請求

May I borrow the car tomorrow?

我明天可以借用你的車嗎？

May we come a little later?

我們可以晚一點到嗎？

3. may not 可用在表達強烈的拒絕

A: May I borrow the car tomorrow?

A: 我明天可以跟你借車嗎？

B: You may not borrow the car until you can be more careful with it.

B: 直到你開車能更小心一點，你才可以借。

A: May we come a little later?

A: 我可以晚一點到嗎？

B: No. You may not!

B: 你不行！

4. might 使用在不很確定一件事的時候。跟 may 一樣可用在現在式中

I might see you tomorrow. 我可能明天會去看你。

The tie looks nice, but it might be very expensive.

這領帶看起來很好，但是可能太貴。

5. 用在禮貌請求 may 的過去式

He asked if he might borrow the car.

他想問他是否可以借車。

They wanted to know if they might come later.

他們想知道是否可以晚一點到。

6. 非常有禮貌的請求

Might I ask how you heard about our company?

請問一下您是怎麼知道我們公司的？

Might we just interrupt for a second?

請問我們可以打擾一下嗎？

7. may have 與 might have 表是對已發生的事情的推測，而事情有持續的狀態

It's ten o'clock. They might have arrived now.

現在十點了。他們可能已經到了。

Olivia wasn't in class today. She may have been sick.

Olivia 今天沒有來上課。她可能生病了。

8. 注意： might have 也用在假設語氣中與過去事實相反的假設。

He might have been here if you had asked him to come.

他本來可以在這如果你有叫他來的話。

You didn't ask him to come and he wasn't here.

你沒有叫他所以他不在這。

換你選選看：

(　) 1. _____ I have your attention, please? Ⓐ May 　Ⓑ Might

(　) 2. Polly wondered if she _____ borrow some money. Ⓐ may
Ⓑ might

(　) 3. They _____ come see me this weekend. Ⓐ may 　Ⓑ might

(　) 4. No one _____ not read my diary. Ⓐ may 　Ⓑ might

(　) 5. He _____ have forgotten all about the incident. Ⓐ may
Ⓑ might

(　) 6. _____ I talk to you in private? Ⓐ May 　Ⓑ Might

答案與中譯解析：

1. 請大家注意一下這邊！（答：Ａ，禮貌請求。）

2. Polly 不確定她是否能借一些錢。（答：Ｂ，禮貌請求過去式。）

3. 他們這星期也許會來看我。（答：Ｂ，表示不確定。）

4. 沒有人可以讀我的日記。（答：Ａ，強烈的拒絕。）

5. 他可能已經忘了事件所有經過。（答：Ａ　Ｂ皆可，事情的推測。）

6. 我可以私底下跟你講一下嗎？（答：Ａ，非常禮貌的請求。）

    D. shall & should

       1. shall 用在問句中，表示一禮貌的問句

         Shall we dance?

         我們跳舞好嗎？

         Shall I go now?

         我該現在走嗎？

         Let's go, shall we?

         走吧，好嗎？

       2. shall 在正式用法裡代表要求與義務

         Everyone shall obey the law.

         每個人都該遵守法律。

         There shall be no trespassing on this property.

         我們不能非法入侵他人的土地。

         Visitors shall not enter this room.

         旅客不能進入這間房間。

       3. should 表示意見、建議、偏好、或想法

         You should stay home and rest today.

         你今天該待在家裡休息。

         I should take a taxi this time.

         我這次應該要搭計程車。

He should be more careful in the process.

他在流程中應該要更小心。

4. 表示對過去曾經或不曾發生的事情一個相反的假設（should + have + Vpp）

You should have seen it. It was really beautiful.

= You didn't see it.

你應該要去看。這真的很漂亮。 ＝你沒有去看。

I should have completed it earlier to meet the deadline.

= I didn't complete it early.

我應該在期限之前要早點做完。 ＝你沒有早點做完。

We should have visited the place on the way.

= We didn't visit the place on the way.

我們在途中應該要參觀那地方的。 ＝我們在途中沒有參觀那地方。

5. 詢問意見

What should we do now?

我們現在應該怎麼做好？

Should we continue our meeting?

我們應該繼續我們的會議嗎？

Should we go this way?

我們應該這樣做嗎？

6. 表達期望發生或預期正確的事情

There should be an old building here.

這裡應該會有一棟老舊的建築。

Everybody should arrive by 6 p.m.

大家應該在六點抵達。

We should be there this evening.

我們今天下午應該要在那。

E. must & have to

1. must 表示基於合理的推測與充分的證據而做確定的推論

There's no air conditioning on. You must be hot.

這裡沒有空調。你一定很熱。

You must be proud of yourself that you've gotten this far.

你一定很自豪你自己已經堅持這麼久。

I can't remember when I did it. I must be getting old.

我不記得我什麼時候做的。我一定在變老的。

2. 對於過去的推論則使用 must have

Sue was working nonstop on the assignment. She must have been tired. Sue 一直沒有休息地執行計劃。她一定很累了。

3. must 表示必須的義務與必須去做的事情

I must go to bed earlier.

我必須早點睡覺。

They must do something about it.

他們必須在這件事上做點什麼。

You must come and see us some time.

你必須找時間來看我們。

4. have to 在肯定時與 must 意思相同，但 have to 可作時態的變化

He has to arrive at work at 9 am. （現在式）

他必須在 9 am 上班。

They'll have to do something about it.（未來式）

他們將勢必在這件事上做點什麼。

I had to send a report to the head office every week last year.（過去式）

我去年必須要每個禮拜寄報告到總公司。

5. have got to = have to

I've got to take this book back to the library today.

我今天必須要把這本書還給圖書館。

We've got to finish the preparation for the dinner soon.

我們必須盡快完成晚餐的準備。

在口語中，have／has 經常會省略，got to 合併成 gotta

I gotta go now. = I've got to go now. = I have to go now. 我們必須
要走了。

注意：have to 與 must 在肯定句裡時意思相同，但注意在否定句中代表
不同解釋

6. must not（mustn't）表示必須的義務，為一定不能做的事情

We mustn't talk about our salaries. They are confidential.

我們絕不能討論薪水。這是保密的。

I mustn't eat too much sweet. It's bad for my teeth.

我絕不能吃太多甜食。這對我的牙齒不好。

They mustn't see us talking or they'll suspect something.

他們絕對不能看到我們對談；不然他們會懷疑我們。

7. don't／doesn't have to 表示不一定需要去做的事

We don't have to get there on time.

我們不必準時到那裡。

You don't have to come if you don't want to.

你不需要來，如果你不想要來的話。

He doesn't have to sign anything.

他不需要簽任何東西。

F. need

1. need 當作必須解釋：可當作一般動詞使用，後面加不定詞 to

He needs to see a doctor.

他需要去看醫生。

Do you need to go to work tomorrow?

你明天需要上班嗎？

You don't need to be here.

你不需要在這裡。

2. need 也可當助動詞：一般用在否定句與疑問句，表示不必要的動作或詢
問是否有此必要

You needn't do the dishes. I'll wash them later.

你不需要洗碗。我待會會洗。

A: Need I lock the door when I leave the office?

A: 我離開辦公室之前需要鎖門嗎？

B: No, you needn't. Sarah will be back soon.

B: 不，你不用。Sarah 待會就會回來。

3. needn't 與 don't need to 的差別

You needn't come if you don't want to.

若你不想來，就不用來。

<u>不用當成一個義務。</u>

You don't need to be a genius to understand this.

你不必是天才才能了解這件事。

<u>不一定需要是這個狀態。</u>

G. had better

1. had better & should

had better 比較起 should 是給予更強烈的建議，已經有警告的語氣。

had better 並不是一過去式的使用，主要是現在或未來的建議。

You'd better tell her everything.

你最好跟她坦白。

I'd better get back to work.

我最好回去工作。

We'd better meet early in the morning.

我們最好早點在早上時相見。

注意：使用 had better 後不需加 to

2. 否定型式 had better not

You'd better not say anything.

你最好不要說任何話。

I'd better not come.

我最好不要去。

We'd better not miss the beginning of the presentation.

我們最好不要錯過報告的開頭。

3. 一般狀況的建議則使用 should

You shouldn't say anything.

你不應該說任何話的。

He should dress more appropriately for work.

他應該上班穿正式一點。

4. had better 建議一件事情如未照此情形發生，另一相反狀況則會發生

You'd better do what I say or else you will get into trouble.

你最好找我的話做，不然你會有麻煩。

I'd better get back to work or my boss will be angry with me

我最好回去上班，不然我的老闆會對我生氣。

We'd better get to the airport by five or else we may miss the flight.

我們最好在五點之前到機場，不然我們會錯過航班。

✎ **換你選選看：**

( ) 1. I've finished my work, so I _____ stay up late again tonight.
    Ⓐ don't must
    Ⓑ don't have to
    Ⓒ must not

( ) 2. You _____ try the shoes on, but it might be a good idea.
    Ⓐ don't have to
    Ⓑ must not
    Ⓒ don't must

( ) 3. This appliance _____ be used in the bathroom. It's dangerous.
    Ⓐ don't must
    Ⓑ don't have to
    Ⓒ must not

( ) 4. You _____ have a passport to travel to a foreign country.
    Ⓐ don't have to
    Ⓑ must not
    Ⓒ have to

( ) 5. Baggage _____ be left unattended.
    Ⓐ don't have to
    Ⓑ must not
    Ⓒ must

( ) 6. You _____ smoke. It is not good for you.
    Ⓐ don't have to
    Ⓑ mustn't
    Ⓒ haven't to

答案與中譯解析：

1. 我已經做完我的工作，所以我今天晚上不用再熬夜了。（答：B，don't ／ doesn't have to 表示不一定需要去做的事。）

2. 你不一定要試穿這鞋子，但是這可能是個好主意。（答：A，don't ／ doesn't have to 表示不一定需要去做的事。）

3. 這個電器絕對不能在浴室使用。這很危險。（答：C，must not（mustn't）表示必須的義務，為一定不能做的事情。）

4. 你必須要有護照去到別的國家旅遊。（答：C，have to 在肯定時與 must 意思相同。）

5. 行李絕對禁止無人看管。（答：B，must not（mustn't）表示一定不能做的事情。）

6. 你絕對不能吸菸，這對你不好。（答：B，must not（mustn't）表示一定不能做的事。）

Unit 24
連接詞

 搶先看名句學文法：

I have frequently experienced myself the mood in which I felt that all is vanity. I have emerged from it not by means of any philosophy, but owing to some imperative necessity of action. 我時常沉入一種情緒中，感覺一切都是虛幻。使我從中解脫出來的不是什麼哲學，而是不得不採取行動的需要。

本句出現 **but**，為連接詞的用法。

 英文達人小筆記！

英文的連接詞就像中文的標點符號，除了有喘一口氣的作用，也有轉折的效果，能突顯文句中的上下文因果、邏輯關係，懂得如何使用對於寫作有很大的幫助。

關於連接詞的詳細說明：

I have frequently experienced myself the mood in which I felt that all is vanity. I have emerged from it not by means of

any philosophy, but owing to some imperative necessity of action. 我時常沉入一種情緒中，感覺一切都是虛幻。使我從中解脫出來的不是什麼哲學，而是不得不採取行動的需要。

名言背景：英國哲學家、數學家和邏輯學家，致力於哲學的大眾化、普及化。1950 年，羅素（Russell）獲得諾貝爾文學獎，以表彰其「西歐思想，言論自由最勇敢的鬥士，卓越的活力，勇氣，智慧與感受性，代表了諾貝爾獎的原意和精神」。1921 年羅素曾於中國講學，對中國學術界有相當影響。

■ 連接詞的文法解析：

A. 連接詞的種類

1. 連接獨立子句

（關於獨立子句定義請參照第六單元附屬子句）

a. 對等連接詞：對等連接詞連接文法性質相同的單字、片語、子句等。

對等連接詞有 and、but、or、yet、nor、for 與 so。

I will eat a sandwich and some chocolate. （連接名詞）

我會吃一個三明治和一些巧克力。

I did not call nor email my mother. （連接動詞）

我沒有打電話也沒有寄信給我的母親。

The man was nice but weird. （連接形容詞）

這個男人很好但是很奇怪。

Today is Tuesday, and my projects due Thursday. （連接獨立子句中間需有逗號）

今天是星期二，而我的計畫截止日是星期四。

b. 連接副詞（關於連接副詞的使用請參照第十九單元副詞）

I need to study for my test; in fact, I am going to the library now.

我需要準備我的考試；事實上，我現在正要去圖書館。

c. 相關連接詞：相關連接詞為一組或一對的連接詞，其中包含 both...and、not...but、not only...but also、either...or、

Part I 句型文法

Part II 字詞文法

Part III 文法矯正篇

neither...nor、although...yet、whether...or。與對等連接詞相同的是，相關連接詞連接文法性質相同的單字、片語、子句等。

The name of the book is not New Moon but Breaking Dawn. （連接名詞）

這本書的書名不是新月而是破曉。

You should feel both excited and proud of your new achievement. （連接形容詞）

你應該為你的成就感到興奮與驕傲。

You can either make the payment online or make a wire transfer at a bank. （連接動詞）

你可以線上付款或者線上銀行轉帳。

Peggy not only finished her paper on time, but she also got an A+. （連接獨立子句時中間需有逗號）

Peggy 不只準時完成她的報告，也得到了 A+。

2. 非獨立子句（關於非獨立子句定義請參照第六單元附屬子句）

   a. 形容詞子句

      形容詞子句位於所修飾的名詞之後，由關係代名詞作連接，常見的關係代名詞有 which、that、who、whom、whose、where 與 when。形容詞子句其中又分作限定與非限定用法。

      The woman whom I talked to was my best friend at high school. （whom I talked to 修飾 the woman）

      跟我說話的女人是我高中最好的朋友。

      The class, which meets once a week, discusses the importance and use of grammar. （which meets once a week 修飾 the class。前後逗號代表形容詞子句為非限定。）

      這個班，每周一次課，是研討文法的重要與使用方法。

   b. 副詞子句

      副詞子句可以修飾定詞、形容詞、副詞、片語或整個句子。副詞子句由從屬連接詞連接。其中分成時間，假設，條件等。副詞子句在主要子句之前中間需用逗號隔開。

When she called, he had already eaten lunch.（when she called 在說明前後兩個事件的時間關係。）

當她打過來時,他剛吃完他的午餐。

I wouldn't take that job offer if I were you.（if I were you 在此作一條件的假設,此條件句在做與現在事實相反的假設。）

我不會接受這份工作,如果我是你的話。

c. 名詞子句

名詞子句可作為句子中的主詞,動詞或介系詞的動詞。一般名詞子句的連接詞為 wh 疑問詞、if／whether 或 wh 疑問詞加 ever。

Whoever wins the competition will receive the reward.（whoever wins the competition 名詞子句在此作為句子的主詞）

任何贏得比賽的人會得到獎品。

I don't know where the car key is.（where the car key is 名詞子句在此作為動詞 know 的受詞）

我不知道車鑰匙在哪。

3. 連接詞的比較

a. 對等連接詞可用分號取代

Jill didn't want any money; she didn't ask for it.（直接使用分號連接兩個句子）

Jill 不想要任何錢;她沒有去追求。

分號的作用如同連接詞 nor,nor 的用法如下:

Jill didn't want any money.

She didn't ask for it.

結合成為→ Jill didn't want any money, nor did she ask for it.

Jill 不想要任何錢,而她並未有所有求。

注意:nor 用來連接兩個否定句。使用時將第二句倒裝,並將否定字 not 去掉

b. 比較 although（從屬連接詞）、but（對等連接詞）與 however（連

接副詞），並將 although、but 與 however 與下面兩句結合：

The typhoon warning has been issued.

颱風警報已經發佈。

There are a lot of people in the beach.

有許多人在海灘上。

but 對等連接詞

The typhoon warning has been issued, but there are a lot of people in the beach.

颱風警報已經發佈，但是還是很多人在海邊。

→ but 對等連接詞連接兩個獨立的子句，but 一定放在句子中間，中間用逗號隔開。兩個獨立子句可互換位置

= There are a lot of people in the beach, but the typhoon warning has been issued.

還是有很多人在海邊，但是颱風警報已經發佈。

although 從屬連接詞

Although the typhoon warning has been issued, there are a lot of people in the beach.

雖然颱風警報已經發佈，還是有很多人待在海邊。

→ 此句 there are a lot of people in the beach 是主要子句，although 一定要放在副詞子句 the typhoon warning has been issued

= There are a lot of people in the beach although the typhoon warning has been issued.

還是有很多人待在海邊，雖然颱風警報已經發佈。

主要子句在前中間不需加逗號

however 連接副詞

The typhoon warning has been issued; however, there are a lot of people in the beach.

颱風警報已經發佈；然而，還是有很多人待在海邊。

however 作為兩句子的轉折詞，可出現在不同的位置
= The typhoon warning has been issued; there are a lot of people, however, in the beach.
= The typhoon warning has been issued; there are a lot of people in the beach, however

 換你選選看：

(　) 1. I asked everybody to calm down, _____ they still seemed to be angry. Ⓐ but 　 Ⓑ although 　 Ⓒ however

(　) 2. I asked everybody to calm down; _____, they still seemed to be angry. Ⓐ but 　 Ⓑ although 　 Ⓒ however

(　) 3. I asked everybody to calm down _____ they still seemed to be angry. Ⓐ but 　 Ⓑ although 　 Ⓒ however

(　) 4. I was so tired, _____ I still finished my work anyway. Ⓐ but Ⓑ although 　 Ⓒ however

(　) 5. _____ I was so tired, I still finished my work anyway. Ⓐ But Ⓑ Although 　 Ⓒ However

(　) 6. He studied hard _____ he was sick. Ⓐ but 　 Ⓑ although Ⓒ however

 答案與中譯解析：

1. 我要求每個人鎮靜下來，不過他們依然看起來很生氣。（答：Ⓐ。）
2. 我要求每個人鎮靜下來；然而他們看起來還是很生氣。（答：Ⓒ。）
3. 我要求每個人鎮靜下來，雖然他們依然看起來很生氣。（答：Ⓑ。）
4. 我覺得好累，但是我還是把我的工作完成了。（答：Ⓐ。）
5. 雖然我覺得好累，我還是把我的工作完成了。（答：Ⓑ。）
6. 雖然他生病了，但他還是努力唸書。（答：Ⓑ。）

Unit 25
介系詞與介系詞片語

 搶先看名句學文法：

I'd just be the catcher in the rye and all. I know it's crazy, but that's the only thing I'd really like to be. I know it's crazy. 我就只是想當麥田裡的捕手罷了，我知道這很瘋狂，但是這是我唯一想做的事，我知道這很瘋狂。

in 出現了，本句為介系詞的用法。

 英文達人小筆記！

　　英文文法中的介系詞（如 in、on、at…等）與由介系詞起頭，名詞或代名詞結尾的介系詞片語（如 in the store、on the sofa…等）皆有清楚表示地點、方位與時間的功能，且某些時間或地點必須接特定的介系詞（如 on Monday、at 10 o'clock），要加什麼介系詞似乎有點難記，但事實上是有規則可循的，且看接下來關於介系詞與介系詞片語的詳細解析與說明吧！

關於介系詞與介系詞片語的詳細說明：

I'd just be the catcher in the rye and all. I know it's crazy, but that's the only thing I'd really like to be. I know it's crazy. 我就只是想當麥田裡的捕手罷了，我知道這很瘋狂，但是這是我唯一想做的事，我知道這很瘋狂。

名言背景：The Catcher in the Rye 是為美國作家傑羅姆·大衛·沙林格於 1951 年發表的長篇小說，中文書名為《麥田捕手》。該書以主角霍爾頓·考爾菲德（Holden Caulfield）講述自己被學校開除後在紐約城遊盪，企圖在成人世界去尋求純潔與真理的經歷。他想要當孩子走進懸崖邊時抓住孩子，即「麥田捕手」。霍爾頓相信「麥田捕手」的任務就是保護孩子們純潔的天真，不要被虛偽的成人世界污染，rye 為裸麥或黑麥，in the rye 為「在裸麥田或黑麥田中」。

■ 介系詞與介系詞片語文法解析：介系詞為一個有語意連接功能的字，介系詞之後一定要接受詞。若介系詞後接動詞，則動詞需變成動名詞，若介系詞後面的受詞省略，則介系詞應跟著省略。介系詞分五類：1. 表時間的介系詞 2. 表地方的介系詞 3. 表相關位置的介系詞 4. 表位置移動的介系詞 5. 其他介系詞。介系詞片語是由介系詞與其後面的名詞片語組成，通常表「時間」或「地點」。

A. 介系詞的種類

1. 表時間的介系詞

in	年代、季節、月份、早上、下午、晚上
on	日期、星期、某特定日子
at	時刻、 at noon、at night
for	表一段時間
during	在…期間

She was born in 2000.
她生於西元 2000 年。

They are going to school in the morning.
他們早上將去學校。

She was born on the morning of October 10th.

在十月十日早上出生。

School starts on August 29th.

學校開學於八月二十九日。

Classes begin at 7:30 every morning.

課程開始於每天早上七點三十分。

We ate our lunch in the cafeteria at noon.

我們中午在自助餐吃午餐。

They have lived in Kaohsiung for three years.

他們已經住在高雄三年了。

During the summer vacation, people usually have a trip abroad.

在暑假期間人們通常去國外旅遊。

2. 表地方的介系詞

in	用於大地方，如國家、城市等。
at	用於小地方，如在學校。

They live in Canada.

他們住在加拿大。

Joe will meet you at school in the afternoon.

下午 Joe 將於學校與你碰面。

3. 表相關位置的介系詞

in	在…範圍之內	over	在…正上方
on	在…之上	under	在…正下方
at	在…正前方	below	在…下方
outside of	在…的外面	off	脫離…
inside of	在…的裡面	in front of	在…前面
between	在…之間	in back of	在…後面
behind	在…後面		

There are fifty students in the classroom.

有五十位學生在教室。

Three boys are sitting on the sofa.

三個男孩正坐在沙發上。

Tom's mother is standing at the door.

Tom 的媽媽正站在門口。

There is a red bridge over the river.

有一座紅橋在河的正上方。

A cat is sleeping under the table.

有一隻貓正睡在桌下。

A big parking space is below the blue building.

一個大的停車場在藍色大樓下。

The teacher is standing in front of the classroom.

老師正站在教室前面。

Let's go inside of the classroom.

讓我們進到教室裡面。

Mary is sitting between John and Jack.

Mary 正坐在 John 和 Jack 之間。

There is a beautiful garden behind the house.

一座美麗花園在房子後面。

Please take off your shoes before entering the room.

進房前請脫掉你的鞋子。

4. 表位置移動的介系詞

from	從…	out of	從…出來
to	到…	through	穿越
into	進入	across	橫越
along	沿著	around	環繞

How long does it take from your home to school?

從你家到學校要花多少時間？

I walk to school every day.

Part I 句型文法

Part II 字詞文法

Part III 文法改正篇

我每天走到學校。

Along the street, you will see a bank next to the post office.

沿著這條街，你將看到一間銀行在郵局隔壁。

He usually walks through a park to take a bus.

他通常走路穿越過一座公園去搭公車。

Be careful when you walk across the road.

當你走路橫越馬路時要小心。

He wants to travel around the world after graduating from the university.

他想要大學畢業後環遊世界。

5. 其他介系詞

with	和、用、有
without	沒有
in	在⋯方面、過一段時間、在⋯氣候中
for	給、交換、為了⋯、總價
about	關於、大約
of	⋯的、在⋯之中

Scott went to the party with Daniel.

Scott 和 Daniel 去派對。

I wrote the letter with a green pen.

我用一隻綠筆寫那一封信。

Rachel is the girl with long hair.

Rachel 是那位留長髮的女孩。

I never go to school without eating my breakfast.

我沒吃早餐絕不上學。

I bought the bag for two thousand dollars.

我花兩千元買這個袋子。

It is about five o'clock.

大約五點。

Students can learn about the basic knowledge of nature.

學生可以學習有關大自然的基本知識。

One of my friends is a doctor.

我的朋友之中有一位是醫生。

6. 介系詞片語

功能	説明
主詞補語	主詞的位置
副詞	動作的地點和時間
形容詞	修飾名詞

a. 當主詞補語

Those chairs are in the living room.

那些椅子在客廳。

b. 當副詞

Joan is swimming in the swimming pool.

Joan 正在游泳池游泳。

c. 當形容詞

The doll on the sofa is mine.

在沙發上的洋娃娃是我的。

 絕妙好例句：

1. Driving along the road, you'll see the bank.

（表位置移動的介系詞 along）沿著路一直開，你就可以看到銀行。

2. I was born on the morning of July 28th 1997.

（某特定日子的介系詞 on）我出生於 1997 年七月二十八日早上。

3. It is very convenient to live in the big city.

（大都市是大地方，介系詞用 in）生活於大都市是很便利。

4. Remember to pick me up at 10 o'clock.

（十點鐘是小時間介系詞用 at）記得在十點來載我。

5. Next week, we'll have a test on English.

（特定某一科的考試用 on）下週我們將有英文考試。

6. The buns are four for fifty dollars. 餐包四個五十元。

7. They ran out of the house when they heard their father's voice.

（從…跑出來介系詞用 out of）當他們聽到爸爸的聲音，他們從房裡跑出來。

8. Snow White is a beautiful princess with a kind heart.

（有…，介系詞用 with）白雪公主是一位有仁慈心腸的美麗公主。

9. He ran through the forest to search for his son.

（穿越…介系詞用 through）他跑步穿越過森林來尋找他的兒子。

10. Without his answer, I didn't know what I should do.

（沒有…介系詞用 without）沒有他的答案，我不知道我應該做什麼。

換你選選看：

( ) 1. Our teacher asked us not to write _____ green pens?
　　 A in　 B as　 C with

( ) 2. He was born _____ the morning of June 26th, 1997.
　　 A in　 B on　 C at

( ) 3. I am sorry _____ my being late. A for　 B to　 C with

( ) 4. He saw a cat jumping _____ the window.
　　 A along　 B by　 C through

( ) 5. We saw some boats _____ the bridge. A below　 B for　 C to

( ) 6. _____ autumn, the leaves of trees turned yellow.
　　 A On　 B In　 C At

( ) 7. There are some cars running _____ the road.
　　 A at　 B on　 C behind

( ) 8. He opened the door _____ curiosity. A in　 B with　 C out of

（ 　 ）9. His mother bought a house _____ twenty million dollars.
　　　Ⓐ by 　 Ⓑ for 　 Ⓒ with

（ 　 ）10. The earth goes ____ the sun. Ⓐ about 　 Ⓑ around 　 Ⓒ beside

（ 　 ）11. The little girl was sitting ____ her mother.
　　　Ⓐ by 　 Ⓑ besides 　 Ⓒ to

（ 　 ）12. The village lies ____ the mountains.
　　　Ⓐ around 　 Ⓑ among 　 Ⓒ between

 答案與中譯解析：

1. 我們老師要求我們不要用綠筆寫字。（ 答：Ⓒ，介系詞 with 表示「使用…」。）

2. 他生於 1997 六月二十六日早上。（ 答：Ⓑ，某特定日子的早上、下午、晚上，介系詞用 on。）

3. 我為我的遲到感到抱歉。（ 答：Ⓐ，be sorry for ＋ N ／ V-ing 表示「為了…感到抱歉」。）

4. 他看到一隻貓跳著穿過窗戶。（ 答：Ⓒ，介系詞 through 表示「穿越」。）

5. 我們在橋下看到一些船。（ 答：Ⓐ，介系詞 below 表示「在…下方」。）

6. 在秋天，樹葉變黃色。（ 答：Ⓑ，表示「在…季節」，介系詞用 in。）

7. 有一些車在路上跑。（ 答：Ⓑ，表示「在…表面上」，介系詞用 on。）

8. 他打開門是出於好奇。（ 答：Ⓒ，表示「出於…原因」，介系詞用 out of。）

9. 他媽媽用兩千萬買這間房子。（ 答：Ⓑ，表示「用…總價」，介系詞用 for。）

10. 地球繞著太陽運轉。（ 答：Ⓑ，表示「環繞」，介系詞用 around。）

11. 小女孩坐在媽媽旁邊。（ 答：Ⓐ，表示「在…旁邊」，介系詞用 by；選項 Ⓑ besides 表示「此外」，應改為 beside，才有「在旁邊」之意。）

12. 村莊座落在群山之中。（ 答：Ⓑ，表示「在…之中」，若數量超過三個以上，介系詞用 among。）

Unit 26
代名詞

 搶先看名句學文法：

You see I usually find myself among strangers because I drift here and there trying to forget the sad things that happened to me. 你瞧我經常總是在陌生人之中找到我自己我在此漂泊並試圖忘記發生在自己身上的悲傷之事。

myself 為代名詞的用法。

 英文達人小筆記！

　　代名詞包含反身代名詞、不定代名詞與數量代名詞，用來說明句子前方已出現過的名詞。關於反身代名詞、不定代名詞與數量代名詞的用法，以下會有詳細的解析與例句。

關於代名詞的詳細說明：

You see I usually find myself among strangers because I drift here and there trying to forget the sad things that happened to me. 你瞧我經常總是在陌生人之中找到我自己我在此漂泊並試圖忘記發生在自己身上的悲傷之事。

名言背景：《大亨小傳》（The Great Gatsby）是美國作家法蘭西斯·史考特·基·費茲傑羅於 1925 所寫的一部以 1920 年代的紐約市及長島為背景的短篇小說。本書從一位耶魯畢業生 Nick 尼克口中來敘述男主角蓋茲比一生的故事。蓋茲比生活於紙醉金迷的奢侈毫豪門世界中，一心追求自己的浪漫愛情夢想，故事一直圍繞蓋茲心中的執著，卻也為自己帶來悲劇的命運。此段為男主角蓋茲感嘆自己飄浮於陌生人中，試圖忘記發生在自己身上的悲傷之事。而蓋茲比的發跡的故事也代表了美國夢。

■ 代名詞／反身代名詞／不定代名詞／數量代名詞文法解析：代名詞用於代替前面的名詞，以避免同一名詞於句中連續使用，造成文字的累贅，並有承接的作用。代名詞分為六大類：人稱代名詞、指示代名詞、不定代名詞、疑問代名詞、數量代名詞、關係代名詞。本章將就代名詞、反身代名詞、不定代名詞以及數量代名詞加以說明。

代名詞的種類

1. 人稱代名詞的分類

主格		單數形			複數形		
		主格	所有格	受格	主格	所有格	受格
第一人稱		I	my	me	we	our	us
第二人稱		you	your	you	you	your	you
第三人稱	男性	he	his	him	they	their	them
	女性	she	her	her			
	中性	it	its	it			

人稱代名詞主格其用法為當主詞和主詞補語。受格為當及物動詞與介系詞的受詞。所有格當形容詞用，後面接名詞。要注意的是兩個以上的人稱代名詞並用其順序為：單數：2、3、1（you, he／she, I）。複數：1、2、3（we, you, they）。

→ She likes his clothes.（she 主格當主詞）
她喜歡他的衣服。

→ I was often taken to him.（him 受格當主詞補語）
我經常被誤認為是他。

→ He is afraid of her.（her 受格當介系詞的受詞）

他害怕她。

→ You know them.（them 受格當及物動詞的受詞）

你認識他們。

→ My dad bought my brother a bicycle.

（my 所有格當形容詞用，後面接名詞 bicycle）

我父親買給我弟弟一輛腳踏車。

→ You, she and I are in the same class.

（單數人稱代名詞順序為 2, 3, 1）

你、她和我在同一班。

→ We, you and they will go to the same university.

（複數人稱代名詞順序為 1, 2, 3）

我們、你們、他們將去同一所大學。

2. 人稱代名詞 "it" 的用法

　a. 可用於表示「時間、天氣、距離」：

What time is it? It is three o'clock.

幾點了？三點了。

　b. 當形式主詞和形式受詞，代替後面的不定詞片語或 that 子句：

→ It is impossible to master math in one month.

→It 當形式主詞代替後面的不定詞片語 to master math in one month）

一個月內精通數學是不可能的。

→ I found it difficult to catch up with him.

→It 當形式受詞代替後面的不定詞片語 to catch up with him

我發現趕上他是困難的。

3. 所有代名詞所有代名詞用於避免重複，所有代名詞 = 所有格 + 名詞，其用法
如下：

> mine=my+ 名詞我的
> yours= your + 名詞你的
> his= his+ 名詞他的
> hers= her+ 名詞她的
> ours= our+ 名詞我們的
> yours= your+ 名詞你們的
> theirs= their+ 名詞他們的

→ This is my car; that is his.

　這是我車;那是他的。

→ His house is red, and mine is white.

　他的房子是紅色的,而我的是白色的。

→ Their parents want them join the swimming team. Ours don't want us to do it.

→他們的父母要他們加入游泳對隊。而我們的父母卻不要。

4. 反身代名詞當主詞與受詞同一人或物時,則需用反身代名詞。語氣強調時亦用反身代名詞。反身代名詞沒有所有格,故用 one's own+ 名詞。反身代名詞有單複數之分,列表如下:

	單數	複數
第一人稱	myself	ourselves
第二人稱	yourself	yourselves
第三人稱	himself herself itself	themselves

He finished the project by himself. 他自己完成這個計劃。

We ourselves walk home. 我們自己走路回家。

I have my own house in Taipei. 反身代名詞沒有所有格,故用 one's own + 名詞

我在台北有自己的房子。

5. 不定代名詞

a. 不定代名詞有兩部份：

（一）	both, all, neither, none, either, any
（二）	One⋯the other⋯ 一個⋯另一個⋯ One⋯the others⋯ 一個⋯其餘⋯
	One⋯another⋯the other⋯ 一個⋯另一個⋯另一個⋯ One⋯another⋯the others⋯ 一個⋯另一個⋯其餘⋯
	Some⋯ some⋯ 有些⋯有些⋯ Some⋯.some⋯ and still others⋯ 有些⋯有些⋯還有些⋯

b. both, all, neither, none, either, any 的比較用法如下：

	肯定句	否定句	任何一個
二者	both	neither	either
三者或三者以上	all	none	any

c. some（一些）（粗體）用於肯定句；any（任一個）（粗體）用於否定句、疑問句、條件句。

d. another, others, the others 和 the others 的分辨：（粗體）

	單數	複數
不特定	another	others
特定	the other	the others

I know neither of the two students.

這兩位學生我都不認識。

I know both of the students.

這兩位學生我都認識。

None of us can get into the classroom.

我們沒有任何一個可以進入教室。

Do you have any money?

你有任何錢嗎？

I have three sisters; one is a teacher, another is a doctor and the other is a nurse.

我有三個姐妹；一位是老師，一位是醫生，另一位是護士。

Lots of people are in the park in the morning. Some are dancing. Some are jogging. And still others are walking.

早上有很多人在公園。有些正在跳舞。有些正在慢跑。還有些正在散步。

6. 數量代名詞（粗體）

數量代名詞有 many, much, most, both, several, lot of, lots of, some, any,（a）few,（a）little,…等。有些「數量代名詞」用於可數名詞，有些用於不可屬名詞。

many 很多 several 幾個 both 兩者皆 a few 一些 few 一點點、幾乎沒有	＋可數名詞
much 很多 a little. 一些 little 一點點、幾乎沒有	＋不可數名詞
all 全部 most 大部分 a lot of 很多 lots of 很多 some 一些 any 任何一個	＋可數名詞 或 ＋不可數名詞

→ Many people want to join the club.

很多人想要加入這家俱樂部。

→ I only have little money.

我只有一點點錢。

→ Some money is from John.

有些錢是來自約翰。

→ I didn't know any of the students.

這些學生中任何一個我都不認識。

絕妙好例句：

1. To say is one thing; but to do is another.（不特定單一其他——another）
   說是一回事；做又是一回事。

2. None of the students was present yesterday.（三者以上沒有任何一人 —— none）
   昨天這些學生沒有任何一個人出席。

3. Don't speak ill of others behind their backs.（不特定複數的其他人 —— others）
   不要在別人背後說壞話。

4. He used to refresh himself with a cup of coffee.（he 的反身代名詞為 himself）
   他過去習慣用一杯咖啡來提神。

5. Any of us can't get in the library.（沒有任何一個人 any of... not）
   我們之中沒有任何一個人可以進入圖書館。

6. Gold is much more valuable than iron.（金子和鐵是不可數名詞，沒有複數型 不可加 s）
   金子比鐵更值錢。

7. If you have any left, please give me some.（any 用於 if 條件子句）
   如果你有任何留下來請給我一些。

換你選選看：

（　　）1. Five people were present in the meeting. One was a doctor and
　　　　 _____ were engineers.
　　　　 Ⓐ others　Ⓑ the others　Ⓒ another

（　　）2. The cars left one after _____.
　　　　 Ⓐ other　Ⓑ the other　Ⓒ another

（　　）3. Which of the four books does he want? _____ will do.
　　　　 Ⓐ Any　Ⓑ Some　Ⓒ One

（　　）4. We should love_____ family.
　　　　 Ⓐ our own　Ⓑ ours　Ⓒ ourselves

（　　）5. Whose car is it? It is _____.
　　　　 Ⓐ my　Ⓑ myself　Ⓒ theirs

（　　）6. He went his own way and I went _____. We already separated.
　　　　 Ⓐ myself　Ⓑ my　Ⓒ mine

 答案與中譯解析：

1. 五個人出席會議一位是醫生，其他人為工程師。（答：Ⓑ，特定複數的其他人 the others。）

2. 車子一輛接一輛離開。（答：Ⓒ，one after another 一個接一個。）

3. 那四本書之中他要哪一本？任何一本都可以。（答：Ⓐ，任何一個 any。）

4. 我們應該愛自己的家人。（答：Ⓐ，one's own+ 名詞，自己的…。）

5. 車是誰的？他們的。（答：Ⓒ，他們的，所有格代名詞 theirs。）

6. 他走他的路，我走自己的路。我們已經分手了。（答：Ⓒ，my own way=mine。）

Part III 文法糾正篇

Unit 27
常常混淆的時態句型

✓ 搶先看名句學文法：

People have been known to achieve more as a result of working with others than against them. 「我們都知道，人們透過共事能夠完成的比對立還多。」

名言背景：艾倫‧佛洛姆（1916-2003）是美國心理學家及作家，在哥倫比亞大學畢業之後，他在紐約市從事心理治療工作長達五十年。並透過出版書籍，以深入淺出的方式告訴人們如何處理日常生活的問題。本句中的 have been known 同時包含現在完成式（have+ ∨ p.p）和被動式（be+Vp.p），be known to 表示「為人所知」。

💬 易混淆時態句型小預告：

1. have been to ＝ 曾經去過…。
   have gone to ＝ 已經去了…。
2. 主詞 +used to+ 動詞原形 ＝ 過去習慣…。
   主詞 +be used to+ 動詞 ing＝ 現在習慣…。
3. have 和 think 的進行式。
4. just 和 just now 的誤用。
5. 不能用在完成式的時間副詞。
6. be going to 和 be 動詞 +V-ing 的混淆。

1. have been to = 曾經去過…
　have gone to = 已經去了…

have been to 表示曾經去過某地的經驗，have gone to 則是表示某人已經去了某地，因此，have gone to 前面的人稱只有第三人稱是合理的，例如：

- *I have been to Japan.*（我曾經去過日本。）→（O）
  I have gone to Japan.（我已經去了日本。）→（X）
  不合理，「我」不可能同時去日本，同時也在這裡說話。
  He has been to Japan.（他曾經去過日本。）→（O）
  He has gone to Japan.（他已經去了日本。）→（O）

2. 主詞 +used to+ 動詞原形 = 過去習慣…
　主詞 +be used to+ 動詞 ing= 現在習慣…

這個句型很容易產生混淆，如果沒有加上 be 動詞的 used to 後面動詞要使用原形動詞，表示過去習慣做某事，但現在已經沒有這個習慣；有加 be 動詞的 used to 後面動詞要使用動名詞，強調現在仍然習慣，例如：

- *He used to go to work my MRT.*（他之前習慣搭捷運上班。）
- *He is used to going to work by MRT.*（他現在習慣搭捷運上班。）

3. have 和 think 的進行式

have 和 think 用於簡單式和進行式中，所表達的意思不同。

have 若表示「擁有」，是屬於表示狀態的動詞，不可以有進行式的型態。但若作「享用、吃」，則可以有進行式。例如：

- *I am having lunch now.*（我現在正在吃午餐。）
  think 可以表示「認為、想」。若作「認為」解釋，表示的是心裡長期的想法，不可以有進行式，相反地，若表示「想」，則可以有進行式。
- *I think she is pretty.*（我認為她很漂亮。）→心裡長期的想法
- *Be quiet! I am thinking.*（安靜！我正在思考。）→現在正在做的動作

Part I 句型文法

Part II 字詞文法

Part III 文法糾正篇

4. just 和 just now 的誤用

just 可以用於完成式中，表示「剛剛完成」，但 just now 卻只能接過去式，表示「剛才」。兩者在中文的意思上差不多，但英文的語法上卻不同。試比較下列兩句：

- *I have just finished my work.*（我剛剛完成工作。）

  → just 強調剛剛做完的動作。

- *I finished my work just now.*（我剛剛才做完工作。）

  → just now 是強調剛剛做完的時間

5. 不能用完成式的時間副詞

可以明確表示時間的副詞，不能用在現在完成式，例如：last month、yesterday、this morning 等，只能用過去式。

同樣的道理，詢問某特定時間點的 when 和 what time 也不能使用於完成式句型。

但是，如果在特定的時間點前加上 since，便可以用完成式：

- *I have drunk three cups of coffee since this morning.*

  （從早上以來，我已經喝了三杯咖啡。）

6. 不能使用進行式的動詞

有些動詞不能使用進行式，這些動詞通常具有「繼續」的涵義，或是表示狀態、心理情感及知覺，例如：exist（存在）、own（擁有）、need（需要）、prefer（比較喜歡）、hear（聽）、see（看）、forget（忘記）、remember（記得）、belong（屬於）、like（喜歡）、love（愛）、hate（恨）、know（知道）和 want（想要）。以 want 為例：

- *I want a toy car.*（我想要一台玩具車。）→（O）

  I am wanting a toy car. →（X）

雖然「現在想要」，但 want 是屬於心理情感慾望的動詞，所以沒有進行式的形態。

7. be going to 和 be 動詞 + V-ing 的混淆

例如：

- *I am going to school.*（我正要去學校。）
  → go 是動詞，am going 是現在進行式。
- *I am going to go to school.*（我將要去學校。）
  → be going to 等於 will，後面的 go 才是這個句子的動詞。

談論到未來確定會發生的活動或事件時，可以用現在進行式代替未來式，但是記得後面要接有未來的時間，否則句子的意思會不一樣。

換你選選看：

( ) 1. Jason ____ Japan for three times.
   A has been to B has gone C go to

( ) 2. ____ has gone to America six days ago.
   A I B He C You

( ) 3. I ____ drink a cup of coffee every morning.
   A used to B am used to C used

( ) 4. 選出正確的句子

   A I have eaten an apple pie just now.

   B The apple pie makes me thirsty.

   C I am wanting to have some tea.

( ) 5. 選出正確的句子

   A Eric is going to visit Johnson this Friday.

   B They haven't met each other last month.

   C They are liking spend time getting along each other.

( ) 6. 選出正確的句子

   A He wants to plays the computer game.

   B He's owing this computer.

   C His dad has bought him this computer 2 months ago.

你寫對了嗎？

1. Jason 曾經去過日本三次。（答：Ａ，has been to 表示「曾經去過」。）

2. 他六天前前往美國。（答：Ｂ，has gone to 只能用第三人稱當主詞。）

3. 我過去習慣每天早上喝一杯咖啡。（答：Ａ，主詞 +used to+ 動詞原形＝過去習慣；主詞 +be used to+ 動詞 ing= 現在習慣。）

4. 蘋果派使我口渴。（答：Ｂ，Ａ選項 just now 和完成式不能一起使用，此句應改成 I have just eaten an apple.。Ｃ選項 want 不能使用進行式，本句應改成 I want to have some tea. I am wanting to have some tea.。）

5. Eric 計畫週五拜訪 Johnson。（答：Ａ，Ｂ選項 last month 若和完成式一起使用，應加上 since，本句應寫成 They haven't met each other since last month.。Ｃ選項 like 不能使用進行式，應將此句改寫為 They like to spend time getting together.。）

6. 他爸爸兩個月前買了台電腦給他。
   （答：Ｃ，Ａ選項 to 後面要使用原形動詞，Ｂ選項 own 不能使用進行式，本句正確寫法為 He owns this computer.）

Unit 28
常常混淆的名詞

 搶先看名句學文法：

It's fine to celebrate success but it is more important to heed the lessons of failure.「慶祝成功是好事，但記取失敗的教訓更重要。」

名言背景：

比爾・蓋茲（1955-）創立了微軟公司，同時也是美國著名企業家、軟體工程師及慈善家。比爾蓋茲在 13 歲的時候，就開始了電腦程式設計，在哈佛大學求學期間，蓋茲開發了一個程式語言版本，並設計了為第一台微型電腦 - MITS 牛郎星。本句是以虛主詞 It 代替兩個不定詞（to celebrate 和 to heed），因此本句也可以寫成 To celebrate success is fine but to heed the lessons of failure is more important.

 易混淆名詞小預告：

1. 搞不清楚什麼時候要大寫？
2. 名詞單複數與所有格的混淆。
3. 動名詞和不定詞的混淆。
4. can't help 後面到底要用動名詞還是原形動詞。

1. 搞不清楚什麼時候要大寫什麼時候名詞要用大寫呢？

首先，特定的名稱要大寫，這包含了人名、公司品牌、稱謂、地方名稱、歷史事件、宗教、國籍、種族、行星等，例如 Jennifer、Apple、Mom、Japan、World War II、Christian、Chinese、Denmark、Mars。其中，如果稱謂前面有所有格，那麼稱謂就可以小寫，例如 my dad。

其次，單一字母開頭的字要大寫，例如 X-ray、T-shirt、U-turn。

最後，文章、電影、書籍等的標題和表示時間的星期、月份、假日要大寫，例如 Chapter one、Mansfield park、Monday、April、Christmas。但是季節不能大寫，例如 summer、winter。

2. 名詞單複數所有格的混淆

常常有人搞不清楚，究竟兩個人一起的所有格，要把 's 放在後面還是兩個人名後面都放，試比較下面兩個句子：

- *Jason and Ella's bicycle is blue.*（Jason 和 Ella 的腳踏車是藍色的。）
   →兩個人一起擁有，腳踏車只有一台。
- *Jason's and Ella's bicycle are blue.*（Jason 和 Ella 的腳踏車都是藍色的。）
   →兩個人各自都有腳踏車，腳踏車有兩台。

你發現不同了嗎？當只有第二個人名後面加 's，才是表示兩人共有的，因此動詞要用單數動詞，若兩個人名後面各自加 's，那就表示兩個人都獨自擁有，所以用複數動詞。

3. 動名詞和不定詞混淆

不定詞和動名詞兩者都具有名詞的功能，可以做主詞、受詞或補語，例如：

- *To see is to believe.*（眼見為憑。）
   → To see 是句子的主詞，to believe 為主詞補語。
- *Seeing is believing.*（眼見為憑。）
   → seeing 是主詞，believing 是主詞補語。
- *She likes to read.*（她喜歡閱讀。）
   → to read 做 like 的受詞。
- *She likes reading.*（她喜歡閱讀。）
   → reading 做 like 的受詞。

但是只有動名詞可以做介系詞的受詞：

- *Eric doesn't want to spend time in playing computer games.*
  （Eric 不想花時間在打電腦遊戲上。）
  →在介系詞 in 後面的 play 要改為動名詞

有些動詞後面接動名詞或不定詞，表達的意思不同。這些動詞如動詞 stop、remember 和 forget，後面接續動名詞時，分別表示停止正在做的事、記得做過的事和忘記做過的事；若接續不定詞，則代表停止原本做的事，去做另一件事、記得去做某事和忘記去做某事，例如：

- *I remember mopping the floor.*（我記得我有拖地。）
  → remember+ 動名詞，表示記得有做過。
- *I remember to mop the floor.*（我記得要去拖地。）
  → remember+ 不定詞，表示記得要去做。

有些動詞後面接動名詞或不定詞，表達的意思相同

love（喜愛）、like（喜歡）和 hate（恨）後接續動名詞或不定詞，意義大致相同，只是接續動名詞，語氣強烈程度會稍微比不定詞大，例如：

- *I love reading comic book.*
  =*I love to read comic book.*

兩者都是表示「我喜歡閱讀漫畫書。」，但第一句表達喜愛的程度會比第二句來的強烈與確定。

4. can't help 後面到底要用動名詞還是原形動詞

在前面的句型中，我們學到在 can't help 後面加上動名詞，可以表示「忍不住…」，但是如果在 help 後面加上 but，也具有同樣的意思，只是，這時候的動詞就不可以用動名詞，而必須用動詞原形，例如：

- *When Kim heard this news, she can't help but laugh.*
  （當 Kim 聽到這個消息，忍不住笑了起來。）

換你選選看：

1. 選出正確的句子

    Ⓐ Last Summer, my family and I went on a picnic there in M ountain a-li.

    Ⓑ My Mom prepared some sandwiches, hot dogs and orange juice.

    Ⓒ Dad forgot to put them into the trunk.

2. 選出正確的句子

    Ⓐ We were angry but can't do anything about it.

    Ⓑ We decided go hiking.

    Ⓒ Wendy and Stella's shoes are pink and white.

3. 選出正確的句子

    Ⓐ Jimmy saw May eating an ice cream cone.

    Ⓑ Jimmy saw May is eating an ice cream cone.

    Ⓒ Jimmy saw May ate an ice cream cone.

4. My mom made me _____ the floor. Ⓐ swept　Ⓑ sweep　Ⓒ to sweep

5. Do you remember _____ the laundry? Ⓐ to do　Ⓑ do　Ⓒ did

6. She can't help but _____. Ⓐ cry　Ⓑ to cry　Ⓒ crying

 你寫對了嗎？

1. 爸爸忘記把它們放進後車廂。（答：Ⓒ，Ⓐ選項應將 summer 改為小寫，Ⓑ選項應將 mom 改為小寫。）

2. 我們很生氣，但也沒辦法做些什麼。（答：Ⓐ，Ⓑ選項 decided 和 go 之間要加 to，Ⓒ選項應為 Wendy's and Stella's。）

3. Jimmy 看到 May 正在吃冰淇淋甜筒。（答：Ⓐ，感官動詞後可接原形動詞或現在分詞。）

4. 我媽媽叫我掃地。（答：Ⓑ，使役動詞接原形動詞。）

5. 你記得要洗衣服嗎？（答：Ⓐ，remember 後面接動名詞或不定詞。）

6. 她忍不住哭出來。（答：Ⓐ，can't help but ＋原形動詞。）

Unit 29
常常混淆的介系詞

✓ 搶先看名句學文法：

Logic will get you from A to B. Imagination will take you everywhere. 「邏輯可以將你由 A 點帶到 B 點，想像則可以帶你到任何地方。」

名言背景：愛因斯坦（1879-1955）為理論物理學家，創立了相對論，其質能方程式 E = mc2 被稱作「全世界最著名的方程式」。他也因為發現光電效應，對理論物理有顯著的貢獻，在 1921 年獲頒諾貝爾物理學獎，被認作是現代物理學之父。本句中 from 和 to 都是介系詞，分別表示「從…」以及「到…」，from A to B 表示「從地點 A 到 B」，from time to time 表示「有時」。

💬 易混淆介系詞小預告：

1. at ／ in ／ on ＋ 慣用的地方。
2. to 作介系詞使用時，後面的動詞要加 ing。
3. 有些用語的介系詞不能使用或是可以省略的地方。
4. 常用字的混淆：during & during ；with & between；in the way & on the way；dream of & dream about。
5. of ／ with ＋ 抽象名詞怎麼用。
6. 使用錯誤的介系詞。

1. at ／ in ／ on + 慣用的地方

在之前我們提到，這三個介系詞的基本原則為〈at+ 小地方〉、〈in+ 大地方〉而〈on+ 特定地方〉，但有些地點沒有辦法使用這個原則，而是要搭配特定的 at、in 或是 on，在使用上常常會造成混淆。這些地方如下表：

常被混淆的 at ／ in ／ on		
at +	in+	on+
（1）某一點的位置	線狀地點中的一點	線狀地點
（2）娛樂場所	有環繞感的環境	與垂直平面接觸的位置
（3）讀書場所	獨立的環境	面部表情
（4）活動的名稱	柔軟的身體部位	身體表面
（5）地址的號碼	街道名稱（英式英文）	街道名稱（美式英文）
（6）地址的街道和號碼	創傷	樓層

（1）　某一點的位置：at the crossroad、at the desk、at the door 等。

（2）　娛樂場所：at a pub、at a club、at a theater、at a restaurant 等。

（3）　讀書場所：at university、at school 等。

（4）　活動的名稱：at a concert、at a meeting、at a party、at a match 等。

（5）　地址的號碼：at number 50、at number 10 等。

（6）　地址的街道和號碼：只要有號碼出現，都要用 at，例如 at 11 Green Street。

（7）　線狀地點中的一點：in the third row、in the river 等。

（8）　有環繞感的環境：in the cupboard、in the house、in the grass 等。

（9）　獨立的環境：in the field、in the car park 等。

（10）柔軟的身體部位：in the eye ／ mouth ／ stomach 等。

（11）街道名稱（英式英文）：in Green street、in Red Avenue 等。

（12）創傷：was hurt in the shoulder ／ head ／ leg 等。

（13）在上方：on the row、on the river、on the road 等。

（14）與垂直平面接觸的位置：on the table、on the sofa、on the floor 等。

（15）面 部 表 情：an expression of anger ／ cunning ／ eager on one's face。

（16）身體表面：on the skin、on the shoulder、on the face 等。

（17）街道名稱：on Black Road、on Purple Street 等。

（18）樓層：on the second floor、on the tenth floor 等。

2. to 作介系詞使用時，後面的動詞要加 ing

一般而言，to 後面的動作要使用原形，但是作為介系詞使用的 to，後面的動詞卻要使用 V-ing 的形式，這一類型的片語常見的有：

to 後面要加 V-ing 的片語			
look forward to	期待	owing to	由於
in addition to	除…以外	due to	由於
with regard to	關於	as to	至於
with reference to	關於	be used to	（現在）習慣於
according to	根據	get used to	漸漸習慣於
compared to	相較而言	be accustomed to	習慣於
be a key to	為…的關鍵	be relative to	相關
be a way to	通往…的方法	be a pressure to	造成…的壓力

3. 有些用語的介系詞不能使用或是可以省略

介系詞可以使句子中的各個語詞產生關係，但是卻不能濫用，有些用語是不能使用介系詞的，這些語詞有：

不使用介系詞或是介系詞可以省略的用語		
（1）to discuss about（討論）	（4）to+ home ／ here ／ there	（6）（in）the same ／ this way
（2）to marry with（結婚）	（5）on ／ in ／ at + next ／ last ／ this ／ one ／ every ／ each ／ some ／ any ／ all	（7）（on）一週七天
（3）to lack of		（8）（at）what time

（1）to discuss 不能加 about，但是 a discussion 卻要加 about：

- *They discussed the movie.*（他們討論這部電影。）
- *We had a discussion about the movie.*（我們針對這部電影進行討論。）

（2）to marry 後面不能加 with，但是 get married 要加 to：

- *Henry married Jane.*
  =*Henry got married to Jane.*（Henry 和 Jane 結婚。）

（3）to lack 不加 of，但是 a lack 後面加 of，也有 to be lacking in 的用法：

- *I don't lack anything.*
  = *I lack for nothing.*（我什麼都不缺。）
  → lack 不能加 of，但可以加 for。

- *Money is a lack of this family.*
  =*The family is lacking in money.*
  （這個家庭很缺錢。）

（4）在 home ／ here ／ there 前不能有 to：

- *I am going to home ／ there.*（X）
  應改成 I am going home ／ there.（我正要回家／去那裡。）

- *She is coming to here.*（X）
  應改成 She is coming here.（她正要來這裡。）

在正統文法裡，here 和 there 是地方副詞，前面不能加介系詞；在口語中，有時為了強調所在的位置，會在前面加上介系詞，但是這是非正式的用法。

（5）next ／ last ／ this ／ one ／ every ／ each ／ some ／ any ／ all 的前面不加 in、at 或是 on，因為這些語詞並沒有特定點出明確的時間或地點，因此也無從判斷到底用哪一種介系詞，所以乾脆全部都不使用，例如：

- *We have an exam on next Monday.*（X）
- *We have an exam next Monday.*（O）
  （我們下週一有考試。）

在（6）（7）（8）的用法中，這些介系詞可加，也可省略：

- *My home is（in）this way.*（我的家在這個方向。）
- *See you Friday.*（週五見囉！）

Part I 句型文法

Part II 字詞文法

Part III 文法糾正篇

● *What time do you watch TV?*（你什麼時候看電視？）

4. 常用字的混淆

有些用語在使用上容易產生混淆，這些用語有：

（1）during 和 while：

during 表示「…的期間」，後面接名詞；while 表示「當…」，後面加動作，例如：

● *Steven usually reads during a meal.*（*Steven* 通常在吃飯時閱讀。）

→ during 加表示期間的名詞 meal。

● *Steven usually reads while he is eating.*

（當 *Steven* 在吃飯時，他通常會一邊閱讀。）

→ while 加表示動作的句子 he is eating。

（2）with 和 between：

表示關係中，單一對象用 with，兩個對象要用 between。

● *Her friendship with Mia is endless.*（她對 *Mia* 的友誼永不止息。）

→ with 加單一對象 Mia。

● *The friendship between Mia and Ella is endless.*

（*Mia* 和 *Ella* 之間的友誼永不止息。）

→ between 介於兩個對象 Mia 和 Ella 之間。

（3）in the way 和 on the way：

in the way 表示阻擋；on the way 表示在某事在進行中，例如：

● *Sam wanted to go to the bathroom, but the chair was in the way.*
（*Sam* 想去洗手間但椅子擋到他的路。）

● *Flu is on the way.*（現在盛行流感。）

（4）in the end 和 at the end：

in the end 表示「終於」，at the end 表示「在…結束時」。

● *Don't worry, you will be all right in the end.*
（別擔心，你最終會沒事的。）

● *He laughed himself hoarse at the end of this movie.*

（在電影最後，他笑到嗓子都啞了。）

（5）dream of 和 dream about：

dream of 表示「有⋯夢想」，dream about 除了表示夢想，還可以表示「夢見」。

- *I dreamed of being an astronaut.*（我以前夢想當太空人。）
- *I dreamed about being rich last night.*（我昨天夢見我變有錢了。）

（6）in time 和 on time：

in time 表示「及時」，有比預定時間略早的語感，on time 表示「準時」，有在時間上剛剛好的感覺。

- *I will be home in time for lunch.*（我會及時趕回家吃午餐。）
- *The 10:30 plane didn't take off on time.*（這班十點半的班機沒有準時起飛。）

5. of ／ with + 抽象名詞，代表的詞性不同

of+ 抽象名詞，具有形容詞的作用；with+ 抽象名詞，具有副詞的作用。例如：

- *He is a man of importance.*（他是一個很重要的人。）

  → of+ 抽象名詞，具有形容詞的功能，修飾前面的名詞 man。

- *He teaches his students with patience.*（他很有耐心地教導學生。）

  → with+ 抽象名詞，具有副詞的功能，修飾前面的動作 teach。

6. 使用錯誤的介系詞

下列情況或用語中的介系詞，常常被誤用：

（1）good ／ bad 是用 at，不是用 in：

- *My Mom is good in playing the piano.* →（X）
- 應寫成 *My mom is good at playing the piano.* →（O）

  （我的媽媽很會彈鋼琴。）

（2）arrive 是用 at，不是用 in：

- *Eric finally arrived in school at ten o'clock.* →（X）

  應寫成 *Eric finally arrived at school at ten o'clock.* →（O）

  （Eric 終於在十點鐘時抵達學校。）

（3）borrow 是用 from，不是用 to：

- *My sister borrows some books to me.* → （X）

  應寫成 *My sister borrows some book from me.* → （O）

  （我妹妹向我借了一些書。）

  若把動詞 *borrow* 換成 *lend*，就可以使用 *to* 作為介系詞，例如：

- *I lend some books to my sister.*（我借了一些書給我妹妹。）

（4）bump ／ run ／ drive ／ crash 是用 into，不是用 against：

- *The sport car bumped against the tree.* → （X）

  應改成 *The sport car bumped into the tree.* → （O）

  （這輛跑車撞上了這棵樹。）

（5）對於某件事的 idea 是用 of，不是用 to：

- *I have an idea to travel the world in 100 days.* → （X）

  應改成 *I have an idea of traveling the world in 100 days.* → （O）

  （我想要在一百天內環遊世界。）

（6）音量是用 in，不是用 with：

- *The children are sleeping, please talk with a quiet voice.* → （X）

  應改成 *The children are sleeping, please talk in a quiet voice.* → （O）

  （孩子們都睡了，請講話小聲一點。）

（7）收音機、電視、電話是用 on，不是用 in：

- *The music in the radio is beautiful.* → （X）

  應改成 *The music on the radio is beautiful.* → （O）

  （收音機播放的音樂很優美。）

  當 radio 與 telephone 和 on 一起使用時，要有定冠詞 the，例如 on the radio、on the telephone、on the phone，on TV 和 on the TV 卻有不一樣的解釋。on TV 表示電視正在播放的節目，on the TV 則表示在電視這件物體的上方，試比較下列兩句：

- *The show on TV is so funny.*（這個電視節目真有趣。）

  → on TV 表示電視播出的節目。

- *The vase on the TV is colorful.*（放在電視上的花瓶顏色珍鮮豔。）

  → on the TV 表示電視上方的位置。

換你選選看：

(　　) 1. Wen is good _____ cooking. Ⓐ in　Ⓑ at　Ⓒ on

(　　) 2. There is a magazine _____ the desk. Ⓐ at　Ⓑ in　Ⓒ from

(　　) 3. There is a stone _____ the river. Ⓐ on　Ⓑ at　Ⓒ to

(　　) 4. I live _____ 116 White Avenue. Ⓐ at　Ⓑ in　Ⓒ on

(　　) 5. I am looking forward _____ to the movies with you.
Ⓐ to go　Ⓑ go　Ⓒ to going

(　　) 6. In addition _____ bikes, they also went mountain climbing.
Ⓐ to ride　Ⓑ ride　Ⓒ to riding

✔ 你寫對了嗎？

1. Wen 很擅長烹飪。（答：Ⓑ，good at 表示「擅長」。）

2. 桌上有一本雜誌。（答：Ⓐ，某一點的位置用 at。）

3. 河流裏有一顆石頭。（答：Ⓐ，線狀地點中的某一點用 in。）

4. 我住在 White 大道 116 號。（答：Ⓐ，只要地址中有號碼的都要用 at。）

5. 我很期待與妳一同去看電影。（答：Ⓒ，look forward to 的 to 為介系詞，後面
要使用現在分詞。）

6. 除了騎腳踏車，他們也去爬山。（答：Ⓒ，in addition to 的 to 為介系詞，後面
要使用現在分詞。）

Part I 句型文法

Part II 字詞文法

Part III 文法糾正篇

Unit 30
常常混淆的形容詞和副詞

✓ 搶先看名句學文法：

I generally think if you do good things for people in the world, that comes back and you benefit from it over time. 「我覺得如果你為世人做善事，你將收到回饋並逐漸從中受益。」

名言背景：馬克·祖克柏（1984-）是知名社群網站 Facebook 的創始人、董事長兼執行長，2010 年被《時代》雜誌選為「年度風雲人物」，2014 年被富比士評比為史上最年輕的前十大億萬富豪。本句中的 good 是非常實用的形容詞，可以表示「好的、漂亮的、新鮮的、十分的、可靠的」，也可以作名詞使用，表示「好處、好事、優點」。

💬 易混淆形容詞與副詞小預告：

1. 形容詞和副詞的混淆。
2. 動詞和形容詞或副詞一起使用，有不同的意思。
3. 只能放在動詞後面的形容詞。
4. 分詞的位置不同，意思也不同。
5. how ／ so ／ too 和名詞連用時，要有不定冠詞。
6. 副詞位置的混淆。
7. 副詞的特殊位置。

1. 形容詞和副詞的混淆

大部分的副詞結尾為 ly，但有些形容詞的結尾也有 ly，因此常常和副詞產生混淆，例如：

- *He is very friendly.*（他很友善。）

  →正確的用法。

- *He talks to me friendly.*

  →誤將 friendly 當成副詞修飾動詞，錯誤的用法。

這類的形容詞有：friendly（友善的）、lovely（可愛的）、lonely（寂寞的）、likely（很有可能的）、lively（活潑的）、ugly（醜的）、deadly（致命的）、cowardly（膽小的）、silly（愚蠢的）等。

有些結尾為 ly 的語詞，可以同時做形容詞或副詞使用，例如：

- *A weekly magazine is published weekly.*（週刊每週都會出版。）

  →第一個 weekly 為形容詞，修飾名詞 magazine；第二個 weekly 為副詞，修飾動詞 publish。

這類形容詞和副詞都是 ly 結尾的語詞如：daily（每天的／地）、weekly（每週的／地）、monthly（每月的／地）、yearly（每年的／地）、early（早的／地）等。

2. 動詞和形容詞或副詞一起使用，有不同的意思

這類的動詞如：be 動詞、appear（顯現／出現）、sound（聽起來／聽）、taste（嚐起來／嚐）、feel（感覺／觸摸）、look（看起來／看）、smell（聞起來／聞）等，在和形容詞或副詞一起使用時，會代表不同的意思，例如：

- *He looks happy.*（他看起來很快樂。）

  → look 和形容詞 happy 一起使用，中文翻成「看起來…」。

- *He looks at the dog happily.*（他快樂地看著這條狗。）

  → look 和副詞 happily 一起使用，中文翻成「看」。

再看一個例子：

- *The cake tastes sweet.*（蛋糕嚐起來很甜。）

  → taste 和形容詞 sweet 一起使用，中文翻成「嚐起來」。

- *She tasted the cake quickly.*（她很快地品嘗了一下蛋糕。）

  → taste 和副詞 quickly 一起使用，表示「品嘗」的動作。

3. 只能放在動詞後面的形容詞 有些形容詞只能出現在動詞後面，例如：

- *The child is afraid.*（這個小孩很害怕。）

  → afraid 在動詞的後面。

- *The afraid child is Tom.*

  →將 afraid 放在名詞前修飾名詞，是錯誤的用法。

- *The frightened child is Tom.*（這個感到害怕的小孩是 Tom。）

  →若想要修飾名詞，可以用 frightened 取代 afraid。

這些形容詞有：awake（醒著的）、afloat（漂浮著的）、afraid（害怕的）、alike（相像的）、alight（點亮著的）、alive（活著的）、alone（單獨的）和 asleep（睡著的）等。

通常，這些形容詞也不會和 very 一起使用，例如：

- *The boy is very awake.*

  →用 very 來修飾 awake，是錯誤的用法。

- *The boy is wide awake.*（這個小男孩徹底醒了。）

  →用 wide 來修飾 awake 的狀態。

- *The baby is very asleep.*

  →不會用 very 來修飾 asleep。

- *The baby is fast asleep.*（小寶寶很快睡著了。）

  →用 fast 來修飾 asleep。

4. 分詞的位置不同，意思也不同

我們已經瞭解了分詞有現在分詞和過去分詞兩種。現在分詞多半帶有主動意味，過去分詞則表示被動意味，例如：

- *an interesting movie*（令人感到有趣的電影）

  →現在分詞表示主動。

- *a broken window*（被打破的窗戶）

  →過去分詞表示被動。

若分詞在句子中的位置不同，代表的涵義也會略也改變，例如：

- *the students laughing in the classroom*（在教室笑的學生們）
  - →現在分詞 laughing 放在名詞 students 後面，不僅可以讓我們知道學生在笑，也讓我們可以感受到在笑的動作。
- *a glass broken yesterday*（昨天打破的玻璃杯）
  - →過去分詞 broken 放在名詞 glass 後修飾，不僅讓我們知道杯子打破了，也幫助我們聯想到杯子打破的動作。

這種在句子中又像形容詞，又像動詞的分詞，可以表達狀態，也可以讓我們聯想到動作本身，使句子更具有動感。

5. how ／ so ／ too 和名詞連用時，要有不定冠詞

當 how、so 和 too 與形容詞一起使用時，後面若有名詞，名詞前面要有不定冠詞 a 或是 an，例如：

- *How pretty a woman she is!*（她是多美的一個女人啊！）
  - → woman 前有不定冠詞 a。
- *How pretty woman she is!*
  - → woman 前沒有不定冠詞，是錯誤的寫法。

再看一個例子：

- *It is so cold a day that you had better put on your sweater.*
  （今天很冷，你最好穿上你的毛衣。）
  - → day 前面有不定冠詞 a。
- *It is so cold day that you had better put on your sweater.*
  - → day 前面沒有不定冠詞，是錯誤的寫法。

6. 副詞位置的混淆

副詞在句中的位置，常常產生混淆，比較看看下面的句子：

- *We often play badminton in the afternoon.*
  （我們通常都在下午打羽毛球。）
  - →句中有動詞，副詞要放在動詞的前面。
- *She speaks Japanese well.*（她日文說得很好。）

→若動詞後有受詞，副詞應放在受詞的後面。

- *She speaks well Japanese.*

   →先寫副詞才寫受詞，是錯誤的寫法，也是常犯的錯誤。

- *She is often early.*（她通常都會早到。）

   →句中有 be 動詞，副詞放在 be 動詞的後面。

- *You will never see me again.*（你將不會再看到我。）

   →句中有助動詞，副詞放在助動詞後。

但下列三種情形，副詞可以放在助動詞或動詞的後面，也可以放在前面：

- *I must always to do the laundry.*（我總是必須要洗衣服。）

   →一般習慣將副詞放在助動詞的後面。

- *I always must to do the laundry.*

   →副詞放在助動詞 must 的前面，也是正確的寫法。

must 可以用〈have to〉代換，因此副詞也可以變換位置：

- *I always have to do the laundry.*

   →正確的寫法。

- *I have always to do the laundry.*

   →正確的寫法。

除了助動詞，當動詞是 used to 時，副詞的位置可以改變：

- *We always used to go to the movies on weekends.*

   （我們總是習慣週末去看電影。）

   →副詞放在動詞 used to 的前面。

- *We used always to go to the movies on weekends.*

   →將 always 放在動詞 used 的後面，也是正確的寫法。

7. 副詞的特殊位置

時間副詞，通常會放在句子的最後，例如：

- *He went to the library yesterday.*（他昨天去圖書館。）

   →時間副詞放在句尾。

- *He yesterday went to the library.*

   →將時間副詞放在一般動詞前，是很常見的錯誤。

地方副詞也多放在句子的最後面，但若句子中同時有時間副詞怎麼辦呢？看看下面這個句子：

- *They went there yesterday.*（他們昨天去那裡。）
  →先寫地方副詞，在寫時間副詞。

表示規律的頻率副詞，也多習慣放在句尾，例如：

- *They have a meeting weekly.*（他們每週開一次會。）
  → weekly 是規律性的頻率副詞，放在句尾。

- *They weekly have a meeting.*
  →將 weekly 等副詞放在一般動詞前，是錯誤的用法。

表示不定時間的頻率副詞，可以放在句中，例如：

- *She seldom goes to the movies.*（她很少去看電影。）
  → seldom 並非規律的頻率副詞，因此放在句子中間。

- *She goes to the movies seldom.*
  → seldom 放在句尾是錯誤的用法。

- *We often rent videos.*（我們常常租影片。）
  → often 表示不定時間的頻率，可以放在句子中間。

- *We rent videos very often.*
  →但是我們卻習慣將 very often 放在句尾。

有些表示評價的副詞，通常也會出現在句子的後面，例如：

- *You sing well.*（你唱得很好。）
  →正確的寫法。

- *You well sing.*
  →錯誤的寫法。

再看一個例子：

- *She dances badly.*（她跳舞跳得很差。）
  →正確的寫法。

- *She badly dances.*
  →錯誤的寫法。

✏️ **換你選選看或選出正確的句子：**

( ) 1. Ⓐ The baby sleeping on the bed is his daughter.

Ⓑ My sister elder called Amy.

Ⓒ Amy is elder than I.

( ) 2. Ⓐ The old man is an ill person.

Ⓑ Today is so hot a day that I want to go swimming.

Ⓒ He likes very much scuba diving.

( ) 3. Ⓐ She runs faster her brother.

Ⓑ He is taller than his small brother.

Ⓒ She can play the piano well.

( ) 4. Ⓐ Jimmy eats his breakfast quickly.

Ⓑ He in the morning drinks a cup of coffee usually.

Ⓒ He daily writes an English article.

( ) 5. The necklace is _____ than that one. Ⓐ beautiful Ⓑ more beautiful Ⓒ much beautiful

( ) 6. Andy is _____ boy in his class. Ⓐ taller Ⓑ tallest Ⓒ the tallest

你寫對了嗎？

1. 睡在床上的嬰兒是他的女兒。（答：A，B 選項形容詞 elder 應放在名詞前修飾名詞，C 選項應將 elder 改為 older，因為在動詞後面，通常會用 older 來表示「比較大的」。）

2. 今天真是熱，我想要去游泳。（答：B，A 選項中的 ill 不會和名詞一起使用，多半放在動詞的後面，本句可寫成：The old man is ill.，C 選項應將副詞放在受詞的後面，正確寫法為：He likes scuba diving very much.。）

3. 她鋼琴彈得很好。（答：C，A 選項測驗比較級，若有兩者進行比較，則中間要加入 than，正確的寫法為：She runs faster than her brother.，B 選項測驗形容詞用法，一般習慣用 little 加名詞，動詞加 small，因此本句正確的寫法應為：He is taller than his little brother.。）

4. Jimmy 吃早餐吃得很快。（答：A，B 選項測驗頻率副詞用法，不定期的頻率副詞放在句中，時間副詞放在句尾，正確的寫法為：He usually drinks a cup of coffee in the morning.，C 選項測驗頻率副詞，定期的頻率副詞放在句尾。）

5. 這條項鍊比那條項鍊漂亮。（答：B，兩個音節以上的形容詞，變成比較級，應在形容詞前面加 more。）

6. Andy 是他班上最高的男生。（答：C，最高級前面要加 the。）

Unit 31
常常混淆的連接詞

 搶先看名句學文法：

The mind is the limit. As long as the mind can envision the fact that you can do something, you can do it – as long as you really believe 100 percent. 「限制存在於心裡，只要你可以想像你要做的事，你就能夠做到 – 只要你真的百分百相信。」

名言背景：阿諾・史瓦辛格（1947-）為著名的健美先生及演員，曾任第三十八任美國加州州長並連任一次。他曾 7 次獲得健美比賽奧林匹亞先生（Mr. Olympia）的頭銜，被認為是健美運動史上的重要人物，並以健美形象進入演藝圈，拍攝膾炙人口的魔鬼終結者系列。本句出現兩次 as long as，做連接詞使用，表示「只要」，其所引導的子句可置於主要子句之前或之後，亦可用 so long as 代替。

 易混淆形容詞與副詞小預告：

1. 對等連接詞連接的語詞不對等。
2. neither…nor…不可以和 not 一起使用。
3. because 和 so 不能在同一個句子中出現。
4. although 不能置於句尾。
5. 容易混淆的 despite ／ in spite of 和 though ／ although。
6. 標點符號的誤用。

7. even though 和 even so 不要搞錯了。

8 有加逗點的是非限定用法（補述用法）＋沒有加逗點的是限定用法。

9 介系詞可以放在受格的關係代名詞前，但不能放在 that 前。

和連接詞有關的錯誤

1. 對等連接詞連接的語詞不對等

例如：*She wants some coffee and happy.*（她想要咖啡和快樂。）（X）

在 and 前後連接的語詞結構應該一致，若是單字對單字，詞性也應相等。本句
and 前連接 coffee，為名詞，則後面的 happy 不能以形容詞的狀態出現，應該為
happiness：

- *She wants some coffee and happiness.*（O）
  →名詞＋名詞，結構正確。

- *She wants some coffee and wants to be happy.*（O）
  → and 前後都是〈動詞＋名詞〉，結構正確。

在這種句型中，除了注意詞性要一致，也要注意類型是否對等。以上述句子來看，
咖啡和快樂是完全不相干的名詞，所以雖然在文法結構上沒有問題，但在語意邏
輯上卻顯得怪怪的。

- *She wants coffee and milk.*（她想要咖啡和牛奶。）

- *She wants to be a smart and pretty girl.*（她想要當一個聰明又漂亮的女
  孩。）

這兩句是不是合理許多呢？

2. neither…nor…不可以和 not 一起使用

請你想想看，當你看到這兩個句子，你會怎麼連接呢？

- *I don't like reading detective novels.*（我不喜歡閱讀偵探小說。）

- *My sister doesn't like reading detective novels.*（我妹妹不喜歡閱讀偵
  探小說。）

你想到了嗎？

- *I don't like reading detective novels, and my sister doesn't like, either.*（我和妹妹都不喜歡閱讀偵探小說。）

  →用連接詞 and 將兩句連接

- *Both my sister and I don't like reading detective novels.*

  →使用〈both…and…〉的句型，記得在動詞前加上 not 表示否定。

當然也可以用〈neither…nor…〉改寫，但下面這個句子是錯誤的寫法：

- *Neither my sister nor I don'tlike reading detective novels.*

  → neither 和 nor 已表示否定，不用在 like 前面加上 not。

neither 和 nor 本身就具有否定的意涵，若再加入表示否定的 not，就會形成雙重否定的句子，因此正確的寫法為：

- *Neither my sister nor I like reading detective novels.*

  （不論我妹妹或是我都不喜歡閱讀偵探小說。）

3. because 和 so 不能在同一個句子中出現

例如：

- *Because I was tired, so I went to bed early last night.*

  →在英文語法中，在一個句子中同時使用 because 和 so 是錯誤的。

這個句子可以這樣寫：

- *Because I was tired, I went to bed early last night.*

  （因為我很累，昨晚我很早就上床睡覺了。）

  → 用 because 表示原因

- *I was tired, so I went to bed early last night.*（我很累，所以我昨晚很早就睡了。）

  → 用 so 表示結果

4. although 不能置於句尾

though 表示「雖然」，位置多放在句子的結尾。although 和 though 意思相似，若置於句子中間，兩者可以代換，但 although 不可以放在句尾，看看下面的例句：

- *I drank some coffee yesterday, although I don't like coffee actually.*
  =*I drank some coffee yesterday, though I don't like coffee actually.*
  （雖然我不是很喜歡咖啡，但我昨天還是喝了一些。）
  → though 和 although 都在句子中間，可以互相代換。

- *I drank some coffee yesterday, but I don't like coffee actually.*
  =*I drank some coffee yesterday, I don't like coffee though.*
  （我昨天喝了一些咖啡，但是其實我不喜歡咖啡。）
  → though 放在句尾，除表示「雖然」，更強調「但是」的語氣

- *I drank some coffee yesterday, I don't like coffee although.*
  →將 although 放在句尾是錯誤的用法。

5. 容易混淆的 despite／in spite of 和 though／although

though 和 although 是連接詞，後面要連接完整的句子，但 despite 和 in spite of 則是介系詞，後面要接名詞或是名詞的相關語。其基本句型為〈despite／in spite of+ 名詞／代名詞／ V-ing 〉＝「儘管」

- *In spite of what I said, I still love you very much.*
  （不論我說過什麼，但我還是很愛你。）
  → in spite of 後面接疑問詞開頭的名詞片語 what I said。

- *I didn't get up early this morning, in spite of having lots of things to do.*
  （儘管有很多事情要做，我今天還是沒有早起。）
  → in spite of 後面接動名詞 having。

- *My little brother loves his toy car, in spite of its oldness.*
  （即使這台玩具車很老舊，我的弟弟還是對它愛不釋手。）
  → in spite of 後面接名詞 oldness。

因為 despite／in spite of 和 though／although 的意思非常接近，很容易在用法上產生混淆，試比較下列各句：

- *I didn't get up early this morning, in spite of having lots of things to do.*

  （儘管有很多事情要做，我今天還是沒有早起。）

- *I didn't get up early this morning, in spite of I have lots of things to do.*

  → despite ／ in spite of 連接名詞或動詞轉化為名詞型態的動名詞，本句為錯誤的寫法。

- *I didn't get up early this morning, although I have lots of things to do.*

  → though ／ although 連接句子，為正確的寫法。

和連接副詞有關的錯誤

6. 標點符號的誤用

標點符號於連接詞和連接副詞中的使用常常產生混淆。

對等連接詞中，若舉例兩個語詞以上，則最後的語詞前要加上連接詞，連接詞前要有逗號，例如：

- *She likes apples, banana, and watermelons.*

  （她喜歡蘋果、香蕉和西瓜。）

  →連接詞 and 前有逗號

- *Which one do you want, coffee, tea, or juice?*

  （你想要咖啡、茶還是牛奶？）

  →連接詞 or 前有逗號

但若只有兩樣語詞，則不用逗號。

- *I love cats and rabbits.*（我喜歡貓咪和兔子。）

  →連接詞 and 前沒有逗號

- *I won't tell anyone but you.*（除了你以外，我不會告訴任何人。）

  →連接詞 but 前沒有逗號

當連接詞連接兩個具有主詞的句子，連接詞前要加上逗號，例如：

- *My dad is a doctor, and my mom is a nurse.*

  （我爸爸是醫生，我媽媽是護士。）

  →兩個句子中有主詞，連接詞前要加逗號。

because 是一個例外，雖然連接的兩個句子都有主詞，但位於句子中間的 because 前不用加逗號，只有將 because 放在句首時，才需要用逗號將兩個句子隔開：

- *I don't want to talk to her anymore because she is so selfish.*

  = Because she is so selfish, I don't want to talk to her anymore.

  （我再也不想跟她說話，因為她太自私了。）

連接副詞在意思上可以使兩個句子發生關連，但應用分號或句號將其分隔，同時，應於連接副詞後加上逗點：

- *I was sick; however, I went to work yesterday.*

  = I was sick. However, I went to work yesterday.

  （我昨天不舒服，但還是去工作。）

7. even though 和 even so 不要搞錯了

請看下面的句子，這三句都是表示「即使下雨，我還是要去兜風」：

- *I go for a rideeven though it is raining outside.*

  → even though 是連接詞，可以連接兩個句子。

- *I go for a ride even so it is raining outside.*

  → Even so 連接兩個句子錯誤的用法。

- *I go for a ride. Even so, it is raining outside.*

  → even so 做連接副詞使用時，只能與一個句子連接。

和關係代名詞有關的錯誤

8. 有加逗點的是非限定用法（補述用法）
沒有加逗點的是限定用法

在關係代名詞前面加上逗號，表示針對先行詞補充說明，稱為非限定用法或補述

Part I 句型文法

Part II 字詞文法

Part III 文法紗正篇

用法；關係代名詞前沒有加上逗號，表示限定用法，試比較下列兩個句子：

- *My brother, who is in Japan, will come back next week.*
  （我的哥哥，他住在日本，下週要回來。）
- *My brother who is in Japan will come back next week.*
  （我住在日本的哥哥下週要回來。）

第一句的關係代名詞前面有加逗號，是補充説明哥哥住在日本的補述用法，因為是補充説明，如果省略，對句子結構不構成影響；第二句中的關係代名詞前面沒有逗號，是限定用法，説明哥哥不只有一個，而是有好多個，下週要回來的是住在日本的哥哥。

9. 介系詞可以放在受格的關係代名詞前，但不能放在 that 前。

例如：

- *Jason is the student（whom）I talked of last night.*
  （這就是昨晚我提到的學生 Jason。）
  → whom 為 talked of 的受詞，可以省略。

可以將介系詞 of 放在關係代名詞的前面，這時候的 whom 不可以省略。

- *Jason is the student of whom I talked last night.*

通常，我們可以用 that 取代 whom，但若前面有介系詞，則不能以 that 進行取代：

- *Jason is the student that I talked of last night.* →（O）
  Jason is the student of that I talked last night. →（X）

換你選選看（選出正確的句子）：

（　　）1. A We both like to play badminton and play dodge ball.

　　　　　B What would you like, ice cream and milk shake?

　　　　　C I can't play the piano, but she.

（　　）2. A Because hungry, I went out to grab a bite.

　　　　　B Neither David nor Kelly is happy.

　　　　　C You cannot eat neither ice cream nor French fries because you are sick.

（　　）3. A Both she and I don't like spiders.

　　　　　B Neither I nor my sister watch romantic movies.

　　　　　C Both she wants and I want to see this movie.

（　　）4. A Because she won the lottery, so she bought a sport car.

　　　　　B He doesn't believe because her lie.

　　　　　C Because her boss asked her to manage the branch company, she went to Japan.

（　　）5. A My girl friend is angry so I bought her a bouquet of flowers.

　　　　　B My mom is busy, therefore I need to prepare the dinner by myself.

　　　　　C I am not hungry although I didn't eat anything since last night.

（　　）6. A The movie isn't popular. I like it, although.

　　　　　B Neither Kelly or David got up early in the morning.

　　　　　C He can't play the piano or the violin.

Part I 句型文法

Part II 字詞文法

Part III 文法改正篇

你寫對了嗎？

1. 我們都喜歡打羽毛球和躲避球。（答：Ⓐ，Ⓑ選項應使用表示「或者」的 or，Ⓒ選項中，but 是對等連接詞，若前面為句子，後面連接的也應該是句子，本句 but 後面只有主詞，不能構成句子，是錯誤的文法，正確應寫成 I can't play the piano, but she can play the piano.（我不會彈鋼琴，但是她會彈鋼琴。）

2. 不論 David 或是 Kelly 都不快樂。（答：Ⓑ，Ⓐ選項中，because 後面要連接句子，本句應於 hungry 前加上主詞 I 和動詞 was，若不接句子，則應將 because 改為 because of，hungry 改為 hunger。本句正確的寫法是：Because I was hungry, I went out to grab a bite. 或 Because of hunger I went out to grab a bite.，Ⓒ選項中，因為 neither 和 nor 已經表示否定，不需在前面的動詞使用否定形態。本句應寫成：You can eat neither ice cream nor French fries because you are sick.）

3. 她和我都不喜歡蜘蛛。（答：Ⓐ，Ⓑ選項在測驗 neither…nor…的句型，在這個巨型中，動詞應依據較為靠近的人稱做變化，本句的動詞 watch 靠近 my sister，應將 watch 做第三人稱單數的動詞變化，因此這句應寫成：Neither I nor my sister watches romantic movies. 此外，若有兩個以上的人稱出現，一般習慣將第一人稱放在最後，故這句最為正確的寫法是：Neither my sister nor I watch romantic movies.，Ⓒ選項應將 wants 去掉。）

4. 因為她老闆要求他管理分公司，因此她去了日本。（答：Ⓒ，Ⓐ選項中，because 和 so 不能在同一個句子中使用，因此本句應改寫成 Because she won the lottery, she bought a sport car. 或是 She won the lottery, so she bought a sport car.，Ⓑ選項中，because 後面應連接句子，若要連接名詞，則應於 because 後面加上 of，因此本句可以寫成 He doesn't believe because she lies. 或是 He doesn't believe because of her lie.）

5. 我不餓，雖然從昨晚我就沒有吃任何東西。（答：C，A 選項中，若用 so 表示兩個句子的因果關係，so 的前面要有逗點，B 選項中，therefore 是連接副詞，用於連接句子時，前面的標點符號應為分號或是句號，同時，在連接副詞的後面要加上逗號，因此本句正確的寫法為 My mom is busy; therefore, I need to prepare the dinner by myself. 或是 My mom is busy. Therefore, I need to prepare the dinner by myself.）

6. 他不會彈鋼琴，也不會拉小提琴。（答：C，A 選項中，although 雖然和 though 在意思上可以互相代換，但是若 though 表示「但是」且置於句尾時，不可以用 although 代換，應將 although 改為 though，B 選項中，neither 和 nor 為一組的連接詞，不可以個別單獨使用。這句應該這樣寫：Neither Kelly nor David got up early in the morning.）

Unit 32
常常混淆的否定句文法

 搶先看名句學文法：

What is not started today is never finished tomorrow. 「今天沒有開始的事，明天絕不會完成。」

名言背景：歌德（1749-1832）出生於德國法蘭克福，是西方重要思想家之一，其作品含蓋詩、戲劇、文學、神學、及科學著作，最有名的即為《少年維特的煩惱》，是一部書信體的小說。本句中 never 屬於否定詞，即本身具有否定意味的詞，表示「絕不…」。

 易混淆否定句文法小預告：

1. not 的位置會影響句子的意思。
2. 部分否定不代表完全沒有。
3. I don't think 而不是 I think you don't。
4. any 開頭的否定詞 + but，but 具有 except 的涵義。

1. not 的位置會影響句子的意思

not 在句子中的位置會影響整個句子的涵義，比較看看下面的句子：

- *He tried not to lose the game.*
- *He didn't try to lose the game.*

你發現有什麼不同了嗎？

- *He tried not to lose the game.*

  → tried not 翻譯成「試著不要⋯」，這句的中文翻譯是「他試著不要輸掉
    比賽。」

- *He didn't try to lose the game.*

  → didn't try 是「沒有試著⋯」，這句的中文翻譯是「他沒有試圖輸掉比
  賽。」

但有些動詞不論 not 放在什麼位置，都不影響句子的意思。這類的動詞常見的有：
appear（顯現）、intend（試圖）、except（除了）、wish（希望）、want（想
要）、seem（似乎）、happen（發生）等，例如：

- *I wish not to lose the game.*（我希望不要輸掉比賽。）

也可以說成：

- *I don't wish to lose the game.*

2. 部分否定不代表完全沒有

若句子裡有 very、always、every 和 not 一起使用時，表示部分否定，例如：

- *The American doesn't speak Chinese very well.*

  （這個美國人中文說得不是很好。）

  → not very well 代表「不會不好，但也沒有很好」的涵義。

- *The rich man is not always happy.*（這位有錢人並不是總是感到快樂。）

廣義否定詞，舉凡 rarely、hardly、seldom、barely 等，也具有部分否定的涵
義，但卻不是完全的否定，例如：

- *He rarely makes breakfast for his daughter.*（他很少做早餐給女兒吃。）

  →很少不代表沒有。

- *She seldom plays basketball.*（她很少打籃球。）

還有一種句型〈almost+ no／never〉，也可以代表部分否定，例如：

- *There is almost no coffee in the cup.*（杯子裡幾乎沒有咖啡。）

  →幾乎沒有不代表完全沒有。

- *I almost never play dodge ball.*（我幾乎沒有打躲避球。）

3. I don't think 而不是 I think you don't

例如：

- *I think she isn't at home.*

  →句子中有 think 和 not 的時候，習慣將 think 改為否定使用。此句文法錯誤。

- *I don't think she is at home.*（我不認為她在家。）

  → think 改為否定語意，句子正確。

這類用法的動詞有：believe（相信）、suppose（推測）、imaging（想像）。

再舉一個例子：

- *He believes he hasn't met Tracy.*

  → believe 要改為否定型。

- *He doesn't believe he has met Tracy.*（他不相信他見過 Tracy。）

  →正確的句型。

這些動詞也可以用在簡答句中，例如：

- *I suppose not.*（我希望不會。）

  → suppose 後面直接加 not，形成否定簡答。

- *She believes not.*（她相信不會。）

4. any 開頭的否定詞 + but，but 具有 except 的涵義

no 開頭的否定詞若加上 but 一起使用，but 具有 only 的涵義，但是 any 開頭的否定詞和 but 一起使用，卻有不同的意思：

- *I can't speak any language but English.*

  （我除了英文，什麼語言都不會說。）

  → any 開頭的否定詞和 but 一起使用時，but 代表「除了…」。

- *He didn't talk to anyone but this young lady.*

  （他除了和這位年輕小姐說話，沒有和任何人說話。）

換你選選看：

( ) 1. I don't eat ＿＿＿ but a hamburger. Ⓐ nothing　Ⓑ anything
　　　　 Ⓒ everything

( ) 2. I won't believe you ＿＿＿. Ⓐ more　Ⓑ any　Ⓒ anymore

( ) 3. He ＿＿＿＿ but beer. Ⓐ drank anything　Ⓑ didn't drink anything
　　　　 Ⓒ didn't drink nothing

( ) 4. 選出正確的句子。
　　　　 Ⓐ I think she isn't stupid.
　　　　 Ⓑ The Japanese can't speak Chinese very well.
　　　　 Ⓒ He doesn't never ask Mia out.

( ) 5. The boss is far from ＿＿＿. Ⓐ satisfied　Ⓑ to satisfy
　　　　 Ⓒ satisfactory

( ) 6. There is no use ＿＿＿ this letter to her. Ⓐ write　Ⓑ to write
　　　　 Ⓒ writing

你寫對了嗎？

1. 我什麼都沒有吃，只吃了漢堡。（答：Ⓑ，nothing 和 don't 不可以一起使用。）

2. 我不會再相信你了。（答：Ⓒ，anymore 和否定句連用，表示「再也不」。）

3. 他除了啤酒，什麼都沒有喝。（答：Ⓒ，如果要使用 anything，則句子中要加否定詞 not，若使用 nothing，則句中不可出現否定詞。）

4. 這個日本人的中文說得不是很好。（答：Ⓑ，Ⓐ選項中，I think 連接的子句若有否定，則應將 think 改為否定，這個句子正確的寫法是：I don't think she is stupid.，Ⓒ選項在測驗雙重否定，若句子中出現兩個否定詞，就不具有否定句的涵義。本句應改寫為：He doesn't ask Mia out. 或是 He never asks Mia out.，但兩句的中文意思略有不同，前者表示「他沒有邀請 Mia 出去。」，後者表示「他從不邀請 Mia 出去。」。）

5. 老闆並不滿意。（答：Ⓒ，far from 後面要接名詞或動名詞。）

6. 寫信給她沒有用。（答：Ⓒ，There is no use 後面的動作要變成動名詞。）

Part I 句型文法　Part II 字詞文法　Part III 文法糾正篇

Unit 33
常常混淆的疑問句文法

 搶先看名句學文法：

But every time she asks me "do I look okay", I say, when I see your face, there's not a thing that I would change, Cause you're amazing, just the way you are. 「但每回她問起我 " 我看起來好嗎？ "，我回答，當我凝視妳的臉龐時，我一點也不想改變它，因為妳好美──就是妳現在的樣子。」

名言背景：這句歌詞摘自火星人布魯諾的〈就是你這個樣子（Just the way you are）〉。整首歌敘述男孩在說服女孩在他眼中是多麼美麗，不需要任何改變，最真實自然的樣子就是最美的。歌詞中的 Do I look ok? 意為「我看起來還可以嗎？」每當女孩這樣問男孩，男孩都會回答說「你現在的樣子很美（you are amazing, just the way you are）」。

 易混淆疑問句文法小預告：

1. 疑問句中的助動詞順序錯誤。
2. 疑問句中沒有助動詞。
3. 助動詞和情態動詞一起出現。
4. 疑問句的主詞是 who、what 和 which 時，不用助動詞。
5. 主要子句用什麼助動詞，附加問句也要用相同的助動詞。

1. 疑問句中的助動詞順序錯誤

助動詞在疑問句中的位置，是放在句首或是疑問詞的後面，這是一個很簡單的概念，但在使用上卻常常發生錯誤，例如：

- *You do want to take a trip?*（你想要去旅行嗎？）

  →錯誤的語序，助動詞要放句首。

  Do you want to take a trip?

  →正確的寫法。

- *What he did go last night?*（他昨晚去哪裡了？）

  → Did 應放在疑問詞的後面，這句是錯誤的寫法。

  What did he go last night?

  →正確的寫法。

但是在間接問句中，疑問詞帶領的子句卻要用直述句的語序：

- *I know what he had done.*（我知道他做了什麼。）

  →〈what+ 主詞 + 動詞〉是間接問句正確的寫法。

  I know what had he done.

  →錯誤的用法。

2. 疑問句中沒有助動詞

當句子中只有動詞時，變成問句要找助動詞幫忙，不同的人稱和時態，助動詞也會隨著改變，例如：

- *She plays the badminton every week?*（她每星期打羽毛球嗎？）

  →疑問句中，應將助動詞置於主詞的前面，本句的文法錯誤。

- *Does she play the badminton every week?*

  → she 的助動詞為 does，當句子中有助動詞時，後面的動詞要使用原形動詞。

上述的句子：She plays the badminton every week? 我們不能說是錯誤的寫法，因為在非正式的場合或口語中，直述句若結尾的語調上揚，也可以表示疑問的口吻，但這不是正確的文法，在書面或正式的場合，要謹慎使用。

若加入疑問詞時，要記得疑問詞後面也要有助動詞：

- *What you eat for breakfast?*（你早餐吃什麼？）

  →應在疑問詞後加入助動詞 do 或是 did，本句的文法錯誤。

  What did you eat for breakfast?

  →助動詞用過去式的 did，表示問發生過的動作。

  What do you eat for breakfast?

  →助動詞用現在式的 do，表示問習慣或事實。

3. 助動詞和情態動詞一起出現

當句子中已經有情態動詞時，變成疑問句不需要在加入助動詞，例如：

- *Leo can speak English well.*（Leo 的英文說得很好。）

  → can 本身就是助動詞，直接移到句首就可以形成疑問句。

  Can Leo speak English well?

  →正確的寫法。

  Does Leo can speak English well?

  → does 和 can 在同一個句子中出現，是錯誤的用法。

完成式的句子特別容易犯這種錯誤，例如：

- *You have called your mom?*（你已經打電話給你媽媽了嗎？）

  → have 是助動詞，移到句首即構成疑問句。

  Do you have called your mom?

  →句子中不能有兩個助動詞。這句為錯誤的寫法。

  Have you called your mom?

  →正確的寫法。

再看一個例子：

- *He has gone to Thailand?*（他去泰國了嗎？）

  → Has 應放在句首構成疑問句。

  Does he have gone to Thailand?

  →錯誤的寫法。

  Has he gone to Thailand?

  →正確的使用。

4. 疑問句的主詞是 who、what 和 which 時，不用助動詞

例如：

- *Who left the cell phone on the table?*（誰把手機留在桌上？）
  → who 扮演主詞的角色，直接加動詞。
- *What happened?*（發生什麼事了？）
  → what 是句子中的主詞，後面銜接動詞。
- *Which is Mike's coat?*（哪一件是 Mike 的外套？）
  → which 當主詞，後面直接加動詞。

但是，當這些疑問詞做為受詞時，還是要和助動詞一起使用，例如：

- *Who do you want to invite?*（你想要邀請誰？）
  → who 是動詞 invite 的受詞。
- *What do you want?*（你想要什麼？）
  → what 是動詞 want 的受詞。
- *Which one do you like?*（你喜歡哪一個？）
  → which one 是動詞 like 的受詞。

5. 主要子句用什麼助動詞，附加問句也要用相同的助動詞

例如：

- *You don't like hamburger, do you?*（你不喜歡漢堡，對吧？）
  →主要子句中的助動詞用 do，附加問句的助動詞也要用 do。
  You don't like hamburger, will you?
  →主要子句和附加問句的助動詞不一致，是錯誤的寫法。

再舉一個例子：

- *He can't play dodge ball, can he?*（他不會打躲避球，對吧？）
  →主要子句中的助動詞用 can，附加問句的助動詞也要用 can。
- *She is very nice, isn't she?*（她人真好，不是嗎？）
  → be 動詞也要一致。

但是若主要子句中沒有助動詞，附加問句的助動詞一律用 do、does 或 did：

- *You like reading, don't you?*（你喜歡閱讀，不是嗎？）

- *He wants to go to the party, doesn't he?*（他想要去這個派對，不是嗎？）

- *She went to the concert last night, didn't she?*（她昨晚去聽演唱會了，不是嗎？）

換你選選看：

(   ) 1. He didn't go to the library, _____?

       A does he   B did he   C is he

(   ) 2. Who _____ you this morning?

       A call   B did call   C called

(   ) 3. _____ the piano well?

       A Does Vicky play   B Vicky does play   C Vicky play does

(   ) 4. Do you happen to know who _____?

       A is she   B is her   C she is

(   ) 5. Do you mind _____ the TV down?

       A turn   B turning   C to turn

(   ) 6. Let's not go to the movies, _____?

       A shall we   B shall you   C OK

你寫對了嗎？

1. 他沒有去圖書館，對嗎？（答：B，附加問句和主要子句的助動詞要一致）

2. 今天早上是誰打電話給你？（答：C，疑問詞若當主詞，後面可直接加動詞）

3. Vicky 的鋼琴彈得好嗎？（答：A，疑問句中的助動詞應放在主詞前面，同時，句中的動詞要改成原形動詞）

4. 你剛好知道她是誰嗎？（答：C，間接問句中，要先寫主詞再寫動詞）

5. 你介意把電視轉小聲嗎？（答：B，mind 後面若加動詞，要使用動名詞）

6. 我們不要去看電影，好嗎？（答：C，祈使句若使用否定型態，附加問句習慣用 OK 或是 all right 來表達，本句正確的寫法是 Let's not go to the movies, OK ／ all right?）

Unit 34
常常混淆的加強語氣文法

 搶先看名句學文法：

Be determined to handle any challenge in a way that will make you grow. 「下定決心以能讓你成長的方式處理任何挑戰。」

名言背景：萊斯‧布朗（1945-）曾被華盛頓郵報譽為世界上最有影響力的思想家，他率先提出環境永續發展的概念，其於 1984 年創刊的世界觀察年度報告，被認為是全球環境運動的聖經。本句以原形動詞 Be 開頭，為祈使句句型。

 易混淆祈使句文法小預告：

1. 〈Why don't we…?〉和〈Why don't you…?〉不一樣。
2. Let's 和 Let 不一樣。
3. No 後面的動詞要加上 ing。
4. 和 and ／ or 一起的特別用法。
5. 祈使句的 go，可以直接加原形動詞。
6. What 和 How 開頭的感嘆句，主詞要在動詞前面。
7. What 後面要有 a 或是名詞變為複數；How 後面要緊連著形容詞或副詞。
8. 倒裝的順序錯誤。
9. Only 或否定詞的倒裝，改寫時應加入助動詞。
10. 否定詞本身具有否定意味，改寫時要特別注意 not 的使用。

11. 不是問句卻用了問號。

祈使句錯誤用法

1.〈Why don't we…?〉和〈Why don't you…?〉不一樣

在使用〈Why don't we+ 動詞原形…?〉時,要特別小心人稱的使用:如果將 we 改成 you 時,會產生完全不一樣的意思,試比較下面的句子:

- *Why don't we marry?*(為什麼我們不結婚呢?)
  → why don't we 用於建議你和我之間來做某事。
- *Why don't you marry him?*(為什麼你不嫁給他呢?)
  → why don't you 用於向對方提出建議。

2. Let's 和 Let 不一樣

Let's 是 let us 的縮寫,表示包含說話者在內的一群人;而 Let 表示「讓…」,後面要接受詞,比較看看下面的句子:

- *Let's go to the party.*(讓我們參加派對吧!)
  → Let's 表示說話的人和說話的對象都要去。
- *Let me go to the party.*(讓我參加派對。)
  → Let me 表示只有說話的人要去,正在請求聽者的同意。

如果是否定句的話,只要加 Don't 放在 let 的前面,例如:

- *Don't let him wait too long.*(不要讓他等太久。)

3.No 後面的動詞要加上 ing

No 加上動詞,可以用來表示強烈的禁止,但要記得動詞要改為現在分詞的形式:

- *No parking!*(禁止停車!)
  →動詞 park 接在 No 後面要加 ing。

No 後面加名詞,也表示強烈的禁止,這時候的名詞不需要特別的變化:

- *No way!*(不行!)

4. 和 and ╱ or 一起的特別用法

和祈使句一起使用的 and 和 or,具有談論條件的意味,and 和 or 表示相反的語氣，例如：

- *Study hard, and you will succeed one day.*

  （認真讀書，有一天一定會成功。）

  →只要認真念書，一定會成功，and 承接前一句的語氣。

- *Study hard, or you will get a bad grade.*

  （認真念書，否則你將會得到壞成績。）

  → or 表示「否則」，用來連接前後對立或是具有因果關係的狀況。

你發現了嗎？儘管 and 和 or 表示的語氣不同，它們所帶領的句子，都要用未來式。

5. 祈使句的 go，可以直接加原形動詞

在祈使句中，如果有兩個動作，中間要用 and 將兩個動作分開，例如：

- *Wait and see.*（走著瞧！）

  →兩個動作用 and 相連。

- *Open your student book and turn to page 11.*

  （打開課本並翻到第十一頁。）

  →兩個祈使句用 and 相連。

但是，若其中的動作有 go，則可以不用加 and，例如：

- *Go and take a shower.*

  → Go take a shower.（去洗澡。）

感嘆句的錯誤用法

1.What 和 How 開頭的感嘆句，主詞要在動詞前面

在這樣的句型裡，我們很容易把 What 和 How 想成疑問詞，而把後面的動詞和主詞的位置顛倒，然而，應該要先將主詞置於動詞前才是正確的寫法：

- *What a strong man is he.*

  →（X）要把主詞 he 放在動詞 is 的前面。

  What a strong man he is. →（O）

  （他是一個多麼強壯的男人啊！）

- *How pale look you!*

  →（X）要把主詞 you 放在動詞 look 前。

  How pale you look! →（O）

  （你看起來好蒼白呀！）

2. What 後面要有 a 或是名詞變為複數
   How 後面要緊連著形容詞或副詞

What 開頭的感嘆句，如果名詞為單數，後面要有不定冠詞 a 或是 an；如果名詞為複數，則不寫不定冠詞，例如：

- *What polite girl!* →（X）

這句有兩種改法，可以在 polite 前加上 a，或是在 girl 後面加上 s：

- *What a polite girl!*（多麼有禮貌的女孩呀！）

  →（O）女孩只有一個。

- *What polite girls!*（這一群女孩多有禮貌呀！）

  →（O）女孩有好多個。

How 開頭的感嘆句，後面要銜接形容詞或副詞，而不能將主詞和動詞置於形容詞或副詞之前，例如：

- *How the grapes are sweet!* →（X）

  How 後面應該先寫形容詞 sweet，才寫主詞 the grapes 和動詞 are：

  How sweet the grapes are!（葡萄多甜啊！）→（O）

倒裝句的錯誤用法

1. 倒裝的順序錯誤

當句子中有助動詞時，應將助動詞置於主詞前，而非動詞置於主詞前，例如：

- *I have never read this book before.*（我之前從來沒有讀過這本書。）

  →原本的句子中有否定詞 never，可以倒裝。

  Never have read I this book before.

  →助動詞＋動詞＋主詞，是錯誤的倒裝句型。

  Never read I have this book before.

→動詞＋主詞＋助動詞，是錯誤的倒裝句型。

- *Never have I read this book before.*

  →助動詞＋主詞＋動詞，才是正確的倒裝。

2. Only 或否定詞的倒裝，改寫時應加入助動詞

例如：

- *Kevin feels easy only at home.*（只有在家時，*Kevin* 才覺得自在。）

  →原本的句子。

  Only at home feels Kevin easy.

  →錯誤的倒裝句型。這個句子中有 only，但沒有助動詞，變成倒裝時，要加入配合人稱的助動詞。

  Only at home does Kevin feel easy.（O）

  →記得助動詞後面的動詞要使用原形動詞。

  再來看一個例子：

- *I rarely hear my sister sing this song.*（我很少聽到我姐姐唱這首歌。）

  →原本的句子。

  Rarely hear I my sister sing this song.

  →句子中有否定詞 rarely，要在倒裝時加入適當的助動詞。

  Rarely do I hear my sister sing this song.

  →加了助動詞後才是正確的倒裝句型。

3. 否定詞本身具有否定意味，改寫時要特別注意 not 的使用。

例如：

- *I don't like watching TV at all.*

  →原本的句型。

  Not at all don't I like watching.

  →句子中有兩的 not，是錯誤的文法。

  Not at all do I like watching TV.

  → Not 移到句首形成倒裝句，後面的助動詞的 not 要刪掉。

再看一個例子：

- *I didn't realize what had happened until I read the newspaper.*

  （我不知道發生什麼事，直到我讀了報紙。）

  →原本的句子。

你可以判斷哪一個句子是正確的嗎？

- *Not until I read the newspaper did I realize what had happened.*
- *Not until read I the newspaper I didn't realize what had happened.*

你答對了嗎？第一個句子才是正確的句型。同時，你有沒有發現，這兩個句子倒裝得地方不一樣？當句子中有兩的子句的時候，主要的子句才要倒裝：

- *Not until read I the newspaper I did realize what had happened.*

  →「不知道發生什麼事」是主要陳述的內容，這個句型倒裝的地方錯誤。

- *Not until I read the newspaper did I realize what had happened.*

  →有兩個句子時，在主要子句進行倒裝。

4. 不是問句卻用了問號

在倒裝句中，雖然有助動詞置於主詞之前的情況，但仍為一般陳述句，而非問句。故標點符號應為句號而非問號，例如：

- *You can't go into my room without my permission.*

  沒有我的允許，你不可以進我的房間。

  →原本的句子。

  By no means can you go into my room without my permission?

  →以為助動詞在助詞前是問句而加了問號是錯誤的。

  By no means can you go into my room without my permission.

  →倒裝句仍是一般的陳述句，用句號即可。

換你選選看：

(　) 1. How ＿＿ !

    Ⓐ your mom is graceful

    Ⓑ your mom is graceful

    Ⓒ graceful your mom is

(　) 2. What ＿＿＿＿.

    Ⓐ nice person

    Ⓑ a nice person

    Ⓒ nice a person

(　) 3. Don't do that again, ＿＿ you will be in trouble.

    Ⓐ or

    Ⓑ and

    Ⓒ but

(　) 4. No ＿＿ here!

    Ⓐ park

    Ⓑ to park

    Ⓒ parking

(　) 5. Don't let ＿＿ open the door.

    Ⓐ she

    Ⓑ her

    Ⓒ hers

(　) 6. Stop ＿＿ me around.

    Ⓐ jerk

    Ⓑ to jerk

    Ⓒ jerking

你寫對了嗎？

1. 你的媽媽多麼優雅啊！（答：C，形容詞要放在 How 的後面。）

2. 多麼好的一個人啊！（答：B，person 是單數，要在 nice 前面加上 a。）

3. 不要再那樣做，否則你會惹上麻煩。（答：A，or 表示「否則」，用來連接前後對立或是具有因果關係的狀況。）

4. 不准在這裡停車！（答：C，No + V-ing 表示強烈的禁止。）

5. 不要讓她把門打開。（答：B，Let 後面的人稱若是代名詞要改為受格，這句正確的寫法是：Don't let her open the door.。）

6. 不要再欺騙我了。（答：C，stop 後面的動詞可以使用動名詞或不定詞，兩者表示的意思不同。若銜接不定詞，表示「停下原本正在做的事來欺騙我」，不合邏輯，故本句根據語意判斷應填寫動名詞。）

Unit 35
常常混淆的假設句文法

 搶先看名句學文法：

The first rule in life is that everyone can, in the end, gets what he wants if he only tries. 「人生的第一個原則是，每個人最終都能得到他想要的，只要他願意嘗試。」

名言背景：塞繆爾・巴特勒（1835-1902）活躍於英國維多利亞時代的反傳統作家，著名作品為半自傳體小說《眾生之路》和烏托邦是諷刺小說《Erewhon》。同時，他也是演化思想史和義大利藝術的研究者，至今人們仍沿用其所翻譯的希臘史詩《伊利亞特》和《奧德賽》版本。本句中的 if 用於假設句，表示「假如、要是」。

 易混淆假設句文法小預告：

1. If 子句中可以有 would 或 will 嗎？
2. As if 後面若接簡單式動詞，和假設語氣沒有關係。
3. 搞不清楚到底是和現在事實相反還是和過去事實相反。

1. If 子句中可以有 would 或 will 嗎？

一般而言，if 引導的子句中不可以出現 would 或 will，例如：

- *I f I were he, I would cycling around Taiwan.*
  （如果我是他，我會騎腳踏車環島。）

→ would 在主要子句中出現。

- *If she had got up earlier, she wouldn't missed the bus.*

  （如果她早一點起床，她就不會錯過巴士。）

  → if 子句中沒有 would。

但若是表示主詞的意願或某種堅持，if 子句中可以有 would 或 will：

- *If he lend me ten thousand dollars, I will be thankful.*

  （如果他肯借我一萬元的話，我會對他心存感激的。）

  →在 if 子句中的 would 代表主詞 he 的意願。

- *If she practices the piano every day, she will be a great musician.*

  （如果她堅持每天練習鋼琴，她會是一個偉大的音樂家。）

2. As if 後面若接簡單式動詞，和假設語氣沒有關係

例如：

It seems as if the typhoon will hit Taiwan the day after tomorrow.

（看起來颱風會在後天登陸台灣。）

→ as if 子句中的動詞使用簡單式，表示實際上會發生的事，而非假設的狀況。

再看一個例子：

- *The train has left; it looks as if we will have to take the bus.*

  （火車開走了，看來我們只好搭公車了。）

  → will have to take 也表示未來將會發生的動作。

有時候，我們可以把 as if 後面的主詞和動詞省略，例如：

- *He raised his hand as if to speak.*（他舉手彷彿有什麼話要說。）

  →這句原本寫成 He raises his hand as if he wants to speak. 省略了 as if

  後面的主詞和動詞。

3. 搞不清楚到底是和現在事實相反還是和過去事實相反

在假設句中，常常讓人困擾得就是搞不清楚到底是和現在的事實相反，還是和過去的事實相反。有一個小訣竅就是，把假設句的時間往後推一格，什麼意思呢？

例如：

- *If I were you, I wouldn't talk back to my parents like that.*

（如果我是你，我不會向我父母這樣頂嘴。）

→假設句的動詞是過去式，過去式往後推一格時間，就是現在，所以這個句子是和現在事實相反。

● *If I had taken the note, I wouldn't forget to do homework.*

（如果當時我有抄筆記，我就不會忘記要寫功課。）

→當句子中有兩個動作，比較早完成的動作要用完成式，因此，在這個句子中，比較早完成的是抄筆記的動作，把時間往後推一格，就是過去式。這樣就可以判斷，這個句子和過去事實相反。

換你選選看：

( ) 1. She looks shock as if the mouse _____ in front of her.
A will B run C ran

( ) 2. If I _____ this talk show, I would know what they said.
A had watched B watched C watch

( ) 3. If Dad drinks too much beer, he _____ uncomfortable.
A would feel B will feel C feel

( ) 4. If I arrived home before six o'clock, I would help her make dinner.
A would help B helped C help

( ) 5. If she _____ here, she would know what to do.
A was B is C were

( ) 6. If I were_____, I would sing a song for Lisa.
A him B his C he

你寫對了嗎？

1. 她看起來很震驚，彷彿有老鼠從她前面跑過。（答：C，as if 後面銜接的若為假設語氣，應將 will run 改為過去式動詞。）

2. 如果當時我有看這個脫口秀節目，我就會知道他們在講什麼。（答：A，had watched 表示「如果當時有看」。）

3. 如果爸爸喝太多啤酒，他會覺得不舒服。（答：B，如果假設句用簡單式動詞，那麼主要子句的助動詞一般習慣用 will。）

4. 如果我六點之前到家，我會幫她做晚餐。（答：A，would help 表示「想要幫忙，但實際上沒有幫忙」。）

5. 如果她在這裡，她會知道該怎麼做。（答：C，假設句中的 be 動詞，不論人稱都用 were，只有在非正式用法中才會有使用 was 的情況出現。）

6. 要是我是他，我會唱一首歌獻給 Lisa。（答：C，因為 be 動詞後面接主詞補語，但受詞並不能作為主詞補語，因此要使用 he，雖然現在口語的英文中，常常有 him 代替 he 的狀況出現，不過是屬於非正式的用法。）

Unit 36
常常混淆的被動句文法

 搶先看名句學文法：

I believe the unarmed truth and unconditional love will have the final word in reality. This is why right, temporarily defeated, is stronger than evil triumphant. 「我相信未武裝的真相與無條的愛，將在現實世界下最後結論。這是為什麼正當性，即使暫時被擊敗，也比邪惡的的勝利還要強大。」

名言背景：馬丁・路德・金恩（1929-1968）是史上最年輕的諾貝爾和平獎得主，領導美國黑人以非暴力方式抗爭種族歧視，成為美國漸進主義的象徵。他在 1963 年發表《我有一個夢想（I have a dream）》演講，迫使美國國會於 1964 年通過《民權法案》，宣佈種族隔離和歧視政策為非法政策，並賦予黑人選舉權。句中 temporarily defeated 為被動句型 is temporarily defeated 的省略。

 易混淆被動句文法小預告：

1. 授與動詞的順序錯誤
2. by+ 給予動作的人；with+ 做某動作使用的工具。
3. 不是所有的動詞都可以改為被動語態。
4. 現在分詞表示主動，過去分詞表示被動。
5. 分辨不出主動或是被動語態。

1. 授與動詞的順序錯誤

授與動詞的句型有兩種：

- *My mom bought me a dress.*（我媽媽買了一件洋裝給我。）

  →〈授與動詞＋間接受詞＋直接受詞〉。

  My mom bought a dress for me.（我媽媽買給我一件洋裝。）

  →先寫直接受詞時，在間接受詞前要有介系詞。

但是，當這種句型變成被動式時，很容易在順序產生混淆，試比較看看下列的句子，你能判斷哪一句才正確嗎？

- *A dress was bought for me by Mom.* →（　　）
- *A dress was bought by Mom.* →（　　）
- *I was bought a dress by Mom.* →（　　）

上面的句子中，第一句和第二句是正確的句子，但第三句的語序是錯誤的。

再看看另一個例子：

- *Amy sang Jack a song.*（Amy 為 Jack 唱了一首歌。）

  Amy sang a song for Jack.

改成被動式：

- *A song was sung by Amy.*

  A song was sung for Jack by Amy.

  →被授與的對象要放在給予動作的人前面。

2. by+ 給予動作的人
   with+ 做某動作使用的工具

例如：

- *Tim was hit by Jason.*（Tim 被 Jason 打。）

  → by+ 給予動作的人

- *Tim was hit with a stone.*（Tim 被一顆石頭打到。）

  → with+ 做某動作使用的工具

再看另一個例子：

- *The thief was shot by a police officer.*（小偷被警察射擊。）

- *The thief was shot with a gun.*（小偷被手槍射擊。）
- *The thief was shot by a police officer with a gun.*

  （小偷被警察用手槍射擊。）

  →如果同時有給予動作的人和做某動作使用的工具，要先寫 by 再寫 with。

3. 不是所有的動詞都可以改為被動語態

不及物動詞因為沒有受詞，如果改成被動語態，就沒有可以做主詞的語詞，所以不及物動詞沒有被動語態，例如：

- *She walks.*（她走路。）

  Is walked by her.（她被走路。）

  →人不可能被走路，是錯誤的寫法

- *He arrived.*（他到了。）

  Was arrived by him.（他被到了。）

  →人不可能被到了，是錯誤的寫法。

有些及物動詞，特別是表示狀態的動詞，也不行改成被動語態，例如：

- *He is a wise man.*（他是一個睿智的男人。）

  → be 動詞表示狀態，這種用法沒有被動語態。

- *They have a beautiful garden.*（他們有一個漂亮的花園。）

  → have 雖然是及物動詞，但表示擁有的狀態，不能有被動語態。

  The garden is had by them.（花園被他們有。）

  →錯誤的用法。

- *The dress doesn't fit me.*（這件洋裝不符合我的尺寸。）

  → fit 表示合適與否，也是表示狀態的一種。

  I wasn't fit by the dress.（我不被這件洋裝符合。）

  →錯誤的用法。

4. 現在分詞表示主動，過去分詞表示被動

例如：

- *a sleeping baby*（正在睡覺的嬰兒）

  →現在分詞表示主動語態。

- *a crying boy*（正在哭的男孩）
- *a broken glass*（被打破的玻璃杯）

  →過去分詞表示被動語態。

- *the invited children*（被邀請的小孩）

有些過去分詞，仍然是主動語態，例如：

- *a retired woman*（退休的女人）

  →雖然 retired 是過去分詞，但卻不帶有被動的涵義。

- *a fallen ball*（掉落的球）

  → fallen 也是具主動意味的過去分詞。

有時，同一個語詞會同時有現在分詞和過去分詞的型態，例如：

- *This movie is interesting.*（這部電影很有趣。）

  → interesting 是現在分詞，中文翻譯成「令人覺得有趣的」。

- *She is interested in this movie.*（她對於這部電影很感興趣。）

  → interested 是過去分詞，中文翻譯成「（某人）感到有趣的」。

- *The baseball game is exciting.*（這場棒球賽很令人興奮。）

- *The baseball game is exciting to Amanda.*（這場棒球賽很令 Amanda 感到興奮。）

  →使用現在分詞時，想要描述人物為何時，使用介系詞 to。

- *She is excited about the baseball game.*（她對於這場棒球賽感到很興奮。）

  →過去分詞後面通常會銜接介系詞，每個過去分詞搭配的介系詞不一樣。

- *Amy is interesting to me.*（我覺得 Amy 很有趣。）

  →人也會令人覺得有趣，所以現在分詞的主詞可以是人物。

但是不能這樣用：

- *The baseball game is interested.*（棒球比賽感到有趣。）

  →事物不會感到有趣，所以將無生命的語詞做為過去分詞的主詞是錯誤的用法。

這類的語詞例如：boring（令人厭煩的）／ bored with（感到厭煩的）、surprising（令人驚訝的）／ surprised at（感到驚訝的）、tiring（令人厭煩的）／ tired of（感到厭煩的）、exciting（令人興奮的）／ excited about（感到興奮的）、 interesting（令人覺得有趣的）／ interested in（感到有趣的）、impressing（令人印象深刻的）／ impressed by（感到印象深刻的）、frightening（令人害怕的）／ frightened at（感到害怕的）等。

5. 分辨不出主動或是被動語態

你可以分辨出來下面的句子是主動或被動嗎？

- *She is asking a question.* →（　　）
- *She has asked the question.* →（　　）
- *She is asked for money.* →（　　）

你分辨出來了嗎？

- *She is asking a question.*（她正在問一個問題。）

  →〈be 動詞＋現在分詞〉表示現在進行式，是主動語態。

- *She has asked the question.*（她已經問了問題。）

  →〈has+ 過去分詞〉是現在完成式，也是主動語態。

- *She is asked by the students.*（她被學生問問題。）

  →〈be 動詞＋過去分詞〉才是被動語態。

再來比較看看另一個句子：

- *She is called by the teacher.*（她被老師叫過去。）

  →正確的寫法。

  She is calling by the teacher.

  →雖然中文句子表示「正在被叫」，但卻不能用現在分詞。

當句子中有做形容詞用的過去分詞時，特別容易搞不清楚主動或被動：

- *I am frightened at cockroach.*（我對蟑螂感到害怕。）

  →雖然中文沒有翻出「被…」的被動語態，但這樣才是正確的寫法。

  I am frightening at cockroach.

  →錯誤的寫法。

換你選選看：

（ ）1. The violin ＿＿ by Emily.
　　Ⓐ played　Ⓑ was played　Ⓒ was playing

（ ）2. He was＿＿＿ in the video game.
　　Ⓐ interested　Ⓑ interesting　Ⓒ interest

（ ）3. The clothes was ＿＿＿.
　　Ⓐ wash　Ⓑ washing　Ⓒ washed

（ ）4. The shoes are ＿＿＿ well.
　　Ⓐ sell　Ⓑ sold　Ⓒ selling

（ ）5. There is a ＿＿ baby.
　　Ⓐ crying　Ⓑ cried　Ⓒ cry

（ ）6. The book ＿＿＿ many years ago.
　　Ⓐ had been written　Ⓑ had written　Ⓒ was written

✓ 你寫對了嗎？

1. 小提琴被 Emily 演奏。（答：Ⓑ，was+ 過去分詞為被動語態。）

2. 他對電動遊戲很感興趣。（答：Ⓐ，過去分詞做形容詞用。）

3. 衣服被洗。（答：Ⓒ，was+ 過去分詞為被動語態。）

4. 鞋子賣得很好。（答：Ⓒ，有些動詞儘管寫成主動形式，但卻帶有被動語態的涵義，這些動詞如 sell（賣）、read（讀）、wash（洗）等，因此 selling 雖然是現在分詞，但卻是被動語態。）

5. 有一個嬰兒正在哭。（答：Ⓐ，現在分詞做形容詞用，表示「正在哭的」。）

6. 這本書在幾年前（被）寫完。（答：Ⓐ，had 和 written 中間要加入 been 才是被動語態。）

Learn Smart! 045

那些年我們一起熟悉的英文文法：藏在電影、小說、歌詞裡

作 者	倍斯特編輯部
發 行 人	周瑞德
企 劃 編 輯	倍斯特編輯部
執 行 編 輯	饒美君
封 面 設 計	高鍾琪
內 文 排 版	華漢電腦排版有限公司
校 對	陳欣慧、陳韋佑

印 製	大亞彩色印刷製版股份有限公司
初 版	2015 年 4 月
出 版	倍斯特出版事業有限公司
電 話	(02) 2351-2007
傳 真	(02) 2351-0887
地 址	100 台北市中正區福州街 1 號 10 樓之 2
E - m a i l	best.books.service@gmail.com
定 價	新台幣 329 元

港澳地區總經銷 泛華發行代理有限公司

地 址	香港新界將軍澳工業邨駿昌街 7 號 2 樓
電 話	(852) 2798-2323
傳 真	(852) 2796-5471

國家圖書館出版品預行編目(CIP)資料

那些年我們一起熟悉的英文文法 : 藏在電影、小
說、歌詞裡 / 倍斯特編輯部著. -- 初版. -- 臺北
市 : 倍斯特, 2015.04
　面 ;　　公分. -- (Learn smart! ; 45)
ISBN 978-986-90883-8-1(平裝)

1.英語 2.語法

　805.16　　　　　　　　　104004980